The Sullivan House

Lanna Richards

For my mother, her love of all things
beautiful, and her abiding love for me,

And for my grandmother who taught me
The Word every day of my life,

And for all my dear readers, especially
The Naomi Sunday School class,
thank you for your love and support.

AUTHOR'S NOTE

This is the third novel in the series. To get a better understanding of the Sullivans and their journey during a tumultuous time in history, reading the first two books might give you a better glimpse into their lives, though not necessary. *Heart of Stones* is the first, and *An Uncertain Horizon* is the second one in the series.

PROLOGUE

The Civil War wreaked havoc on America and divided the country for a time. Plantations in the South were destroyed or broken up into smaller farms, and people eked out a living as best they could. What lives the war didn't take or maim, the hardships, devastation, and death of those who remained behind left a scar on the country that would not soon heal.

The Sullivans, immigrants from Ireland, became one of the richest families in Scottsville, Mississippi on Oak Hollow Plantation with its majestic mansion, stately trees, and fertile fields. They endured the joys and tragedies of the history of this great nation until they relocated back to Ireland. Even though the family came back to America, Oak Hollow as a plantation fell by the wayside, broken up into small parcels of land. The buildings and half the land remained in the family, but time, weather, and neglect claimed a toll on them after the family moved in different directions.

Now more than a hundred years later, the antebellum mansion, that grand lady, that housed their family and protected their secrets for decades, lies desolate, sad, and in need of repair. Only love can save her, but will it come in time? Could her heart beat again, vibrant and full of hope? Could laughter and joy replace the sadness and tears, or would the scars of an act of war forever haunt the mansion?

CHAPTER ONE

Bright sunshine woke Braden Cunningham, but it didn't dispel the gloom settling over his thoughts. Pulling himself out of bed, he moved his two over-stuffed bags to the hall. Whether he liked it or not, he had made his decision. It was bittersweet to leave a home he'd known all his life, except for the four years he'd spent at the University of Alabama.

Walking through the house, he said goodbye to his parents and his beloved grandmother before throwing his bags into his car on top of his stereo system and the bare necessities for moving into his first apartment. He was hoping to find a furnished one.

Cranking the motor, he didn't hear his mother shouting, "Call when you get there. Be safe."

Driving as fast as he dared, the radio blasting classical music, Braden let it sink into his soul and relieve the trepidation he felt. The only good thing was his car. He had spotted the '56 Thunderbird on the back lot of a used car dealer. It was his dream car, and when he saw it, he had to have it. He had worked after school and on weekends to pay for it, and he and his dad had restored it.

Now this car was speeding him toward Scottsville, Mississippi and his first job as a third-grade teacher. What unknown future faced him in a small nondescript town? Sadly, he couldn't join his best friend, Justin, in Dallas, but there had been no job offers there for a male elementary school teacher. So, he had accepted the only offer he had from Scottsville, Mississippi.

"I should never have listened to Missus Porter telling me there weren't enough male elementary teachers. I've also learned that there aren't many openings either." Sarcasm tinted his speech. A breeze blowing through the open window ushered in a blanket of humidity causing sweat to pour down Braden's face. He yelled to the landscape as the car sped by. "Why couldn't I have gone to Dallas with Justin, got my culinary degree like he did, and put our band back together. Instead, I'm trading big city lights for a Podunk town in the middle of nowhere."

While he wasn't happy, he was content to have a job, even in a small town, and felt in time, he could get his certificate to teach junior high or high school. Teaching English, especially literature and writing, or even history was an elusive dream at the moment. He would take whatever courses he needed, but he was not going to teach elementary school forever. To make matters worse, he had no idea what kind of amenities the town offered and what caliber of students he would have.

A small voice seemed to be on a loop constantly replaying the phrase, "You chose this. Now make the best of it. Teach a year and move on."

Braden hit the brakes, slowing to the speed limit when he saw Scottsville's welcome sign.

Chiding himself, Braden cast off the negativity he felt and focused on the positive. As he cruised down Main Street, he was struck by the cleanliness of the streets, even though the dingy buildings looked like they had been transplanted from the early 1900s as they sat side by side trying to hold each other up. Not at all what he had imagined. The once painted buildings looked like an old woman who slathered on makeup to hide her wrinkles. Now he understood. There was no future to living here.

He shook depressing thoughts that kept creeping into his mind as he located Knight Real Estate Agency on his right. Three crape myrtle trees planted in large concrete containers graced every block as far as he could see. Many of the merchants had flower boxes brimming with red, white, and pink geraniums attached to their front windows and benches to sit and relax. Awnings provided shade over most of the stores, and shopkeepers were outside sweeping off the wide sidewalks. Straightening his shoulders, he mumbled, "Here goes nothing" as he entered the lobby.

Overhead fluorescent lights seemed futile in their attempt to lighten the dim interior, reflecting how he felt. To his right, he saw colored polaroids of houses for sale thumbtacked on a cork bulletin board on the wall above a much-used floral sofa. Two mismatched wing-back chairs, and a large oak coffee table completed the waiting area. Real estate brochures obscured most of the surface of the table. A small bell chimed when he opened the door, and from somewhere in the bowels of the establishment, Elizabeth Addison appeared. She smiled and extended her hand.

"You must be Braden Cunningham. I've been looking forward to meeting you, but I wasn't expecting you until tomorrow."

"Yes, I'm Braden. I decided to come early to acquaint myself with Scottsville and the school. I hope you have found something for me to rent." He followed Elizabeth to her desk and sat in the chair she offered him.

"I'm afraid I have bad news, Braden. This is a small town, and there aren't any apartment complexes as I told you on the phone. I have scouted around for rental houses and haven't been very successful at that, either. I was going to call you this afternoon, but you got here early. I wish I could have saved you the trip."

More discouraging news. "I don't know what I'll do now, but I'll figure it out." Braden yawned as he covered his mouth. "I'm tired and was hoping to get settled today. Thank you for trying." A large sigh escaped his lips mirroring his disappointment.

"You told me you are a new teacher here. I'm so sorry, but I'm a little confused. Didn't you look over the town when you had your interview?"

"No, I drove into Vicksburg, spent the night, and came for the interview the next morning. As soon as it was over, I headed back out of town. Since the school is located just off the road coming in, I didn't go through town."

Elizabeth nodded. "I do have some places for sale. I warned you it would be hard."

"You did. I suppose I'll have to commute from Vicksburg. It won't be all that bad because I've heard there are some nice places to go in the city. It's just that I'm not a morning person, and it would've been nice

3

not to have to get up so early. It's okay. It is what it is. I'll deal with it." Braden rose and started toward the door. "Thanks anyway."

"Wait. I have another solution, and if you don't like it, please say so. You certainly won't hurt my feelings." Elizabeth had shifted in her chair, and a slight blush crept up to color her face.

"And what might that be?" Braden retraced his steps and sat down again.

"I purchased a property a couple of weeks ago at a ridiculous price, sight unseen. I have no idea what it looks like inside because the auctioneer said no one was allowed to view it before making a bid. Turns out I was the only bidder on the courthouse steps, and now I'm the proud owner of an antebellum mansion with about ninety acres of land. I had planned to renovate it and either live there or sell it. If it didn't sell at auction, they were going to tear it down and sell the land. Call me sentimental, but I could not see letting a grand old mansion bite the dust, even though it's very creepy looking."

Braden's thoughts went immediately to his mother and grandmother. They both loved antiques, and Braden had helped his mother, Emma, restore more pieces than he cared to remember. She'd be in her element in an antebellum home. Elizabeth's voice brought him back to the present.

"When I had this bright idea to restore it, I drove out to look at it after I purchased it. It looks pretty bad. I have no idea how expensive repairs and updating will be, but everyone I talked to thinks I've lost my mind. I'm hoping all it needs inside is just a good cleaning. If it's more than that, then time and money will alter my plans. But you may be the answer to my prayers."

"What do you mean?"

Elizabeth ignored his question and gushed on, seemingly unaware Braden had asked a question. "I've had the utilities turned on and am planning to move there this weekend to see what needs to be done to make it livable. I'm just thankful there's electricity. I found out there's no city water, but there is a well, so I hope the pump is electric and that there's still water."

Braden frowned, wondering where she was leading with this conversation. He wasn't interested in her ramblings. He just wanted to leave and drive to Vicksburg to find an apartment. She was still talking.

4

"I would be happy to rent you a bedroom with kitchen privileges. If you're any kind of handyman, we could exchange part of the rent if you will help me. You don't have to answer right now. Think it over and let me know. I really hope you will move in because living in such a Big House by myself is a little scary. Kind of like living with ghosts of the past."

So that's what she meant about my being the answer to her prayers. She expects me to repair a decades old home. Maybe I should just decline now. Still, it might be a fun challenge.

Suddenly Braden smiled and thought of his father. Though Braden's dad, Mason, worked as a salesman, his first love was carpentry, and he was always tinkering with wood. In junior high, Braden and his dad had built a room in the attic for Braden, giving his old bedroom to his paternal grandmother who moved in with them. It was the only bedroom on the ground level, and the other bedrooms upstairs were occupied by his parents and one Emma had turned into a craft room. The remaining room had been his sister's, and now was the guest room.

His father was an excellent woodworker and had a shop in a building behind their home. Braden's grandfather also had a passion for woodworking, and Braden had helped his dad with some of their projects.

As Mason told him. "Once sawdust gets in your veins, you're hooked." Braden hadn't gotten the sawdust bug yet, but perhaps he could be of some help, and it might be neat to live in a home with a history, but then again….

"Braden, what are you thinking? Would you like to look at it?"

Looking at this woman, Braden noticed an almost child-like anticipation. Though she looked to be close to his age, her exuberance reminded Braden of his twelve-year-old cousin. Did he want to live with an effervescent girl, who would probably greet the weekend mornings singing and playing rock music while he tried to sleep in? Weighing his options, he could commute from Vicksburg or live with her close to work with cheap rent. In the end, he decided if it wasn't too rundown, he would take Elizabeth up on her offer. He had already made up his mind he'd fulfill his contract for a year and move on, even if he had to change careers. Maybe he'd go to culinary school like Justin, and they could open an upscale restaurant. He was not going to rot in a tiny town.

5

He focused on the young realtor. "If it works out, I could get settled in school, and in a month if I decide it's too much work, we could part with no hard feelings, huh? Would you be agreeable to a month-to-month rent?"

"Sure, but I have to warn you. It may be a dump, since to my knowledge, it hasn't been lived in for ages now."

"May I ask, what prompted you to buy a mansion without going inside besides the fact that you are sentimental?"

"I thought it would be a good investment."

"So would it just be you and me, or are there other people who might move in with you?"

"No, there's no one. I'm single and have been living with a college roommate and her husband. He works at the bank here and told me about the auction. He gave me a loan at a very good interest rate. They're newlyweds, so I need to get out of their house."

"Is this your hometown?"

"No, my family lives in Jackson, but a friend of the family told me I could make good money in real estate. I got my license and worked in Jackson for a while. But my best friend was moving here, so she convinced me to come to Scottsville. She thought I'd have more opportunities here since there is only one real estate office." Elizabeth didn't elaborate further details of why she had moved.

Braden didn't know why he felt so let down. He thought graduating from college and getting his first job after his internship would give him an exhilarated feeling, but instead he felt annoyed that not only was he in a small town, but in a house which was probably falling down with a roommate he didn't know, and whose overabundance of energy irritated him.

Braden focused his attention back to the present. "Okay, I'll look at it, but don't get your hopes up. If it's in too bad a shape, I may not want to take you up on your offer."

"I understand. Let me clock out, and we can go right now." Elizabeth hung a sign in the window that she would be back in an hour, transferred the phones to the answering system, and grabbed her keys.

"Mine is the little white Toyota," she said, pointing down the street. She swished her full skirt and almost skipped to her car. "Hop in, and I'll drive, unless you want to follow me."

A large sigh escaped Braden's lips, a resigned look on his face. "Okay, Elizabeth, lead on. I'll follow."

The road led out of town about a mile or so. Thoughts of home surfaced. He had gone through his home one last time before leaving for Scottsville. His mother had followed him as if he were taking a tour of the White House as he looked at the antiques he had helped her refinish. Going through his restored home felt like taking a dive back to another time and place.

CHAPTER TWO

Elizabeth's turn signal brought him back to awareness of his surroundings. She turned down a winding dirt path leading to a semi-circular drive, or what was once a drive. It had been cleared enough to get cars in and out, but the overgrowth gave the mansion a sad appearance. Braden looked at the rock-lined walkway leading up to the massive columned veranda of the two-story mansion. What was he thinking? His mother and grandmother would love this place. They were both history buffs and loved all things old. He could picture them donning huge bell-shaped gowns, swishing from room to room like the women in *Gone with the Wind.* This certainly wasn't the modern apartment he had visualized.

Bramble bushes of wild raspberries had almost taken over the veranda winding through the rails, and the house had deteriorated over the years. Elizabeth didn't paint a false picture. Tearing it down and starting over might be a better option, but Braden kept his thoughts to himself.

"Here we go!" Elizabeth was energetic and as full of life as Braden was depressed. "Your choice, upstairs or down…that is, if you decide to take me up on my offer." As she put her hand on the once beautiful double door with etched panels of oak trees, it flew open before she could insert the key. A smell unlike anything she had ever experienced assaulted her. Apparently, squatters had been living here. Her first vision was dirty clothes scattered haphazardly over the floor or draped over furniture, full ashtrays and empty liquor bottles on the floor. Sacks full of trash littered the interior. From what she could see, squatters had left everything and moved on. Elizabeth gagged, grabbed her throat, and backed out of the doorway. "Oh, no. This is terrible. I don't know if we can live here."

Braden held his breath and entered the house to open windows. He prayed they still worked. A breeze wafted through the house as he went back to the veranda. "Let's let it air out for a little while. I dread seeing the upstairs."

Looking around the veranda, Braden noticed Elizabeth leaning against a column, her shoulders stooped, despair covering her face as a tear slipped down her cheek. He actually felt sorry for her, and it puzzled him that she would follow a friend here to such a small town. Her explanation really didn't make sense, but that wasn't his problem. His problem was whether he could live in the trashed-out house.

Braden pulled some raspberries from the vines. "Want some fresh fruit?"

Elizabeth took his offering. "Are they edible?"

"Yeah, they should be" Braden wanted to lighten her mood. "Now if we only had some ice cream to put these on."

Elizabeth didn't smile. "Braden, I'm so sorry. I had no idea how bad this is. If you want to back out now, I wouldn't blame you."

"I'm not a quitter, Elizabeth, but I think we need to go get some cleaning supplies and gloves. We should get something to cover our faces, too, before we begin the clean-up and exploring any further. We can take my car."

Elizabeth's eyes widened. "This is a vintage car, right?"

Braden grinned as he ran his hand over the peacock-blue hood. "My pride and joy!"

"I hate to sound dumb, but is it a Corvette, I think it's called?"

"No, it's '56 Thunderbird, loving called by aficionados as a T-Bird."

Elizabeth nodded and opened the passenger side door. "I guess it doesn't have a trunk?"

Braden's eyebrows knitted together in confusion. "Why would you say that?"

"It has the spare on the back, but I love the little round windows!"

Braden laughed for the first time since he'd entered this thing called a town. "It's built that way! Obviously, you don't know much about cars." He regained his composure. "Thank you for brightening my day!"

10

"Whatever. And no, I don't know a thing about cars. My dad picks out my cars."

After shopping, they armed themselves with cleaning supplies and braved their way back inside. The air blowing through the windows had diminished the smell a little. There were two large bedrooms where mildewed clothes lay on the floor or were draped over antique furniture. In the larger of the two, a mattress on the large four poster bed had stains on it, visible through a layer of dust. The other bedroom was just as bad. Someone had tried to modernize an outdated bathroom, but it left a lot to be desired.

A shower head faced the toilet, separated only by a thin curtain hanging from a sagging rod. There was very little room between the shower curtain and the toilet, even though it was a large room. A claw foot tub sat rusting on the warped linoleum next to the toilet. Elizabeth scooted from the room. "I'm going to poke around and see what else is down here."

Standing there taking in the condition of the bathroom, Braden thought of his mother. This bathroom might be too much of a challenge, depending on what else they found. He thought even his mother would balk at the monumental task of bringing this grand old home back to its former glory.

Elizabeth came back to the door of the bathroom. Her hangdog expression told Braden the rest of the downstairs was not much better. Braden gritted his teeth. "Let's see what surprises the upstairs is hiding."

Elizabeth just nodded, holding back tears as she followed him.

Reaching the top, they discovered eight oversized bedrooms. Each held an odd assortment of furniture that in the distant past would have been opulent and splendid, but now every piece had a sheet over it as if waiting in a morgue to be embalmed and buried.

Seeing the condition of the house, Braden's disappointment turned to nausea and then to a profound feeling of sadness. This house had a story to tell, and it might be interesting to find out more about it. History had fascinated Braden, a love of old things instilled in him by his mother and grandmother. Renovating it would be right up his mother's alley if the repairs were not too extensive, but Braden wasn't sure he was up to the task, and he wondered whether his father would have time to help him.

11

Trying to get a feel for who might have lived here, why so many bedrooms, and why it was in such disrepair piqued his curiosity. Research about the history of this old mansion would pass the time and make a good story for a novel he wanted to write.

Ideas twirled through his brain. With so many spacious bedrooms, they could easily make a couple of roomy apartments. There would be plenty of room for a bathroom in each apartment along with a small kitchen and sitting area. But would modernizing the upstairs destroy the character and the very soul of the house? Pushing his thoughts aside, he turned to Elizabeth who stood, hope evident in her deep blue eyes.

Elizabeth's voice quivered. "Well? What do you think?"

They were standing in the southwest corner bedroom. Braden took in the view from the large windows that abutted each other. "I think this will do fine. At least most of the rooms have some furniture, so that's one thing we wouldn't have to buy. From the looks of it, I don't think anyone has occupied the upstairs for a long time. Most of the filth is downstairs." He raised the windows. "I feel this may be cooler than downstairs. If you want the one across the hall, it won't bother me. There's just a lot of work ahead of us."

"It looks that way. I don't see a bathroom up here, so I guess we have to share the one downstairs."

Share a bathroom? Judging by his sister's time in a bathroom they had shared growing up, Braden could not imagine how that would work, but maybe a second bathroom would be the next project. They would have to work out a time schedule. Aloud, he said, "Not a problem."

Moving to the open windows, Braden blew out a repressed breath. "This view would be impressive if the land were cleared of the weeds, which must be over waist high right now." He took in the room's furnishings while Elizabeth shifted from one foot to the other.

The room held a double bed, a wardrobe, a chest, a dresser, and a small desk tucked under a window looking over the back acreage. A wicker rocking chair sat huddled in a corner as if it were trying to hide. Faded lavender-colored flowers on the wallpaper indicated this may have been a girl's room.

"I think this room will do nicely for me, but I'll have to do something about this wallpaper."

A small laugh escaped Elizabeth's lips. "I can see why this wouldn't fit a man. I'll take the downstairs then. I wish now I had never bought this. I thought it would be an easy fix. A little paint, mowing the yard, and modernizing it a little would be all it would take, but I didn't realize how hard it would be. Guess you can tell, I haven't been in the real estate business very long. I'll see if I can take off early to help with the cleaning."

"Don't worry about it. I'll make myself useful while you go back to work. I may wander around the grounds, clean a little, and do some shopping. Right now, the mattresses are my main concern. I don't want to sleep on the ones here for obvious reasons."

"I can go to the furniture store and have them deliver a couple."

"That would be fine, but I like to try one out before buying. I like a firm feel."

"I like that, too. See if Mister Dawson will put it on an account for me if you would feel like picking out a couple of sets. I really need to check back in at work." Elizabeth fidgeted through her purse to find her keys. How could she tell Braden that she might not have enough money in the bank? "I have no idea how much the mattresses will cost, but if for some reason Mister Dawson doesn't want to open an account for me, drop by the office and let me know."

Braden had saved most of his salary after restoring his car. It was obvious that Elizabeth was having some financial problems. "I doubt he would open an account for you if you're not there. Tell you what. I'll buy my mattress and box springs and pick up a few groceries. And you can pick out a mattress that feels best to you."

"Sounds great, if you're sure. I can pay you back once I get a commission check. I'll be home around five-thirty unless I get caught showing a property, which is unlikely."

"No matter where I live, Elizabeth, I'm going to need a mattress. I'm just glad I don't have to buy furniture." Braden thought she would be better off to go back to Jackson, but he didn't say anything.

He walked to the top of the stairs and waited until he heard Elizabeth's car heading down the driveway. He walked back into the bedroom upstairs, pulled back the muslin covering the old mattress. It looked like a thin mattress with a feather bed on top. He plopped down in the rocking chair that had not been covered. Clouds of dust enveloped him. He jumped up and dusted himself off. "Why, oh why, didn't I follow Justin to Dallas and enroll in culinary school? We could have opened a restaurant together," he muttered. "What's done is done. I need to make the most of this. Time to find the furniture store and locate a grocery."

CHAPTER THREE

The furniture store had a surprising array of furniture and a decent selection of mattresses and box springs. Braden picked out the firmest one and was surprised that it was on sale. He paid for it and asked about delivery.

The owner nodded his head. "I haven't sold a mattress set in months. You're the second person who's bought one today. What address do you want us to deliver your set to?"

"Do you know the old plantation a mile or so from town?"

"The one Elizabeth Addison bought?"

"Yes. Can you deliver it there? I'm renting a room from her."

"Sure thing. She ordered this same mattress. Would late afternoon work for you?"

"That would be fine." Braden smiled, thinking they bought the same set.

"I don't believe I've seen you around these parts. You must be new here."

"I'm the new third grade teacher. Since there are no apartments here, Miss Addison was kind enough to rent me a room."

"She's a fine young lady. I heard she bought that place, and it kind of worried me that she'd be living out there alone, isolated from everyone. I know she's glad for the company."

"Thank you. It may just be temporary." All Braden needed was for this man to shout it all over town that he was living with a woman. Could tarnish his reputation and cause problems at school. But he had more to worry about at the present time.

Braden decided to familiarize himself with the town and find something to eat.

A quaint little house served as a restaurant. The painted sign in the window looked amateurish and proclaimed the title The Greenhouse.

15

While it had a tea room ambience, it was decorated in an artsy sort of way. "I could write here if I ever start on that novel," he muttered.

"I'm sorry, did you say something?" The waitress, who looked to be in her late teens or early twenties stood with her pad ready to take his order from the menu already on the table. She was tall, slim, and had beautiful hazel eyes.

"No, I was just looking over the menu. You serve breakfast all day?"

"Yes, we do."

"I'll have the breakfast special with coffee."

"My name is Harriet. I'll bring your coffee and water right away."

When she returned with his food, Braden asked, "I'm curious. This house is white, but the name of this restaurant is The Greenhouse. Is there a story behind the name?"

"You must be new in town. The owners love to garden, and most of the vegetables we serve come from their garden and greenhouse."

"I can't wait to try lunch. And yes, I'm new. Name's Braden Cunningham. I'm the new third grade teacher." Braden smiled. He might change his mind about dating.

Harriet set his plate in front of him and refreshed his coffee. "Welcome. Let me know if you need anything else."

At a local department store, Braden found a set of white sheets, some fluffy pillows, and a navy and white striped coverlet. White towels, a loofa, and wash cloths completed his shopping for the bedroom and bath. He also found a blue cushion for the rocking chair. Contemplating what he would need to stock the kitchen, Braden drove down the two busiest streets until he found a locally-owned grocery store. He filled his cart with a few canned goods, staples, and some chicken breasts. He decided on enough fresh food to last for a day in case the refrigerator and stove didn't work. Hopefully, he could cook dinner on the stove, but if not, he'd build a campfire to cook their dinner.

Back home, Braden donned gloves and covered his mouth and nose with a large bandana he had purchased. After filling two trash sacks, he lugged them outside and cleared away enough weeds to make a fire. He piled the trash sacks on it once the fire blazed. He dragged the mattresses and box springs from his room and the one he assumed Elizabeth would use. Mattresses would take a long time to burn, so he'd leave them for

16

another day. As the trash disintegrated, he considered whether he really wanted to stay. Did he love history enough to warrant trying to find out about this mansion? Still, something gnawed at his brain. Was the house getting to him? His thoughts wandered back to his family, settled in a beautifully restored 1930's home in Tuscaloosa, Alabama where he grew up with antique furniture and vintage dishes. Braden smiled as he recalled the tree house his dad had helped Justin and him build. It was in that magical place where they had slain dragons, fought pirates, and learned about girls before abandoning it in junior high. Angst bubbled just below the surface, at finding himself in such a deteriorating house in a tiny town with not much future ahead of him. Even though he loved historical homes, he vowed he'd have a modern apartment. Yet here he was surrounded by history, and he almost felt guilty for bad-mouthing the mansion. What secrets did it hold, and what hold did it have over him?

By the time the fire had burned down to a few embers, Braden moved upstairs to his bedroom. He swept down the walls and ceiling, dusted and polished the furniture, and swept the floor. Turning on the faucet in the bathroom, water gurgled and spewed forth foul-smelling brown water. Letting it run for a few minutes, it turned clear. Braden let out a sigh of relief. At least they had water. He grabbed an old mop and dented bucket, filled it with water, and mopped the floor.

After cleaning his room, he surveyed his work. While it wasn't a poshly designed room, it was now, at least, livable and somewhat comfortable. He didn't bother with curtains since Elizabeth would definitely not be traipsing through the weeds to watch him undress. Plopping down in the rocking chair to cool off after replacing the cushion, he let out a sigh. Something would have to be done about the peeling wallpaper with lavender and purple flowers splashed all over it. It was enough to turn his stomach to wake up in a flower patch of faded flowers looking as if they had been planted there from a dying garden. He could almost smell the putrid odor, or perhaps it was the old wallpaper paste that was visible from where the wallpaper had peeled. He envisioned a young girl playing with hand carved wooden toys or porcelain dolls. Or perhaps an older girl, who would sit at the small desk and do her homework, if girls were allowed to go to school. Something felt odd and unsettling about the room, sending a chill down his spine, but he chalked it up to the house having been vacant for so long. Admonishing himself for letting his thoughts run wild, Braden moved downstairs.

He entered the larger bedroom downstairs and gave it the same thorough cleaning as his. The furniture in this bedroom was much finer than the one he chose, and he assumed it was the master. He ran his hands over the furniture. The detail of the work, and the fine wood were priceless antiques. How could anyone just leave such treasures and move on? Opening the drawers, he discovered that they hadn't been used by the squatters, so he wouldn't have to deal with moldy clothes.

In the bathroom, he scrubbed and sanitized the fixtures. Disgust at how human beings could live in such squalor overcame him. He surmised they had only stayed for a short time.

Trudging to the kitchen, he noticed an arched fireplace with a raised hearth. It looked almost like one he'd seen in a pizza restaurant, except there was no door. A somewhat modern stove jutted out from a row of cabinets situated underneath a window looking out to the back veranda and a walkway to another building. Looking up, Braden noticed a flue that was vented to the outside.

"Must have been for an old iron cookstove," he mused.

A large tin tub hung on a hook at the end of the cabinet. Talking to the air, he said, "This must have been what they used to wash dishes." Sticking out from another set of cabinets looming like a giant white shark was an outdated refrigerator. All the cabinets looked to have been created by a master craftsman, and Braden wondered if the original owner had built them. Opening drawers. he was not surprised to note that all of them had dovetail joints. Even though there were forks and spoons in one drawer and some mismatched plastic dishes in the cabinet, there was no way he was going to use them. He went to his car and brought in a box of kitchen ware he and his mother had selected. Dumping the ones in the house into the box he had just emptied, Braden would ask Elizabeth if she wanted them. He made a mental note to have the well inspected and the water tested. In the meantime, he'd use the bottled water he bought for cooking and drinking and boil water for washing dishes. Running his hand along the shelves of the refrigerator, it felt cold, which relieved him. He shook his head that the only thing the squatters left in the refrigerator were a few cans of beer, but it smelled musty and needed a good cleaning. He tried the stove and was delighted to find it worked as well, but it was also filthy and had not been cleaned in a long time.

After cleaning the stove and refrigerator and disinfecting the counter tops, Braden declared the kitchen fit for cooking.

He swept and mopped the kitchen before starting dinner. His mother had taught him to cook basic foods when he was a teen. He and Justin had fancied themselves world-famous chefs. Justin had always been interested in food, and between them, they experimented with making up recipes. Sometimes they had to throw out their endeavors, but other times, they made some surprisingly good food. The idea of creating special dishes is what prompted Justin to go to culinary school.

Braden could still hear his mother's words as clearly as if she had been in the room.

"You never know if you'll get married. You're so picky, you need to learn to cook and clean."

Her words still incensed him. Being a bookworm, his mother felt he'd never find a girlfriend. Unfortunately, she was probably right. He had dated some girls in high school, but either they were too flighty, too hung up on looks, or wanted to date the local football boys. None of them liked classical music or fine literature. He didn't have any better luck in college.

Testing the oven, it felt hot enough for him to put together a meal of basil and spinach stuffed chicken breasts with rice pilaf and fresh green beans. He found a kettle and put on water to boil for iced tea.

Just as he finished, the front door opened, and Elizabeth called out, "What's that wonderful smell?"

Braden yelled, "Dinner."

Elizabeth stood taking in the sight of the handsome man who had just agreed to live with her. "What can I do to help?"

"I didn't know if you wanted what was left here in the kitchen, but I put everything in a box for you."

"I don't think I want to use anything that was left."

"My feelings exactly. You can set the table."

"Mmm, I think I'm going to like having you for a roommate."

Braden ignored her comment and put the meal on the table. "I hope you don't mind, but I've always said the blessing before a meal." And oh, how I need some blessings, he thought, and patience, too, Lord.

19

"I'm so glad you said that. My family always prayed before we ate. I got out of the habit when I lived with my friend."

Braden held her hand and said a quick prayer. "Hope you like it."

"This is delicious." She gushed over every item, even the green beans which Braden had seasoned with salt and pepper and just pinch of sugar. "I don't want to pry, but I'm wondering why you chose to come here."

Braden fought to keep his anxiety under control. "It's kind of strange. This was the only offer I had because I found out there's not much demand for male elementary teachers. I'll stay a year because I signed a contract, but then I plan to either get my certificate to teach at the high school level or go to culinary school in Dallas like my friend, Justin. Another reason, I have decided to stay is because of my grandmother. She and I are close, and she used to tell me bedtime stories and would make up names of towns, both here and in Ireland. I always thought Scottsville was a made-up town. She said she had been here and went to family reunions at a large plantation house. Imagine my surprise to find out the town really exists! Wouldn't it be a hoot if she was in this very house?"

"It must have been a while back because this isn't exactly a tourist area. Did she mention why? Did she have family here?"

"I don't know, and I don't know if she really ever came here or if it was something she made up. She didn't elaborate as to why she was ever here, but I know her family traveled to do revivals. Maybe she visited here. Obviously, I have a lot of questions to ask her!"

"I'm having second thoughts about staying here."

"I'm surprised you bought the house if you have thoughts of leaving."

"In all honesty, I sometimes act before I think. I guess the princess in me always wanted to live in a castle, and this was the nearest thing. I imagined how grand it would be and how much fun I'd have decorating it, and now I'm stuck with it."

Braden nodded his head. He could certainly relate to her spontaneity. "Look, Elizabeth, I don't mind living here for a little while, but I'm kind of a neat freak. This house is going to take a lot of time to keep clean, not to mention the repairs."

20

Elizabeth's lips formed a pout. "I can't say I didn't expect this. I keep looking to see if anyone has a house for rent, but so far, no luck."

"As I said, we'll take it one day at a time." He watched Elizabeth's face go from dejected to excitement. If only he could curb some of her electrified personality, maybe he could make this work.

CHAPTER FOUR

Lying in bed, Braden tossed and turned. He would talk to Elizabeth about a window unit since the bedroom felt like a steam bath, leaving him wet from sweat. He had tested the one in the parlor downstairs. It seemed to work fairly well, but the air didn't reach upstairs. The windows he had opened, did not help. There was not a breeze to be had. He berated himself again for accepting Elizabeth's offer. But he was here, and he'd paid the first month's rent, so he was stuck for a month or so. Besides he had invested in a nice mattress set.

Looking around with moonlight streaming through the windows, the hideous flowers on the wallpaper looked like a black aberration. Should he modernize his room? He needed to strip the wallpaper and find something neutral that would still reflect the beauty of a once lovely home. But did he even want to help Elizabeth?

A cold breeze swirled over him. It circled his bare chest but no other part of his body. He figured it was the sweat drying. He got up and closed the windows. The minute he got back into bed, the cold air started again. Going back to the windows, he checked to be sure he had closed them all the way. They were closed tight. How did the cold air circulate when the windows were closed? He raised the windows again. The air was still, and in the moonlight, he could make out the trees. No leaves moved on them. Goosebumps raised on his arms. He felt something in the room he couldn't define. Surely the downstairs window unit would not create such a drastic temperature drop, and why was the bedroom so hot until now? "Maybe it's just this old house, and there's a draft coming in somewhere from another part of the house, or maybe the frames are loose. I'll find out tomorrow where it's coming from," he mused. He pulled the coverlet up to his chin. The cold air seemed to still swirl underneath the coverlet. Braden shivered until sleep finally overtook him.

Getting ready for school the next morning, he walked into the school and checked in with the office to see where his room was located. Fifteen third graders sat, their eyes shining, waiting for their new teacher.

"Good morning!" he said and was met with an echo of the same words. Looking at his roll, surprise registered when he noticed a few boys were absent. He quizzed the class and found out they always came a few weeks late to school because they had to help pick cotton.

The first day was awkward as students summed up Braden. He still felt unnerved from the night before, but he forced a happy demeanor to try to give a positive attitude.

A young girl approached him at lunch. "I'm Janet. We never had a man teacher before, but we think you're gonna do okay."

"Thank you, Janet. I'm looking forward to a wonderful year. I have some fun things planned that I hope you will like."

"Yippee! See ya." She joined her friends at a long table reserved for students. The staff had their tables set apart from the noisy interaction of the children but where they could still watch over them. Braden sat between two women, who looked to be his mother's age. One was so thin, she reminded Braden of dogs he's rescued whose bodies were little more than skin stretched over bones. The other woman was obese and had trouble breathing. What a mixture, Braden thought. Though they were chatty and seemed excited to have a male staff member, Braden felt no camaraderie with any of them. Not one of them was near his age, not that he'd want to date right away, but it would have been nice to find someone with some commonality. Dealing with Elizabeth was enough for now. He could never tell her mood. Either she was Miss Perky Peggy or Miss Debbie Downer.

Two boys stood out as trouble makers, disrupting the class, trying Braden's patience. Jed Adams and Donald Denning. Not having been around young children except during his internship, Braden racked his brain to figure out how to deal with them. If this was any indication of what lay in store for him, he might have picked the wrong vocation.

Though exhausted after school, Braden was eager to make his bedroom more to his liking. Stopping by the hardware store, he picked up some basic tools and headed home. The first thing he wanted to do was find out where the cold air came from last night. He took out a notepad and began making a list of the most pressing repairs. In his bedroom, armed with his tools, he examined the window frames to see if they were loose. Confused, he found the frames were intact, and he could feel no air coming through them. All of a sudden, the room felt old and creepy reminding Braden of some of the old Hitchcock's suspense movies he'd watched. Could it be someone was murdered in this room? He'd heard that the essence of a person could hang around for a while. To his way of thinking, that was a lot of nonsense, but he felt as if he were being watched by the character, Jeff Jefferies, in the movie *Rear Window*. He turned to see if Elizabeth had come home early and was in the room with him, but he was alone. Or was he?

Moving through each bedroom, he was somewhat bewildered that the house felt sound except for the floor boards that needed sanding, but he hadn't examined the attic or done any in depth investigation. Things could look good on the surface but there might be underlying issues.

Downstairs, a small room across from the large parlor held an oversized desk and chair, a floor to ceiling bookcase along with a fine leather sofa, and a beautiful marble surround fireplace. "Another place to do lesson plans and start on my novel," he remarked. Problem was he had no idea of the premise of a book, except he always thought he would write historical fiction. Maybe the history of this grand old lady would provide a backdrop for the novel. Taking his time in the room, he noticed, stuck in the darkest corner, an old easel. "Maybe an artist lived here."

Going to the parlor, it was as if he were in two worlds. An antique olive-green velvet sofa and matching chairs had been pushed against the wall and a modern red faux leather sofa sat across from the fireplace. It was covered in what looked like cigarette burns, and in a few places, there were splits in the cushions.

In the dining room, a huge china cabinet kept watch over the room as it was the only piece of furniture.

The kitchen had a cheap wooden table that seemed as out of place as Braden felt.

Visions of his mother flitting through the house oohing and awing over the antiques put a smile on his face. His mother was good at finding bargains. Perhaps she could find an antique table that would replace the rickety one where he and Elizabeth ate. Mainly, he wanted his dad to see if he could find the source of the cold air. Maybe he shouldn't worry. Elizabeth had not purchased a new window unit to replace the one that was about to give up the ghost, so to speak, but it was better to have some cold air coming from somewhere than being engulfed in sweat all night for as long as it worked.

Outside, a few limestone bricks had fallen and lay haphazardly around the perimeter of the house. Some had cracked and would need to be replaced if they could match them. The wraparound veranda had suffered a lot of damage, but with a power wash, some boards replaced, and a couple of coats of stain, it would be a great place to sit and listen to music or talk. He and Elizabeth had not had a lot of time to visit, but Braden needed to see what she had in mind for the first project. He made a pitcher of iced tea and sat on the back veranda trying to relax.

The building across the walkway from the kitchen intrigued him. He decided to take a look. Pushing the large door open, he gasped! It was a very large kitchen with the same detailed cabinets, a large iron cookstove, and another huge fireplace. Windows on three sides let in a lot of light, even through dust-encrusted windows. One of the cabinets had a built-in tin sink. Why would a family need such a large kitchen? Four people could move around in it and not bump into each other. Did the family have large feasts so that they needed this large kitchen? It looked as though it had not been used for decades. He wanted to renovate it, but it would be last on the list. How much fun would it be to try cooking on an old woodburning stove?

He moved back to the veranda and sat in a wicker chair, enjoying the quiet before Miss Hyper Sunshine came home.

Elizabeth bounced out of her car to join him. She removed her heels and plopped into another wicker chair beside him. "I took off early today. There's nothing like sitting all day with nothing to do, no buyers, no sellers. Wonder if I'm in the wrong business?"

"What else would you like to do?"

"Buy a restaurant, I suppose."

Braden couldn't hold his laughter. "Elizabeth, you said you can't cook. How could you possibly own a restaurant?"

"I wouldn't cook. I'd just watch the front and manage the people who'd work for me."

26

"Oh, well, that makes perfect sense." His sarcasm was lost on Elizabeth.

Despondency showed on her face. "But I don't have any money to get started."

"You think you'd need to learn some basic skills first? And what about this house? Isn't it enough to keep you busy and drain your bank account? And you don't know how to cook because?"

"My mother is a fabulous cook, but she never wanted me in the kitchen. I tried my hand a few times at making cookies, and made a mess of everything." Her demeanor brightened. "You could teach me! You're a fabulous cook!".

"Elizabeth, I teach third graders. I don't teach adults, and especially if you want me to do repairs. Speaking of which, what do you want me to tackle first?"

"What would you suggest?"

"The veranda would be one of the easiest repairs without too much expense. Some boards and nails should do it. I'll look it over and see what we'll need." Calculations started whirling in Braden's brain.

"What do you think about the inside repairs?"

"I thought the window frames were loose, but I've checked all of them. None of them need repairing. Some of the windows are pretty thick with grime, though. I'll rent a pressure washer and see if we can clean them enough not to have to replace them. That would be a big expense. I can also use the washer on the veranda."

"I hate to ruin your weekend."

Braden laughed. "I've got the first week of school behind me. I don't know another adult in this town, except you, so I need something to keep me busy."

"Can I help?"

Braden couldn't resist. "Can I? You mean, may I?"

"No, I meant, can I? Am I capable?"

"Oops, sorry. The teacher in me. Yes, if you have time."

"I've taken the weekend off from the office and just put the phone on the answering service. They will call the house if I have an important call. I had the phone here activated yesterday. I wrote down the number for you. It's on the counter."

"Great, grab your purse, and let's go to the lumber yard. In your car."

"Why mine?"

"Don't want mine scratched with the lumber." Could he even do this? After his first night in this run down, depressive old manor, probably filled with ghostly beings, if he had believed in that, Braden had decided to stick out the first month and leave. Still there was somewhat of a mystery surrounding this place that pulled him in, and he still wondered why his grandmother visited here.

Memories surfaced as he recalled how he had sat, enthralled with the stories she told him, magical tales of Ireland and Scotland, and fairies and leprechauns. Braden knew some or most of them were figments of her imagination to thrill him when he was little, and maybe some of them were embellished truth. She also created fictional towns and countries, and one that now rose to the front of his memories was Scottsville. But when Braden had learned Scottsville was an actual town, his curiosity was further captivated. Why Scottsville?

It was always their special time. Charity's eyesight dimmed a little as she aged, but her stories fascinated Braden, wanting to know more about her life before he was born. Her cognitive function seemed intact, and Braden prayed she would never lose her memory. Her presence soothed him more than any other person. The tears he shed alone in his room as he watched her frail smile fade a little more each day tore at Braden's heart. It was only when he told her he was moving to Scottsville, that her eyes had brightened, and a smile illuminated her face.

She took his hand and held it as if she didn't want to let go, and he would have been content to sit there forever, but life called. As much as he loved her and couldn't stand to be away from her, he knew she wanted him to spread his wings.

"Nannie, I'll write to you and call you when I can. Be a good girl, and don't into any trouble, or I'll have to come home and ground you."

His grandmother laughed. "Now, Braden, you know you can't curtail my actions! After you're in Scottsville for a while, come home, and tell me how you like it."

There it was again. Scottsville. "Okay. You think I'll like a small town?"

"I hope you will. It's kind of a neat town."

28

"You've been there?"

"Yes, a long time ago."

"Tell me about it, Nannie."

"It's not the time now. Experience Scottsville, and go with an open mind. I would love to know how it's changed. It's been many many years since I was there."

"I'll let you know. I love you Nannie, and I'll see you soon."

Leaving her room, Braden mulled over what she'd said.

He had put his curiosity to the back of his mind. But now he was here. Someday, he'd find out more of why she had mentioned it.

"Braden? Are you having second thoughts about the veranda? You seemed to be in la la land."

"Oh, sorry. I guess I was just letting my thoughts wander. Let's go." He moved to her car.

CHAPTER FIVE

Armed with a pressure washer, boards, a couple of pounds of nails, and a huge container of iced tea, Braden and Elizabeth worked all day Saturday. Elizabeth handed Braden boards, and he nailed them. By six o'clock they had finished the walkway to the Big Kitchen and replaced all the loose boards on the veranda.

Elizabeth stood admiring their work. I didn't know pressure washing would help this old wood. I'm amazed you knew how to do that."

Braden joined her, wiping his face with a bandana. "My dad loves working with wood. I want to be sure everything is dry before we apply the stain and polyurethane. How about dinner?"

"You are not going to cook. It will be my treat at The Greenhouse."

"I'm too tired to get dressed. How about you have your first go at making something?"

"Like what?"

"There's a couple of steaks in the refrigerator I picked up yesterday on my way home. I'll put those on my new charcoal grill I had delivered. You can practice making baked potatoes and salad."

Sitting down, Braden unwrapped his baked potato. "My goodness, you certainly poked enough holes in this poor potato."

"I didn't want to burn them. You said to poke them."

"You did great. Best meal I've had in a long time." Braden smiled, a tease sparkling his eyes. "After we do the dishes, I'm ready to turn in."

"I'm doing the dishes. You've done enough."

"By the way, I'm wondering if you ever feel cold air. I think there may be some place that air is getting through."

31

"I just feel a breeze because I always have the windows open. I'm afraid to use the window unit in my bedroom because I don't know if being so old, it might short out and cause a fire. I should see about getting you a new one because it does still get hot, even in September. I will tell you, though, I'm glad you're here. Sometimes, I get a spooky feeling. I guess it's because the house is old and creaky."

"A window unit would be great, but I'm sure the weather will cool off soon, and I like the idea of opening the windows. I'll ask my dad who knows everything about remodeling how much trouble it would be to install a window unit if I can't stand the heat."

Lying in bed, Braden shifted trying to get comfortable to assuage his muscles. He could feel his body rebelling from the repairs on the veranda and walkway, but it was a good kind of sore. He made a mental list of things he hoped to accomplish to help Elizabeth and bring this grand old mansion back to life. Though Elizabeth wasn't what he envisioned as his type, she was pleasant to be around when she wasn't wired and hyperactive. She mentioned almost every day how grateful for any effort he expended. Until he could move on to bigger things, he found he enjoyed helping her. She gushed to excess over everything he did with an almost childlike look lighting up her face. Repairing the veranda was kind of like bringing history back to life. Visions of what the house might look like, once they were finished, painted a picture of a long-gone era, and he fell asleep dreaming of throngs of people gathering for a party in the grand parlor.

Something woke him in the middle of the night disturbing a pleasant dream. The sound of branches scraping against a window. He waited to see if it occurred again. It was a subtle noise, but it repeated three times. Braden crept to the window. No tree outside his windows grew close enough to have made the noise.

"Strange," he murmured. "I'll check tomorrow and see if there are branches too close to the other bedrooms." Sleepiness and sore muscles prompted him back to bed. He finally got back to sleep, but the dream did not reappear which annoyed Braden.

Checking the next morning, there were no trees anywhere close enough to the house for a branch to scratch a window, but he saw broken branches on the ground. "Must have been the wind throwing them against the window and breaking them," he mumbled. Looking closer, he swore the branches formed a heart. "My imagination is working overtime," he said. He ambled to the kitchen. Surprise registered on his face as he saw Elizabeth with a dish towel tied around her waist, her hands wrist-deep in flour, and a cookbook propped up on the counter to her right. Ingredients sat clumped together against the cookbook to hold it open. A can of lard, a tin of baking powder, and an opened sack with flour spilling all over the counter greeted him. The smell of bacon sizzling in a pan and a carton of eggs next to the stove prompted a smile.

Elizabeth heard him, but she didn't turn around. "Good morning."

"What are you making?"

"Breakfast. Do you like biscuits?" It took Elizabeth a good hour to make the meal. The bacon was so crisp, it broke and resembled dried cranberries as she scooped it onto a platter without a paper towel to drain it. The scrambled eggs were a little underdone, but edible. The biscuits were as hard as a concrete parking lot.

"I'm impressed that you are interested in learning to cook, Elizabeth."

"I don't know what I did wrong, but I've decided you're right. I need to learn to cook before I think about giving up real estate for a restaurant. You can see why my mother never wanted me in the kitchen."

"Giving up real estate for a restaurant probably isn't a good idea at the moment. Let me ask you something. Did you hear anything strange last night?"

"I hear things every night. That's another reason I'm glad you're here. This far from town I get scared sometimes. I guess it's just the house settling. At least that's what I've been told."

"It appears to have had over a hundred years of time to settle. I'd like to look over the grounds today. I usually go to church, but since I don't know much about the town, and my muscles are chastising me for overworking them, I think I'll skip."

"Me, too, but I had decided to make you a world-famous breakfast. That didn't turn out too well."

Braden rose and took his dishes to the tub. "Want to explore with me?"

"Sure."

Braden ushered Elizabeth to the side of the house and showed her the branches. "Must have been a powerful wind last night to break these branches, but I found it strange that they formed a heart on the ground."

"That is odd, and gives me the heebie jeebies for some reason."

"I don't think it's important. Just wanted to show you. Let's go to the back of the house and start there."

Armed with a sickle he found in an old stable, Braden cut through the weeds enough to forge a makeshift path. Elizabeth followed and raked the path clean. The weeds were waist high. With their sweat, and the sun beating down on them, they drew an army of mosquitos and other insects to feast on their arms and legs not covered in shorts and shirts.

Braden glanced at Elizabeth from time to time. Judging from her face and the occasional loud sigh, he could tell she was not enjoying this. Just as he was about to stop and turn around, he noticed a river. Sunlight reflected on small ripples shining like diamonds, making happy gurgling sounds near the bank as it sped along to who knows where.

"Look, Elizabeth. Did you know this was here?"

She clapped her hands and yelled, "Last one in's a rotten egg!" She sat on the bank and pulled off her shoes. Braden followed suit.

"Haven't heard that expression since I was about ten. Let me test the water and see how deep it is before you drown yourself." He slid down a small embankment and put his feet into the water. Venturing farther, he realized that it sloped from shallow to much deeper in the middle.

"I think it's okay. You can swim, can't you?"

"Yeah, I was on the swim team in high school."

An afternoon of splashing, swimming, lazing on the bank, and talking about the renovations they planned for the house seemed a fitting reward for the hard work of clearing a path.

"Elizabeth, seriously, I may not stay in Scottsville long enough to see all the renovations done because it will take a lot of time and money to get this property where you want it."

"But you will finish out the school year, won't you?"

"Of course. I've found that I really enjoy having a small class for my first assignment, but I have a dream of a nice apartment in a city. I may join my friend, Justin, in Dallas."

"I can't do everything by myself, and I can't hire it done, so I guess I'll have to live with whatever we get finished before you leave. Then I'll

34

put it on the market. I'm sure some farmer will buy it for the land. And, for all the help and hard work you're doing, I'm not charging you one cent for rent."

"That's kind, but you shouldn't short yourself. I rather enjoyed working on the deck, or the veranda as you call it."

"I just wonder what secrets this house has, who lived here, why they left, and why it was vacant for so long." Elizabeth started for the house.

Braden pulled at a weed rubbing against his elbow. "One of my minors was in history, so my curiosity is aroused as well. And why they left the furniture. Maybe I'll research it. There's bound to be a nice library in Vicksburg or Jackson, both equidistant from here. I wonder why whoever lived here in more modern times put in cheap modern furniture and that horrible bathroom. It does seem, though that a farmer would buy it for the land." Unless he had the weird feelings I'm having, he thought.

"Please let me know what you find out at the library. I'd be happy to go with you if you go to Vicksburg. I'm not crazy about Jackson."

"Why not? Isn't it your hometown?"

"Yes. It's a long story, but I like Vicksburg better."

Braden didn't want to be rude, but Elizabeth just wasn't his type. She was either bubbly like a child or depressed and looked as if she were ready for a pity party. Some days, she sounded more normal, and he enjoyed talking to her. He could never tell what her mood would be any given day, but there would never be sparks between them.

"Thanks for the offer. I may spend the weekend there, but I'll let you know."

CHAPTER SIX

Midweek, the loud speaker in Braden's room summoned him to the office. A secretary walked in to watch his class. "What's this about?' he asked her.

"I don't know. I was just told to come watch the kids."

Braden hurried to the office, wondering if he had violated some rule and was about to receive his first reprimand. Braden knocked on the door. The principal, Mister Patton, ushered him into the room. Four people sat on a sofa and chairs across from the large desk.

Mister Patton greeted Braden. "You look puzzled. We'll clear this up shortly. Please have a seat." He indicated a chair he had pulled up so Braden was facing the two couples. "I'd like to introduce you to Mister and Missus Adams and Mister and Missus Denning."

Braden shook hands with the men and nodded to the women before sitting down. "Nice to meet you." Maybe, he thought. What had those two trouble makers told their parents?

Mister Denning spoke first. "Although you have only been here a few weeks, I thought it important enough to take off work to talk to you. Our son, Donald, has been a trouble maker from the time he was born. We've seen numerous specialists, and he's had a different diagnosis with each one. He hates school, he hates homework, he hates…."

Missus Denning interrupted, "It's easier to say what he likes because he hates almost everything, including us. Now that you're his teacher, he doesn't fret as much about school. In fact, he gets his homework without complaining. We don't know what you have done to cause a change in him. We'd like to ask you, so maybe we could deal with him at home."

Braden smiled. "I hated school in elementary, myself, until I had a great third grade teacher. I've tried to do some of the things that she did to make school enjoyable and fun while still challenging us. Donald likes to be on top of everything and doesn't make friends easily. I've created

37

some contests, and they have to pair up. Donald and his partner, Jed Adams have teamed up and win a lot of the time." He glanced at Jed's parents, both nodding their heads.

"How do you think that has changed his behavior?" Missus Denning asked.

"He's bright, very bright. I'm no psychologist, but I feel he's bored. That's why I challenge him."

Mister Adams said, "We have the same complaints. Our son isn't rebellious, but he has had no interest in anything other than building model cars and airplanes. Now, he's excited about school. He talks a lot about what he and Donald are doing. They have become close. We're here today to tell you how grateful we are for you and what you've done with our children."

Braden sat stunned. "Thank you very much. It has been my pleasure to have your sons. I try to get into each student's head, so to speak, and see if I can find a way to encourage them in a way that isn't boring."

Mister Patton spoke, "As you know, we had reservations about hiring a male for elementary, but you were our only choice. I guess you have cemented your place! So nice to have you on board. I hope you'll stay until retirement!"

The two couples rose and shook hands with Braden. Mister Denning said, "If you need any outside supplies for your projects, you let me know. I'll be happy to supply them."

"Thank you, sir. I'm honored that you're pleased with my teaching."

The day passed in a blur. Braden reflected on the conversations on the way home. He had come to this pokey little town, thinking he'd last maybe a year or two and move on. He had no idea he would become so attached to the town, to a sad old house, and to students who challenged him in a good sort of way. Maybe he wouldn't be too eager to leave. A thought occurred to him, but he'd run it by Elizabeth before putting his plan into action.

Elizabeth met him at the door. "I wonder if you would grill some hamburgers. I have everything else ready. I have some news to share."

"Let me change into something more casual."

Wearing shorts and a Roll Tide t-shirt, Braden walked out to the back veranda. "I also have some news. You first." He set about getting the grill ready.

Elizabeth watched him. "I'm closing the real estate office. I talked to Mister Knight. He's content to let me run the office from home since the lease is up this month. It will save him a ton in expenses, and we haven't been that busy. He also got me on the board of the Chamber of Commerce to see if we can come up with a way to grow Scottsville."

"That's wonderful, Elizabeth." He told her about the meeting with the two couples. "I have decided not to leave, at least for the time being, so I'm at your service for when you want to do more work on this house. The other news is I was thinking about asking my parents to come for a visit. My mother is great at knowing how to restore antiques, even down to the fabric. My dad is a salesman, and his hobby is construction."

"That's how you learned? Should we fix up the second bedroom downstairs or one upstairs for them?"

"Downstairs would be fine. I bought a new mattress set for them."

"I'll pay you for it."

"No need. Let me know when you sell your next home, and we'll talk about it. Braden watched her as they ate. She seemed deep in thought, and her mood had changed. She looked happy, but not giddy. Maybe working from home would be good for her, and in turn, good for him.

Preparations were made for the second weekend. Elizabeth spent the entire week cleaning the house from top to bottom. She bought fresh linens for the extra bedroom and more towels and wash cloths for the bathroom.

Emma and Mason Cunningham arrived right on time the next morning as Braden knew they would. Emma followed Elizabeth through the house, stopping to run her hands over the fabric on chairs and sofas that sat in a corner, examining the antique furniture in other rooms and dating them for her.

Sitting in the parlor with a glass of iced tea, Emma said, "Elizabeth, you have a goldmine here. This place could be restored so beautifully. You are lucky that most of the furniture is original. Some of the cheap stuff will have to be replaced, and some of the antiques will have to be repaired, but I think Mason could help with some repairs on the structure, if you'd like."

"That would be wonderful, but I have to save money to afford the repairs. That's why I haven't done it yet. I didn't know anyone who knew about antiques."

"I guess Mason and Braden are looking at the out buildings. Mason will be as happy as a puppy with a shoe. He has his own business now, so he can take off when he wants to, and I'm a stay-at-home crafter, so maybe we can work out something. Braden told me you aren't charging him rent, so it's the least we can do to help out."

"What can I do?"

"Let's go through the house. You write down what we have and what we need to do. Let's begin in here."

They spent the better part of the morning working in the parlor and dining room, assessing furniture, repairs needed, rugs, fabric, and the fireplace repairs.

Emma poked her head into the bathroom. "Oh, my. This is sad. I'd say we make remodeling this our top priority. It's a nice size, but we need to rearrange it and get new fixtures. Mason is good at that sort of thing. He should have been an architect as well as a construction genius. I can't abide this bathroom in this condition."

Mason and Braden braved chest high weeds and found a beautiful house near the river with a bridge and a path leading to the bigger mansion as well as a stables and a woodworking shed. The river meandered around a curve, apparently through a grove of trees.

"Do you think this house was for slaves, Dad?"

"It looks more like a single-family dwelling. Slave quarters were usually single cabins or sometimes a long building, but not with distinct rooms like this. It's almost as large as the bigger house. Why they would vacate the mansion is a mystery. Of course, the research would be interesting. I'd love to work with you on this, but you are just a renter."

"I never thought I'd want to live in such a small town and certainly not want to save money to invest in a decrepit house."

"But it's growing on you, isn't it?"

Braden grinned, "Maybe. Right now, I'm hungry. I think we should go in and eat. I put a meal in the oven, so it should be ready now. There's

40

only one restaurant here, and they are so busy on the weekend, I decided we could eat here."

Over dinner, Braden told them about the meeting at school he had with the parents. "I've thought of several different ways to engage the kids in some academic contests as well as some fun activities. My principal told me he would raise my salary next year, even though they don't usually do that for new teachers."

Emma's eyes sparkled. "Good for you. You can make your mark here, Braden. We are very proud of you. We'll be visiting often because I have fallen in love with this place."

Braden smiled. He'd had no doubt that his mother would be thrilled the minute she entered the home.

"I'm delighted as well, Braden." A fleeting look crossed Mason's face. "Your grandmother is going to be beside herself."

"Dad, you seemed so eager for me to take this job. I know it gave you and Mom some time alone, but I'm wondering why you seemed so happy for me to take this particular job. Was it Nannie?"

"Your grandmother has mentioned Scottsville numerous times. I think she wanted you to live here, and frankly, I kind of wanted to see what the town looked like since I thought it was a figment of her imagination."

"How is she?"

She's frail, but her memory seems to be intact most of the time. Her appetite isn't as good as it used to be, but she doesn't seem to be in pain, so I attribute everything to her advancing age."

"She's really not that old, Dad. She can still walk, can't she?"

"She uses a walker if she has to go very far, and we hired a caregiver to stay with her while we're gone. We didn't want her to turn on the stove and cook."

"That's a good idea. I couldn't stand it if she got burned."

Emma pushed her hair back. "Or burned the house to the ground."

"The last time I was home, she told me she wanted to sit down and talk. I'll try to come as often as I can."

Emma changed the subject. "Now about this bathroom. Something has to be done. Mason, look it over. See if we can move that shower and get some decent fixtures. I would like to keep the tub if it can be salvaged."

41

"Yes, ma'am. Braden and I will get right on it. I know how fastidious you are. I surely would not want you to have to bathe in an old metal shower stall." Mason's lips turned up in a grin.

Elizabeth put her napkin to her lips to hide a giggle.

Emma shot Mason a look. "You know me well."

Mason assessed the bathroom. "Look, Braden, we could have that clawfoot tub refinished, put in a large shower, and counter with a sink if Elizabeth has the money. It's big enough, but not arranged properly."

"I didn't want to say anything, Dad, but I've been thinking about this house. I'd like to research it, but I'm also thinking maybe I'd like to stay here. My class is small, the kids are adjusting well to me, and most of all Mister Patton is pleased with me. I'm considering making Elizabeth an offer to buy half of the property and turn it into an inn or a museum."

"I think that's a great idea, as long as you trust Elizabeth. Let me know what you find out about this property when you research it. And you have to think about whether Elizabeth will up and move on, leaving you with a large mortgage. That said, your mama will be overjoyed. Her wheels are already turning as to how to renovate this place."

"I can tell. I guess I'll talk to Elizabeth."

After they left the next morning, Elizabeth and Braden took their coffee and sat on the back veranda. Sweeping her eyes over the landscape, Elizabeth exclaimed, "There's so much to do. Where do we start?"

"To begin, I have a question for you. It seems to me my parents and I are going to be doing a lot of work, so don't you think I should have part ownership?"

Shock stilled Elizabeth's voice for a few minutes. "I would have been willing to sell you the whole thing the minute you got here, but you didn't seem interested. Your parents have made me believe I…we…could turn this in to something wonderful. I would love to have you as part owner with the stipulation that if it doesn't work, we can buy each other out. But even if we restore it, it's still going to be too big for just the two of us, unless one of us gets married and fills this house with kids."

"Maybe we could either sell it or turn it into an inn."

"I love the inn idea. We'd have to advertise a lot, though, to get guests."

"I'm sure. So, do we have a deal?" Braden's eyes took in the forlorn vista. What was he thinking? And where did this offer come from? He hadn't even had time to really think about his decision. But his mouth overrode his brain.

"Yes." Elizabeth clapped her hands. "Thank you."

The proposal was a done deal. Elizabeth looked too excited for him to back out. "You're the realtor. You draw up the papers, but remember you told me how much you paid for this, so I'm willing to go for half of what you paid."

"I would not think of trying to make a profit, Braden."

Braden looked hard at Elizabeth. Since she had been working from home and joined the Chamber of Commerce, she had changed into a different person. She acted more mature and let her intelligence shine through. She had come up with several ideas to garner interest in the town, and several businesses from Vicksburg had expressed interest in moving. The city had added a park along the river that ran through town, complete with playground equipment and picnic tables.

CHAPTER SEVEN

Braden and Elizabeth decided to spend a weekend in Vicksburg. Braden paid for two rooms in a nice hotel. They explored the city so Elizabeth could get some ideas for the planning committee, and after a deli lunch, they perused the library to see if they could find out about the mansion. They found the antebellum mansion they called home was named Oak Hollow Plantation and was built around 1840 by a doctor and later occupied by the Sullivan family from Cork, Ireland who bought it sight unseen.

Walking back to the hotel, Elizabeth said, "I've been thinking about your idea to turn the mansion into an inn. I'll bet we could get the house on the National Registry, which might make it more attractive to history buffs. It seems to have been an important plantation."

"I believe the only reason there was an article about it was that it was used as headquarters during the Civil War by the Confederates."

"I'm glad it wasn't a hospital. I read that some soldiers took over large houses as hospitals. No telling what germs were spread, and some houses had to be burned. Lots of men died." Elizabeth shivered.

"That's true." Braden didn't mention he had thoughts of whether a murder had taken place inside the walls. Maybe it was dead soldiers. After all, they were close to Vicksburg where a major battle happened, and it was rumored to be haunted. Talk at the Chamber was Vicksburg might look to annex Scottsville.

Elizabeth's eyes sparkled. "Shall we restore its name?"

"Let's think about it. It's no longer a plantation, but it does have a sizeable amount of land. To name it a plantation doesn't seem right. Maybe Oak Hollow Inn or something like that."

"I like that. It could also be The Sullivan House or Scottsville on the River."

"Lots of possibilities."

A week later, after a particularly stressful Friday, Braden turned in early. He had not had time to really work on the house, though he was eager to start clearing some of the weeds around the perimeter. No telling what kind of critters had taken up residence. His mind flitted from one project to another until he felt sleepiness creeping up. Suddenly he heard Elizabeth scream and heard her running up the stairs. Braden sat up, but before he could get out of bed, Elizabeth burst into his room and jumped on his bed, grabbing him around the neck.

"What the heck?" Elizabeth grabbed his arms and put them around her. "You're shaking. What's going on?"

Finding her voice, she whispered, "There's a man in the house."

"Probably not now. You scared me half to death screaming. He probably ran." Braden kept a revolver in a chest in his room. He grabbed it, ignoring the fact that he was in his underwear, and crept downstairs. Examining every room, he found no forced entry, and the doors were locked.

"Thank you. I'm sorry I screamed and scared you. I'm fine now, though." Her mood settled down. She smiled. Braden was standing in boxer shorts decorated with red hearts and chocolate kisses holding a gun. "Cute boxers!"

Braden's face turned as bright as the hearts. "Gag gift from a frat brother. I need to do laundry." He bolted upstairs. After throwing on some jeans and a t-shirt, he came back down.

Elizabeth was sitting at the table. "Why are you dressed? It's three o'clock in the morning."

"Can't sleep now, and apparently you can't, either. Maybe some hot chocolate will help. Besides I want to know about this man you saw."

"He looked to be about sixty or so, tall and skinny, had on a weird long coat, and his eyes were like steel just staring at me. He raised his hand and said, 'Abe,' and I ran upstairs."

"Are you sure you weren't dreaming about Abraham Lincoln?"

"Maybe, but it was so real."

"I don't believe in ghosts, but maybe all this research we've been doing has spurred your dreams. I doubt President Lincoln was in the house during the Civil War, though, since he was on the other side."

"If so, that's the most vivid dream I've ever had. Sorry I destroyed your sleep."

Braden worked all morning Saturday with a scythe. He had an area around the house cleared enough to use an old push lawn mower he found in the woodworking shed. Taking a break, he looked up and saw Elizabeth carrying a tray with fresh lemonade. "Thought you could use a little refreshment."

"Thanks. What have you been doing besides making lemonade?"

I bought a new cookbook. I've been planning dinner. I'm determined to learn to cook if you're game. You didn't die with my breakfast as bad as it was. I also thought I'd go down to those trees and see if they might have pecans."

"I don't want you to go by yourself. There may be snakes. I'll grab my revolver."

Midafternoon, they took a dip in the river and explored the house Braden and his dad had found.

"This house is built out of the same limestone bricks as the main house and looks roomy enough for a large family. Another mystery." Braden shook water from his hair and towel dried it. "Let's go see about the pecan trees."

A few of the trees were old and had fallen, but many newer trees had clusters of green nuts. "Looks like we may have a crop this year. I'll try my hand at pecan pie."

From the house, they trudged through shoulder high brambles. The thorns scratched their own brand of art on their arms, making them look like red tattoos. Braden tried to shield Elizabeth from the larger ones. He felt them pierce his back through his thin shirt as he held them back for her. He decided to call a halt to their adventure when he heard Elizabeth let out a delighted squeal.

"Look, Braden, these bushes have blackberries on them. Pecans can wait." She pulled up her shirt from the bottom and made a pouch. She started picking the berries until she had a pouchful. "We'll have these for breakfast tomorrow. Maybe blackberry pancakes or just a side of fruit with toast."

Braden smiled at her enthusiasm. "We're finding treasures all over the place. I believe, though, there may be a better way to get to the woods. I need to prune these bushes back once the blackberries are finished making. For now, I'm tired after my lawn work this morning. Makes me appreciate gas powered mowers."

"You're right, Braden. We'll look for another way. Let's go back to the house."

"I just want to shower, shave, and crash."

"I'll warm up some soup. Would a light supper be okay?"

"Yeah, that shouldn't take too long."

For once, Braden had no trouble falling asleep. Turning to his side, he woke with a start. He'd been dreaming again. He looked at the clock. Three o'clock. "What's with the three in the morning deal?" he mumbled. He sat with his head in his hands trying to remember the dream.

He recalled a thin girl with long blonde hair in a lavender dress with a huge skirt. She carried a basket with books sticking out of it and seemed to float around a meadow. She had a beautiful face, but she wasn't smiling. He felt he knew her, but couldn't put a name to her. "Guess it was just a dream, probably from all those purple flowers on this girly wallpaper, and maybe on the cover of one of those romance novels in the grocery store." Braden usually forgot dreams, but he couldn't shake this one. "Maybe Mother can come up with better wallpaper when she comes again. These flowers are too much." He relayed his dream to Elizabeth the next morning at breakfast.

"I forgot to tell you. Your mom called and wanted to know when they could come again."

Braden said, "That's up to you. I don't exactly have a social calendar."

"I don't either. The guy I dated for two years decided he didn't want to be in a serious relationship."

"After two years?"

Elizabeth's face turned dark, almost as if a shadow fell across her. "Let's say, I was in a relationship. He was in several. Kind of soured me on getting serious with anyone."

"What a jerk. I had never asked about your personal life, but thanks for telling me. I guess next weekend is fine with me if you don't have plans. Want me to call my parents?"

"Sure. Thanks. Do you have a girlfriend back home?"

"No, I'm too artsy for most of the girls I've met."

"I like artsy."

The middle of October provided warm days and cool nights. A few of the oak trees had begun to turn, and leaves of gold and orange gave a colorful backdrop to the otherwise drab fields. Braden had thought about asking Harriet at The Greenhouse out, but the few times he had been there, she was nowhere to be seen. He assumed he just kept missing her shift. Though he had been to church and a movie every once in a while, but there was limited social interaction. Braden hadn't found anyone who interested him, other than Harriet, and he had not asked Elizabeth to accompany him on any of his excursions because he didn't want to encourage her.

Roaming around upstairs, he had discovered a large rolltop desk in one of the other bedrooms, but the room was hot and stuffy with only one window. He decided to use the small desk already in his room to do lesson plans and maybe start on his novel. Thinking about a premise, he thought the house would make a good story. "I doubt I'll find enough material for a nonfiction book, so I'll just fictionalize it," he said to the desk.

Elizabeth had given him a journal for his birthday to make notes of the progress of the restoration. Sitting at the desk one afternoon, Braden started itemizing the repairs they needed to do. Something caught his attention. He expected to see Elizabeth standing beside him. He turned, but no one was there. He went downstairs to see if she had come up and left when she saw he was busy, but she was gone. She left a note saying she was going to the grocery store. The presence of someone in the room with him continued and spooked him.

"Okay, this house is getting to me." He decided to go for a walk and sit by the river for a while. Watching the water as it sped along, it played a song of peace. Relaxation washed over him. He postulated it might be headed toward the mighty Mississippi River. The small limestone house intrigued him. Why would a house made from the same stone be placed in this location? On his walks around the property, he and Elizabeth had found some remnants of what might have been slave cabins. Mostly they were just random piles of rotted logs, but some of them had partial fireplaces still standing. Research showed that overseers sometimes had better houses, but this one looked too grand for an overseer. So many questions, but one that took precedence over the others at the present time was Elizabeth. She wasn't his type. While he felt a deep friendship and camaraderie with her, he felt no romantic leanings. She had continued subtle flirting, and it made him a little uneasy.

Speaking as if the small house could hear him, he said, "This could complicate things. If she feels more about me, and we are partners, what will happen to our business deal if she feels rejected?"

Braden rose and walked slowly, feeling his way through the weeds to watch for his parents. Surely Elizabeth would pick up something for lunch because everything in the house was earmarked for dinner. The Greenhouse was a good little restaurant, but this visit from his parents was to ascertain what needed to be done to the house. Braden didn't want to take time to sit and visit in a restaurant, especially since Harriet was no longer there.

Elizabeth rushed in with an armload of groceries and more in the car. She began putting things away while Braden welcomed his parents, then went to help her.

Not surprisingly, Emma had prioritized the list she and Elizabeth had made on their last visit. She handed a copy to both Braden and Elizabeth.

Sitting in the parlor, Braden addressed his mother. "Did Dad tell you that I have decided to go into partnership with Elizabeth, so I am now half owner of this property, or will be when I get the mortgage paid?"

A frown formed between Emma's eyebrows. "He did tell me. I thought you wanted to move to a bigger city in a year or so. I'm surprised you want to stay here."

"We talked about that. If I decide to move, Elizabeth would be in charge of the house, and I'd pay her a salary. Same thing if Elizabeth decides to leave."

50

Elizabeth spoke, "And we are thinking about making this into sort of retreat or an inn with breakfast served. I'm learning to cook. I got a cookbook on brunches, so cooking shouldn't be too hard."

Emma beamed. "I think that's a splendid idea. How clever you two are. All the more reason to get started on the interior."

Mason had quietly eaten his lunch, a puzzled look residing on his face. "You've got a lot of land, and if weeds were a commodity, you two would be rolling in money. Have you thought of what to do with the grounds and fields?"

"That's where we need your advice, Dad."

Mason focused his eyes out the window and waited for what seemed hours before speaking. "This could be a fairly large farm, so I would suggest you find a local farmer to come in, clear the land, and plant a crop. It could be cotton or maize or wheat or vegetables, whatever his preference and give you half the profits. That way the fields would look nice without any work on your part, and you would have a little income. The other thing I thought about was raising horses, but with you teaching and Elizabeth having her hands full, that wouldn't be an option."

Elizabeth and Braden looked at each other. Elizabeth's eyes were dancing. "I like that idea of horses. Maybe we could hire someone who knows about horses and offer that as an activity for our guests. And in our research, we could see what kind of lawn games people played in that era and offer that as well. The horseman and his family could live in that other house we found if we fix it up."

Emma smiled. "Spoken like a true realtor." She rose. "Come, Elizabeth. We have things to do while the guys discuss what needs to be done structurally." She retrieved a tote from the bedroom they'd be occupying.

Emma pulled out a large catalogue of fabric swatches. "I borrowed this from an interior decorator friend. I don't know what colors you prefer, so I thought we could put some of the swatches over the sofa and chairs and see what you think. We need to keep it authentic."

"I was thinking maybe a sea theme. Turquoise, pink, and navy blue with pictures of ships and the ocean. We could have each room a different theme."

"Antebellum homes did not use those kinds of themes, dear, but we could certainly use your color scheme. I believe the walls should be more muted colors and the furnishings brighter. I also brought wallpaper samples." Emma held up a swatch of a sea green and taupe wallpaper. We could combine that with either a solid velvet fabric or a paisley with soft burgundy, yellow, ochre, and green. Or we could go more muted with a light blue ceiling, eggshell white walls and light blue and white fabric on the furniture. That would make the room look larger."

"What do you think would look best?" Elizabeth fingered the swatches.

"I like the lighter, softer colors for the parlor and dining room and brighter, bold colors for the study across the hall. In fact, if it's structurally possible, what do you think about opening up the wall and having either an arched wall or columns so the dining room and parlor are open to each other?"

"I'd love it."

They spent the better part of the afternoon going over plans for the two rooms, the study, and even a couple of the bedrooms.

Elizabeth sighed. "With everything we need to do, it's going to cost a lot of money."

"We could loan you the money to get started until you start making a profit."

"We already owe you for the bathroom that Braden and Mason are working on. I'd have to talk to Braden. He doesn't think I'm good with finances, but I'm studying a book I bought."

Emma smiled. "It's just that I want to get started. Let's see what the guys think we need to do first. Outside or inside of the house…after they do the bathroom."

Braden and Mason came in from outside. Mason plopped down in a chair. "I'm hungry, and there's no need to cook. Let's go try out that restaurant in town. My treat."

Braden sat down opposite him. "I put a roast in the oven which should be ready now, and I don't feel like taking the time for each of us to shower and get dressed. With only one bathroom, that would take forever. Let's do lunch tomorrow before you leave." Braden wanted to see if Harriet was working, and he figured she would be there on Sunday if she hadn't quit.

"Remodeling that bathroom has to be done for your mother!"

Emma popped up and gazed out the window as if she could visualize what the finished restoration would look like. "We're staying until Tuesday. Your dad can start on what needs to be done, maybe find a farmer, and Elizabeth and I can look into an upholsterer while you're teaching, Braden. Can you spare the time, Elizabeth?"

"Yes, I'd love it."

Mason had brought in his tool box, measured floor boards, and examined the posts and beams in the attic. Muttering to himself, he said, "I can't believe the house is so well built to have withstood weather, war, and wear for over a hundred years. We need to replace a few posts, but the beams seem to have held up well. All in all, there's not as much work to do as I had expected." He figured how much lumber they'd need.

He went back downstairs. Emma met him as he took the last few steps. "You've been busy. Why don't you rest until Braden gets home?" Emma started putting her samples back into her tote. "Elizabeth and I found an upholsterer, and he's coming to get the parlor furniture next week."

"I'll go see about buying a horse or two and a groom. The weeds are so high, we are going to need someone to clear the fields, plant some grass for the horses and maybe grow a crop of some kind. I guess I'll need to see about a farmer, too."

CHAPTER EIGHT

Braden came home from school mid-morning Tuesday. His face was flushed, and his eyes looked red as if he'd been crying. Emma rushed to him. "What's happened?"

"Nothing, Mother. I didn't feel good yesterday, but I thought it was soreness from the work Dad and I did, but after I got to school this morning, I realized I'm coming down with something. Several of the students have been coughing and have runny noses."

Emma felt his head. "You're burning up. Straight to bed, son. She found some aspirin in her purse gave him two."

Braden grinned. "No telling what else you've got in that purse, but I know it's heavy!"

After they got Braden situated in bed, Emma made sure Elizabeth knew what to do. "If he gets worse, take him to a doctor and call us."

"Yes, ma'am."

"We're going to go ahead and leave, but call me tomorrow, and let me know how he's doing, or sooner if he doesn't get better."

Braden lay on his back, staring at the faded feminine wallpaper with the awful purple flowers and startled when Elizabeth entered with a tray of chicken soup, a jar of Vicks, and some soft cloths.

"I don't want to upset you, but my grandmother always rubbed Vicks on me when I was little, and chicken soup is a known remedy, according to my grandmother. Eat your soup, and I'll be back." Elizabeth hated for Braden to be sick, but rubbing the Vicks on his chest would be a highlight of her day. His chest reminded her of handsome men on the covers of romance novels. Besides that, he made her feel safe. She had been having some strange feelings, hearing some weird noises, and

55

seeing shadows in her bedroom. She didn't say anything because she didn't want Braden to think she was being silly after she had screamed and jumped onto his bed earlier. The shadows never materialized into discernible shapes, so she attributed it to the moon shining through swaying branches. Knowing Braden was in the house gave her a sense of comfort.

Just as she started up the stairs to administer the Vicks, it started raining, and a chill traveled down her arms. A cool front had moved in.

"Look at the window, Elizabeth. It seems as if the rain is going around a circle that almost has the shape of a tree. Wonder if there's an oily spot where the rain won't stick."

"That's strange. It looks more like a heart to me."

Their eyes were glued to the window. None of the other windows had the same effect. The rain poured down in sheets.

"It does resemble a heart now that you mention it. No telling how many years of grime and maybe some oily substances have accumulated on these windows. Maybe a young girl had greasy fingers and made a heart and it was never cleaned." A deep cough interrupted Braden's conversation.

"Maybe." Elizabeth didn't mention it gave her an eerie feeling. She finished applying the Vicks, and placed soft flannel cloths over the salve to keep from staining the t-shirt she helped him with. "I'm going to leave you alone. Get some rest. I brought up a bell I found, so if you need anything, just ring."

Braden stayed out of school the rest of the week. Much to his delight, the cold wind had stopped swirling. He didn't know exactly what his dad had done in the attic, but it must have stopped the source of the air. Elizabeth had a business trip for the Chamber in Vicksburg, and Braden asked her to see if she could find any additional information on Oak Hollow or the Sullivans.

She returned with a stack of books and some articles they copied for her. Braden read when he could keep his eyes open. He learned a few facts, but not anything enlightening.

Elizabeth entered the bedroom. "How are you feeling? Did you learn anything more about this place?"

"I'm better. I've been up and down the stairs to see if I can gain some of my strength back. Most of the books are on the founding of Scottsville, the businesses, and the most influential people. I found out Abraham Sullivan was one of the wealthiest planters, and in fact, at one time, he owned two plantations. Most of the articles are about activities he participated in. There's not much about what happened during the Civil War, though. Only that one article that said the house was used as a headquarters for the Confederacy, which we already knew."

"I ran into Hiram Parker. He said your dad made a deal with him, and he's going to start clearing the fields tomorrow before cold weather sets in. If you hear loud noises, it's probably his tractor or whatever he uses."

"Wonder why he didn't buy it when it went to auction?"

"Said he didn't want to outlay the money to buy it, clear it, and have to deal with the house. He said people would have been mad if he'd torn it down. This way, he said, he could just farm the land, giving us half the profits."

"That makes sense."

Friday morning, Braden was jarred out of bed with a vibration that shook the house. He strode to the window to see what caused such commotion. Hiram had some kind of machine attached to the back of his tractor and was clearing land around the house that Braden had left when he cleared the perimeter. He stood, mesmerized at how quickly the machine worked, even though the cacophony was enough to deafen a person.

Elizabeth had become quite the cook, and Braden had survived her earlier attempts without food poisoning. She prepared a light lunch, inviting Hiram to take a break and eat. Braden felt like coming to the table, which was good because Ellie felt like he would want to talk to Hiram.

"Sure does look good, Miss Elizabeth. Ya know, my folks have been in Scottsville for as long as anyone can remember. My wife loves digging into the past. She told me this place used to be called Oak Hollow. Fellow by the name of Sullivan owned it. I believe she said he was a

57

foreigner. The wife wanted to buy it, but it was in too bad a shape to my way of thinking. Seems my kin owned the plantation next to it."

"What was the name of that plantation?" Braden gave his full attention to Hiram.

"Let's see. I think she said it was called Walnut Hill and was owned by the Sullivans. But my kin way back was a guy named James Noble, and he bought it. 'Course all the plantations got split up after the war. It was used as a hospital. Wife's into findin' out about our ancestors."

"Thank you for the information. We've read a lot of the large houses were used as hospitals. We are trying to do some research on this place. Is Walnut Hill still standing?" Elizabeth's refilled his iced tea glass.

"Naw, it burned to the ground. Twice. First time was some slave hunters, but Noble rebuilt it. Last time, they said it was caused by a patient, that went crazy and knocked over a couple of lamps. Had the devil of a time gettin' the patients out. Guess I'd better get on about my rat killin' as they say. They's a lot of land to clear. Don't think it's been touched in a good long spell. It'll be good for crops 'cause it's almost like virgin land."

Braden smiled. "I don't know about rat killing, but watch for snakes. While you're clearing it, feel free to come in any time you get tired or need some water. Elizabeth always has a light meal prepared, and you're free to join us."

"Thank you. I've a right smart to get done, so I'd best get after it."

Braden coughed, the tail end of the upper respiratory illness he had. "Been fallow probably longer than we know. Glad you've got on high top boots. I'm sure there are rattlers hiding in those weeds."

"Yeah, funny thing is, there are some farmers who eat those things. Never appealed to me. We ain't got that hungry yet!"

After Hiram left, Braden and Elizabeth sat over another glass of iced tea. Braden got his journal and started writing what Hiram told them. "We learn a little more each day. I'd like to ride out and see if we can find any remnants of the house still standing after the fire."

"Writing down everything that we're doing is a good idea. Maybe we could turn it into a booklet that guests might like to read. Mind if I go with you to Walnut Hill?"

"I'd like the company. I also wonder if the Sullivans owned any other plantations." Braden tucked his journal into a small backpack. "Might find something interesting to write down."

They weren't sure which direction to go, but assuming that Oak Hollow was one of the largest, they decided to drive away from town. While there weren't plantations, there were several large farms with fields now stripped of cotton. A few farmers were out clearing the fields in preparation for the next crop.

Braden had removed the detachable top and maneuvered his car over a roughly paved road. He chastised himself for putting his beloved car through such a seldom traveled road with small pebbles flying up and hitting the windshield. Driving for what seemed an hour, they found no trace of Walnut Hill.

"Guess the debris from the fire was cleared a long time ago." Braden turned the car around.

"The fields look so ugly now that the pretty white cotton is gone." Elizabeth scanned the horizon.

"Mother wrote and said they would be here Friday. I think she said you two are working on the parlor?"

"Yes, and the dining room."

"Dad mentioned knocking out the wall between the two."

"Depends on how much it costs." Elizabeth had calculated their expenses, and it frightened her that they might not be able to pay his parents back.

Shedding their lightweight jackets, Elizabeth called Braden to the parlor. "I found a book on bookkeeping. I've started keeping a profit and loss statement of our expenses and will add our profits if we ever get this place opened up for guests."

A shocked look spread over Braden's face. Elizabeth had definitely changed over the last few months. No longer the flighty girl, her focus was on the house and her real estate business. Joining the Chamber had been the best thing for her. Most of the men in town accepted her, even though she was the only female on the board.

"See," she said, "I've put the amount of the loan your parents gave us, the materials we've bought, and how much everything cost. The only thing is we need to pay your parents back. We should also pay them for their time."

59

"They are enjoying working on the restoration. We'll pay them back as soon as we can for the loan."

Late morning, Friday, Emma breezed through the door, tote in hand, followed by Mason lugging a tool box. Braden went to help him.

Setting her tote down, Emma brushed her hair back where the wind had whipped it into her face. "Goodness, that wind is strong."

"Would you like something to eat?" Elizabeth followed her as she entered the parlor from the foyer.

"No, dear. We stopped on the way."

Mason looked over the wall. He knocked on it in several places to ascertain if it was a load bearing wall. "I think I can knock this wall out to open up the two rooms. It's up to you, my dear, but have you and Elizabeth decided if you want an arched entrance or columns between the two rooms?"

Braden stood, taking in all the activity and marveled that his petite mother could be such a whirlwind of activity. "Do I have any say so in any of this?"

"Of course, dear. What do you think we should do?" Emma frowned, fearing she had excluded her son from their decisions.

"I don't care one flip for what happens down here, but could you please get rid of that ghastly wallpaper with those purple flowers in my bedroom?"

Emma and Elizabeth burst out laughing. Elizabeth wiped her eyes. "You mean you wouldn't like us to add a bit more lavender? I saw a really pretty bedspread in Cumming's Department Store that has lavender flowers on it." Elizabeth's eyes were dancing.

"That's not funny, Elizabeth. I can barely sleep. It reminds me of a funeral, and I swear I can smell them. They smell rotten."

Emma said, "We'll make that our next priority." She turned her head to shade her grin.

Mason had a large hammer and started punching holes in the wall. "Archway or columns?"

Elizabeth looked at Emma. "I think columns to match the ones on the veranda, though I do love arches."

Emma chimed in, "I think either would be perfect."

Mason measured the wall with Braden's help. Why not both? You could have a couple of columns, which would also give integrity to the structure and have an arched top."

"Yes, yes!" Elizabeth clapped her hands.

Emma agreed.

By late afternoon, the old wallpaper in the two rooms had been stripped. Dust and odd smells from the paste used so many years ago to hang the wallpaper permeated the entire house. The family decided it was time for a nice meal out. They went to The Greenhouse.

Braden noticed Harriet was working again. "Nice to see you, Harriet. Haven't seen you around for a while."

"I've been busy." She glanced at Elizabeth. "Have you found us a house, yet?"

Elizabeth smiled. "I was going to call you Monday. I have a three bedroom that might be a possibility. Are you sure you want only two bedrooms? I found one in your price range that has three bedrooms."

Braden looked confused. "House? You're buying a house?"

"Yes, my husband and I are tired of living with his parents."

Elizabeth introduced Emma and Mason. "Harriet married Hiram's son, Rodney, a few months ago. She's been helping with their farm now that Hiram's taken over our fields."

"Everything's cleared now, thank goodness, and I can get back to this job. Rod's going to Jackson for the spring semester. I hope to go later."

Braden, though disappointed, looked at her closely and realized that she was older than she looked. There goes that possibility for dating.

CHAPTER NINE

By the time the Cunninghams left, the parlor and dining room were in shambles. Elizabeth had swept and mopped the floors, but the walls were bare and the holes in the wall looked like a giant rat had chewed through it. A few scraps of wallpaper remained, and no matter how many times she swept, dust kept falling out of the holes.

Braden sat with his head in his hands. "What have we taken on, Elizabeth?"

"I don't know. The fields look wonderful, and it's nice to see the river. I hope the parlor and dining room will look great when they're finished, but I'm sorry we didn't get to your bedroom. I had a call from my mother. She wants me to visit them. My cousin is getting married. They want me to help with her bridal shower."

"How long will you be gone?"

"Probably a week. You'll probably enjoy some peace and quiet after all this banging around. Maybe you can work on your novel."

"How's your father feeling?"

"He's doing as well as can be expected. His diabetes acts up every now and then, but my mother is a great nurse and keeps him on a strict diet. Dad works at an accounting firm in Jackson. When he feels too bad, he takes work home."

"I'm sorry they haven't been able to visit. I'd like to meet them, but I know your dad is proud of you, especially your bookkeeping skills, following in his footsteps."

"They rarely visit because of his diet. Mom has to weigh his food, and he can only eat certain things. I'm going to take the books I've been keeping to show him."

Elizabeth left early Monday morning. Braden wandered from room to room after school. The house had evidently settled since Mason had repaired some beams and had eradicated a large rat's nest in the attic. Now it seemed too quiet, even though school was a good diversion. Braden threw himself into planning some activities since they were studying the pilgrims and the first Thanksgiving. He decided to have the children make some decorations for the classroom, and he would furnish snacks.

Sitting at his desk, he put down his pen and stared out the window. He couldn't keep his thoughts off of Elizabeth. She had been all business ever since they decided to co-own the property, and he missed her. What he thought would be a real annoyance with her bubbly personality when he moved in had now turned into a real friendship. Her self-confidence had soared, and her intelligence amazed Braden. She had learned to keep the books, had turned into a good cook, and his parents really liked her. His mother hadn't said anything directly, but she had left hints.

Braden had saved some money. Speaking to the empty house, he asked, "I wonder what it would be like to date Elizabeth? Would that ruin the friendship? She has stopped flirting, so would she even be interested?" Braden slapped his cheek. "What am I thinking? I don't want to date a friend and business partner."

Thanksgiving week excited the kids. Braden's efforts paid off. Decorations filled the room, and his snacks were well received. Donald and Jed had soared to the top of the class academically. Instead of bullying, they had started helping slower kids. Life was good at school, and things were progressing at home. Braden's sister, Susan, though she wanted to go home, had to work Thanksgiving, so she suggested her parents visit Braden and Elizabeth. Emma offered to prepare the meal. Braden didn't know if Elizabeth would go to her parents, but it would be nice to eat his mama's famous dressing and pumpkin pie.

Walking in the front door, Braden saw Elizabeth poring over a book in the parlor. "What are you reading?"

"A cookbook. I wanted to do a Thanksgiving meal, but it looks like a lot of work for one person."

"I thought maybe you'd go home for the holiday."

64

"No, my dad can't eat traditional stuff, and I told Mom I wanted to cook here. Now, I'm having doubts."

"My parents have invited themselves. My mom has offered to cook. Maybe you two could work together. They'll be here tomorrow. Mom wants to do some work on the parlor and dining room."

"Great! Maybe she could show me how to make dressing."

Emma flurried through the house Wednesday morning followed by Mason, his arms loaded down with paper sacks of groceries. Braden ran to help him. "What is all this?"

"I have no idea. I suppose it's for the meal."

"We're not feeding an army. I guess it's a woman's thing."

Elizabeth and Emma put the groceries away. Emma sat at the rickety table in the kitchen with a folder. "I have some pictures that I found in a magazine. I like the ivory wallpaper we talked about, but I'm thinking painting the walls might be easier, faster, and prettier. And the upholsterer wrote me that they have the fabric in and wants our approval."

"Let's go."

When they entered the shop, Elizabeth gasped. They had polished and refinished the wood on the chairs and sofa and they gleamed with a soft patina. The fabric draped over the sofa and chairs was perfect. They had selected a deep blue velvet for the sofa and a brocade floral of pale peach, subtle yellow, and ivory on a cerulean background for the chairs.

"When can you have this finished?" Emma ran her hands over the fabric.

"In a couple of weeks. The holiday, you know."

"Wonderful." She turned to Elizabeth. "Do you have a paint store?"

"The hardware store sells paint."

Lugging a couple of cans of paint into the house, they walked in to ask Braden to get the rest of them out of the car. He took them to the parlor.

Mason looked at her. "I don't know if you would like it, but there are a couple of tables in the attic."

Everyone climbed up to see what treasures Mason found. The opening to the attic was huge. Two dormers shed enough light as four pair of eyes swept the oversized attic full of antique furniture.

"Mom, your mind is racing faster than the Indianapolis 500. We're not finishing this attic right now." Braden grinned.

"Oh, but it has such possibilities."

Mason guided her to a table. "Look at this. Looks like some kind of pattern on the edges. Will this do?"

"Yes! Look, Elizabeth, and here's a smaller round one."

Braden focused a beam from his flashlight on both tables.

Elizabeth and Braden both gasped.

"What is it?" Emma asked as both men moved closer.

Mason said, "This small one looks like it was made from a tree with the rings in the center. And look at the way there are cutouts around the leaves on the edge."

Braden commented, "But, more importantly, look at the name Sullivan. We found out they bought this house and probably finished it the way they wanted it."

Elizabeth exclaimed, "We have to take them down. I can't wait to see what else is up here. Looks like boxes of stuff. Maybe some dishes or something?"

Mason shone his light around and noticed chairs that might match the large table. "Let's take these, too, because I'm afraid I'm going to fall through those flimsy things we're sitting on."

It took some maneuvering to get the tables and chairs down from the attic, but it was well worth the trouble.

The dining room table and chairs were stored in the study until the parlor and dining room were finished. Elizabeth polished the chairs and dining room table. The tree-ringed table was placed in the kitchen. They decided the designs on the dining room table were Celtic in origin.

Emma motioned Elizabeth down the hall. "I'll start putting the dressing together for tomorrow. I always like to mix all the dry ingredients and store them in the fridge until I have the turkey cooked."

"What can I do?"

"We can go ahead and get as much prep done as possible. You can peel and chop the sweet potatoes and the Irish potatoes. We'll store them in water in the fridge so they won't turn color."

The men had returned to their work in the parlor and dining room. Strange noise emitted from the room, but Emma and Elizabeth had been warned not to enter.

"I can't imagine what they're doing in there to make so much noise. It certainly has my curiosity up." Emma wiped her hands on her apron. "And hanging a sheet over the door makes me even more curious."

Elizabeth stopped chopping. "I was thinking the same thing, but I know nothing about construction."

Putting the bowls of potatoes and dressing mix in the fridge, Emma wiped her brow. "Let's get a light supper together for the guys. If I know Mason, he's going to want to shower and eat the minute they take a break."

Braden and Mason had been working all day behind the sheet over the parlor door. They emerged fifteen minutes later.

Mason yelled, "We're going to take a shower. How long till dinner?" He walked into the kitchen followed by Braden.

Emma's eyes sparkled. "Do I assume since you said 'we' you and Braden are going to shower together?" She and Elizabeth bent over laughing.

"Okay, smarty pants. I'm going first and then Braden."

"How long will it take?" Elizabeth was wiping the tears of mirth from her eyes.

Half an hour later, they were sitting around the beautiful kitchen table laughing and joking.

Elizabeth wiped her mouth. "We don't need a TV. We are more fun than anything on the tube."

Braden rose to take his dishes to the sink. "I can't speak for all of you, but I'm ready for bed."

Emma said, "We're right behind you."

Thanksgiving morning dawned bright and beautiful, and the sunshine streaming through her window woke Elizabeth. She wanted to just snuggle under her cover and go back to sleep, but she heard noise coming from the kitchen, so she knew people were already up. Throwing on her robe, she shuffled down the hall. Emma was in the kitchen humming some song Elizabeth didn't recognize.

"Hey sleepyhead. I hope I didn't wake you." Emma put a cup of coffee on the table as Elizabeth glanced around the room. "Where is everybody?"

"Mason is back in the parlor, and I assume Braden is still asleep."

"Should I go wake him up? And why are you up so early?"

"No, let him sleep. I had to put the turkey on to bake."

Emma put bacon on while Elizabeth whipped up a dozen eggs. The smell of bacon and coffee stirred Braden and Mason to the kitchen for a simple breakfast.

Finishing their meal, Mason and Braden moved back to the parlor.

The rest of the day was spent with the women putting together the Thanksgiving meal while Mason and Braden returned to the parlor with more banging ensuing.

After a big Thanksgiving meal, Elizabeth and Emma cleaned up, put leftovers in the fridge, and did the dishes while the men busied themselves in the parlor. Emma sat at the little round table in the kitchen planning out some of the other rooms and getting Elizabeth's opinion. After an hour, the men took a break and sat on the front veranda.

"Braden, I haven't said much to you, but I want you to know how proud I am of you and all the things you've learned that have nothing to do with college."

"Thank you, Dad. I guess the sawdust has entered my veins!"

Mason chuckled. "You seem happy here. Elizabeth is such a sweet girl. Have you two developed a relationship? Your mom wanted me to ask since she knew you'd throw up your hands and roll your eyes if she asked."

"She knows me well. Elizabeth and I haven't discussed anything other than business and friendship, but I must admit, I do feel drawn to her a little."

"We had hoped you would come back to Tuscaloosa after you got some experience, but now you've bought this house."

"Who knows what the future will bring? We have a lot to do. Let's work off some of that meal Mom cooked."

Mason winked with a gleam in his eye. "Shall we?"

"Yes, but how do we keep them from barging in?"

"I told Emma for her and Elizabeth to look at the bedrooms upstairs and see what they need done. I saw some sales advertised in the paper starting tomorrow and suggested they go over the paper and decide which ones they want to go to. Let's finish up what we can tonight and start fresh tomorrow while the girls shop."

"Great. I can't wait to see their faces when we reveal our surprise!"

"Yes, it's going to be fun."

CHAPTER TEN

Emma and Elizabeth had been asked to shop as long as they wanted. They hit flea markets, thrift stores, department stores, and finally a small pastry shop to recover from all the shopping. Over coffee and a cherry scone, they put their heads together to decide where each item they bought would fit.

When Emma and Elizabeth got home, they dumped their treasures on the sofa in the study. By the time they sorted everything as to which room it would go to, they decided on a light supper.

Leftovers were brought out from the Thanksgiving dinner, warmed, and dishes were set on the counter in the small kitchen. Elizabeth turned to Braden and Mason. "We're going to eat buffet style, so help yourselves."

During the meal, Emma and Elizabeth talked almost non-stop about what they'd found. Braden and Mason sat with mischievous eyes sparkling, listening, but didn't say a word, not that they could have eased a word into the conversation anyway.

After a break in the conversation, Braden rose and said, "Follow me." He led them to the parlor where a sheet had hung for days. As he pulled the sheet down, loud gasps punctuated the room as the ladies took in the opulence of the rooms. The archway and columns with the eggshell white walls opened up the space, and the sofa and chairs that had been delivered on Wednesday sat regally in the parlor. Large crown molding gleamed from the top of the walls. Braden had secreted large windows and stored them in the stables. They were now installed. The floor to ceiling windows held a beautiful view of the grounds and the woods beyond, almost bringing in the outside. They had placed lit candles on the mantle and hearth and dimmed the lights in the chandelier over the dining table, giving the rooms a warm glow.

Elizabeth hugged Mason. "These are the most beautiful rooms I've ever seen. I love the light blue ceiling and the furniture looks perfect."

Mason and Braden grinned like two silly monkeys. Braden spoke, "Next on the list is another bathroom, but that will have to wait."

Emma looked shocked. "How? When? I don't understand."

Elizabeth's gaze took in the whole room. "How did you get it painted? We only bought home the paint yesterday." She seemed to fall into a trance.

Braden put his arm around her. "What are you thinking?"

Elizabeth shook her head to come back to reality. "I just pictured grand ladies with their huge skirts dancing around our parlor."

"Maybe we can make that happen. To answer your question, Mom, we worked fast while you were out shopping."

Mason nodded. "By doing a lot of work ourselves, this didn't cost that much. I made a deal on the windows."

After the Cunninghams left, Elizabeth and Braden sat down at the kitchen table. Elizabeth rose, waiting for the percolator to stop so she could pour coffee for them before they looked over Emma's list. An eerie silence filled the house, and then they heard it. A soft giggle seemed to float down the hall.

Elizabeth grabbed Braden's arm. "Did you hear that?" Goosebumps flared on her arms.

"Could it be the coffee brewing that made that sound?"

Elizabeth stiffened. "No, it was definitely a giggle."

They moved cautiously down the hall and entered the parlor. Silence greeted them, but as they started back to the kitchen nook, another round of barely audible giggles stopped them.

"I don't know what's going on, but something is definitely different about this house." Elizabeth moved her chair closer to Braden in the kitchen. "It sounds as if someone approves of the renovations, but it still freaks me out."

"I don't believe in ghosts, but there is some kind of essence in this house. I don't know if it's our imagination, but both of us hearing it makes me wonder."

"Okay, Braden. I haven't wanted to say anything because you already think I'm half crazy, but I've been having dreams. I see shadows all the time. A lot of nights I don't sleep because I'm so scared."

"Elizabeth, I will admit, you came across as kind of scattered and flighty when I first met you, but as the months have gone by, I realize you were hiding your true self from me. You are smart, creative, caring, and a real pleasure to be around. I'm happy we're together, not just as business partners, but as close friends."

Elizabeth brushed her eyes. "Me, too. I don't want to leave this house, but I feel better since you're here. I just wish the freaky stuff would stop."

"It's up to you, but my bedroom is huge. There's enough room for two regular beds in there, so if you'd like to move up there with me, we could be in the same room, or there's a connecting door to another bedroom if you would be more comfortable."

"It would be good to see if we experience the same things, but I don't want to interfere with your lesson plans or if you're working on your novel. Sometimes I toss and turn. Are you sure that won't bother you?"

"You won't disturb me since you'll be in your bed, and I'll be in mine. I can work on paperwork in one of the other bedrooms. Now tell me about your dreams."

"In one, I saw a girl. She had long blonde hair, very blue eyes, and wore a lavender dress with a corseted top and a full skirt. She was talking to a black boy, but I couldn't understand what they were saying. It wasn't scary, but I wanted to know more. Then I woke up."

Braden clinked his cup on the table. In a whisper, he said, "I've seen the same girl."

"Another time, I saw a girl with very curly hair who looked younger and was flitting around on the veranda. The scary thing I dreamed was about people fighting. I guess it was the Civil War."

"You decide what you want to do about where you want to sleep."

"I want to be in your room until we figure out what's going on. If it doesn't work out, just tell me. I can always come back down here."

"We can move one of the beds from the other rooms, or see what we can find in the attic. The one you're sleeping on now is too massive to haul upstairs."

"We might find a treasure." Elizabeth grabbed a flashlight.

In the attic, they found a brass bed frame which looked to be in excellent condition along with chests, chifforobes, dressers, boxes, mirrors, and trunks. There was a large rectangle of something covered in sheeting. Elizabeth pulled the sheet off. Dust flew everywhere, but what greeted them were paintings of landscapes in all sizes.

"I wonder if someone was an artist?" Elizabeth began looking through the canvasses as well as ones that were framed.

Braden coughed. "This dust really gets to me. I'm allergic to it. I suggest we move a bed from here to my bedroom and leave all this for another time."

Braden disassembled the brass bed frame and started to set it up in his room. Elizabeth stopped him.

"You've been waiting a long time to get rid of this wallpaper. Let's do that first."

"Sounds good to me. I'll run into town and get the supplies we need. Dad taught me how to strip the wallpaper in the parlor, so I know what to buy. We had quite a bit of paint left over, so I'm sure we won't have to buy that. You have made me a happy man."

"Braden, one more thing. Thank you for letting me be with you. I was seriously thinking about asking you if you want to buy me out because of all the weird stuff going on that scares me."

"We started this together. Let's finish it together, and if we decide to sell it, then it will bring a better price." Braden gave her a quick hug and bounded through the doorway.

Armed with the supplies, Braden put on an old t-shirt and started scraping.

"I know it's my imagination, but that scraping sounds like someone crying." Elizabeth picked up pieces of wallpaper that fell on the floor and stuffed them into a trash bag.

Braden stopped. They put their ears to the wall he had scraped and listened. A decided sound emanated from the wall. It sounded like something softly crying, but with a squeaky sniffling.

"I think we're letting our imaginations run wild. It's probably a mouse. Maybe we should set a trap. Dad found that nest in the attic, and we thought he had gotten rid of all of them."

74

Braden resumed scraping. "I don't know if we can sleep in here tonight. The smell of the old paste as well as the musty wallpaper is pretty strong."

"It doesn't matter. Wherever you sleep, I'm going to be there, too, even if I have to sleep sitting up in a chair." She began raising the windows, and cold air rushed in. "This breeze should clear it out."

They worked steadily, and by the end of the day, the walls were bare, the bed frame had been put together, and they had brought up the mattress and box springs from Elizabeth's room downstairs. She swept and mopped and made both beds with fresh linens.

"Let's eat in the little kitchen instead of the dining room." Elizabeth began pulling leftovers from the refrigerator.

"I'd like that a lot."

"It'll be cozy. I want a special dinner to celebrate our new dining room, not that these leftovers aren't delicious. I think we'll postpone the celebrating until we're rested."

"Let's make an early night of it. I'm bushed." Braden raked his fingers through his hair.

Elizabeth usually slept in a shortie gown. She went to her bedroom to see what else she could sleep in and not expose herself. She settled on the longest short gown and pulled a robe from her wardrobe. When she got upstairs, she realized Braden was already in bed but had turned back her covers.

"Thank you. How sweet of you." Elizabeth smiled. Her heart skipped a beat as she noticed Braden's bare chest framed by the glow of the lamp on his night table.

"You're welcome. Sweet dreams." Braden noticed she had let her hair loose from the pony tail, and it trailed down her back in soft curls. Her blue eyes, the color of the ocean, intrigued him. Could they become more than friends? When he met her, she definitely wasn't his type, but the more he was around her, the more he felt himself drawn to her. Her sweet disposition soothed him when he had a trying day at school. Maybe a modern apartment was not what he really wanted. Besides this was a perfect setting to start on his novel.

Something woke him in the middle of the night. He glanced at the clock. Three o'clock again. Elizabeth was sitting straight up in bed, her hands covering each side of her face. After a few minutes, she snuggled back under the covers. Was she having another dream?

Warm sunshine greeted them the next morning. Tiny dust particles swirled around the room, and a light breeze invigorated them.

Braden stretched. "Did you have a dream last night?"

"Yeah. I kept seeing hearts floating around. Maybe it was those cute boxers with all the hearts on them you had on a while back," Elizabeth's eyes sparkled, remembering how handsome he looked that day, standing there with a gun. Could have been a calendar photo, except Braden would never pose like that. Elizabeth had toyed with the idea of a relationship, but Braden had made it clear he wasn't interested in dating anyone, so she reined in her feelings.

"Hearts, huh?" Braden's face reddened remembering how embarrassed he'd been.

Over breakfast, Braden suggested they look at Emma's list again. "Mom wants to finish the downstairs, but I want to measure the bedrooms upstairs. I think they are all large enough to do a small bathroom with each one, especially if we want to turn this into an inn."

"I think that's a great idea. We could do one for now. I've made some big commissions this month, so I could afford it if we don't reimburse your parents."

"I've saved some money, too, but I want to see about air conditioning this place."

"I'm seeing a lot of time and money before we turn this house into our dream. I mean, I guess it's my dream, but I don't know about you. You're here because of the future of this place, right, and half the headaches?"

Braden looked hard at Elizabeth. The way her eyes reflected the light on a bright day, almost as if someone had sprinkled glitter in them drew him in, and the Cupid's bow lips that could turn from a pout to a wide smile with just a word had him wondering how those lips would feel if he kissed her. She probably wouldn't win the Miss America crown, but her beauty was natural and seemed to bubble up like a balloon being filled with helium. And her kindness, the way she and his mother bonded, and her eagerness to learn amazed him. Why hadn't he seen all this? Would she settle for an overinflated third grade teacher who wanted big city life? Or did he? Her words brought him out of his reverie.

"Just for half ownership, Braden?"

"Elizabeth, I wouldn't do the work we've been doing if I didn't share your dream. I've come to love this place. It's spooky, and I'd like to know more history, but you've brought the spirit of this house to life. Maybe the sounds are the loud sighs this wonderful old home emits because we've shown her love. I don't feel anything sinister about it."

"I've done very little to bring life to this house, Braden. Your mom is the one who brought my vision into existence. Would I be selfish if I said I wish you would never leave? I feel safe when you're here, you're fun when you let yourself, and you inspire me. But I know you love the big city life, so I can't help but dread the day you'll leave."

"What if I said I'd like to ask you out on a date, Miss Ellie?"

Confusion created a frown between her eyebrows. "Wha…what did you say?"

Braden grinned. "Ellie, if I may call you that, would you do me the honor of having dinner with me?"

"You mean a date where we don't just talk about our next project?"

"Yes, ma'am."

"I'd be delighted, and I love my new nickname." Ellie's hands fumbled with her hair to hide her nervousness.

CHAPTER ELEVEN

Saturday evening, Braden walked downstairs to see if Elizabeth was ready. She sat in the parlor on a newly covered chair in a sapphire blue dress, which brought out the color of her eyes. The soft folds of the ankle-length dress cascaded to a puddle on the floor. She had her eyes fixed on the dining room chandelier and didn't see Braden standing in the arched entrance to the parlor. For a moment in time and space, it was as if he were transported back to when this home was new, and the mistress of the house was waiting for their guests. She took his breath away.

Ellie pulled her eyes away from the dining room and noticed Braden. "Oh, I didn't hear you come down."

"You look beautiful," he whispered as he held her coat.

A blush crept up. "Thank you."

Braden had chosen a restaurant in Vicksburg. Ahead of time, he had ordered a dozen deep red roses to be placed around an oil lamp on the table. The décor was done in vintage style with antebellum paintings gracing the walls. Some were of ladies in grand ballgowns, their hair coiffed in tight chignons, others of landscapes, and early plantation scenes. Walking through a cloistered entrance into a secluded alcove, a fireplace crackled, sending golden sparks up the chimney. The oil lamp emitted a soft glow, giving the table with its circle of roses a soft vintage look. The walls were a dark burgundy framed with soft golden woodwork.

"Oh, Braden, this is magical. I feel as if I've stepped back in time."

"I wanted it to be memorable for our first official date."

"It's so calming, I'd like to spend the whole night here, just taking in the beauty!"

The food was exquisitely prepared and served with aplomb befitting a grand lady. The ambience of the small room provided a perfect backdrop for the talk and laughter of two people who seemed to have just discovered each other.

On the drive home, Braden remarked, "I've wanted to ask you out for a long time, but I was afraid you would say no since you've seemed all business lately. I hope you enjoyed the evening." He didn't mention that it took everything he had not to kiss her, but he didn't want to rush her and ruin his chances for another date.

Elizabeth touched his arm. "It has been the best evening of my life. I sensed you didn't want anything more than friendship, so I pulled back."

"Don't do it any longer, okay?"

"Deal."

"One thing I want to make clear, though. If you ever change your mind about dating me, just say so, and we'll go back to a platonic friendship." Braden found her hand and squeezed it.

"As of right now, that won't happen, but I like the control." Ellie giggled.

Sunday morning dawned cold with a mist enveloping the old house as a norther moved through. Braden was building a fire in the small kitchen fireplace before turning on electric heaters. He wanted to warm it before Elizabeth got up. As he was tending the fire, Elizabeth walked in snuggled in a fleecy robe.

"How sweet of you, Braden."

"To build a fire?"

"No, the window."

Braden looked. There was a heart in the middle of the window as if someone had drawn it on the frost. It took Braden back to his childhood when he drew pictures on cold, mist-covered windows. But this. This was different and strange enough to raise goosebumps. In a quiet voice as if ghosts in the house could hear, he whispered, "I didn't do that, Elizabeth."

She ran to him and threw her arms around him. "We haven't had any strange activity since I moved into your room until this. Why now? This is creepy, Braden. Maybe they want us out of this house. I'm sure it's haunted."

"We have to get to the bottom of this. I wonder if there's a clue in those boxes in the attic? We've put too much into this to leave. A heart signifies warmth and love. I don't think they are forcing us to leave."

Elizabeth pulled away from him to pop a couple of slices of bread into the toaster. "After church, let's go to the attic like you suggested."

After church, they changed clothes and trudged up the ladder to the attic. Braden looked behind him at Elizabeth.

"We need stairs. This ladder is getting tedious and hard to maneuver furniture and boxes down."

"And the opening is big enough for an oversized door, and correct me if I'm wrong, but every time we come up here with your mother, I think she envisions finishing this attic as another room!"

"You know her well."

Using a flashlight, they noticed the boxes had dates on them. Elizabeth dusted the top of them. They decided to start with the earliest one. Braden shook dust from his shorts. "I don't want to put it in the parlor. Let's open it in the kitchen."

Tucked among elegant dresses and petticoats, Elizabeth pulled out ribbons and intricately decorated combs inlaid with pearls or precious gems. She held up a beautiful lavender dress with a lace collar and immediately dropped it, too shocked to speak.

They both stared. It was the dress the girl wore in their dreams. Elizabeth's hand shook as she picked it up again and noticed a small journal had fallen out of the folds of it.

Braden picked it up. "It says Grace's Journal on the first page. Maybe this will give us some history of this place."

Elizabeth made steaming hot chocolate and set their cups on the kitchen table. She ran her hands over the name Sullivan carved into it. Braden handed the journal to Elizabeth. "You read it. It was evidently written by a girl."

Glancing at the window, the outline of the heart was dripping as if crying. Since it was freaking them out, Braden grabbed a dish towel and wiped away the image.

Elizabeth read, "July 13, 1856. Tonight was awful. There was a fire in the lower sixty acres that blazed so hot, we thought it might move to the house. Everyone worked all night, hauling water and stomping out embers. Our dresses got all sooty. Mama nearly fainted from the heat and the work. Papa tried to get her to come back to the house, but she refused. I guess Maggie and I both get a little bit of stubbornness from her. Miss

81

Daisy is the only one who didn't go. She made a good meal, and the workers joined us for an early breakfast on the veranda. I really like our workers. I'm glad Papa doesn't call them slaves or darkies. I like the word workers better since Papa freed them. It's a big secret, though, because we could get in lots of trouble. Papa might even have to go to jail."

Elizabeth looked at Braden, who had picked up the book. "Hmm, wonder what caused the fire? I guess it didn't reach the house. Is there more on that page?"

"No. The next page skips to July 27, 1856."

"I'm guessing that lower sixty is not part of this property now."

"I agree."

Braden said, "I'll read, and you finish your hot chocolate before it gets cold." He lingered on her hand as he opened the book. "The pages are thin and fragile. Some of the ink is blurred, but maybe I can make out what she wrote."

"I guess they used an ink well."

Braden gently handled the page. "July 27, 1856. I am so glad this night is over. Maggie and I had to dress up. The heat was terrible. I felt like my legs were in the river, we were perspiring so much with our heavy petticoats and big skirts. Maggie wanted us to take off our stockings, and we would have, but the Millers got here early. That was the worst part. Mama would have had apoplexy if she had discovered bare ankles. They have this spoiled girl named Jane. She put on airs like she was some elegant queen. Mama would scold me for writing this, but she won't ever see it. I didn't think the night would ever end, especially when Papa asked them to stay over. Thank goodness, they refused. This is so different from Cork. We wore comfortable clothes there and only dressed up every once in a while. Here we have big dresses, corsets, and petticoats. Essie Mae helps us dress, and Lavitica June helps Mama. My favorite dresses are the day dresses with only one soft petticoat. They feel more like the ones in Cork. I don't know if Papa and Mister Miller will have an agreement, but I hope we don't have to be around Jane very often. I wish we could go back to Ireland."

Elizabeth touched Braden's arm. "I guess she was a daughter. Shall we read more or look through the rest of the box?"

"Let's look through the box. I want to make some notes for more research. What caused the fire, and who were the Millers? What kind of agreement would they have had?"

Elizabeth once again pulled the lavender dress from the box. "She must have been a skinny girl."

Braden studied the details of the dress. "Was her waist really that small?"

"Oh, this explains it. Look at this corset."

"What's a corset?"

"It is an undergarment with stays in it, kind of like a man's collar, and it laces up the back. They would cinch it as tight as the girl could stand it."

"Looks very uncomfortable and stiff."

"Didn't you see *Gone with the Wind*?"

"Yes, a long time ago. I probably didn't pay attention to the corset."

"There are lots of dresses in here. Wonder why they packed them? I guess they got tired of them." Elizabeth removed each dress and smoothed it. "These would look great in a museum."

"Apparently, there's not much else in the box that will give us clues as to what happened to the Sullivans. We have some other decisions to make."

"You're talking about a bathroom upstairs?"

"Yes. We either put in another bathroom or install air conditioning."

"I'd say we go for the bathroom because the weather is cooler now, and the electric heaters are warming each room for the winter. A closet would be nice also. And you mentioned stairs to the attic."

Braden glanced at Elizabeth. He loved the girl next door look she had, and in the mornings, her skin took on a dewy glow. He wanted to kiss her. "Why don't we go for a walk this morning? Maybe we could pick some pecans. Since the area has been cleared, I'd like to see what Hiram Parker has done to the fields. Maybe we could find some fallen trees we could use for firewood."

They bundled up and walked toward the pecan grove with a basket for collecting any nuts that were ready for picking. Entering the woods, Elizabeth felt as if they were stepping back in time, enveloped in the arms of nature. The large pecan trees had dropped most of their golden leaves, providing a soft carpet, but a heavy fog had moved in and rose up from the woods. Elizabeth repeated, "The woods are lovely, dark and deep."

"Robert Frost."

"Yes, the woods aren't so deep now, but they are lovely in the spring and summer. As she walked ahead of Braden, she felt a sense of happiness and peace. She glanced toward a stand of trees that set apart from the others. They formed a large circle. "Look, Braden, this is a perfect circle. This would be a perfect meditation spot. We could put some benches where people could come and sit. It's so secluded and peaceful, but also a little sad."

"Why is it sad feeling?"

Elizabeth shivered. "I hope this wasn't a gravesite."

"I don't see any wooden crosses, but they may have deteriorated. Sometimes, they stacked stones or used one large one and carved on it. I don't think anyone is buried here. I agree, though, it has a feeling I can't describe, but being close to nature always does that to me."

Braden moved closer to Elizabeth and without thinking, he drew her to him and kissed her. His heart raced being next to her as he breathed in her essence. "I'm sorry. I hope I haven't offended you. You just looked as if you were a little nervous and needed a kiss."

Elizabeth's eyes sparkled. "It took you long enough!" She pulled his face to hers and kissed him soundly on the lips again. "Since this was our first kiss, let's make this our special place."

Braden pulled her closer. "I'd like that. I think this would be the perfect place to come when we're stressed or just to take a breather."

"I've been thinking about those dresses. We could see if any female guest would like to wear one and have her picture made. We could dress men in clothes kind of like Abraham Lincoln wore."

"That's another avenue of income. You are so brilliant, Miss Ellie. But do you think any lady these days has a waist that small?"

"We can alter them and use a corset. And some of them, could be put on dress forms, and we could stand them in a corner of one or two of the bedrooms, like a display, so it would be kind of like a historical museum."

"You have the neatest ideas."

"Thank you, kind sir." Ellie did a small courtesy.

Walking toward the house, Braden asked, "What are your plans for Christmas?"

"You have some time off for Christmas, and real estate is slow at this time of year. Why don't we visit our parents together and then have our special Christmas, just us, here?"

Braden contemplated her words. "Or we could invite both sets of parents here and have a feast in our grand parlor and dining room. It's almost like a ballroom. That way, they could meet each other."

"What about your grandmother?"

"Mom mentioned the other day that Uncle Dirk and Aunt Julia contacted her and said they'd like to visit with Nannie over Christmas. Maybe they will stay with her."

"That would be great. You don't think our parents will get the wrong idea about us?"

CHAPTER TWELVE

Braden stopped by a large bolder jutting out from the river. "Ellie, I don't know how to say this. When you visited your parents some months ago, I felt lost and rambled around the house looking for something to do. I had plenty of chores, but it was as if part of me was missing. My feelings for you have grown every day, and I don't want to be apart from you."

"Braden, I was attracted to you the minute you walked through the office, but I thought it was just that you were so handsome. You made me all giddy inside. I've also developed those same feelings. I can't wait to get home every evening. When you talked about leaving, I thought my heart would break. I didn't want you to go. Not only because I was scared to be by myself out here away from town, but because you gave me a sense of peace and happiness. That's when I realized that my feelings could develop into more than friendship, but I thought you would never be attracted to me."

"I've never been in love, Ellie. I've had some infatuations, but I have never felt this way. I think I'm falling in love with you." He leaned her against the large boulder and kissed her again. His heart pounded in his chest, and lightheadedness spread through his head.

"I feel the same way. I thought I'd been in love several times, too, but I never felt comfortable like I do with you. I've loved you for a long time." She struggled to quiet the butterflies fluttering inside her chest.

Braden pulled her away from the large rock. Holding hands, they decided to visit the house by the river.

Braden put his hand on the door knob and carefully opened it since one hinge was loose. On one side of the hall, an L shaped staircase with a

87

balcony led to the upstairs. On the left were three rooms, probably a study or library as well as what might have been a bedroom. On the right was a parlor, another room that might have been used as a dining room, and a large kitchen.

Elizabeth fingered the newel posts and banister as she made her way upstairs. "This staircase has held up well. It is so pretty. I like the way it turns the corner with this little landing at the top."

Upstairs were eight large rooms, four on each side of a long hall. It seemed out of place on the property, but judging from the hinges and door knobs, it appeared to have been built using the same materials as the Big House, as they chose to call it.

"Maybe someone had a contagious disease and needed isolating, or maybe it was used as a hospital, but why so many rooms? It's a mystery for sure." Braden was assessing the structure as best he could. "Looks as if the staircase is made of oak, probably from some of the trees here. You know, Elizabeth, if we decided to make the Big House, as we'll call it, an inn, we could live here in this Mystery House. It wouldn't take as much work as the Big House. We would still be on the premises, but away from our guests."

"I like that idea, and I like calling it The Mystery House. The view of the river and the trees beyond is very calming and beautiful."

Braden laughed.

"What's so funny?" Elizabeth looked puzzled.

"I was just thinking about how we're going to make time to keep it clean. I can see you dressed in a scullery maid's rags scrubbing floors and other household chores and me as a footman toiling at other chores."

Elizabeth slapped his arm. "Maybe we'll make enough money to hire a housekeeper. And I'm not dressing up in rags to clean. I'll leave that up to you, Mister Footman!"

"I was only teasing."

Back at the house, Elizabeth and Braden sat down and figured how much money they could put aside for making a bathroom upstairs as well as a closet and stairs to the attic. They agreed to open a checking account and add to it when they could.

Elizabeth pulled out her books. "We really do need more than one bathroom, especially if your mother and dad keep coming to help us. I'll have to start a new ledger for our new account. I think we should give it a business name."

"We talked about The Sullivan House. How about that?"

"That's it. I'll meet you after school at the bank. I'll also call both of our parents and see if they will come for Christmas."

Braden's eyes widened. "It's a week and a half away. We'd better get cracking. I'll invite my sister. I've never asked. Do you have siblings?"

"No, I'm an only child. Where does your sister live?"

"She's in Birmingham."

Preparations got underway without delay. That afternoon, they went traipsing along the carriageway in front of Oak Hollow. Douglas fir trees lined the road behind the magnolia trees on either side. Most of them were asymmetrical and scrawny, but sitting alone, they saw a large tree, which seemed to have been placed right in their line of vision. It wasn't perfect, but it looked just right. Braden sawed it down, and they dragged it to the house. Elizabeth searched the attic and found a large wooden box. It would make the perfect container for the tree. Braden had the tree on the porch, waiting to bring it inside.

Elizabeth looked at it. "Is it too tall to fit in the parlor? Don't forget I want to put a star on the top."

"I just measured it, and I think it will be perfect. It's wider than it is tall."

Together, they managed to get the tree into the box and inside the house. It sat nestled beside the far column, so that it could be seen from the dining room, parlor, and hall. Elizabeth had found some handblown glass ornaments in a small box in the attic. "I'd like to use them as sort of a memorial."

"I wonder if the Sullivans used them?"

"Don't guess we will ever know. I'm going to think they did."

Elizabeth drove to town. She picked up more decorations, candles, and a centerpiece. Winding artificial lengths of evergreen along the banister of the staircase, hanging mistletoe above the parlor arch, and heating hot cider on the stove made for a happy day. She and Braden finished the tree and sat in the parlor admiring their work. Tipping their cups as a toast for a job well done, they sipped their cider until Braden broke the spell.

"I didn't tell you, but the man we talked to about making a closet and bathroom said he could come next week and have it done before Christmas."

"Even the stairs?"

"Yes. I gave him the go ahead. He quoted me a reasonable price. But that brings up something else. We can't expect to be in the same room with my parents and sister here."

Elizabeth went to get her ledger. "I thought about that. Your parents can use my room, my parents can be in the bedroom beside them, and Susan can be across the hall from your bedroom upstairs. I'll take the one next to you with that connecting door. We need new mattresses anyway for the inn. How much will the remodeling cost?"

Braden gave her the figure. "I'll go pick out the mattresses and box springs for the downstairs if you will take care of the linens. Girls are better at that type of thing."

Two days before Christmas, Braden's bedroom was painted a soft eggshell white with a staircase in the hall for access to the attic, a walk-in closet in Braden's room, and an en suite bathroom. They found a clawfoot bathtub and had a shower installed. Ellie poked around and found a washstand and a beautiful pitcher and bowl set in the attic. "I'd like to use this pitcher and bowl somewhere. It says Belleek, but when I looked it up, I don't think they made these sets. I thought they were reproductions, but they have their china mark on them. Maybe they used to make the pitcher and bowl sets and stopped because people don't use them now."

"That sounds reasonable. Are they still in business? Perhaps, we could put them in one of the bedrooms. That would add to the opulence of yesteryear, especially if they are authentic."

"Yes, they are still in business. Everything is handmade in Northern Ireland in the city of, guess where? Belleek!"

Ellie and Braden had moved furniture around until each of the bedrooms looked as if they had come from an antique magazine. She had used a different palette for each bedroom. Most of the walls were a muted cream color, but she used some earth-toned comforters for his parent's bedroom in a random patchwork quilt pattern. She found drapes in a soft beige color with a valance edged in gold fringe. The tie backs matched the fringe. For Susan's room, Ellie chose a comforter with a pastel coral background. A paisley design popped up from the background. Solid drapes of the same coral color completed the decor. For what had been a nursery, Ellie chose Braden's blue and white striped comforter and curtains and moved them downstairs into what she chose for her parents. Upstairs for Braden's room, she chose a comforter of sky blue, muted greens, and dark navy blended together, resembling a watercolor. She hung matching drapes. For variety, she had Braden paint the ceiling blue in the bedroom next to his where she would be staying. "I've heard that keeps ghosts away." She moved her bedding from his room to hers.

Braden laughed. "I think we've had our share of other worldly experiences, but if it makes you feel better, I'm happy to do it. You may decide you like having your own bedroom."

"I may, but it is really comforting to look across and see you in your bed."

Braden said, "I feel the same way. As silly as it sounds, I want to protect you."

"You know, we can refer to each room as the Autumn Room, Spring Room, Blue Room, White Room, and Watercolor Room, and give guests their choice if the room is available. I'll come up with some other colors as we redo the rest of the bedrooms. Also, we could charge more if there is a tub and a separate shower. We could even name the bigger ones as names of the Sullivan family."

"Like I said, you're brilliant."

"I hope your mom thinks so."

"I read some more of Grace's journal last night when I couldn't sleep in my new room."

"Anything interesting?"

"I'd say! A boy by the name of Daniel Winston set the fire because he was furious that Grace wouldn't date him. And there was bad blood between the Winstons and Sullivans for a long time."

"A lover scorned."

The weather turned colder as the deciduous trees lost the rest of their leaves, but the pine, spruce, and fir trees added welcome color to the drab

91

landscape. The Winterberry shrubs that lined the driveway, or as Elizabeth still referred to it as the carriageway, popped with bright red berries. Massive Southern Magnolia trees stood behind the shrubs as silent sentinels of protection, their waxy leaves shining as if they'd been polished for the holidays.

Elizabeth stood with her back to the front window in the parlor to get the whole picture of the tree. Braden was on a ladder attaching the star to the top. "It looks beautiful." She turned to look out the window. "Looking at the red berries and the evergreens, it seems as if God has decorated the outside! Red and Green everywhere."

Climbing back down the ladder, Braden joined her. "We are blessed, sweetheart."

Elizabeth had placed some pine cones scented with cinnamon on the coffee table in the parlor and warmed by the fire Braden started, the aroma filled their senses. Ellie had purchased some Christmas dishes on sale and stocked the pantry and freezer with ingredients for the meal. In spite of the bitter weather that had come down from the north, the house looked inviting and cozy. Braden set about starting a fire in each bedroom as well as the kitchen. Soon warmth spread throughout the house.

Elizabeth's eyes sparkled as the fire cast a rosy glow on her cheeks.

"I never knew that fireplaces would really keep a home warm, but I guess that's why we have so many."

Braden smiled as he stoked the parlor fire. "I kind of worried that we haven't had time to install heating and air conditioning, but I think we'll do just fine until we can afford it."

"I have a surprise. When I was in the antique store the other day looking for decorations for the house, I found a whole box of round metal containers with a hinged top and a long handle. I thought they were used to pop corn, but I found out they were used for bed warmers. The people would put hot coals in them, and the handle allowed them to move the warmer up and down on the bed. I stuck them in the pantry and thought we could fill them with small embers and tuck them into the beds so everyone could warm their feet, or the whole bed before they climb in. We would have to wrap them in a cloth, so people wouldn't get burned."

"Just as they did when the Sullivans lived here. What a neat idea."

Elizabeth had a bowl of apples, oranges, and bananas on the kitchen table flanked by two red candles. Braden sat down and watched Ellie putting on a pot of coffee. He picked up a banana from the bowl and started peeling it.

"I'm glad I got more than enough for the fruit salad. I knew you'd grab something."

"A growing boy's gotta eat!"

"Sure, Braden."

Braden's laugh warmed Ellie's heart. She could never begrudge him anything…well, almost anything.

CHAPTER THIRTEEN

Their guests arrived midafternoon on Christmas Eve. Ellie's father and mother sat in the parlor while Braden retrieved their luggage. His parents arrived shortly afterward, and introductions were made all around. Braden's father initiated it. He walked over to Elizabeth's father and extended his hand. "Hello, I'm Mason, and this is my wife, Emma. Pleased to meet you at last."

Ellie's father stood. "Pleased to meet you, too." He returned the handshake. "I'm Preston Addison, and this is my wife, Cynthia." Both men grinned as if they had a secret known only to them. Braden watched the interaction, but couldn't figure out why the men acted as if they had met before.

Susan Cunningham showed up late, hurtled into the house, her hair all askew with her gifts flying helter-skelter across the room. Braden ran to help her. "You seem flustered."

"I am. I hate being late. I got behind traffic. Who in their right mind rides a bicycle in the middle of the street in freezing winter weather going to the grocery store?"

"Welcome to small town Scottsville."

Sitting at the dining table with the beautiful Celtic designs outlining the edges, Braden asked his father to say the blessing.

Mason rose and delivered a prayer that touched every heart around the table. "Dear Father, as we come together today to celebrate the birth of our Savior, Jesus Christ, may we all feel the joy the world must have felt on that glorious day. May we be reminded of why He came to earth, and remember that this day is meant to honor Him, not exploit worldly pleasures. Thank you for this food, and those that prepared it, that we are about to partake, and keep us safe in Your arms. In Jesus' name, I pray. Amen."

Emma asked, "I wonder who made this table and what the Christmases were like in their time. Did they have a tree? Did they exchange gifts?"

Susan looked around. "There's seven of us here, and we have plenty of room, but can you imagine being in huge skirts with petticoats? How would they all fit here if they had this many people?"

Braden grinned. "Leave it to my sister to think about fashion."

Turning serious, Elizabeth told them about the journal and what they had found so far at the library. "We did learn that it was used as headquarters for the Confederacy during the Civil War, and I looked up some history of this property in deeds. Apparently, the house by the river was built to house the Sullivans when the Confederate officers took over this house.

Preston put his fork down. "I love history. Many of the grand mansions were taken over by the military for hospitals. I'm glad to know this wasn't a hospital. It makes sense the family constructed a temporary house until the war was over. You've done a lot of research."

"The smaller one has a much prettier view than the main house."

Cynthia looked at Ellie and took a sip of iced tea. "I believe you may find out more from that journal you found. I wonder if Grace was an only child or perhaps the older one."

"I think Grace was older. She talked about her sister, Maggie. I got the feeling she was younger."

Preston wiped his mouth. "You said the journal mentioned Ireland. They were probably O'Sullivan before coming to America. Many Irish dropped 'O' and 'Mc' or 'Mac' from their names. Our surname Addison is Scottish and English. Studying ancestry is one of my hobbies."

Mason said, "Cunningham is a mix of English, Irish, and mostly Scottish."

Elizabeth rose to take plates from the table. Emma and Cynthia helped.

As they brought dessert in, Braden said, "I wonder if Elizabeth and I are related. Wouldn't that be a hoot if we're cousins?"

"Braden Cunningham, we are most decidedly not cousins!" Elizabeth gave him a look that squelched further conversation from him.

Preston laughed. "That would be funny, indeed. Might be interesting to do a little research."

Elizabeth said, "Dad, if you want to investigate our surname, I would be interested, but Braden and I have our hands full at the moment. And, we are not cousins."

Emma pushed her chair back. "I think it's time for opening gifts!"

Ellie poured coffee for everyone and took the tray to the parlor.

Braden went to a side table and opened a drawer. He pulled out his well-read Bible. "It was always our tradition when I was growing up to read Luke, Chapter Two before opening gifts. If everyone is agreeable, I'd like to read it."

A round of yesses filled the room as Braden found his place in the Bible and began to read.

When he finished, everyone got comfortable to await their gifts while Braden started doling them out. He and Ellie gave each father a tie and cuff links, and their mothers got a pearl necklace and a beautiful shawl. They gave Susan a cable knit sweater. Their parents gave each person a sweater.

Braden stretched and yawned. "This has been a great evening. We can either play a board game, watch something on the new television in the study, or turn in early."

Mason nodded to Preston. Both men stood up and exited the parlor. Frowns followed them since they didn't say a word.

Braden asked, "Wonder where they're going?"

"Maybe to get another cup of coffee?" Ellie rose to go help them, but before she took one step, they came back in. Mason handed Braden an envelope, and Preston handed one to Elizabeth. They were both grinning that same grin Braden had noticed earlier when they were introducing each other.

Mason said, "Preston and I have been visiting on the telephone. We didn't get you much for Christmas, but maybe this will make up for it. This is for both of you from our families."

Elizabeth moved her chair closer to Braden's. He opened his envelope and a folded piece of paper fell out. It was a note from Mason saying the loan he had given them, and their work was paid in full.

Mason turned to Susan. "And we're giving you the same amount in case you want to buy a new car."

Elizabeth opened hers and a check fell out. It was for the same amount as the original loan Mason and Emma had given them plus more for their labor.

Preston said, "This check is from both your mother and me."

Elizabeth and Braden both had shock written all over their faces.

Preston smiled. "We couldn't let Mason fund you all the money. We want to help, too. We feel you have a great idea for this house and for a great friendship. There's only one stipulation." He turned to Mason.

Mason's eyes gleamed, and a mischievous grin crossed his face. "Yes, we both agree. We will be the first guests when this magnificent house is finished, and we expect a gourmet dinner!"

Ellie laughed. "That I can guarantee. Now, mind you, I don't know how the gourmet meal will taste, but it will look pretty!"

Everyone laughed.

Preston sat down again. "I don't have a lot of strength to help Mason and you, Braden, but I can certainly offer any assistance with books or financial advice that you need."

Braden and Ellie rose and hugged both fathers. Susan followed suit.

Elizabeth lingered in her father's hug. "Daddy, we're just so glad you came for Christmas. Your presence is worth more than any money. I guess Braden and I are both overwhelmed that our two families would give us such support. Thank you all so much."

Susan spoke up. "I don't have any leverage, but I want to be with them as the first guests!"

Braden hugged his sister. "Of course, all of you will be our first guests. We are more than grateful and so blessed to have such wonderful families."

Picking up the coffee cups, the women moved into the kitchen to discuss further plans for the house.

Christmas Day dawned sunny and warmer than usual. Braden and Ellie invited their guests to tour the grounds. They showed off the limestone house down by the river. Preston declined since diabetes had caused neuropathy in his legs, and walking any distance tired him. Cynthia and Emma formed a bond right away as did Susan and Ellie. They all followed Braden as he led the way, his scythe in hand in case it was needed.

98

Emma commented, "There is so much antique furniture in the Big House. I wonder why there's none in this house?"

"Another mystery," Braden said. "We assume they moved their furniture here when the Big House was made the Confederate Headquarters, and then moved everything back once the war was over."

Elizabeth said, "That's why we have decided to call this place The Mystery House for lack of a better title. Even with our assumption, it seems strange that they would just abandon it."

On the way back to the main house, Cynthia turned to Ellie. "Darling, we have enjoyed seeing you and sharing Christmas with you and Braden's family. It's been a real pleasure to meet all of you. Emma, we must keep in touch, but I need to get Preston back home, so he can rest before he has to go to work on Monday."

Emma said, "Let's write, and perhaps we can meet here again soon. Did you say you're from Jackson?"

"Actually, we're from Brandon, a suburb east of Jackson. Even though it isn't that far away, it pushes Preston's limits. He's thinking about seeing if he can pick up work two or three days a week and work from home."

Braden's family left soon after Preston and Cynthia. Susan stumbled descending the front steps. She didn't fall, but her suitcase went flying. She yelled to Braden and Elizabeth, "No, I didn't look where I was going. You'd better not laugh." All three broke into peals of laughter.

"What a sendoff." Braden pulled Ellie into the house.

They sat in front of a fire in the parlor. "I enjoyed our parents, but I'm happy to be alone again." Ellie put her head on Braden's chest.

"Me, too, Cous!"

"Braden Cunningham, we're not cousins!" Elizabeth slapped his arm.

"Oh, I was hoping you'd say we could be kissing cousins." Braden had that impish grin, and couldn't resist teasing Ellie. He planted a soft kiss on her lips.

"Funny. I want to read more in that journal."

"Seems like that would be a good project for tomorrow since it's Sunday. After church, let's settle down in front of a fire and read."

Sunday afternoon, Elizabeth poured their coffee and sat in the parlor with a blazing fire going. Blue flames released golden sparks going up the chimney.

Ellie snuggled up to Braden. "I love sitting in here. I almost feel like this is where Grace would sit. The fireplace is so cozy."

"What's the next entry?"

"It's just her talking about Cork, Ireland, and a conversation with her sister, Maggie, and their mother."

"It sounds as if they were close."

"Yes, and apparently, the girls were allowed to go to public school. Grace talks about getting dresses ready." She refreshed their coffee. "The next thing of any importance is an entry in late August." She started at the top of the page, though she had already read part of it. "August 28, 1856. Today I went for a walk, and it was such a nice day, I found myself lying on my back staring at the clouds and closed my eyes thinking of Cork. Jim, one of the workers, saw me and stood over me to see if I was breathing. It scared me when I opened my eyes, but as we talked, I realized the Negroes can't read or write. I'd like to teach him, but I know that's dangerous."

Braden interrupted. "Okay, this is getting interesting. She wants to teach a slave." He took the journal from Elizabeth. "Let me read. Here it is. August 30, 1856. Jim and I met in a grove of pecan trees away from prying eyes. There is a special place where the trees form a large circle. We feel it's the best place to meet. Even though we know we could be punished severely, Jim agreed to let me teach him. We hid a primer in the woods, so if Jim has time, he can practice. He's a very fast learner and one of the most beautiful souls I've ever met. We have to be careful, but it's kind of exciting to break the law! I've never done anything so risky. I don't want us to get in trouble. Jim could have his hands chopped off, and I could go to jail, even though Papa has freed all our slaves. Papa would be angry and embarrassed, and probably disown me, but he would try to protect both of us. I think if it gets too dangerous, we will stop. At least Jim knows the alphabet and the sounds the letters make. I have to hide this, so Maggie doesn't see it." Braden took a long sip of his cooled coffee. "She must have been a brave girl. We were taught in junior high slaves were treated as nothing more than property." Braden closed the journal. "Secrets this house held for so long are coming to light."

"Yes, I was horrified when we read about slaves. Braden, do you suppose that circle of trees we found when we were picking pecans might be the very same circle they found?"

"Would they last this long?"

"I've got a book on trees and flowers. I'll be right back."

Elizabeth went to her old bedroom and pulled a book from her bookcase. Braden poured fresh cups of coffee as she thumbed through the book. "It says pecan trees can live up to three hundred years."

Elizabeth and Braden talked about what they had learned so far and what other secrets might be hiding in the attic. They decided to investigate after lunch.

Braden poked around uncovering furniture under sheets and quilts. One box he opened held crystal wine glasses and a set of china. Another box held books and papers of some sort. Braden took a step back from the box. Stale cigar or pipe tobacco assaulted his nose. He would have to air out the box before they could see what papers it contained. Feeling a little lightheaded, he looked at Elizabeth who was across the room looking at other relics. She stirred up some dust, and Braden started coughing. Making his way to the opening of the attic, he paused.

"Elizabeth, can you come here, please." Braden straightened from his bent position.

Elizabeth rushed over. "What's the matter?"

"The smells and dust got to me, but I want to take that box of dishes down. I think we could use them. With my asthma and an allergy to dust, I need some fresh air."

"I'll come with you."

They walked along a path Hiram had cleared toward the river, but the cold temperatures got to them, as they accelerated their walk.

CHAPTER FOURTEEN

Back at the table in the breakfast room, Braden said, "Let's look at the journal again."

Ellie looked at Braden. "This journal is pretty thick. If we read the whole thing together, it will take us a long time, time we could be spending on the house. I have more spare time than you. What if I read while you're at school when real estate is slow and tell you what I've found?"

"That sounds good, but I'd like to read some of it together."

"I'll note the entries I think you would like. We'll read them together."

"Don't leave out any juicy details!" Braden's face reddened.

"I doubt there's anything remotely juicy. This was in the 1800's. They didn't do juicy stuff."

"Oh, but they did, my dear. You should read some of the accounts of affairs that went on, especially men of wealth and even presidents. Some plantation owners were notorious for raping their slave women."

"How awful. I do remember reading about that." She turned her attention to the large box and opened it. "Braden, these dishes and crystal are beautiful. I wonder why they were packed away. I guess the squatters didn't investigate the attic. Except for the Christmas dishes we bought, and your dishes, I'd like to store these in the beautiful china cabinet."

"These dishes will bring back some of the glory of this old house, especially if we use them to serve guests."

Ellie's eyes lit up. "I can't wait to show your mom. She will probably know the pattern."

"I'm sure."

103

Ellie had a pensive look. "I searched some records at the court house and found out it was in Abraham Sullivan's name when they foreclosed on it the first time. I met a clerk who has been there for a long time. She told me this property was foreclosed a long time ago, but a young couple bought it in 1958. She knew the man's mother and said he was a disgrace to the family. He was arrested for multiple DUIs, he assaulted the postmaster, and severely injured a young girl in an accident. The man went to prison, his wife was evicted, and the bank foreclosed again and the property reverted back to Abraham. They couldn't find him, so it was abandoned. It kind of fell through the cracks until my friend's husband from the bank was investigating old foreclosures and agreed to put it up for auction instead of tearing it down."

"That's quite a bit of history."

"They could have taken their horrible furniture we found down here, but I guess the lady just wanted to just walk away." Ellie unwrapped a cup and saucer.

"I'm glad the woman walked away and apparently didn't like antiques."

As days grew longer, a hint of spring warmed the air, and trees festooned themselves with leaves and new branches. Wild flowers popped up in unexpected places, almost as if an artist had painted a landscape and spread the canvas over the ground. It was a sea of tiny white, yellow, and pink flowers. Ellie and Braden painted the rest of the bedrooms in the same creamy eggshell color to match the other rooms.

Emma and Mason had come every other weekend to help. Chifforobes, wash stands, dressers, and chests were brought from the attic and placed in each bedroom upstairs that didn't have much furniture. The excess was moved to The Mystery House. Emma and Ellie had polished every piece with loving care, delighted when the wood practically came to life.

Emma stood up from cleaning drawers in a dresser. She turned to Ellie. "I wonder why the Sullivans left some furniture downstairs, but stored everything else in the attic."

Ellie relayed the information the clerk at the courthouse told her.

"That makes sense. I guess they didn't bother since they were here for such a short time. I'm really glad Mason and Braden got the floors refinished before we moved all this furniture in. I'd really like to go through everything in the attic."

"I'm getting more excited to think we can actually turn this place into an inn." Ellie ran her hand over a chest they had just polished. "And I know you want to make an attic bedroom!"

Emma smiled. "Yes, but we need to put finishing touches on each room, and see how long it will take to flesh out more bathrooms."

Ellie nodded. "I found out the pitcher and bowls and the other pieces we found with Belleek on them were handmade in Belleek, a little village in Northern Ireland, and they are still in business today. They are real treasures. Since I didn't see any pitchers and bowls for sale in the articles I read, I wonder if they were commissioned, or if they just stopped making them since people don't use them any longer?"

"Probably. The Sullivans were quite affluent from the look of things and what you've learned. I hope the washstands are sturdy enough to hold a pitcher and bowl, and I hope your guests don't break them. Since there are only four of them, maybe we should put American made ones in the guest rooms and save the others for The Mystery House if you move there." Emma made a note that she needed to ask Braden his intentions toward Ellie. She already felt like she was her daughter-in-law, but Braden hadn't proposed. Mason didn't get very far with that request, so she'd do it herself. She heard him in the hall. "Ellie, I'll be right back."

Emma cornered Braden. "Let's go to the kitchen."

"Something on your mind, Mom?" He noted Emma's determined look.

"Yes, sit down. I'm wondering when you are going to propose to Ellie, and don't roll your eyes at me. A mother can tell these things."

"I'll admit, I've been thinking about it, but we've been so busy. I want to make it memorable, so I am trying to think of a good way to do it."

"Don't wait too long. If you need help, let me know. I really love her."

"So do I."

Emma went back to Ellie who was still polishing and cleaning. "Ellie, all that's left to do after we finish cleaning here is the kitchen.

105

Have you and Braden talked about the Big Kitchen, or do you want to just use the kitchen attached to this house?"

"We've talked about it. We are thinking we could serve a small breakfast if guests want to come down and eat. Maybe cinnamon rolls, banana bread, toast and jelly, something simple until we can afford to redo the Big Kitchen. We want to update it and hire a chef to do three meals a day. No menu, just his choice. If the guests don't like what's served, they don't have to eat. We would post the menu each morning on a chalk board."

"That sounds wonderful. I love your creative mind."

Sitting at the table after Emma and Mason left, Ellie rubbed the front of the journal. "I thought I'd bring you up to date on what I've read."

"Good. Anything interesting?"

"Abe got sick, but recovered and wanted the girls to have a coming out or debut party. They rebelled. The really interesting thing is that Jim broke off his and Grace's relationship because he was a Negro. Grace was heartbroken and took to her bed for three days. She wrote the most tender message about her feelings. I sat here and cried like a baby. She said she would never love anyone except him."

"It was unheard of for Negroes to marry whites, and unfortunately, there is still a stigma today, but one day, maybe that will change."

"I want to read what she wrote." A tear slipped down her cheek.

"I can't wait to hear."

"It's very sad." She wiped her eyes and read, "I'm finally able to write in my journal. I don't know that I will ever get over the pain of losing the one person in the world that I love beyond words, beyond touching his soft, beautiful skin, beyond his clean smell of lavender soap Miss Daisy makes, beyond his eyes that look into my soul, beyond my heart where he resides, beyond the soft kiss that has to last a lifetime because we can't change our colors, beyond my world which has crumbled, and will never be the same. I feel his every emotion, and he feels mine. We are so connected that we can tell when one of us needs to talk or when we need to go to the circle. How can I live in a world that is so cruel to not understand love? Do hearts ever heal? I know mine never will, so from now on, I'll survive, but nothing will ever matter again in my life. I am his. He is mine, and I'll wait until my dying day to spend just one more minute with him, even if it is in Heaven. I pray every day that God will provide a way for us to be together."

Braden's eyes misted. He quickly wiped them. "That's how I feel about you, Ellie. I love you so much. I wonder if they ever got together again?"

"I love you, too, Braden. I haven't read enough to see if they got back together. Her sister, Maggie asked her to go for a walk, and they found a heart made out of river washed stones. Grace knew Jim had made it. That gave her some comfort just to touch it."

"And you want to see if we can find the heart?"

Ellie's eyes sparkled through her tears. "Can we go now?"

Making their way to the pecan grove, Ellie felt something in her soul being lifted. The strength of ancient trees still standing no matter what nature threw at them, the rebirth of leaves appearing each spring as they had now, the branches providing for a place to house a bird family, the little flowers peeking up through the forest floor made the world seem right and peaceful as butterflies darted to and fro among the flowers. It wasn't the Garden of Eden, but God created this forest just as He did that garden. He created that circle, and Ellie was determined to find the heart.

Braden stood still listening to the sounds of nature. The steady gurgle of the river as it curved around the trees and rushed to parts unknown, the rustle of crisp leaves on the ground as the wind picked them up and swirled them, revealing tiny flowers of orange, pink, purple, and yellow shyly opening to the warmth of a sunshiny day, and the sound of birdcalls far and near touched his soul. He looked around and etched this magical place in his mind. He caught up with Ellie, who was on her knees moving leaves with both hands.

"I feel like an archeologist searching for a lost ruin."

Braden bent to help her. "In a way, we are. We're looking for a lost treasure. A heart of stones."

They moved leaves for over an hour. Standing up, they stretched and dusted their hands. Braden exclaimed, "Maybe we've been looking in the wrong place. There's another circle of trees over there that's a little larger."

"And it's farther away from the perimeter of the grove."

"We'll look later. I think we need a break. Since we aren't going anywhere, it will be there when we have more time. We need to focus on the house."

"You're right, Braden. Okay, I'll wait, but I have a feeling it is in that larger grove."

The next two months were spent planning and remodeling the kitchen attached to the house, but they had to forego the Big Kitchen. Money was scarce since Ellie wasn't selling or listing many homes, and they were basically living on Braden's salary. She had a lot of time to reflect on her life. She had shared a lot of things with Braden, but he still didn't know her deepest secret. No one did, not even her parents. Although she had tried to move past it by putting on a happy-go-lucky attitude, she couldn't get on top of the pain, and she couldn't bring herself to reveal it. She had read books on self-esteem, sought a counselor in another town, and had gone to church every Sunday. She kept telling herself it wasn't her fault, but deep down, she blamed herself. A small part of her wondered if Braden would love her anyway, and if she could let him, but she dared not dream.

Although she loved Braden, she could never marry him. She just wasn't good enough, but she felt more like her old self around him than any other person. Her parents cared for her, but they were not a demonstrative couple. They provided her with almost everything she wanted, made sure she got a good education, and kept up her dental and doctor appointments.

Braden's parents were the opposite. They doted on him. Love just oozed out of them. She felt closer to them than to her own parents.

Braden walked in from school, interrupting her thoughts. "Hi, beautiful. How was your day?"

"I read more of Grace's journal."

"Oh, great. Anything to give us a clue?"

"Not much. Just family stuff, but the love she and Jim shared just breaks my heart. I wish they could have been together. That was such a hard time."

"Not much has changed, especially in Mississippi. Even though it's mandated, my school has not desegregated. Mixed marriages are still frowned upon, though they don't punish people who choose to buck the system."

"I hope we find out if they got together." Ellie's eyes wandered to the window where they first saw the heart materialize last winter. She rose and stared out the window.

Braden's eyes followed Ellie. "Or if we'll ever find the heart. I guess it's been too many years."

"We have all weekend and not much else to do around here. Let's look again." Ellie sought Braden's eyes. "Please?"

"You win!"

They spent Friday evening going through the journal trying to figure out if they could pinpoint an area.

"There must be something in the journal that will give us a clue. I don't think it's near the edge since Jim wanted it hidden. Maybe we should go deeper into the woods."

Braden took the journal. "I don't think she intended for anyone to read her entries, especially not over a hundred years later!" He flipped through the pages. "From what I can tell, the last half of the journal is about her brothers and sister."

"Yes, apparently Matthew was high-strung and arrogant. He was jealous of the younger brother, Joseph and their sisters, and wanted to get Oak Hollow's deed in his name. He decided when Abe died, he was not going to divide it among his brother and sisters as Abe and Sarah wanted. He cheated in college and abused a sweet girl named Mary. Joesph finished college and wanted to go to medical school."

"That's terrible. Did Matthew get his name on the title, I wonder?"

"I don't know. I'll keep reading."

"Greed and jealousy are so insidious. It permeates everything around a person."

Ellie said, "It seems there was a lot of turmoil and tragedy within the family as well as the country. Looks like they had a lot of obstacles within the entire family."

"Right now, though, with all the spooky stuff going on, I feel like it's Grace's story that is causing all the uneasiness we feel." Braden's face reflected his worry.

Ellie smiled. "It is creepy, but you're my big protector. It's such a sad story. It breaks my heart to know they can never get married. I feel

Grace couldn't divulge her feelings, so she put it all in the journal, and now we're reading it. I feel we are betraying her and exposing her deepest secrets." Ellie crossed her arms over her heart and tried to erase the thoughts that bombarded her. *Just like I can't have the man I love more than anything.*

Braden noticed Elizabeth's face had changed. "Are you thinking about Grace?"

"Yes. Just wondering since the journal ended if something happened to Grace. Maybe she died of a broken heart."

Braden rose and refreshed their coffee. "My feeling is if she didn't want us to read her journal, she wouldn't be leaving all these signs. Perhaps she wanted to leave a bit of history for future generations. We need to do some more exploring in the attic. Maybe there's another journal."

Elizabeth brightened. "Yes, maybe you're right. But tomorrow I want to look for the heart."

Though the weather whispered of spring, the breeze kicking up dead leaves warranted a jacket. After a breakfast of blackberry pancakes, Ellie and Braden threw on light sweats, grabbed gloves, and headed to the woods.

CHAPTER FIFTEEN

Ellie talked as they walked. "The woods were special to Grace and Joseph both. Lots of secrets hiding there. That's where he had an epiphany and decided to become a doctor."

They found traces of a path that Braden had uncovered when he had cleared the weeds. It led them beside the river and turned just after they came to a large boulder.

Ellie stopped and ran her hands over the large rock. "What a beautiful rock this is. It's almost like a sentinel of protection or something."

"Sentinel? Aren't you being a big dramatic? You should write a novel with that imagination."

"That's your dream, not mine." Ellie placed a quick kiss on his cheek.

Braden smiled. "I hope we find the heart. Maybe that will stop things that are happening. It might not be intact, but the woods don't look like they have been disturbed for a long time."

Ellie frowned. "You mean by ghostly encounters. Though it's frightening sometimes, you don't get a sense of evil, do you?"

"No, more one of sadness. I wonder what has happened in the house in the last hundred years. Was there a murder, or did someone die a horrible death? I read a long time ago in a literature class I took that sometimes houses carry memories, especially negative ones. Not haunting a place, but kind of leaving a thumbprint. I think they call it residual memories. I never put much stock in it, but Oak Hollow is beginning to make a believer out of me."

Ellie nodded. "Me, too. Almost everywhere I turn, I see hearts. In store windows, in magazines, and I find myself doodling them. That makes me think maybe the house holds good memories. Still, some of the things that have happened here frighten me."

As they walked deeper into the woods, Braden suddenly stopped. "Look, Ellie." He pointed to their right. "We've come to that larger circle of trees over there."

"Yes, we have. I'm going to go over there and start clearing the leaves."

Braden wanted Ellie to find the heart if it existed because he knew how determined she was to uncover it. A feeling he had sometimes when things seem to fall into place clicked in his brain, and he felt she might find it. "While you look there, I'm going to go a little deeper and see if I see anything else that might resemble the grove Grace talked about."

Braden stood just beyond where Ellie was on her knees moving leaves and debris carefully, her hands as gentle as a feather. He leaned against a tree soaking up the beauty of the woods and the sights and sounds that it emitted. A loud scream penetrated the air and Braden's thoughts.

He ran, thinking Ellie had seen or been bitten by a rattlesnake. "Are you okay? Are you hurt?" Collecting his senses when he saw her sitting on the ground smiling, he waited for an answer.

"Look, I think I found it!"

Braden looked where she pointed. "I think you're right. Looks like some of the stones are missing or maybe misplaced, but it is definitely a heart. Good work, Ellie."

"Let's clear the rest of the debris from here, and maybe we could find some pink or white rocks by the river to fill in the heart."

"Good idea."

They worked all afternoon restoring the heart and clearing the grove. Over a light supper, Ellie said, "I'd like to get one of those white wrought iron benches, so that our guests can go there to relax."

Braden nodded. He had been thinking for a while about proposing, and wanted it to be special. What could be more perfect than the grove with the heart of stones? He would go look for a ring the next day. Ellie had described her cousin's ring when she went to her bridal shower, so he knew what she liked. He had also lifted a ring from her jewelry box and found out her size.

The next Saturday, Braden had a white wrought iron bench delivered and set up in the grove. Ellie ran to him and jumped into his arms. "This is so perfect. Our guests are going to love it. Thank you for doing this."

"You're welcome. How about I take you out for dinner to celebrate our accomplishment?"

"I'll never turn down dinner. Where are we going so I know how to dress?"

"I'm thinking that little Italian place we love in Vicksburg."

"Okay, I'll wear a nice dress."

An hour later, Ellie appeared at the top of the stairs. Braden sucked in a breath. She looked more beautiful than he had ever seen her. Her pale sage-colored dress highlighted her eyes, and he swore he could see flecks of green sparkling in them, making them appear turquoise. As she descended the stairs, he said, "I know you are dressed to the nines, but how about you put on some tennis shoes, and let's go look at the heart and bench before we go? I'd like to see how it would feel if we were guests."

"Now?"

"Yes, I have an idea I'd like to run by you while we're there."

"Can't it wait? I don't want to get my dress wrinkled. And I can't walk in high heels very well over uneven ground."

Braden held up a pair of her tennis shoes. "Wear these, and we'll come back for your heels."

"Braden, those are new tennis shoes, and I don't want to get them dirty."

Braden tried to look disheartened. "It wouldn't take long, and we did clear the path."

Ellie locked eyes with him and realized, for some reason, this was important. "Okay, but if my dress gets dirty or wrinkled, you have to buy me a new one."

Braden grinned. "Deal. Let's go."

Sitting on the bench, Braden turned to her. "I was thinking this would be a perfect place for a man to propose. And later, we could build a gazebo or maybe have an arch-like trellis covered with flowers where they could get married. The grove is big enough to bring in some chairs for their guests, or if there is an overflow, we can set up chairs in a circle around it. That way, they would have to book rooms to come back for the wedding."

Ellie's eyes sparkled. "Aren't you the romantic one? I love it. I'll start looking for flowers that will grow in the shade to line the path if it's in the spring, or they could decorate it to fit their colors and bring their own flowers for the trellis. Or we could put pots of mums if it's a fall wedding. Now I'm excited that you wanted to come here."

Braden rose. "Stand up just a minute. I think there was a dirty leaf on the bench, and I want to be sure it didn't stain the back of your dress and I'd have to buy you another one!" He brushed the back of her dress. Ellie looked over her shoulder to see if she could see anything. Braden slipped around to the front of her. When she turned her head back, she gasped when she saw Braden had dropped to one knee.

"Ellie, when I first came to Scottsville, I had every intention of spending all my spare time looking for a teaching position in a larger city. I could not imagine living in a Podunk town like this for more than a year. When you showed me this mansion and the lands, they looked so sad, I wanted to turn around and go to Vicksburg, but you had such enthusiasm and optimism, I decided to stay. I had visions of waking up every morning to frantic music, but that was my preconceived idea. Imagine my surprise when I found out you like classical and retro music and old movies. What I didn't expect was that I would fall in love with you, and now, I can't live without you. No matter what we have each been through in the past, nothing matters except that I'm with you. You bring out the best in me and inspire me every day. I didn't know one guy could be this happy. So, in front of this heart of stones, and with God's blessing, my beautiful Elizabeth Addison, will you be my wife for the rest of our lives?" Braden held up a box with a beautiful one carat diamond.

What did he say? Nothing in the past mattered. Maybe he would love me no matter what. Maybe I can let my secret fade away. Ellie squealed. "Yes, yes, yes, a thousand times yes!"

Braden slipped the ring on her finger. "Whew, you don't know how nervous I was. Now, let's go eat!"

"How did you know my size and what I wanted? This ring cost a fortune."

Braden explained. "I listened very carefully when you talked about your cousin's ring. I've been saving my money. On the side during lunch and after school, I have been doing private tutoring for elementary and middle school kids. If you would rather have something else, we can exchange this one."

"NO! I love this. It is the most perfect ring ever. You really surprised me. This was so romantic. When we get married, I want it to be right here under the trellis we are going to build."

Ellie changed her shoes, and Braden drove to Vicksburg. He ushered her into the vintage restaurant where they had their first official date. He had ordered deep red roses to be placed on the table, just as he had done on their first date and had hired a trio to play and sing "The Twelfth of Never" that Johnny Mathis had made famous. It had become "their song." To complete the magic of the evening, bright stars shining in a cloudless sky led them home.

Ellie stepped out of her heels and ran for the telephone.

"What are you doing?"

"I'm calling my parents to tell them the good news."

"Ellie, it's almost eleven o'clock. Don't you think they'll be asleep?"

"I don't care. It's not every day a girl gets engaged!" Ellie held the phone where Braden could hear.

After two rings, Ellie's mom answered the phone. "What is it, Ellie? Are you all right? Is Braden okay? Why are you calling so late? Are you sick?" Panic tinged her voice.

"Everything's wonderful, Mom. Put your phone to Daddy's ear. How would feel about going shopping?"

"What? Have you been drinking? It's eleven o'clock at night. Are you sure you're okay?"

"Yes ma'am, but I might need some help."

"Okay." She raised her voice. "Wake up, Preston. Something's wrong. Ellie needs help. Preston! Ellie isn't making any sense. I think she may have been drinking."

Braden and Ellie both giggled.

"What's so funny?" Preston's voice sounded gravelly from being awakened so abruptly.

"Mom, I need help…finding the perfect wedding gown. Dad, will you give me away?"

115

Cynthia Addison screamed. "Oh, my goodness, I am so happy. We wondered when Braden would get around to it."

"I'm sorry to wake you so late, but I'm too excited to sleep and thought you'd want to know right away."

"With news like this, we are delighted to have our sleep interrupted! Have you set a date?"

"No, not yet. I'll let you know when we need to go shopping."

"Preston asked, "Braden, it is okay if I reveal the secret?"

Braden beamed. "Of course!"

"Ellie, Braden called me last week at work and asked for your hand in marriage, but he wanted it to be kept secret until you said yes and told your mother. I give my wholehearted blessing to this marriage."

Cynthia gave off a noise indicating her surprise. "Preston Addison, you kept this secret from me? How could you?" Her laughter assured everyone she wasn't really upset.

"Oh, and I have been researching our ancestry, and you are definitely not cousins!"

"Dad! I wouldn't care."

Preston's laugh reverberated through time and space, tickling sound waves of happiness as Ellie held the phone.

Coming home from school each day, it seemed bridal magazines, brochures of china and silver, flyers of cake designs, and myriad other bridal things cluttered every flat surface in the house.

"My goodness, I thought we just got rings, you got a gown, I got a suit, and we got married." Braden shook his head, confused about all the fuss. "I didn't know it was such a production."

"I only plan to be married once, Braden so I want it to be memorable."

"What part do I play in this?"

"We need to decide a date, you need to ask Pastor Denton if he will be available to perform the ceremony, and you need to make a list of people you want to invite. Then you need to plan the honeymoon."

"Okay, I can do that. How does next week sound? I can get a substitute teacher, and I have an idea of where to go on the honeymoon."

"Oh, no, Braden. It will take close to six months to a year to finalize everything."

"Why?"

"Well, I have to decide on invitations, coordinate our lists of people to invite, how I want the cake decorated, the colors we will use, my bridesmaid's dresses, my gown, my mother's…"

"Okay, okay. That's a lot. Do you have a date in mind?"

"I was thinking the Saturday before Easter Sunday in April. The days should be fairly warm if we want it outside. We will have a bigger selection of flowers then, too."

"Am I the 'we' in all of this?"

"No, silly, my mom."

Braden sighed and went to grade papers.

The next afternoon, Braden pulled into the circular carriageway and trudged up the steps to the front door. His arms were loaded with papers and books. Exhaustion covered his face. Ellie ran to him to help him.

"You look awful. Was it a hard day?"

"I had heard the last day of the school year is always draining, but I had no idea. They set up activities for the kids to participate in. A lot of it involved physical exertion as the kids were pitted against the teachers in a lot of the games. I'm not as fit as I once was, but it was good, all in all, just tiring. I hope I never have to do a sack race with a kid again."

"Why don't you take a shower. I have something to tell you."

"What is it?"

"Go unwind. I'll have tea on the veranda when you're ready."

Ater a relaxing shower, Braden joined Ellie on the veranda. A cool breeze stirred the air and blew away the past school year's worry.

"Okay, so tell me what's on your mind."

Ellie pulled out Grace's journal.

"I thought you had read all of it. Did you miss something?"

"No, I was rummaging around in the attic, trying to organize it a little so we could decide what to keep and what to donate. I found a whole box of Grace's journals."

"Wow! So, what have you learned?"

"She describes the town and a guy named Paul Scott wanting to court her. She doesn't like him, but his family is prominent in Scottsville. In fact, his grandfather founded the town and named it. They owned the bank."

117

"You read a lot."

"Grace did mention that they treated their workers, as she called their freed slaves, more like family than employees. They had to keep their freed status a secret, so in town, they referred to them as slaves."

Braden looked in a trance as if he were picturing how they must have felt. "I guess life was hard back then. Just renovating this home makes me think of what it would have been like to live here with no electricity, no running water, no bathrooms, and no air conditioning in the summer. And the girls and women wearing those huge dresses and petticoats must have been stifling. I can hardly bear to think what the slaves must have endured in the hot sun doing back breaking work, dragging those heavy cotton sacks."

Ellie agreed, "And in the cold winters with drafty cabins. It wasn't idyllic as some novels and movies would have us believe."

"Yes, textbooks I've read talk about maintaining the houses all year round. The plantations were mostly self-sufficient, so there was firewood to be chopped, livestock tended to, and sometimes they were loaned out to other plantations or to work on roads."

"I'm sure they didn't have adequate clothes to be out in the weather."

"Must have been horrible. Did you find out if Matthew got his name on the title?"

"No, he didn't, but he got his name on the bank account. He gambled away a lot of money. And left them almost bankrupt. He had come home saying he had finished college, but he hadn't. He was a liar and a thief. He had a horrible accident and was left crippled."

Braden blew out a breath. "So he abused his power, as the male heir, so to speak?"

"Yes, but that girl named Mary was really good to him when he was in college, and she came to visit him."

"She must have been an angel to him."

"Well, she wasn't in the business of being an angel. She was more in the business of satisfying men."

"Oh, remember, I told you there was some juicy stuff!" Braden laughed.

"It wasn't juicy. It was sad. She had no other way to support her brother. Matt gave her large tips to help her get by."

"Well, he redeemed himself a little, I guess."

"And Joseph proposed to a girl named Rebecca, or Becca, as they called her. Another really sweet girl."

"I'm happy for him. As for Matthew, I don't know. That accident was maybe a good thing to take him off his high horse."

"Speaking of horses, that's how he got crippled. He got drunk and fell off his horse."

"I see what you mean about happy times and sad times. I'm thinking this would make a great novel! A lot of history in Grace's journals. Changing the subject, I forgot to tell you, Mom and Dad are coming tomorrow."

"Good, I have some ideas to run by your mother."

"And I suppose this has something to do with the wedding?"

"Could be. We also need to finish cleaning the remaining bedrooms if a lot of people want to spend the night." Ellie shot Braden a little impish grin.

CHAPTER SIXTEEN

Emma and Mason arrived the next morning. They both grabbed Ellie in a hug.

"Your ring is stunning." Emma held up Ellie's left hand.

Mason nodded and grinned.

Ellie blushed, but tried to hold in her excitement.

In the kitchen, Mason and Braden had a quick cup of coffee to make plans for the next project, while Emma and Ellie went upstairs to look at the bedrooms. Five more of them begged for attention. Some of the furniture needed repairing, but most of the pieces were intact, needing only to be cleaned and polished.

Emma rubbed her hands over a large chest. "They don't make furniture like they used to. I doubt many modern tables or bedsteads would last twenty-five years, much less over a hundred."

After a quick salad, Emma and Ellie bent over the furniture in the other bedrooms. By evening, they had two more bedrooms ready to be dressed in a color Ellie would pick out and purchase.

Ellie wiped her brow with a clean cloth. "I can picture the ad now. Come to The Sullivan House for a relaxing vacation and step back into another era. Choose your room, whether it is The Blue Room, The Spring Room or any other bedroom of your preference. Come relax in the fragrant flower garden with a spot of tea, or sit on our expansive veranda, play croquet on our beautiful green lawn, or go horseback riding with guidance from our groom. Slip away to a place of solitude and sit on our beautiful wrought iron bench in the orchard as you wait for a gourmet meal from our chef."

Emma stood with her eyes dancing. "You should write advertisements for a living. That had me wanting to come visit right away."

Ellie laughed. "If real estate keeps declining, I might have to do that. I thought we could put pictures in the brochure of a bedroom, the parlor and dining room, and the grounds."

"I think we have done enough for one day! I'd say let's have a light supper, get a good night's sleep and start fresh in the morning.

Ellie nodded. "I didn't realize this would be so tiring. I have a left-over roast in the refrigerator. Think the guys would like a hot beef sandwich with mashed potatoes?"

Emma laughed. "They both love those. They'll think they're eating gourmet food!"

The next morning, after a small breakfast, Emma and Ellie decided to go shopping for accessories for the bedrooms they had worked on. They found some beautiful quilts in an antique store and some new bedding sets that looked vintage. Their arms loaded with shopping bags, they sat down and wiped perspiration from their faces.

Ellie laughed. "I guess this is what the old Southern women called glowing?"

Emma returned her laughter. "Yes, Nannie still says that! Men sweat. Women glow!"

They moved upstairs, putting bags of bedding in each bedroom after they decided on which colors to use for each one.

Emma looked at her watch. "Where does time go? We need to start lunch."

As if they heard her, Mason and Braden walked in. "When is lunch?" Mason walked to Emma who was busy making the gravy for the sandwiches. He embraced her from behind.

Emma eased out of his arms. "Mason, you don't exactly smell nice. Go take a shower. By that time the hot beef sandwiches will be ready."

Mason looked at Braden. "You'd better do the same thing. I guess the girls don't like our earthy aroma."

Braden nodded, a big grin on his face. "Guess you're right."

After lunch, Emma mentioned that they were going home. "We left your grandmother with a sitter. I know she doesn't like it, so we need to get there before dinner and relieve the poor woman."

Braden asked between bites of his sandwich, "Is it the same lady you always hire?"

"No, she was busy. This is a new one. Your grandmother doesn't like change." Emma started removing the dishes.

Ellie stepped up. "Leave all this. I'll clean up. You probably need to get on the road."

Emma kissed Ellie's cheek. "Thank you."

They gathered their things and were on the road before Ellie got the dishes finished.

Sitting on the veranda, Braden turned to Ellie. "I have some news."

'Somehow, I think this might involve work." A confused look peppered Ellie's face.

"You guessed it, sort of. I need to go home this weekend. I'd like you to go with me. Nannie will want to see your ring, and Dad wants to drive a truck."

"What? Truck?"

Braden laughed. "He has a wholesale license. He found some bathroom fixtures that someone ordered but reneged on at the last minute. He got them cheap because the plumber wanted to get rid of them. There are eight sets, so the remaining seven bedrooms upstairs, plus the one down here, next to my parents, would all have bathrooms."

"Where do I fit into this?"

"You and Mom need to figure out which walls to tear down to build the bathrooms. Dad wants to rent a big commercial truck to bring all of them. I need to help him load and follow him here in his pickup so he will have a way back home. I need you to follow me in my car, so we have my car back here. There's a service station here he can drop off the truck after we unload it."

"I can do that. Might be a lot of fun."

"Don't get reckless with my baby!"

Ellie sighed. "It's a car, Braden."

"Yeah, but she's my baby."

"Whatever." Ellie rolled her eyes, and under her breath, she muttered, "Men!"

"Dad's also hired a plumber to be ready when we give the word."

"Okay, I'd like to meet your grandmother."

"You'll love Nannie."

Walking into the Cunningham's home, Ellie felt she had been wrapped in love. Exclamations over her ring again, and long hugs welcomed her. She turned to Braden. "Where is Nannie?"

"Come. I'll take you to her room." They walked down a hall decorated with family pictures on both walls.

Ellie stopped. "I want to look at these. I see one when you were little."

"Not now." He stood in the doorway of a bright, cheery room.

Charity sat in an overstuffed chair by a window with sunshine streaming in. When she saw Braden in the doorway, her hands flew to cover her mouth. "Braden! Come give me a hug." She looked around him. "Ellie! They told me you were coming. I want to see your ring."

They walked in and after hugs and seeing the ring, Charity said, "Tell me about Scottsville. I understand you are not wanting to find a big city any longer?"

Braden laughed. He and Ellie relayed their journey with the mansion and Grace's journals.

"Remember I told you I'd tell you a story? My mother took me to Oak Hollow many times. I loved the river."

Braden looked confused. "You knew the people who lived there?"

"Oh yes. It's long story, and I'll tell you more one of these days, but I want to know if the river is still flowing. And is there a big boulder jutting out into the water?"

Ellie took her hand. "Yes, to both. The whole place was so sad looking when I bought it. I thought I had made a horrible mistake and would lose my money. Braden, Mason, and Emma brought it back to life. Now Braden has brought me back to life." She flashed her ring. "I hope you will let me call you Nannie when we marry."

"You can call me that, now, young lady. It's a name more precious to me than any jewel."

Braden saw her eyes droop. "You're getting tired. We'll let you rest, but I'll hold you to more stories about your connection to Oak Hollow."

Charity nodded. "Read the journals. I'm glad they're still there. Maybe you could take me to Scottsville some time."

"You just tell me when you feel up to it. Now take a little nap. We're heading out early in the morning, so we may not see you before we leave.

Just remember we love you, and I'll have your carriage ready when you want to come visit."

Charity grinned. "I am tired, but I don't think that little blue car is my idea of a carriage!"

Braden bent and kissed her on the cheek. "Wait till you ride in her!"

As they walked back toward the living room, something gnawed at Braden. Why had his grandmother never mentioned visiting Oak Hollow that was a real place during his childhood? He thought it was just a figment of her imagination. Who owned it, and why was she in Scottsville? How did she know about Grace and her journals? Did they live in Scottsville for a while when they first married? She and his grandfather lived in Alabama and had for as long as Braden could remember. He would sometimes walk down to their house after school or in the summer. He vowed to press her for more details when she felt up to it.

In the kitchen, Braden cornered his mother. "Is Nannie okay? She looks kind of pale, and her eyes are droopy."

"She has an appointment in two weeks with her doctor. I'm thinking about seeing if I can get her in earlier. I don't think she rested very well when we were with you."

"Keep us posted. Dad said he wanted to leave early in the morning, so don't fix a big breakfast."

"You definitely know your dad."

The trip back home was uneventful though Braden kept looking in his rear-view mirror to be sure Ellie was driving his baby carefully. After they unloaded the bathroom fixtures, he followed Mason to drop off the truck.

"Why don't you spend the night with us, Dad?"

"I'd like that, but I have a morning meeting with client, so I need to get back. I'll come next weekend and see if we can't get the bathrooms prepped. I hope the plumber will be available."

"We have given him more business than he's had in a while, and he told me he is putting us at the top of his list for anything we need."

Mason smiled. "I figured as much. That's good to know. Give him a heads up, and I'll see you in a few days.

By the middle of May, all the bedrooms had bathrooms attached. Some were smaller than others, but all were a nice size and it didn't cut down on the size of the huge bedrooms too much.

Ellie and Braden made payments to their account when they could. Ellie just needed to sell five or six expensive homes, and their debt would be paid. Problem was there weren't that many large homes in Scottsville that had been renovated, claiming a high dollar price tag. Braden didn't contribute much since he was saving for their honeymoon. He had decided to surprise her with a trip to Los Angeles and Hollywood. There was so much to do there. Ellie loved movies. She would be able to visit the Walk of Fame, maybe see some actresses and actors, and shop where the stars did. In addition, there were many activities and places to see. They would be gone a week. He had scouted places to stay and the cost of flights, and figured the amount he'd need to save. He could do it and still put some toward their debt.

CHAPTER SEVENTEEN

The gentle spring saw June blast in, windy, sultry, and kicking up dust in a temper tantrum. It was the driest season people had seen in a long time. Sweat woke Braden early. Their bedroom felt damp from the humidity pouring through the open window. When he stumbled downstairs, surprise registered when he saw Ellie on the telephone.

She hung up smiling. "Good morning, sleepyhead."

"I'd still be sleeping if I hadn't been drowning in sweat."

She poured him a cup of coffee and turned the floor fan toward him. "Don't be so grumpy. We'll have air conditioning soon."

"Who was that on the phone? I didn't even hear it ring."

"It didn't. I had a phone call from Thomas Chandler in Jackson late yesterday. I was calling him back. He's the one that got me into real estate. He lost one of his agents and wanted to know if I'd have time to help him out if real estate is slow here. A few companies have moved into Jackson, so his agency is busy, and he needs another agent. It would only be temporary."

"What about Mister Knight?"

"I talked to him after Thomas called. We are so slow, he told me if I need to take any time off, he could handle the agency by himself. He knows we're remodeling and thought I could use the time off to accumulate some funds."

"Are you going to Jackson? What did you tell Mister Chandler?"

"Braden, it's an answer to prayer. If I can make enough, we can pay off our debt to your parents. I told Thomas I'd call him back after I discussed it with you."

Braden mulled over Ellie's announcement. "I want to pay off my parents, but if you make enough, I'd rather have air conditioning and heating put in. But then I'd be in your debt until I can pay my half."

127

Ellie laughed. "Don't be silly. We're not exactly keeping score on who owes what, though I am making a record so we will know how much we've spent, who it's to, how much each of us has paid, and how much we owe your parents."

"You are so organized. I think you should have been an accountant."

"No, that's my daddy's bailiwick. If real estate here doesn't pick up, I may consider it."

"How long will you be gone?"

"I guess I'll see how things go. You can always come visit, or I can come home for a few days every once in a while."

"I'll miss you like crazy, but I know you're frustrated with the real estate market here."

"Yes, I am. I'll call him back and go ahead and leave in a day or two."

Braden thought it might break all records if they didn't get rain in the next few days. He wiped his brow with the bottom of his t-shirt and moved to the window looking out over the meadow. There wasn't even the tiniest hint of a breeze.

Ellie made toast and an omelet and halved it with Braden. "I need to water my garden. It looks sad. A few plants have already died. At the Chamber meeting the other day, I learned farmers and ranchers are hurting. The bank has offered to reduce interest rates on their loans."

Braden nodded. "I ran into Hiram the other day. He said the same thing. I can only imagine what it would have been like for Abraham Sullivan if his cotton didn't make."

"I think he must have been a frugal man and probably had enough saved to see them through the lean years."

"I'm thinking of starting on The Mystery House. Since Dad has his own construction company, he told me any time I need him, he's free to come. Maybe he will tell me what needs to be done. I want to be sure the stairs are stable. I know the walls need paint, but thank goodness, there's no wallpaper."

"Good idea. I'm hoping we can open by Thanksgiving. It's going to be exciting to have Christmas here, too."

"It couldn't be any better than last year. Have you found any more journals?"

"No. I've looked. Grace must have stored the rest in another box, or maybe they got destroyed. I don't have time to look today. Big meeting at the Chamber and then the Park Committee."

The phone rang. Braden answered it and mouthed to Ellie, "Dad." She nodded.

"Okay, Dad, see you tomorrow."

Braden rose and kissed her cheek before going to take a shower. "Don't worry about dinner. We can throw together a salad or something. I think Dad is as excited as we are about our big adventure."

Ellie laughed and grabbed her purse. "See you this afternoon, and then I need to pack. I'll leave early in the morning. If I don't see your dad, tell him hello."

Mason drove up mid-morning the next day. Singing "Heigh-Ho," the dwarf's song, he hurried up the steps. Braden was just cleaning up the breakfast dishes. He had put a fresh pot of coffee on since Mason drank it all day long.

"Hi, Dad. You're in a good mood."

"Your mother is having some kind of hen party where the women buy plastic containers and bowls, and I don't know what all. I'm glad not to have to be around that. That's just too many gabbing women in one house. I also just finished a big project, so we're in the money for at least a few months."

"How is the business going?"

"Better than I expected. I've signed a contract with a major building firm. That will keep me as busy as I want to be."

Braden poured two cups of coffee. "Where do we start?"

"You mentioned the Mystery House. As she always does, your mother said bathrooms were the first priority. For once, I agree with her. She could always use the ones in here, but when she and Ellie are working at the Mystery House, she wants a bathroom."

"Dad, you always agree with her. That's how I am with Ellie, too. Guess you passed on your passivity to me."

"Son, I learned a long time ago giving in to Emma just made my life easier. On big issues, we compromise, but it's her way on small things."

They spent the rest of the morning going through The Mystery House, planning bathrooms, assessing the stability of the house, and making notes of what they needed to buy.

"Dad, I don't want you to buy everything. We would have you paid off, but real estate is slow, and I'm trying to save for a honeymoon. Let's just get what I can afford."

"I'm not worried about your paying me back. I know after the honeymoon, you'll have more money to work with. I'd say, we frame out the bathrooms this week. I would like to buy at least one toilet and see if we can get the plumber to connect it to the septic tank as soon as he has time."

"So, we need a few two by fours and some nails?"

"Maybe a few other things. It won't be too expensive, though. We need to fix the hinge on the front door." Mason hit the button on his tape measure and put the notepad with the measurements in his shirt pocket.

"Later down the road, I'd like to get a new door with panels like the one in the Big House."

"I'll keep that in mind." Mason unscrewed the lower hinge of the door since it wasn't holding the door. "Let's go see if we can match this."

Braden looked at his dad. He seemed to be animated every time he came to visit. "Okay, I guess we take your truck."

After getting what they needed, including a new toilet, they started working in earnest. By late afternoon, they had one bathroom framed in, ready for sheet rock. Braden spoke with the plumber. He made an appointment for the next week.

"I guess when you and Mom come back, The Mystery House will have a working toilet."

"That will please her. I'm thinking of going home tomorrow, but we'll be back if I don't have a lot of work with the Baker Brothers Construction Company."

Braden explained that Ellie had left for Jackson for a few weeks, but was planning to come home for the weekend. "I'll start painting as soon as Ellie leaves again."

"You'd better check with the girls before you decide on the color. You know how they are."

"Good idea. Speaking of girls, Ellie just pulled in. I'm sure she's as tired as we are. How about I fire up the grill and throw a couple of hamburgers on for dinner?"

Ellie breezed in the house carrying a paper sack of groceries. "I don't feel like cooking tonight, so I stopped and got the fixings for hamburgers. I hope that's okay with you two."

Braden and Mason started laughing.

"What's so funny?"

Braden said, "I just started the grill and took out some hamburger patties from the freezer!"

Mason smiled. "This is exactly what Emma and I do. She finishes my sentences, and if I have a thought about something, she gets it. You two are going to have a great marriage."

After dinner and clean up, everyone said goodnight. Braden turned out all the lights and made his way upstairs. Just as he got to sleep, the phone rang. He rushed down as fast as he could, stumbling a time or two in the dark and silently mouthing some strong words for a wrong number. It was his mother. He felt chills race up and down his spine.

"Braden, tell Mason to come home now. Your grandmother has been taken to the ER." Emma's voice broke. "Tell him to hurry."

"Okay, Mom, I'm coming, too."

Braden woke his father and Ellie. "Get dressed, Dad. I'm going with you. I'll take my car." He turned to Ellie. "Will you be all right here, or do you want to come with me?"

"I want to go with you. I'll call Thomas when we get there." She dressed and grabbed a couple of changes of clothes for each of them. In her haste, she didn't realize she had packed Braden's underwear with the hearts as she didn't pay attention to what she put in the suitcase. Within twenty minutes, they were on the road.

Braden's hands gripped the steering wheel so hard, his knuckles turned white. Ellie could see by the moonlight that he was struggling to maintain his composure. She wanted to do something to ease his anxiety. "What can I do to help, sweetheart?"

"Being with me helps. Maybe say a prayer." He moved a hand to his eyes and swiped away a tear. "I can't lose her, Ellie. I just can't. We have so much more living to do together."

"Let's wait and see what the doctors say before we go thinking negative thoughts."

"You're right. She's a feisty little thing. Always has been. She's the one who would organize a swim party for no reason, and supervise all my friends. She helped me make a kite when I was in second grade. We would go to open fields, and she'd run with me to get it airborne. She was the one who took care of me while my parents worked. If a teacher or anyone else did something she felt was unfair, she had no trouble telling them off. All my friends love her."

"I remember she didn't dilly dally with words when I met her!"

"She is a good judge of character. She summed you up in a couple of minutes! And she's made it known, she's ready for a wedding!" Braden voice broke. "I hope she can make it to our wedding."

Ellie looked at her watch as they drove into the hospital's parking lot. "It's a little after two. Do you see your mother's car? Your grandmother may have been discharged."

"Yeah, I see it."

Mason joined Braden and Ellie, and they walked into the ER. The receptionist at the front desk told them Charity had been admitted and gave them the room number. No words were spoken as they walked down a long hall, the smell of strong antiseptic assaulting their noses. Entering her room, Braden and Mason walked to her bedside. Charity had her eyes closed. Ellie stood at the foot of the bed. Emma was sitting in a chair but rose, and hugs were exchanged.

Mason whispered, "Mom, it's Mason. We're here if you feel like talking."

Braden bent and kissed her cheek. "Nannie, hang in there. Don't give up."

"Emma, what happened?" Mason asked.

"She was fine. We were having a light supper at her request. She wanted a lettuce salad with green olives in it. I thought that was a strange combination, but I fixed it for her. She took about three bites and started talking about you, Braden. Wanted to know where you were and what you were doing, and if you were spending the night with someone. I think she thought you were young. Then she asked about Mason. She mumbled some other incoherent words and put her hand over her chest. I thought it might be indigestion with that weird salad, but to be safe, I called an ambulance. Her blood pressure was elevated, and she seemed perturbed. The ER doctor said he thought she had the beginning stages of congestive heart failure or a stroke and recommended admitting her. She fell asleep almost as soon as the nurses got her settled."

"Her color looks good, and her breathing is regular. How long does the doctor say before he knows anything?" Mason steadied himself against Braden.

Emma sighed. "He said if she's stable, he'll discharge her tomorrow. I'm sorry I frightened you, but I thought you'd want to be here."

Braden sighed. "We wouldn't be anywhere else, Mom."

Ellie spoke up. "Is there anything I can do? I could go get coffee for everyone."

Mason spoke, "Why don't all of you go home? I'll sit up with her the rest of the night."

Braden put his hand on his father's shoulder. "No. I'll sit up. I'm younger than you, Dad."

"I guess you noticed." Mason's wearied body denied his attempt at sarcastic humor. "Okay. Call if she wakes up. You know we'll sleep with one eye open."

Braden watched them go down the long hall with Ellie trailing them before he gave into the feeling of despair. As he walked back into the room, Charity stirred. He rushed to the bed. She was whispering something. "What is it, Nannie?"

"Braden. Scotts."

Confused, Braden bent closer to her mouth. "Are you talking about Scottsville, Nannie? I live there now."

"Gotta talk."

"Okay, Nannie. We'll talk, but everything's fine. Get some sleep. When you wake up, we'll talk as long as you want."

CHAPTER EIGHTEEN

Charity didn't wake or mumble the rest of the night. Sitting in the dark room, Braden felt somewhat baffled. His grandmother mentioned Scottsville when he told her he was going to move there. Now, again, she seemed anxious to talk to him. When she mentioned Scotts, did she mean Scottsville? What secret did Scottsville hold? Or maybe she had Scottsville mixed up with Scotland. He'd ask his dad. Surely, Nannie had talked to his dad. If he could find a minute to get him alone, he'd see what he knew.

Muttering his thoughts out loud, he said, "I don't remember them ever saying where Granddaddy was from. Maybe he was from the area...maybe Vicksburg or Jackson, and they went to Scottsville for little get-a-ways, but they probably lived in a bigger city. That's it. She's just reliving some memories with my grandfather." Having settled his theory in his mind, his thoughts turned to other things.

Given how much money his dad was spending on The Mystery House, Braden rethought Los Angeles as a honeymoon. New Orleans was a lot closer, and he could drive there. They wouldn't have to fly or get a rental car. Since he hadn't told Ellie about Hollywood, he decided that would be a better option. There were as many things to do and see there as there were in Los Angeles. Braden couldn't still his mind. Nurses were in and out throughout the night, so dozing was impossible. When he got up to stretch his legs, he noticed the sun was peeking over the horizon. He glanced at his grandmother. She seemed to be sleeping peacefully. He walked down to the nurses' station and got a cup of coffee. It seared his throat and tasted burned, but it would keep him alert until someone relieved him.

Braden turned at the slight sound the door made. His dad and Ellie walked in followed by his mother carrying a large tote. "You are not really drinking hospital coffee, are you? Pour that out. I have a thermos of the good stuff."

"What else is in that tote? You could carry a week's worth of clothes in there."

"I brought a change of clothes for your grandmother in case they let her go home. I have a couple of books to read while I wait, and I have some knitting to do." She closed the tote and sat in the chair Braden offered her. "Has the doctor made rounds yet?"

"No. Nannie has been sleeping."

As the clock on the wall hit seven o'clock, the doctor and two nurses walked in. They went to Charity's bedside. After a cursory exam, the doctor took her hand and woke her. "Missus Cunningham, do you know where you are?"

Charity cleared her throat as she reached for a glass of water. Taking a sip, she looked at the doctor and nurses. "'Peers I'm in the hospital. Do you not know where you are, Doctor?"

"Good point. What day of the week is it?"

"Let's see. I had that salad last night with olives, and I've been asleep. Must be Tuesday." She focused her eyes on his.

"That's right. Can you tell me who is president?"

"Of course, I know. And our country is in a mess. I don't have time to fill you in on all the shenanigans going on, but you should read up on it. A doctor needs to be informed. Not to be rude, but you seem a little confused since you're asking all these questions. And you might need to get a calendar."

A huge grin spanned his face. Turning to Emma and Braden, he said, "She's the cutest patient I've had in a long time. She just made my day. I've looked at all her tests. Her heart and lungs are fine. She's a little anemic, but I feel the biggest thing is dehydration. It causes all kinds of symptoms. I'm going to send her home, but I want her to drink a lot of water. You can pick up some iron tablets over the counter and have her take two a day. I'd like to see her back in a couple of weeks to recheck her labs." He went back to her bed. "You take care. It's been a real pleasure to have you as a patient."

"Thank you. You need to go rest so you can remember better."

On the way home, Emma tried to explain about the questions. Braden tried to suppress laughter. That was his Nannie. Sassy as all get out.

Braden went to his father's carpentry shop. Mason, concentrating on a project with his scroll saw, didn't hear him come in. Braden waited until he finished. "Hey Dad, have you got a minute?"

"Sure. Are you and Ellie headed out? I'll come in and say goodbye."

"No, not yet. We are going to leave tomorrow. Nannie has mentioned Scottsville several times. The latest was in the hospital, but she didn't elaborate. What do you know about her connection?"

"As you know, I grew up right here in Tuscaloosa. When we were little, we loved to visit my grandparents…Chi Chi and Popsi, as we called them. When you came along, Popsi had already passed from a tractor accident, and Chi Chi wasn't far behind. We were going to call your grandmother the same, but we didn't. We stuck with Nannie. At any rate, Mom used to love to tell us made-up stories. She created fairy tales when we were young, and scary stories when we were older. Many of the stories revolved around Ireland and Scotland, but sometimes, she told stories of towns, mostly ones she created, but there was one called Scottsville, Mississippi. We thought that was a play on Scot Land. It was only after your uncle Dirk and I were teens that we discovered there was an actual town by that name. She claims to have visited there, but whether she really did, we don't know."

"I remember the stories she told. Do you remember going there for a reunion or anything?"

"No, the only reunion I remember was a trip to County Cork in Ireland. Chi Chi had a sister named Cara who moved to Ireland. She met and married a man named Pat Kelly, who refused to come to America. That broke Chi Chi's heart, so Popsi took all of us to meet the family. Dirk and I were little, but I vaguely remember meeting our cousins, Cian and Oscar that one time, but I haven't heard from any of that family since, and I think your Nannie only had a few letters. The thing I remember most is that they talked funny. Chi Chi went into a depression over losing Popsi and Cara being so far away." Mason wiped sawdust from his shirt and face. "Remember, take what your Nannie says with the realization that it may all be made up. She may have confused the Ireland trip with Scottsville that she created in her mind. I don't think she ever knew there was a real town by that name. When you mentioned you were going to teach there, it stimulated Nannie's imagination and my curiosity."

"I thought the same thing about Scotland, but she knows about the river. Why didn't we call Nannie Chi Chi? We called our grandfather Popsi."

"Someone told us it had a bad connotation in Spanish."

"That it does. I think I'll see what the girls are up to." Braden walked to the house, not aware of his steps. His mind was deep in thought about his father's words. Nannie did have an active imagination, but she seemed lucid and sure of what she told him. He found Ellie helping his mom with brunch.

He gave Ellie a silent message. "Hey, Mom, how about Ellie and I take a tray to Nannie. I'd like to spend a little more time with her before we leave tomorrow."

Ellie smiled. "I'd like to see her, too. She may not get to come to our wedding, so I'd like to talk to her before we go home. She's such a sweet lady."

Emma giggled, "She is sweet, but she's can be a little cheeky."

Braden picked up the tray, and Ellie took a tea towel. They knocked on her door. She was sitting up in bed reading.

"Oh, my. I'm getting waited on. I'm perfectly fine to go to the table. I'm old but not an invalid."

Ellie placed the tea towel over the old woman's lap, and Braden set the tray down. "You said you wanted to talk to me. Ellie would like to hear what you have to say as well. I thought your room would have less distractions."

"You're right. When is the wedding?"

Ellie smiled and put her hand on Charity's arm. "Depends on the weather. We want to have it outside, so if it's warm enough, maybe around Easter. We have a perfect place."

"Where is that?"

Ellie told her about finding Grace's journals and the heart of stones."

"That sounds lovely."

"Do you feel up to talking and telling us what you know?"

"It's a long story, Braden. I want to take my time and visit Scottsville. Maybe we'll sit in Oak Hollow, and it will bring back memories I have forgotten."

Braden lifted the tray. "That's a good idea, Nannie. When you're rested, I'll come get you, and you can tell us more stories."

Braden and Ellie kissed the old woman's cheek and went back to the living room.

After Charity had a nap, Braden and Ellie went back to her room.

Charity's eyes held a faraway look. "You'll marry in the woods?"

"Yes." Braden said, "You told me you visited Scottsville when you were little."

"Yes, my cousins and I loved the river. We used to catch frogs and soft-shelled turtles. We loved to play with them, but my mother would not let me take them home because she said they would be lonely and miss their natural home. She was right. They never venture far from where they were born, and if they do, they try to find their way back. They say turtles feel lonely away from their family I don't like people to keep them as pets. It's cruel."

"Why did you go there?"

"We had family reunions there until I turned seven. Lots of people would come. I liked the Big House, as we called it, but there was a smaller house down by the river. I liked to stay there. I'd sneak out at night and go to a big boulder that jutted out into the river and look at the stars. I'd pretend it was place of magic, and when I was on top of it, I could fly. Fly, I did one night. I slipped right into the river. I was scared I was going to drown because I couldn't see in the dark very well, and I didn't know how to swim. I made my way to the bank. I clawed my way up to solid ground, but I was wet and cold, and my clothes were covered in mud. I didn't know how I'd explain my wet clothes, so I hung them over a low hanging bush and tiptoed into the house as naked as a new born babe. I groped in the dark and found my bed."

Ellie looked puzzled. "But how did you explain your clothes on the branch?"

"I got up early the next morning and got them before she saw them. They dried stiff as a broomstick, but I managed to work with them and get them somewhat soft. I told my mom I had been playing in the mud the day before and didn't want to hang them in the house."

139

Braden saw Charity's eyes dull a bit. "We've tired you. I want to know more when you are up to it."

"I'll come with Mason and Emma early before the wedding, and we'll have lots of time to talk. I want to see the place one more time before I..."

"Don't say it, Nannie. You'd better live a long time."

"Duly noted." Braden noticed she ate all the fruit, most of the waffle and a third of the omelet. As he picked up the tray, her eyes closed. There would be more time later.

Ellie wandered to the kitchen to talk to Emma about The Sullivan House and to see if she could help with preparations for dinner.

"That's sweet of you. I guess you could set the table and throw these greens together for a salad."

"I can do that. I also wanted to talk to you. My mom and I are going wedding shopping soon. If you'd like to join us, I would be honored."

Emma's eyes misted. "I love weddings. I have been waiting for Susan to get married, so I could help with all the details. I would very much like to go with you and Cynthia. I'll make sure Mason stays home to keep an eye on Charity."

Early the next morning, Braden and Ellie started home. Ellie grew pensive as she stared out the window. Breaking her silence, Braden asked, "What do you think of what Nannie said?"

"I find it strange. Did she really visit there? Were her parents good friends to the Sullivans and allowed them to have their family reunions there? You know I wonder..."

"What?" Braden glanced at her before turning his attention back to the road.

"Is it possible that they used The Mystery House as sort of a gathering place for people to have reunions? Wouldn't that be ironic?"

"I didn't think of that. I want to write that down to ask Nannie if she gets to come with Mom and Dad the next time they visit."

"I'd like to be here when you talk to her. Unfortunately, I'm planning to leave tomorrow to go back to Jackson. Thomas was very patient to let me stay with you while Nannie was sick."

"Okay. You will keep me posted, so I know what's going on?"

"Of course."

CHAPTER NINETEEN

Once they arrived back at home, Braden took their luggage inside and then settled himself in one of the wicker chairs on the veranda. Ellie poured large glasses of iced tea and joined him.

"I have something to tell you. Mom and I are going shopping for my wedding gown soon. Before we do, I'd like to know how many friends you want to stand up with you, so I'll know how many bridesmaids to have. I'd like to look for their dresses, too."

"The circle isn't big enough for a lot of guests, so I'd say we keep the attendants to two or three and the guests to about twenty. If you want more, we could set some in a semicircle outside the circle."

"I like that. So, a best man and two groomsmen?"

"Are you going to shop for all the wedding things when you're there?"

"I'd like to, but I doubt I'll have time. I spend a lot of time running around showing property. When I get home, I try to prepare most of the evening meals, do my laundry, and fall into bed. My dad is a horrible patient, and my mother is just about ready to hit him over the head with an iron skillet."

"Well, that paints a picture. I know she must be exhausted, though."

"Even though she'd like to, she never says an unkind word to him. I think that is the definition of lasting love."

The next morning, Braden carried Ellie's suitcase to her car. "Please be careful. Call me when you get there. Remember I love you. I'm just sad I have the whole summer off, and you won't be here to spend it with me."

"I love you, too. Think positively. Maybe the market is still busy, and I'll sell a lot of houses soon."

Two days later, Emma and Mason drove up unannounced. Braden helped his father take their things into their bedroom. Emma gave Braden a hug. "I guess you think we've moved in. We just pop in and claim this bedroom downstairs as ours."

"You're family. You don't need an invitation."

Emma smiled. "Where's Ellie?"

Braden explained her absence. "That's why I'm glad you're here. You and Ellie have the same tastes, so you can help me decide on the color of paint for The Mystery House."

"I hate to do that without Ellie."

"When she called to tell me she got to her parents' house, I told her that I might ask you and Dad to come keep me company. But you got here before I could call. Maybe it was mental telepathy? We are really eager to get The Mystery House finished. She said you two had discussed some general things that you thought should be done. She said to trust whatever you said."

"Yes, when you were home, she and I did discuss some things. I think the first thing would be to do the repairs and make sure the walls are ready for paint. I'll go tomorrow and look for what Ellie and I thought might work."

Braden nodded. "How is Nannie? Did you get the sitter she likes?"

Mason laughed. "Yes. That woman is a miracle worker. She got Mom dressed up and convinced her to go to lunch at a small cafe. Of course, she took her walker. It really perked up Mom's spirits."

The three of them set around the kitchen table making plans.

Mason put his pencil down and gazed out the window.

"What's on your mind, Dad?"

"I was just thinking. If you are going to turn this into an inn, it might be wiser to start on the Big Kitchen. Ellie said something about hiring a chef, so you could serve three meals a day."

"Yes, we talked about that, but we don't have the money right now. We thought we'd start with just some breakfast items and let them do what they want to during the day. There's a lot to do in Vicksburg and also Jackson."

Emma looked around. "This kitchen is good sized, but we'd need to set up the buffet in the dining room with all the things you want to offer. They would have to eat in the dining room. Serving them in the kitchen where the cooking is done wouldn't be a good idea."

"True, Mom. What would you think about having some tables with umbrellas on the veranda? With it wrapping around, we could fit several tables outside in the summer. When it gets cool in the fall, that dining table will seat ten people comfortably. I don't think they would all get up at the same time. We might have certain hours that we serve, say seven to ten o'clock. And we could also provide room service between those hours if they don't want to come down."

Mason said, "Too bad we didn't build a banquette before we found the table. That would have seated six more people."

"But I'm glad we didn't. I like this table with the Sullivan name on it." Braden ran his hands over the edge of the table.

"Let's go look at the big monstrosity." Mason pulled Emma's chair out for her.

Braden followed them down the walkway. He gasped. "I'd forgotten how big this kitchen is."

Emma studied the room. "We need all new appliances. There is room here for a long work counter, a small rectangular table for prep work, and room for a large refrigerator and freezer. This could be a chef's dream kitchen. I love all the windows, too. I'll map out how to remodel it."

Braden shot a serious look at his mother. "How long can you stay?"

Emma looked at Mason before answering. "We talked about this on the way here. Of course, we thought Ellie would be here, so we'd just stay a few days. If your grandmother's sitter will stay, we could extend our visit."

Mason nodded. "For all I know, she'll have Mom up dancing before we get home."

Emma laughed. "She did talk about taking her to a center for senior-aged people where they have a heated pool to let Nannie get some exercise!"

"Okay, then. Let's organize chores, and see what I can afford to get done."

"Son, I told you. Do not worry about the money. The main thing is to get everything ready for your guests. We don't want to do too much, though, without consulting Ellie."

"I talk to her every night. I'll run our plans by her. Are you sure you and Mom don't want to move in here? You could have The Mystery House."

Mason locked eyes with Emma. "What do you think? We could be here to supervise these young people, and be sure they don't stay out too late!"

"Mason! You know that's not funny."

"I know we spend a lot of time here, but there is something about this place that speaks to me. I get a real sense of peace, even with all the chaos. I guess it's really that it is so quiet, it's like stepping back in time to a gentler way of life."

Emma put her hands on her hips. "Way of life? Humph. As for me, I love it here, too, but I'm glad we installed bathrooms as well as air conditioning and heating. I cannot imagine wearing those heavy dresses, all those petticoats, and especially the corsets in the hot, humid weather in the summer. In the winter, it might not be so bad, but thankfully, the winter is short. Seriously, though, I wouldn't mind having a bedroom in The Mystery House if you and Ellie move in there. I like the one we've designated ours in this house, too. Since we have a kitchen in this Mystery House, and the Big Kitchen will be easy to renovate, so let's start on The Mystery House first."

Within the next two weeks, Mason had employed a plumber to do the plumbing of the bathrooms. He and Braden put in a master suite with an attached bathroom upstairs as well as small bathrooms in the other seven bedrooms. Downstairs, they enlarged another master bedroom by taking some space from the study and attached a bathroom as well.

Emma selected warm colors of light buttery paint for the entire house. The color was called Lemon Frost, and by the time they finished painting, Braden didn't even want to look at the fruit for a long time. He had lugged in more paint and primer cans than he wanted to count.

Emma went shopping and found a sofa and two arm chairs with hand-carved detail on the exposed wooden areas of the arms. The fabric on the sofa was a subtle shade of sage green, but it was still muted enough that any color would go with it if Ellie didn't like the wall color. The chairs had random flowers of pale orange, light lemony yellow, and barely blue with sage-colored leaves on a light ivory background. She decided to confer with Ellie before tackling the bedrooms. They would select bedding, drapes, and pictures when Ellie found time to go shopping. Braden looked around. "I'm glad we delayed the kitchen remodel. This looks fantastic."

"Braden, you may want to offer the chef a room here, and maybe any other staff you might employ. Ellie did tell me she wants to bring down some of those paintings from the attic to put throughout the house."

"They were on her to do list, so I brought them down. I stored them in the study."

Mason cleared his throat. "I thought we talked about getting some horses."

Braden slapped his leg. "We did. I forgot. I'll run it by Ellie when we talk tonight."

Emma nodded. "How's it going? I'd like to talk to her, too, and tell her what all I've decided on."

"She knows we are working, but I kind of wanted everything to be a surprise. Have you talked to Nannie?"

"Yes, we call her every night as well. She is really enjoying the center and wants to swim, as she calls it, every day. We may have to join her when we get home."

Braden put a pot of coffee on and fired up the grill. "How about a good juicy steak to reward us for our efforts?"

Mason agreed. "I never turn down a good steak. Make mine medium rare, please, and your mother's a touch more toward well done."

"Yes, I remember. You taught me well."

The phone rang. Ellie's voice lifted Braden's spirits. He didn't mention the surprise they had planned. "She's planning to come home in the next day or two."

"Braden, I think you and Ellie need to look at Grace's journal. All the paintings have Matthew Sullivan signed on the bottom. I think he was the artist."

"That's really something special. To have one of his paintings in each room would be fabulous, and I know Ellie would love it. I also found some wooden panels that he must have painted. I don't know what purpose they served, but some of them were hinged like a room divider."

Emma said, "I've been reading. They stood in bedrooms, so women could bathe behind them in large tubs and then dress for bed and also to

145

dress behind them any time a woman would change clothes. We'll use them, too."

"In the bathroom? Couldn't they just close the door?"

"No, silly, they bathed in big tin tubs in the bedroom, so we'll put them in bedrooms."

CHAPTER TWENTY

The next morning, Mason and Emma decided to go home and check on Charity. Emma hugged Braden. "If she's up to it, we may bring her with us next time. She may have gained some strength "swimming" with that sitter!"

"That would be great. I know Ellie would be sorry if she missed Nannie. She wanted to be here when Nannie visits, but she will understand."

Mason held up his hand. "No, we won't bring her until Ellie is here. We've already taken more liberty with all this remodeling than we should have without her here."

"Okay. Have a safe trip. Call when you get home."

That night, before Braden had a chance to call, the phone rang. He heard Ellie's sweet voice. "Braden, I've got wonderful news! I've sold six houses." She gave him the figure of what her profit would be.

Braden sat down before he collapsed. "That is fantastic, sweetheart. Does that mean you are coming home?"

"I wanted to talk to you. Thomas has asked me to stay a little longer. He's having a hard time finding agents that he thinks would fit in with his business. At this rate, if the market holds, I may be able to make enough to pay off all our bills. Of course, I don't know how much we owe your parents since they've been there."

Braden had written down all the materials, the plumber's fee, and the hours they had spent, but he didn't want to divulge all the work they had done and ruin the surprise. "I've written down everything, but I didn't put it in our journal. I'll leave that up to you. I just got receipts, but they are kind of disorganized."

"I can't wait to see the progress. I've already made enough to pay them what we owed before this last visit. If I can sell at least ten more houses, I think we can be out of debt with money left over."

147

Braden sighed. "How long will that take? If we do have money left over, we should get the horses we talked about."

"Yes, yes, yes! I hate being away from you. I think I'll come home Monday and stay a couple of days. Weekends are the busiest here, so I can't get away for fear of losing a sale, but weekdays are slower."

"I miss you so much. I'll count the hours until you're home."

"Do you think your mom and dad could come, so Emma and I could go over what she's done?"

"I'll call them. So, you'll be here in three days?"

"Yes. I can hardly wait."

Three days later, Ellie drove into the driveway. Braden had the coffeepot on and the waffle batter ready to pour into the waffle iron. He had fresh fruit and whipped cream along with a stack of baked peppered bacon. He met Ellie at the door.

He embraced her and kissed her until they came up for air. "I hope you haven't eaten."

"You told me not to."

Over breakfast, Ellie filled Braden in on the real estate she had sold, and he gave her a few sketchy details of what they had accomplished in The Mystery House. He wanted to wait to surprise her until his parents arrived. He told her about the paintings with Matthew's signature, and asked if she'd like to decide which rooms to hang them in. "I talked to Mom. She's on her way, but Dad's got a big project he's working on. He'll need to finish that, which will take up most of the week. I know he's tired. We've worked really hard."

After breakfast, they strolled down to the river. Ellie stopped midway and took a deep breath. "It feels so peaceful to be home. I am definitely through with city life. It smells so clean here, so different from the noise and smells of the city. I know we have a lot to do, but I could stay right here for a month!"

They heard a horn. "Mom must be here." They looked toward the carriageway and saw Emma wave. They waved back and started for the house.

As soon as she had time to have a cup of coffee, Emma suggested they go to the Mystery House.

Emma stood behind as Braden urged Ellie forward and stopped at the new front door.

Ellie's hands flew to her face. "I love this door. It's almost like the one at the Big House."

"Yes, except it has etched pecan trees instead of oak trees. Dad made the double doors and had an artist do the panes." He turned the knob and ushered Emma and Ellie inside.

Entering, a gleaming expanse of warm beige terrazzo tile greeted Ellie. A pattern of different colored pebbles of pale shades of orange, yellow, pink, blue, and ivory, picked up the colors of the sofa and chairs. Light shone through the glass etched panels on either side of the double doors giving the entrance a glow of warmth. Ellie stood in the room, seemingly unable to move.

"It's...it's breathtaking."

"Dad got the tile wholesale."

They moved into the parlor. The sofa stood regal and proud in front of a stone fireplace. The two Victorian arm chairs flanked each side of it.

Ellie was speechless. Braden moved to her side. "Did you notice the fireplace?" He saw her nod. "We spent a whole day picking up river stones that had a pearlescent and pale golden color to make the fireplace surround. I'll bet there are ten thousand pebbles in that creek. We didn't have to go far to get what we needed."

Regaining her composure, Ellie whispered, "It's magical. I don't want to leave this room."

"But you must see the rest."

In the kitchen, pale butter-colored walls reflected the light trailing in from a large stained-glass window, casting a magical luminescence, wrapping the room in a cozy ambience of subtle color.

The flowers on the stained glass matched the colors of the parlor chairs. A small fireplace of limestone was centered next to a modern stove perched just below the stained-glass window facing the river. On the other side sat a large refrigerator, and a long counter containing a double sink sat under another large window looking out to the orchard. A floor to ceiling pantry sat against the back wall. Emma had found an antique oak table and chairs, and a Hoosier cabinet to complete the kitchen.

149

"Everything's perfect. I like that the kitchen is open to the parlor, and we can see the orchard and the Big House from here."

The cabinets and pantry were painted military blue and stood out against the pale buttery walls. With the backsplash done in pale pearlized tile, it picked up the colors of the stones in the fireplace. The kitchen took on an atmosphere of sheer joy.

The bedrooms were all done in the same pale paint, so they would fit in with any color scheme they chose. When Ellie looked at the master bedroom on the second floor, she could not contain her tears.

"Braden, the vanities are done in river washed stones also!"

"Yes, love. We found a lot of pale pink to mix with the pearlescent ones. I hope you like it."

"It's beautiful. It gives a faint blush to the room and reminds me of Grace's heart of stones that had pale pink, white, and some with a golden hue. That's why you chose these stones, isn't it?"

Braden smiled.

Ellie paused. "This gives me an idea. I wonder if we could put Grace's heart of stones in a display case or embedded in concrete so that people walking around wouldn't disturb the rocks."

"Great idea. I'm thinking maybe a raised concrete platform with the heart imbedded in it, so that the bride and groom could stand on the heart to say their vows if they wanted." Braden didn't mention he was trying to make the venue for the wedding as special for Ellie as the heart of stones had become to her. He had her in mind when he thought of it.

"I love it!"

Early Thursday morning, Emma started home, and Ellie hit the road for Jackson in order to report to the real estate agency by nine o'clock.

Emma and Ellie had shown Braden a brochure from the furniture store and marked a number by each suite to correspond to a bedroom in the house. They also earmarked what would need to be brought from the attic. Ellie had left Braden all of her checks, so he deposited them and paid cash for the furniture. It arrived several days later. The only things left to do were the Big Kitchen and securing a few horses, but those two things could wait. Braden was exhausted, Mason was covered up with projects, and Emma was busy taking her mother-in-law "swimming." Cynthia had her hands full with Ellie's father, whose diabetes was vacillating between normal and off-the-charts elevated. Ellie would go home each night to cook dinner to give Cynthia a break. In general, everyone, except Braden, were covered up with work and took the rest of the month off from remodeling.

Braden made his way to the heart of stones and sat on the white wrought iron bench. He had to get out of the house. With everyone gone, the house felt as if it closed in on him. It wasn't a warm snuggly feeling. He felt as if the life was being squeezed out of him and that they had been butchering the house. Should they have let it die with no upkeep? Were they destroying memories that should never have been defiled? Or was bringing it back to life with a modern touch something the Sullivans would want? Knowing what tragedies they had observed in Ireland and how they had pulled themselves up to become one of the most prosperous families in town, second only to the Scotts, it would stand to reason they would want their memories preserved, but maybe not their secrets, to stand the test of time. Braden cleared his throat as he glanced at the heart of stones. He knew it was the wind gently moving over the stones, but the heart seemed to vibrate as if answering him. How he wished Grace could talk to him, but maybe she was. Out of his peripheral vision, he thought he saw the figure of a small woman peeking from around a large tree. He focused his eyes to the spot, but no one was there. The wind was playing tricks on him. He knew he had to find out what happened to Grace and the rest of the family. How he wished Ellie were home.

Braden chuckled. How strange that perky little Ellie with her annoying high-pitched voice and hyper antics had irritated him to the point that he considered leaving the Big House after only a week. Sticking it out and watching her change had by some miracle transformed his heart and his goals. He was content, satisfied, for now, with his job, and if a high school English or history teacher spot turned up, he would apply. No matter what, he'd never want to leave this place. It was in his blood now. With Ellie as his wife, he could imagine no greater gift from God. It was amazing how a dose of self-confidence brought out the inner Ellie. She now shone as a brilliant woman who calmed his fears and encouraged his creativity. And he missed her. Clearing his head, he walked back to the house.

He set up his new typewriter in the study, a gift from Nannie when he graduated from college. Pouring a cup of coffee, he inserted a piece of paper and started typing. He wouldn't attempt a novel right now, but he

151

did want to tell the story of the Sullivans. They could hand out a booklet of the ups and downs of the family and reveal a few of the secrets the house had held all these years. He titled it *The Legend of the Sullivan Family and the Secrets of Oak Hollow*. Somehow that sounded more like one of the Nancy Drew books Susan used to bring home from the library. That would belittle what he wanted to reveal. The Sullivans were a phenomenon of the time. A better title would be *The History of the Sullivan Family and Oak Hollow Plantation*. From the research he had done, he knew that Abraham Sullivan had sold a large part of the land of Oak Hollow just before the Civil War commenced. With that sale, there was still a section and a half of land, according to the deeds Ellie had discovered. Braden was shocked. He didn't know where Ellie got her information that there were ninety acres. There were nine hundred and sixty! Braden could only imagine that it was a blow to Abe's ego, as well as the affluent lifestyle he had provided for his family, to sell off part of their estate. Although King Cotton held court over the large plantations, the weather, the decrease in demand for cotton, the war, and lack of slaves forced the abdication of King Cotton. Lowly wheat, maize, corn, and vegetable farms replaced some of the cotton fields. Since the fields were mostly broken up into smaller parcels of land, Braden thought that if Abe's family could have gone up in one of the new hot air balloons that had just come into existence and looked down, Braden was sure it would have looked like a giant patchwork quilt as it did when Braden took a flight to Dallas to visit Justin and gazed out of the airplane's window. Between cities, each plot of land along the way looked different from the next one. He marveled that all the land didn't look the same. Of course, now, cotton was king again with farmers buying many of the small parcels and combining them. He wondered why some farmer hadn't scooped up the land with the mansion, but perhaps tearing down the large home would have been too costly.

He placed his fingers on the keys, but before he could strike a key, the telephone rang. Lately, every time the phone rang, it was bad news. Apprehension gripped him as he hurried to answer.

"Braden, I am so excited. I just closed on a commercial property. It's a building that has sat vacant for years. I hope you aren't mad, but I spent the latest commission check I got and advertised in a couple of business magazines. It paid off! I found a buyer!"

"That's wonderful."

"What this means is I don't have to sell any more houses. The only bad thing is I won't get my commission check until they take possession, and that could be months from now. They did sign a contract, so I know the money will be there eventually. I'm on my way home. I told Thomas if he needs me on the weekends, I could arrange that, but I need to get home."

"It's about time! Oh, by the way, that ninety-acre figure you mentioned about the land is nine hundred and sixty. No wonder it's taking all of Hiram's time to get it ready for planting."

"Oh, I thought a section and a half was about ninety acres. Guess I left off a zero!"

CHAPTER TWENTY-ONE

Summer turned out to be the hottest on record, bringing with it stifling humid heat that seemed to weigh everything down. Flowers and gardens drooped, while cotton flourished. Braden felt as if he were walking through a tunnel of moisture leading to Hades, but there was no brimstone…just his sweat-soaked t-shirt. Though most plants suffered, a new King Cotton came back to rule as the successor to the former king. Once again, the south flourished. Scottsville was growing.

Ellie and Braden sat down with her ledger and estimated their profit and loss. Braden looked at their bank account. He realized most of the money had been contributed by Ellie. Though he knew she didn't mind, it didn't seem fair that he couldn't contribute more. His personal stash was secure in an upper drawer of his chest. He had earmarked it for a special honeymoon for Ellie. Maybe they should forego the honeymoon until after everything was completed, and he could contribute his savings to help with their bills.

He rose and paced the kitchen, his hands clasped behind his back, a frown clouding his face, giving him the appearance of an aging man.

Ellie watched him for a few minutes. His pacing increased. "Braden, come sit down. What is bothering you?"

"I have been keeping a secret for a while, but I need to talk to you."

Ellie's cheeks turned bright red. "We agreed not to ever keep secrets."

"I know."

"What have you been hiding? What's wrong? I thought I could trust you. Now you spring this on me!"

Braden took her hands, but Ellie pulled away and crossed her arms over her chest as if to protect her heart. She refused to cry.

"Please don't be mad. I tutored some students during the school year and have had a few this summer when you have been gone. The extra

155

money, I put into a small pouch to save for a honeymoon. I wanted to surprise you, but now I realize I could contribute that to our bills. I feel terrible that you have supplied most of the cash for our remodel."

Ellie succumbed to her tears. "What? Oh, Braden, I thought you had found someone else. I am so relieved and so very happy that your thoughts were of me. You are a special man. Do not worry about the money. You and your parents have worked so hard for no pay. That's worth more than I could ever contribute. I'm sorry I got the wrong impression from your facial expression."

Braden wiped the tears from her cheek and kissed her. "Ellie, I would never cheat on you, and I could never find anyone as wonderful as you are. You are my soul mate. I spent my days ruminating about Oak Hollow, The Mystery House, and the Sullivans during the time you've been gone. I can't imagine what happened to this grand old house, why the Sullivans just up and left, leaving all this opulence, why they built The Mystery House by the river instead of a smaller one in town, and how the war affected them. I suppose some of them died, but who? I wonder about Jim and Grace and those that survived. Did they go to Ireland, and did they return after the war? Or did the Sullivans sell to another family who enjoyed all this grandeur?"

"I've wondered all those things, too, but I guess I don't dwell as deeply as you do. My mind has been on waking up this house, picturing our guests coming here to relax or have an antebellum vacation. I also think about what our legacy will be a hundred years from now. Will our ancestors tear down everything we've built up, or will the history of Oak Hollow rise majestic again taking the memories of a family that could have been a testament to what hard work and perseverance could do?"

"Between you and the heart of stones, I have my answer. No more guilt about invading their privacy. It is so good to have you home."

Ellie laughed. "I'm glad to be here, but don't get too comfortable. I'll be making another trip as soon as I get rested to go look for my wedding gown and all the other things I need to decide on. First, though, I think we should finish this renovation. We just have the Big Kitchen to finish, right?"

"It won't take much to remodel it. I can start painting, and when Dad comes again, we can build new cabinets and counters and put in the appliances. You know we might need to get a dishwasher. If we are going to have a lot of guests, we might need one of those."

"Braden, I hate to destroy the cabinets, but I know they wouldn't work very well in a modern kitchen we need for a chef. And it isn't really part of the Big House. I can think of so many things to make this a real vacation spot."

"What else?"

"We talked about horses, but I was also thinking about a tennis court and a swimming pool."

"Whoa, Ellie. Those may have to come later. I'm going to call Dad to see when they can come again. I know he's been busy with his new company."

"I'll check in with Mister Knight and see if he will still let me work from home. The last time I talked to him, he said business had picked up. I hope he doesn't want to lease a building again and expect me to come in every day."

"Good. I can start painting the Big Kitchen if you're okay with that."

"Yes, can you use that pale buttery paint like in The Mystery House?"

"Sure, I have enough left over to do it."

"While you do that, I think I'll go select which paintings go in each room, and maybe poke around in the attic to see what else I can find."

"The paintings are in the study."

"Thank you. I'm glad you brought them down, but I want to go poking around up there anyway."

"Be warned. It's going to be hot."

Ellie smiled. "If you can stand the kitchen heat, I can stand the attic heat."

Braden dismantled the cast iron cookstove and stored it in the horse stables. He hated to trash it and had the idea that it would make a good addition to the stables during the winter to warm the horses that they'd buy. Of course, not knowing anything about the beautiful animals, he would leave that up to the man they hired to take care of them. As he painted, he let his thoughts wander. He could imagine a slave woman bustling about the room preparing food for the family. Maybe she fried chicken or baked large roasts and gathered vegetables from the garden.

She probably set pies on the large window sill to cool. When they got the kitchen finished, Braden would ask Ellie to make a pie and cool it just like they did when Oak Hollow was in its prime. But the heat. How did they stand the heat in the summer with a hot stove and no air conditioning? Braden raised all the windows to get some air as he wiped his face with a large cleaning rag. Even though the day felt like an inferno, a breeze drifted though the massive trees just outside the house and swept into the large room. Braden smiled. "Problem solved. A breeze cooled them."

Ellie made her way to the attic and uncovered more boxes of clothes. "They probably stored them when the fashions changed. I wonder if I could fit into any of them," she muttered. She scooted the boxes she wanted to go through to the opening of the attic so Braden could take them down along with the box of Grace's journals. The heat stifled her exploration of the rest of the attic. She climbed down and made iced tea and a salad before strolling across to the Big Kitchen.

"You've done a lot! It looks great…and empty."

"Yes, I'm almost finished."

"Come eat. It's too hot to cook, so I made a big salad."

Together they hurried across the walkway to the air-conditioned Big House. After they ate, Braden retrieved the boxes Ellie wanted and took them to her bedroom. She pulled several dresses out of a box and laid them on her bed. One was a white satin dress with a red sash. Another was a bright green taffeta, and the third was an ivory voile with a brown hooded cape. There were other dresses, but Ellie didn't have room to display all of them at once. She made a note to pick up some sewing forms to display them in the bedrooms when she took the dresses to be dry cleaned.

Braden thought it might break all records if they didn't get rain in the next few days. Striding into the kitchen, sweat poured from his head. He wiped his brow with the bottom of his t-shirt, but it was almost too wet to dry his face. "It's brutal out there."

The next morning, sitting on the veranda with their morning coffee, Braden turned to Ellie and took her hand. "You cannot imagine how much I love you. Sitting here watching the sun rising, lighting up the sky with so many beautiful colors, I am a blessed man. Why can't we just get married now without all the fuss?"

Ellie frowned. She wanted to tell Braden her secret, but she knew it would change everything. She quickly changed her countenance and forced a smile. All that went through her mind every day was that Braden said the past didn't matter when he proposed, but would he feel the same way when he knew her secret. She wiped the thoughts from her mind. "Dear Braden, a wedding is a big deal for women. Don't deny me that."

"I called Dad while you were unpacking those boxes. I gave him a rough idea of what we wanted. He's going to build the cabinets and counters in his shop when he has a break between jobs. Then he and Mom will bring them."

"Did he say how long? I need to look at appliances."

"He indicated it would be soon. I can go with you if you'd like."

"That would be great, but first I have a favor to ask of you."

"Anything. What can I do?"

Ellie dragged Braden by the hand up the stairs to her bedroom. "I'm going to put on these petticoats and this corset. I need you to lace it and pull it tight. I want to see if I can wear any of these dresses. I'll call you when I'm ready."

Seeing Ellie's bare back almost took Braden's breath away, but he willed himself to lace up the contraption she was holding over her front. He managed to get it laced and then pulled gently on the cords.

"No, pull harder."

"I'll cut off your circulation. This looks like some kind of torture device."

Ellie laughed. "Yes, just keep pulling."

When he had pulled enough, she asked Braden to help her pull the white satin dress over her head. It was too small, but not as much as she had thought. She pulled it back over her head. "Okay, unlace me, please."

"Gladly!" He reveled at her beauty and knew he needed to direct his attention elsewhere. He moved back downstairs.

Ellie hurriedly got into her clothes and sat on the bed. Looking at the seams, she thought the dress could be let out and made to fit. She had the notion that she could dress up in one of the dresses and maybe arrange a waltz each Saturday night. If the guests could fit into the dresses, they could borrow ones to dance in. A photographer could capture the scene.

She gathered up six of the dresses and went downstairs, stowing them on Emma and Mason's bed until Braden was ready to go to town.

Arriving in town, Braden went to the hardware store to see if he could find a groom with a couple of horses for sale, and Ellie went to a seamstress's shop.

Bert Kindle rubbed his chin. "They's old man Mabry's son. Doug's the name, I think. He might be interested. I know he likes horses." Braden got his telephone number and sat on a bench in front of the store waiting on Ellie.

He didn't have to wait long. Ellie walked up to him, smiling. "Hi. I found a seamstress who will alter the dresses. She also had some ideas on how to enlarge all the dresses so they would fit most women. We came up with an idea to make them expandable if larger women want to wear them, but also will fit women of any size. I doubt any woman visiting will have a sixteen-inch waist! She will do it with extra fabric that either matches or compliments the dresses. She's going to work on the ones I left her for now. Ready to look at appliances?"

"Sure." They walked down the street to the furniture store which also sold appliances.

Since Braden and Ellie were one of his best customers, John Dalton smiled and greeted them as they walked in. "Good afternoon. How may I help you today?"

"We're looking for some appliances."

"What do you have in mind?"

Ellie looked around at two aisles of appliances on each side. "We need a stove and refrigerator to start with."

Braden added, "It won't be long until we need a dishwasher and a washer and dryer."

John Dalton rubbed his chin. "This is for the old Oak Hollow place you are renovating? Heard you were making it some kind of hotel or something."

Ellie smiled. "It will be a kind of vacation place, but not a hotel."

Braden nodded as he opened an oven door. "This one looks nice, Ellie."

"You know, I was about to send some appliances back. Some of them have some minor damage, but if you could use them, I'll give you a big discount."

Ellie brightened. "May we see them?"

"Sure, come to the back with me."

He led them into a large storage room at the back of the building. Several stoves, refrigerators, dishwashers, washers and dryers sat, some damaged and some not. Ellie examined a beautiful large stove. "Is this an undamaged one?"

"No, this one has a scratch on the side and a small dent."

Braden stepped over and looked. "I can barely see the damage. Besides it will have a cabinet on that side of it."

When they looked at all the damaged appliances, they bought everything they needed at the price of a new stove and refrigerator.

Braden and Mason moved the old cast iron cookstove to one of the larger rooms of the horses' stables, intending to hook it up later. They had decided it would be a good place for the washer and dryer until they could get a laundry room made. Later they'd add a deep freezer to the room.

Braden wrote a check. "We'll come back later for a freezer." As they walked out of the doorway, he said to Ellie, "How about lunch at The Greenhouse?"

"Sounds good. I haven't been there in ages. They've enlarged it. Business must be good."

Braden told her about the horses. "The only thing is buying the horses and hiring a groom may be more than we have in the bank, even with the money Dad loaned us."

"My commission on the commercial property should be coming in soon. Did your dad say when he might come?"

"No, but I also found a croquet set the other day. I think it is what you wanted."

"That's awesome! I'd say, let's get the horses. We can get a loan until my check comes through. I've always wanted horses."

When they drove up, Mason and Emma were sitting in the kitchen drinking iced tea.

Mason spoke, "Welcome home. We made ourselves comfortable. Look out back."

A large panel truck sat adjacent to the veranda walkway to the Big Kitchen. "Come on, Braden, let me show you what I've done." Braden followed Mason outside.

"Where'd you get this truck?"

"One of my clients offered it to me. I hope I made the cabinets to your satisfaction. Emma didn't complain too much riding in the truck, but she hasn't seen the cabinets."

"Let's call the girls."

Both Ellie and Emma raved about the cabinets as they came out of the truck. Ellie shook her head. "They look almost like the original ones. Your detail and workmanship are unsurpassed!"

Mason grinned. "Thank you. Glad they suit you."

As soon as they maneuvered the bottom cabinets into place, Mason pulled out a large sink. Braden called the furniture store, and they said they could deliver the appliances within a couple of hours. Braden smiled. Being probably their best customer came in handy. Braden and Mason scooted the cabinets next to the wall to make room for the appliances.

"We can't stay, Braden. I need to get this truck back, but I'll come later, and we'll finish this."

After they left, Ellie indicated she wanted to sit on the veranda. "I want to talk about The Mystery House. When I walked in and saw all the ways you had used the pebbles, it occurred to me, we could rename it. Does the river have a name?"

"Not that I know of. I think they refer to it as a tributary of the Mississippi."

"Good."

"Why do you ask?"

"I'm thinking about naming the river. Instead of The Mystery House, what do you think about something to do with the river?"

"So, you are going to rename the house, too?"

"Yes, what about Pebble Creek for the river and The Inn at Pebble Creek for the house? If we ever do decide we need more bedrooms to rent, or we have a large reunion, we could move back into the Big House. Since your grandmother talked about going to reunions as a child, we

162

could advertise it for family reunions or conferences or whatever a large group of people would want."

"Brilliant, as always."

CHAPTER TWENTY-TWO

Two weeks later, the renovations were finished along with the new laundry room. The houses bloomed in all their glory as Mason Cunningham's bank account withered to a sad demise.

Mason, Emma, Ellie, and Braden all let out a collective sigh of relief. Braden looked at all of them.

"I have a request before you and Mom go home, Dad. I want to christen the house. Instead of breaking a good bottle of wine, I think we should join hands and christen it with a prayer for all the blessings we had in bringing these homes back to life. Kind of like how Jesus takes us as sinners and His Glory brings us back to life."

Ellie and Emma had tears in their eyes as everyone joined hands. Braden lowered his head. "Father God, how blessed we are that You have been with us and opened doors for us as we started on this journey. Thank you for my mom and dad being Your ambassadors to see our vision through and blessed us in more ways than we can count. Thank you that Ellie and I found love here, and we ask you to bless our union when we marry. Please bless these houses and the guests we will have that they may experience Your peace here. I pray in Jesus' name. Amen."

Mason's voice cracked. "I couldn't have said it any better. Your mother and I are blessed to be part of all you and Ellie have done." Emma nodded and wiped her eyes. "Let us know how the groom works out."

"We will. Call us when you get home."

Braden and Mason had hired a groom who helped them pick out a couple of horses. Doug Mabry jumped at the chance to work for them and came out that day after work to see what kind of set up they had. Braden led him to the stables.

165

"I don't know a thing about horses, so if this isn't satisfactory, please let us know."

Doug looked over the horse stalls. "Someone had horses here before. The stalls need some updating, but nothing major. The tack room looks great, too. And I wonder what this larger room was used for with this large cast iron cookstove?"

Braden shook his head and held his hands out, palms up. "Beats me. Maybe this was a room for the wagons or for the slaves that watched over the animals. I moved the stove in here. Thought it would keep the horses warm in the winter if we opened the door. We just need to vent it."

Doug looked at the floor. Braden quizzed him. "Is something wrong? You look worried. Are you having second thoughts?"

"No, just the opposite. Mister Cunningham, I have some horses that I'm boarding at another man's stables. I have a job in town and live with my parents. Lately, things have been strained at our house. My parents are fighting a lot, and it's usually about me. My father is drinking heavily and is disappointed that I don't want to follow in his footsteps and help him run his auto repair business. I rarely get to see my horses. My job at the grocery store stocking shelves barely pays for their upkeep." He paused and took a deep breath. "I was wondering how much you would charge me to keep my horses here with yours, and if I could maybe buy a bed and rent this large room."

Braden smiled. "Of course, you can keep your horses here, but there won't be a charge. And if you want to stay out here, we can fix up this room. In the meantime, we have some rooms in the Inn, and you could have one of them. There's a parlor and a kitchen. Later if you still want to be out here with the horses, we can make you a small apartment."

"How much would the room rent for?"

"Well, let's see. Since you will be looking after our horses, I'd say we could call it even."

"You mean that?"

Braden laughed. "Of course. When do you want to move in?"

"I have the day off tomorrow. I could go and get my horses and my things from my parents' home. There's just one more thing."

"What's that?"

"I have a pick-up and a horse trailer. Will it be okay to park them beside the stables?"

166

"That would be wonderful. It would come in handy if we ever have to transport the horses to the vet or if we buy more. We are going to insist on paying you a salary, but it may not be much to start with. We also want to build a large garage and a parking area for guests, so we can all have our cars under a shelter."

Doug Mabry pumped Braden's hand until he thought he was going to break it.

"Oh, and call me Braden. When you say Mister Cunningham, I think you are speaking of my dad!"

When Braden came down for breakfast, the next morning, he smiled as Ellie got up and poured him a cup of coffee. "I think we'll just have toast and jelly this morning because I'm on my way to Jackson to finally see about my wedding dress. I talked to your mom last night. She is going to meet me there."

"I didn't know you had talked to her."

"I'm sorry. I was busy collecting all the pictures of dresses I might like and making a list of all the things I need to do. I want to get an early start, so I can be back home soon. I have also been playing with the brochure about the house with pictures of some of the rooms. I want it to go with the booklet you are writing about the family. I'm sure we can open by the middle of September. I also found several pictures of the Sullivan family in that box of papers you brought down. I think we can put some of the smaller ones in your booklet and the brochures, but I'd like to enlarge one of the entire family and put it in the foyer above a small table."

"If you find a dress, do you want to have our wedding before we invite paying guests?"

"I thought of that. Each season can be special, not just June. I'll think about it, but I think I still want an Easter wedding. You know, a new beginning." Ellie took her plate to the sink. "Right now, I need to get going. I'll call you when I get there."

Ellie called just as Braden set down to a quick dinner of a hamburger and chips.

"Sorry I was so short with you when I let you know I got here, but we wanted to get started shopping. We got so much done. Your mom was a big help. I think I have decided on a gown and the bridesmaid dresses, but I want to think about it before I make a final decision. Your mom, my mom, and I looked at cakes. I like the style, but I want to finalize my colors before I place an order. Mom said when I decide, she would take care of that. I need to secure a photographer and decide on wedding invitations. But again, I want to think about it, and I'd like to run what I think I want the invitations to look like, and see if you agree. I'm thinking of coming home tomorrow."

"Best news I've heard. Be careful. I love you."

"Love you, too."

The next day mid-morning, Braden watched the carriageway, thinking Ellie should be home. At noon, she called. Braden answered the phone, and he could tell she'd been crying. "What on earth is wrong, sweetheart?"

"It's Dad. I'm sorry I haven't called you sooner. Mom couldn't wake Dad up this morning. I called an ambulance. He's in the hospital now. I came home to fix a sandwich for Mom because she won't leave him."

"Maybe my mom could help."

"She went home yesterday evening."

Braden felt a dark cloud sweep over him. "Do you know what's wrong?"

"Yes, when they got his blood sugar regulated, he admitted he's been hiding sweets and chips in his desk and getting up in the middle of the night to snack."

"That's not good."

"I told him if he doesn't get well to walk me down the aisle, I'm going to be really mad at him. At any rate, I need to get back to the hospital and take Mom something to eat. I love you, but guess I'll be here a few more days."

"Do you want me to come?"

"No, you've got your hands full there with the horses and the garden."

Braden immediately went to the parlor and knelt in front of the sofa. Clasping his hands in front of his chest, he uttered a prayer. "Please, Father, look down on Preston, and heal him. I don't know how Ellie would handle it if he passes away, and especially before our wedding.

168

Father, I know it says in Your word that You are the Great Physician. Please wrap Your loving arms around Preston, and grant him peace and healing. In Jesus' name I pray. Amen." Tears slipped uncontrolled down Braden's face. What would he do if Preston didn't make it? They could not have a wedding following a funeral. They would have to postpone it. Rising from the floor, he slapped his thigh. "I have to stop thinking negatively. I've turned it over to God, and I need to let Him handle it." He took a deep breath and forced himself to think more pleasant thoughts about their wedding.

Preston Addison stayed in the hospital for three days. The first day was critical, and neither Cynthia or Ellie would leave his side except to grab a bite of food. By the second day, they were able to take turns sitting or going home to take a shower.

His doctor came in and didn't mince words. "Mister Addison, if you don't take care of yourself and stay on the diet and medication I have prescribed, your days are numbered. Right now, you have neuropathy in your right leg and foot. If you vary one bit from what I'm telling you, you will lose your leg and maybe your life. Do you understand?"

Preston nodded. He ducked his head and muttered his agreement. When they arrived home, Ellie called Braden and told him the news. "My mother is exhausted. We're going through the house throwing out all the food that Dad has hidden. We are going to make a menu of foods he should eat and a list of ones to avoid. I'll go to the grocery store and stock up on food, so Mom won't have to leave him alone for a few days. Then I'll come home in a couple of days. The good news is I had a call from Thomas. My commission checks are ready. I'll bring them home, and we can pay off your dad!"

As summer wound down, cooler temperatures in the afternoon made sitting on the veranda more pleasant. Preston rallied, and Ellie made it home as promised. Relaxing on the veranda, she sat two glasses of iced tea on a small table between two wicker chairs. "Are you ready to hear more of Grace's story?"

"Sure."

"I read a little bit. She and Maggie didn't want to make their debut, but under pressure, they agreed. Let me find out where I left off." Ellie flipped through several pages and gasped. "Oh, my goodness!"

"What is it?"

"Grace got married after she and Maggie made their debut."

"That's wonderful. How did they pull that off? That must have shocked the whole town."

"Not to Jim. To Paul Scott. She wasn't happy about it." Ellie read ahead silently. "You won't believe this. One of the dresses I had altered was her wedding dress. It's the one with the red ribbon that tied around her waist." She took a drink of her tea. "And Maggie got married shortly afterward, and I found her wedding dress, also."

"Poor Jim."

"And poor Grace. She didn't love Paul Scott, but did it because her father was having financial troubles, and Paul agreed to bail him out if Grace married him." Ellie put the journal down and got a faraway look in her eye.

She apparently didn't hear Braden talking to her. He waved his hand in front of her eyes. "Ellie?"

"Oh, sorry. I was just thinking about all the dresses I took to the seamstress. Do you remember seeing the white dress with the red sash?"

"Uh, no, not really. Overgrown dresses and those torture devices are not at the top of my thoughts!"

"Well, she wore the red ribbon at the waist as she said in her journal to symbolize her giving up her life's blood to marry a man she didn't love." Ellie had an idea, but she didn't want to share it with Braden. She decided if it could be altered, she would wear Grace's wedding dress. Of course, she would change it up a bit since it wasn't a happy occasion for Grace. Ellie remembered that Grace pricked her finger on a thorn and it bled. She really did shed her blood to marry Paul.

"How sad that she couldn't marry Jim, but Paul sounds like he was a good man."

"He wasn't. He was demanding, but she felt she had to marry him because it was expected by everyone in town. After they married, he abused her as well as some slaves."

"I'm glad you don't have another man you are expected to marry besides me!"

170

"Never, silly." She read a few more pages in silence. "Oh, no!"

"What now?"

"Paul almost killed Grace. Jim saved her life."

"Seems Jim always knew when she needed him."

"Yes, she even says that. They have some kind of mental telepathy, kind of like us and your parents. I guess all married couples have that, even though Jim and Grace weren't married. That's all I've read so far. Now I have some other things to do to tie up everything. I'm going to leave in the morning, but I'll just be gone overnight."

Ellie smiled as she put a small travel bag on the bed and started packing. Thinking about her trip, she decided to cancel the order for her dress and the bridesmaid dresses and see if the seamstress in town could also alter some of the dresses for her attendants. She would take measurements of her friends that were going to stand up with her and see if three of the pastel dresses could be made to fit. They would be different colors, but that would be perfect for a spring wedding, and she would match her bouquet to the colors of the dresses. She wanted to surprise Braden when she wore Grace's wedding dress. She visualized her cake with flowers of those same colors trailing down the side. She wanted to see what Braden thought about putting a picture of a heart of stones made out of pebbles on their invitations.

Braden interrupted her thoughts. "Dad called, and said Mom is having another one of those parties, so he may come up and keep me company. He wants to meet Doug, too, and look over the horses."

"Good. Then you can pay him." She mentioned the invitations and asked his opinion about putting a picture of the heart of stones at the top.

"I think that would be perfect. Thank you for letting me have some say so in all these big plans!"

"I promise to get your opinion on the flavor of the cake we choose."

"I can do that with no problem!"

Mason drove up around noon the next day.

"Has Ellie already gone?"

"Yes, she was going to do something with her friends who are going to be in the wedding and some other girl stuff that I know nothing about."

"Let's eat and go riding. I want to meet Doug and see the horses."

"They're beautiful and very tame. He is delighted to be able to stay in the Inn and board his own horses here. He told me his father drinks a lot, and Doug was happy to get out of their house. He has a job in town, but it doesn't pay much. He told me he can't wait to get back to the peace and quiet here. He said we can use his horses for whatever we need. I'm hoping we can pay him a bigger salary so he can quit his job in town."

"Works out well for everyone. It may not be so quiet when all the guests arrive."

"That's true. We kind of toyed with the idea of making him a small apartment out in the stables. It is a huge room, and he would be near the horses. He could use the smaller room for tack and mixing feed and storing medicine for the horses."

"But would he like that?"

"He suggested it when I first hired him."

"Good idea. That won't take much time."

Thursday morning brought a wide spread blanket of thunder storms across the state, but they hadn't reached Scottsville. Braden and Mason took their coffee to the veranda. Mason pulled on his chin as he scanned the sky. "Looks like a frog-strangler gonna come in for sure. Guess I'll delay going home for a day." Almost before he could get the last word out, the heavens opened up and a torrential downpour, launched the men to the kitchen.

"I'm going to call Ellie and tell her to wait until tomorrow to come home." He picked up the phone in the kitchen and placed a long-distance call. Ellie answered on the first ring. "Hi, honey. I was taking my things to the car so I could leave. What's up?"

"I don't want you to travel in this weather. Please wait until tomorrow. It's coming down in buckets here."

"Yeah, it's raining here, too, but not bad. It was foggy earlier, but it's clearing now. Besides, I want to be home. I miss you."

"I miss you, too, but I'd rather you be safe."

"I'll start out. If the rain gets heavier, I'll turn around. I think it may let up soon."

"As bad as we need the rain, it's like a blessing for the farmers and a curse for drivers."

Ellie laughed. "You worry too much."

Braden hung up the phone. "Dad, I'm not feeling good about Ellie on the road."

"Maybe the rain will slack off. We need the moisture. Hope it's doing this at home."

Forty-five minutes passed. Braden paced, glancing at the clock every few minutes. A foreboding feeling keep nagging at him. "She should have been home by now. Even in the rain, it usually takes no more than a half hour."

Mason didn't like the weather, either, but he didn't want Braden to read his face. "Maybe she started out and turned around. She'll probably be calling you in a few minutes, or maybe she's just going slower."

"I guess I'm borrowing trouble."

CHAPTER TWENTY-THREE

The phone rang, startling both men.

"Must be Ellie." Braden grabbed the receiver. Before he could acknowledge the caller, he heard Preston's voice.

"Braden, sit down." His voice sounded tinged with fear.

"Okay, what's the matter? Is it Ellie?"

"Yes, son, she's been in a terrible accident. We're at the hospital now. Cynthia asked me to call you." His voice broke. "She's in a coma. The weather is bad, so don't try to come until it lets up. We don't need two of you in the hospital."

"What hospital?"

Preston gave him the name and address. "I need to get back to the room. Cynthia is beside herself."

"Okay. I'm on my way." Braden hung up before Preston could protest.

Mason quizzed him with his eyes.

"She's been in a horrible accident. She's in a coma," Braden screamed. "I can't lose her, Dad. I can't stand this. I've got to go."

"I hate for you to drive in this weather. Do you know any details?"

"No. I'm going to go throw some clothes in a suitcase and stay as long as I need to. Would you stay, and ask Doug to look after things?"

"Sure thing. At least, take my truck. You'll be safer. I'll stay another night or two and drive your car home with me. Later, when things settle down, and we have more news, we'll trade."

"Thanks, Dad. I'll let you know more when I find out."

"I'll wait here to hear from you. I'll call Emma and let her know."

The roads were slick, but Mason's truck was easier to handle than Braden's T-bird. He admonished himself not to speed over the road. Cars meeting him slung water onto the truck, but he was high enough up that it didn't obstruct his vision. After what seemed like hours, he arrived at the hospital and rushed into Ellie's room.

Ellie was in a bed hooked up to machines and oxygen. Her eyes were closed. Braden noticed a bandage on her cheek near her ear with traces of blood on it. Her eyes were blackened, and her face was swollen, but she looked peaceful.

"How is she?" Braden hugged both her parents before walking to the bed and picking up Ellie's hand.

"We're waiting on tests now to see what the next step is."

Braden stood by the bedside until Cynthia pushed an extra chair to him. "Sit down, Braden. It's going to be a long day."

"Do you know what happened?"

Preston said, "She hadn't been gone ten minutes and was stopped at a traffic light. The police said witnesses were standing at the corner waiting to cross the street when they saw a car come barreling down the street on the wrong side of the road, ran the red traffic light, and hit her head on. They ducked into a store and called the police."

"Was he drunk?"

"We think so. The police didn't say, but what else could it be? They wouldn't tell us much about his condition, but we know he's alive. Apparently, he is also in the hospital."

"Was it still raining?"

"No, it had let up, the fog had lifted, and we all thought it was safe for her to continue. Right after she left, another cell broke loose dumping another downpour on us. We assumed she was going to turn around and come home, but, of course, she never made it."

The doctor walked in and motioned them to the hall. "She has a severe concussion. So far, we don't believe she has a subdural hematoma." He looked toward the family, whose confused faces led him to explain, "A brain bleed, but we'll watch her. Her left leg is fractured in multiple places. She'll need surgery for that as soon we can get her stabilized. She also has some internal injuries, but at the moment, she isn't bleeding internally as far as we can tell. We'll just take it day by day. She's not stable enough now to withstand surgery. Sorry I can't give you better news."

Braden tried to get past the boulder stuck in his throat. "When will she wake up?"

"Hard to say. Sometimes, it's just a few hours, sometimes longer. We'll know more in twenty-four hours."

Cynthia wiped tears from her eyes. "I want to go to the chapel and pray."

Preston put his arm around her waist. "I'll go with you, sweetheart. Braden, come get us if Ellie wakes up."

Braden nodded. He sat transfixed by the hum of machines, the slow drip of the IV, and the shallow up and down movement of Ellie's chest. Pulling the sheet off of her leg, he almost fell backwards. The black bruises looked as though some evil force had invaded his precious fiancée. Blood seeped out of a huge bandage, but more than anything was the swelling. How could a leg swell that big? Had they injected fluid into it to make it look like an over-inflated balloon? He couldn't stand to look at it any longer, so he pulled the sheet back over her. Thoughts replayed in his mind like a bad song that kept repeating over and over. If only he could go back in time. Why couldn't she have waited just ten minutes? Why didn't he keep her on the phone longer?

Preston and Cynthia walked back in. Cynthia walked to the bed. "You said you left your dad at your house. Have you called him?"

Braden's eyes focused on hers. "No, I forgot. All I could think about was Ellie. I'll go now. Thank you for reminding me."

Braden located a pay phone on the street corner outside the hospital's large lobby. Fumbling in his pocket, he found the change necessary to get the operator to place a collect call to his home. Mason answered on the first ring. "Hi, Dad. Sorry I didn't call you earlier."

"That's okay, son. I knew you probably had a one-track mind and just wanted to get to there. How is she?"

"She's not good. She has a concussion, internal injuries, and a broken leg." He didn't want to elaborate. If he didn't give details, maybe everything would be better by the time he got back to the room. "I don't know when she will have surgery, so I may be here a few days or longer. If you want to bring my car here and take your truck, let me know."

"I may see what I can do to help Doug. He mentioned that he might like to spend more time in the stables. He needs to make a run to the feed store, but one of the mares is about to foal, so he needs to stay close. I'll go to the feed store for him. I wouldn't be surprised if he wouldn't want to take you up on that apartment. You are lucky to have found him. He is one smart guy when it comes to horses."

177

"I can't say I would blame him wanting to be out there. The horses seem to understand our emotions. And I know his are grateful to be with him. But don't work too hard, Dad. We're out of money now, and I know Ellie doesn't want you to put in any more hours."

"Working keeps my mind calm, but I know Emma needs me, too. She said to tell you she is praying for Ellie and wants to be updated when you have time."

"When Ellie gets well…" Braden's throat chocked him so he couldn't continue until he cleared his throat and spoke, "we'll decide about the grand opening and the wedding. Go home and be with Mom. I'll phone both of you when I know more." A lone tear slipped down Braden's cheek. He didn't bother to wipe it away.

Preston looked exhausted. When Braden spoke to him on entering Ellie's room, he nodded but didn't acknowledge. Cynthia was putting something in her purse.

"I asked a nurse to check his blood sugar, and it's low, getting to the dangerous level. I keep a candy bar in my purse, but I couldn't get him to eat much. I need to get him home. Preston…Preston, look at me…Preston, open your eyes."

Preston found Cynthia's eyes, but his were glassy, unable to focus.

"Braden, will you help me get him into my car?" She pulled out a chocolate bar again and got it into Preston's mouth.

"Do you think we should call a nurse to see about him?"

"No, she couldn't treat him since he isn't her patient, and she'd need doctor's orders."

Braden hooked Preston's arm around his shoulder and practically dragged him to Cynthia's car. "Let me know how he is, please. Should I follow you and help you get him into your home?"

"No, I think I'll be fine if I can get a little more candy into him. Please let us know if there's an update on Ellie. I'll get Preston to eat something, and as soon as his blood sugar stabilizes, I'll be back. Are you okay to stay with Ellie?"

"Of course. You couldn't drag me away. I wish the doctor would come back to see if he could wake her up."

Sitting by her bedside, Braden's shock had worn off somewhat. Looking at Ellie, he began to talk to her. "I know you want to have the biggest wedding this side of the Mississippi, but I really hope you have

178

taken care of everything so you won't have to be running back and forth. I've been looking at trellises. I had no idea how many styles there are. You need to wake up, and help me decide. Ellie, squeeze my hand."

Braden was still, concentrating on her hand. Her little finger twitched. Does that mean she heard him or was that an involuntary movement? He couldn't be sure. Again, he said, "Ellie, squeeze harder."

Ellie's eyes fluttered for a second, and she moved her hand but not enough to say she controlled it. Still, any movement was progress in his eyes.

An hour later, Cynthia walked in. Braden told her that Ellie had been having some movement, but he couldn't be sure if it was voluntary. The news seemed to relieve some of the tension Braden noticed in Cynthia's body.

"I'm going to see if the doctor can come in and see what he thinks." Cynthia rushed from the room.

A nurse followed Cynthia back into the room. "Let me check." She took Ellie's hand. "Squeeze my hand, Ellie." She waited. Ellie moved her fingers. It wasn't a bona fide squeeze, but it was something. "I'll page Doctor Drake, and see if he can come in between patients. This is a good sign."

As the day wore on, Cynthia asked Braden, "Have you had anything to eat?"

Braden shook his head. "I had coffee this morning, but I was too nervous to eat."

Cynthia seemed agitated as if moving around would ease her worry. "I'll go get us something to eat from the cafeteria. If you need to go home and trade cars with your dad, I can stay here with Ellie."

Before Braden could answer, she was gone.

Just as she brought in two trays of food, Doctor Drake walked into the room. He acknowledged Cynthia and Braden before walking to Ellie's bedside. He checked her pupils and listened to her chest. Straightening up, he said, "Her pupils are equal, and her chest is clear. Her labs aren't great, but they're not as bad as I had imagined." He took her hand and asked her to squeeze his. Ellie compressed her hand. "Good, Ellie! I think she'll wake up soon. Don't be surprised if she's a little confused. She probably will not remember the accident. I'll assess her again on my evening rounds."

Around five o'clock, the doctor walked back in. "Any progress?" Cynthia and Braden both shook their heads.

Examining her eyes and chest, he said, "I know you've been talking to her. Keep it up. I'll see you in the morning."

Cynthia needed to check on her husband. "I hate to leave, but Preston needs to eat again. Call me if there's a change, no matter what time it is." She hurried from the room, trying to get away from the nightmare.

Braden slipped out of the room and called his parents on the pay phone. Relief washed over him when Mason answered the phone. "Glad you made it home, Dad. I thought you were coming here to trade vehicles."

"No, I thought you needed the truck in case another storm moves in. I made it home fine in that little tin can you call a car. Any update?"

Braden smiled at his dad's humor. "Ellie did squeeze the doctor's hand just a tiny bit. He thinks she'll wake up soon." As soon as he hung up, he went back to Ellie's room. He took her hand and laid his head on the edge of her bed. Fatigue plastered his eyes shut. At midnight, Ellie stirred and made a guttural sound. She began to shake.

Braden ran to the nurses' station. "Come, quick, please. She's shaking."

A nurse walked in. "She's having a seizure."

Braden's eyes widened in fear. "Does she have…what do you call it…epilepsy?"

"No, this is common with brain injuries." The seizing stopped as the nurse addressed Braden. "Her chart shows that she has had some squeezing of her hands. That's a good sign." Ellie's eyelids fluttered, opened for a few seconds, and closed again. "That's another good sign. She's coming around."

Braden realized he hadn't had a deep breath for as long as he could remember and let out a big whoosh. "Thank you." He wanted to call Cynthia, but leaving Ellie meant he could miss something, and he didn't want to wake them until he had more news. The nurse told him they always had fresh coffee at the nurses' station for visitors if he ever wanted a cup. He left Ellie long enough to grab a quick cup, hoping the caffeine would keep him alert. He tested a small sip. It was hot enough to burn his tongue, so he moved away from Ellie's bed in case he accidently spilled any. He didn't like the feel of the Styrofoam cup, but it held coffee.

CHAPTER TWENTY-FOUR

The next morning, a nurse brought Braden a tray. "You look fatigued. Why don't you go home and take a nap? There likely won't be any change for a while."

"No, I'll leave when Ellie is able to go home."

The nurse mentioned the coffee bar again, and Braden hurried to pour himself another cup. While sipping the last of the coffee, Cynthia walked in. She had a paper sack of sandwiches and chips.

"I thought you might need something to eat. Any change? I was going to get you a soda when I got here, but I see you have coffee."

"Thank you. Yes, I slipped away for a couple of minutes to grab a cup so I can stay awake today. And they brought me a breakfast tray." He told her about Ellie's seizure.

"I'm so glad you were with her to alert the nurse. Braden, you are worn out. I have Preston situated with meds and lunch. Why don't you go to our house and rest?"

"Thank you, but I just can't leave her. I might miss something. And…" Braden pointed. "she's moving her hand."

Cynthia rushed to the bed. "She did! She really did. Ellie, it's Mom. Wake up. Open your eyes."

Braden copied her. "Please open your eyes. We want to talk to you."

With slow, almost robotic movements, Elli's hand went to her face as if trying to recognize her own features. Her eyes moved back and forth under closed eyelids and then fluttered open.

Reading her facial expression, Braden could see she was confused and fearful. "Hi, honey. Your mom and I are here with you. You were in a car accident, and you're in the hospital."

Cynthia leaned over and placed a kiss on Ellie's cheek. "Do you understand what Braden said to you, sweetheart? Dad will be up to see you later this afternoon."

Ellie's lips moved, but the sound was so low, it barely penetrated the machine noise in the room. Braden and Cynthia both leaned in closer.

Cynthia asked, "Are you thirsty?" She took some lip balm out of her purse and rubbed Elli's chapped lips. Can you repeat what you said, darling?"

Ellie's eyes darted from Braden to Cynthia and back again. "Leg."

Braden asked, "Does your leg hurt?"

"Yeah." She closed her eyes again.

Braden turned to Cynthia. "I'll go ask the nurse if she can have some pain medication. And I think I'll make a quick call to Mom and Dad if you don't mind."

"Take your time, Braden. Walking around will be good for you."

Just as he walked back from the pay phone, he saw the doctor reading a chart outside Ellie's room. He rushed to see what he had to say.

Doctor Drake sat in a chair in the room and faced Braden and Cynthia. "I know it doesn't seem like it, but she is making excellent progress. I have reviewed the x-rays we repeated. I feel certain there is no permanent damage. Her labs are good, lungs are clear, the swelling in her leg is subsiding, and her heart is strong, so there's no reason not to go ahead with surgery to repair her leg. I have her scheduled as soon as the OR is available…probably about another hour or so."

He moved to the bed. "Ellie, I'm Doctor Drake. Can you wiggle your fingers?" He noticed the fingers on both hands wiggled. "Great job. Can you open your eyes?" Ellie turned her head to follow his voice and opened her eyes. "Good. We're going to get your leg fixed up real soon. Okay?"

Ellie seemed a little brighter. "Leg hurts."

"I know. We're going to give you something shortly." He turned to Braden and Cynthia. "I don't want to sedate her too heavily since we will be doing surgery soon, but I'll order something that will help. Any questions?"

Braden looked him in the eye. "How long will the surgery take, and how long for recovery?"

"Surgery, including recovery room, may take a few hours. It will take a while for her leg to completely heal. Do not be surprised if she has lapses of memory for a few more days or weeks. All of this is up to her

184

and her body. It will be imperative to make sure infection doesn't set in."
He smiled. "Be patient." He walked from the room.

Within the hour, a team of nurses entered the room and started
getting Ellie ready for surgery. Her eyes sought Cynthia's, and she
mumbled something incoherent. Cynthia took her hand. "Honey, they are
going to fix your leg and give you something for pain. Braden and I will
be right here. It's going to be all right." Cynthia thought she saw a slight
smile. "Love you and so does Braden."

After Ellie was wheeled into surgery, Braden ate a sandwich and
stretched out in a chair, spreading his legs straight out. "I can nap here.
Why don't you go see about Preston?"

"I should, I guess. We'll be back in an hour or so. He wants to be
here." In the silence of the room, disturbed only by the faint sounds of a
hospital busy breathing life into patients, Braden uttered a prayer. "Father
God, please direct the surgeons as they repair Ellie's leg. Be with Ellie,
and let her have a complete healing. I need her, Father. She's my other
half. Thank you for the blessings you have bestowed on us. In Jesus'
name, I pray. Amen."

Braden's psyche conjured up myriad scenarios. Would she be able to
heal before their wedding date? Would she walk with a limp? Would she
walk at all or be bound to a wheelchair? Would the leg have to be
amputated? Would she heal completely putting his worries to rest? His
internal script was interrupted by Cynthia and Preston.

Preston looked rested. "Any word?"

"No, and I'm beginning to worry. It's been a long time." Silently
Braden castigated himself for not trusting the Lord after his heartfelt
prayer.

Another hour ticked by. Preston, Cynthia, and Braden sat in stoic
silence waiting for news. No words were spoken. No machines beeped.
Three people sat suspended in a time warp.

As if on cue, Doctor Drake walked in, still in his frog green scrubs.
"Surgery went well. She's in recovery now and should be there another
hour or so."

A chorus of thank you's followed him as he exited the room.

Cynthia spoke to Braden, "I know I sound like a mother, but please
go eat something before the cafeteria closes. Have them put the bill on
Ellie's room."

Braden stretched. Fatigue washed over him like dust kicking up on a unpaved county road. He needed to eat, but his stomach was holding a rushing tidal wave at the moment. More than food, he would like to clean up and change into clean clothes. He'd do that once Ellie was back in the room.

"Thanks, I'll go see what they have." He called his parents before rushing to the cafeteria. He got yet another cup of coffee, a cold ham and cheese sandwich on what tasted and smelled like three-day old bread. He ate half of it and tossed the rest. Taking the coffee back to the room, he noticed Ellie had not made it back from recovery. He exhaled a breath of relief. That meant he would be here when she returned.

Just as he finished his coffee, the door swung wide, and Ellie was wheeled into the room. She looked peaceful. Her leg was enclosed in a wrapping so big, it looked like a fake Halloween costume. A contraption had been attached to her bed while she was in surgery to keep her leg elevated. As soon as her leg was secured to the lift, a nurse brought in an ice pack.

Ellie seemed to be interested in the nurse's movements. When Braden and her parents moved to her bed, she studied them one by one as if trying to recognize them.

Preston took her hand. "Sweetheart, it's Dad. Looks like they got you all fixed up."

Ellie smiled. "Okay."

Cynthia moved to the side of Preston. "I'm right here, too, sweetie."

Confusion dotted Ellie's face.

"It's Mom, baby."

"Oh."

Braden cleared his throat. "Glad to see you're awake."

She looked at him hard. "Uh, uh…"

"Braden. Your fiancé, remember?"

"Yeah." Her voice didn't sound like she fully comprehended Braden. "Where am I?"

Preston nodded to Braden to reply. "You're in the hospital. You had an accident."

"No, I didn't. I don't remember."

Cynthia bent and kissed her cheek. "It's good you don't remember. The doctor said that was normal."

"Where was I going?"

Braden calmed his nerves and lowered his voice, "You were coming back home to Scottsville, to me, to our home."

"I'm tired. Thirsty."

Braden rushed down the hall to the nurses' station. "Can Elizabeth Addison in Room 214 have water?"

"Let me get you some ice chips. Give her a spoonful at a time and go slow."

Since she tolerated the ice chips, they let her have a few sips of water before administering pain meds. "She's going to be asleep all night. Why don't you all go home, get some rest, and come back in the morning."

Preston rose. "Only if you promise to call if there's a change."

The nurse smiled. "Of course."

Entering the Addison's home, Braden noticed a few photos of Ellie on a table in the living room. Though it was clean with a place for everything, he didn't feel the warmth that his home exuded. Looking around, the room was spotless, but emotion was void in this house. He understood why Ellie said his family felt warm and inviting. He shook off his observations and moved to a bedroom that Cynthia pointed to down the hall. Taking clean clothes out of his duffel bag, he let hot water pour over his body in the shower ridding himself of the stress he'd felt and the smells of the hospital. He wanted to scrub away the reality of seeing Ellie hooked up to machines. He wanted to go home and see her in the kitchen fussing over a new recipe, planning the grove where they would hold weddings, and seeing about making some of Grace's dresses fit any size, so photos could be taken.

Making his way to the kitchen, Braden smelled real food cooking. Cynthia had put a roast into the oven to cook at a certain time that morning. It was ready, and she was dishing up vegetables to go with it.

As soon as they finished eating, Braden asked to be excused. He went to the bedroom, peeled off his clothes, and burst out laughing. In his haste, he had picked up his boxer shorts with the red hearts on them. How Ellie would love to see this, he thought. He slipped beneath clean sheets and a light blanket, uttered a prayer, and fell into a deep sleep.

Ellie continued to make progress the next few days. Her memory was sporadic the first couple of days, but by the third day, her cognitive function had returned to normal. The accident never surfaced in her recollection, but she remembered everything else. On the fifth day, Doctor Drake determined the swelling had gone down enough to put her leg in a cast.

He checked Ellie's vital signs. "You're free to go home. I'd like to see you in a week for an x-ray to be sure everything is still in place. The fractures weren't as bad as I first thought, so they were easily fixed. You should be able to start putting some weight on your leg after a few weeks. The cast will stay on for six weeks if all goes as it should. Then you will need to start physical therapy."

As if on cue, a physical therapist walked in. "Hi, my name is Brad." He shook hands with Preston and Braden and nodded to Cynthia. "I'm here to show you how to walk on crutches."

Ellie looked at Braden. "At this rate, I'll he incapacitated until August." Turning to the doctor, she asked, "May I go to Scottsville and just come back for physical therapy?"

"I don't see why not if you have a driver. It will be three times a week at first."

An entourage, made up of Braden and Ellie in Mason's truck, Preston in his car, and Cynthia in hers snaked down winding city streets until they reached the Preston home. Since Ellie had to be back for x-rays in a week, Braden thought they should stay with her parents, and then, depending on how everything looked, Braden would take Ellie home.

Sitting in the living room, Braden glanced at Preston. His eyes looked glassy, and he was sweating profusely. Cynthia had gone to the kitchen to make sandwiches. Braden rose and went to the kitchen.

"Cynthia, Preston doesn't look good. I wonder if his blood sugar has dropped."

Cynthia dropped a slice of bread she was slathering with mayonnaise and rushed to see about her husband. "Preston, are you feeling weak?"

"Weak?" Confusion dotted his face as he drew his eyebrows together.

"Braden, will you go pour him a glass of orange juice, and there is a bottle on the windowsill. Can you bring both?"

Preston looked at her. "Is Elizabeth home?"

Ellie was sitting on the sofa. "I'm right here, Daddy."

Braden rushed in with the orange juice and pills, and within fifteen minutes, Preston's sugar level had increased.

"Sorry, I disrupted everything. Sometimes I just have these spells if I don't take my medicine at the same time every day."

Ellie and Braden returned to The Sullivan House, as they now called it, after the doctor assured them that Ellie was progressing as expected. The groom met them in the driveway. He turned to Braden. "I watered the grass and your garden. Your dad filled me in on what was happening. I also picked some of your produce. I sent some home with your mom and dad, and the rest is in the kitchen. I also picked up the mail every day from the post office. It's on the table in the hall."

"My dad was here?"

"Oh yes, he and your mother have been here a lot of the time that you were gone. He was working on the house. I don't know what your mother was doing, but she was in and out of the house a lot."

A bevy of colorful hanging pots containing various colors of petunias adorned the veranda. Ellie laughed. "I think it's plain to see why she was in and out. The flowers are beautiful."

Braden carried Ellie into the house and eased her onto the sofa in the study. He pulled an ottoman up and piled pillows on it to elevate her leg.

"Braden, I'm hurting." Ellie squirmed, trying to find a position that would relieve the pain. "Will you get me a pain pill?"

Braden ruffled through Ellie's things and found the bottle of little white pills. He marveled that such a tiny pill would relieve pain. After a few minutes, he could see Ellie was tired, so he suggested lying down. She agreed, and Braden carried her to the bed.

"Braden, I'm supposed to walk with crutches, remember?"

"Yes, but those pills may make you groggy. I don't mind carrying you."

Ellie laughed. "I guess you'll be doing most of the cooking for a while."

"I thought I'd make potato soup. Does that sound good?"

"That sounds wonderful. After I have a nap, could we read more in Grace's journal?"

The next few days, between bouts of pain and periods of napping, Ellie read more of Grace's journal and filled Braden in on the details. "It's mostly about family and the secrets some of them kept."

"You've read a lot."

"What else can I do? It helps me ignore the pain."

"What else have you found out?"

"Joseph graduated from college and went to medical school in New Orleans. Maggie was secretly dating Charles, even though her family would not have approved. His family was not affluent, and Maggie knew she would have to go against their expectations to marry him. And of course, Grace kept the secret of Paul abusing her."

Braden sighed. "I wonder if her family ever found out?"

"Yes, Jim heard her in his mind and went to see about her. He rescued her and saved her life."

"And did all these secrets come to light?"

"Yes, Maggie and Charles finally received Abe and Sarah's consent and got married. Charles turned out to be very successful with a construction business, and Maggie became a clothing designer and producer of the latest fashions for women. After the ordeal with Paul, Grace and Matthew returned to the family home. Grace and Charles were in town. Only Joseph was away at medical school."

"It sounded like they were a close-knit family, willing to forgive even the smallest to the largest transgression." Braden bent to kiss Elli's cheek.

"Yes, in the end, I guess love and forgiveness are at the core of their happy family."

"That's a good mantra to live by. I hope we can build a family together and always remember this."

Ellie smiled. "Me, too. That's the last of this journal. Would you bring me that box with those papers and the other journals? Maybe I can find the one that comes after this one."

Braden carried the box into the parlor and helped Ellie go through it. They found what looked to be journals, but on opening them, they were financial records that Abe had kept. They did learn that he sold half of the land of Oak Hollow right before the war, giving credence to what Ellie had found in the deed records.

Ellie sighed. "If we don't find more journals, I guess we have to assume that she stopped writing since the Civil War was imminent."

"That's frustrating. I'm wondering about Grace and Jim. You try to nap. I'll go check on Doug, and see if he needs anything. Call if you need me."

After Braden checked on Doug and the horses, he slipped back into the house, careful not to wake Ellie. Deciding to check on her, he walked down the hall and tiptoed into the bedroom. Ellie sat up in bed, but she seemed in a trance. Her eyes did not track him, and her expression did not change.

Braden moved to the bed. "Ellie?"

Ellie shook her head. "Braden?"

"Yes, sweetheart, what is it?"

The pain medicine had evidently dulled Ellie's pain. She slung her feet to the floor and stood up on her left leg with Braden's help. He handed her the crutches, and she made her way to the breakfast nook with Braden behind her in case she fell. Sitting at the table, tears streamed down her face.

Braden jumped up. "What's the matter. Are you in pain? Is it time for another pill?"

Ellie shook her head. Between sobs, she blurted out, "I can't marry you. I'm sorry to wait so long to tell you."

"What? What are you saying? Are you saying you want to postpone the wedding until you are fully recovered?"

"No." She took off her engagement ring and laid it on the table.

"Ellie, you can't spring this on me out of the blue. I need answers. Is it because of your leg?

"I don't want to talk about it right now. Maybe later. Will you help me back to my room?"

CHAPTER TWENTY-FIVE

After helping Ellie back to bed, Braden took her ring and put it in a small dish and placed it on the mantle in the parlor. His face flushed crimson as anger and depression rose to the surface. He clinched his fists as a tear slid down his cheek. He needed to get away. Without a word to Ellie, he slammed through the breakfast nook's door and went to the stables. Doug had worked hard to restore the stalls and had bought a recliner and a small television set so he could relax while he cared for the horses. His patience had impressed Braden, and within a week of working for them, he had instructed Braden in how to saddle a horse.

Doug had gone into town, so Braden went to the tack room and saddled his favorite horse. He rode as hard and fast as he dared, the wind whipping through his hair and blasting his face. He didn't care. He wanted to run away from whatever had caused Ellie to destroy him. He rode until the wind dried the last of his tears. Stopping by the river, he poured his soul out to the Lord. He rode back to the stables and put Apollo in his stall. He brushed him down and gave him a pat. "Thanks, Apollo." Braden dragged himself to the house. He went to the bedroom where Ellie sat propped up. Her face was blotched, and her eyes were swollen, but she had, apparently, spent her tears as well.

Braden pulled up a chair. "Ellie, I don't know what has happened. I've racked my brain and gone over everything. Is it that you are frustrated that your leg won't heal properly? Is there someone else? Your ex, maybe?"

"What are you talking about?"

"You just broke our engagement. I need to know why."

193

Ellie spoke in a mechanical voice with no emotion as if she were reciting a story of someone else. Her eyes had a strange look. "Braden, when you proposed, I knew I couldn't accept, but then you said the past wouldn't matter. I think you have assumed I can't marry you because I had been in a long-term relationship and was not over those feelings. But that's not it."

"Then what?"

"I'm going to tell you. Then, as we agreed, if one of us moved out, he or she would sell their half or pay a salary to the one left to manage the business."

"But you've paid off my father, so we aren't even. I was saving for a honeymoon, but I'll gladly put that money into making our investments even."

"It isn't that. Either you move out, or I will. We can remain friends and still fulfill our dream for this property."

"I don't see demoting my love to mere friendship. Tell me what you have to say, and I'll leave if that's what you want, but not until I find out why you are breaking up with me."

"Just go, Braden."

"Not until I know why you broke up with me."

Ellie's eyes glazed over, and she appeared in an altered state of consciousness.

"Ellie? Are you okay?"

She didn't answer. She looked past Braden and just started talking as if he were not in the room. "When I was a freshman in high school, my best friend and I went to a fair, and there was a medium there. We wanted to see what she would say. I didn't have quite enough money, but she said she'd do a reading for me for half price. She told me someone had put a curse on me, and that no man would ever survive my love. It scared me."

"I can only imagine. Go on."

"I met Roy Sikes later that year, and we started dating. We went to prom, and he asked me to go to an after party. I knew there would be drinking, and I had a curfew, so I refused. He took me home. The last thing he said to me as he walked me to the door was that he loved me.

"A little after three o'clock in the morning, my mom woke me up. She told me there had been a horrible accident. Roy was going to take three other guys home, but he lost control, and the passenger's side of the car hit a tree. Roy was the only one killed even though he was driving. All the other boys survived. I heard that medium's voice cackling, saying she told me so."

"That's terrible."

"My friends told me that medium had nothing to do with it, so I dated another boy my sophomore year. He was a very nice boy. We mostly went to movies. He didn't drink or smoke or anything. One night he told me he thought he was falling in love with me. I had the worst feeling. Two weeks later, he got sick. He had some kind of bad infection, and he died a month later. I think I killed him."

"But none of this was your fault."

After he died, Tommy Butler and I started dating. We dated the rest of our high school years, and nothing happened, so I put the medium out of my mind."

"Yes, and he cheated on you."

"Yes, he had a roving eye. The first year was wonderful. He was everything I thought I wanted, but as he began to go places without me, one of his friends came and told me he was dating other girls at the same time he was dating me."

"How could he keep track of all those girlfriends at once without your knowing?"

"Some were from out of town, and others had already graduated from high school. At any rate, we fought almost every day until I grew tired of it. Tommy would taunt me about my looks, my figure, and belittled me for being skinny and not having a curvaceous figure. One afternoon, we met a group of couples at the lake." Ellie broke down in sobs.

Braden took her hand and wiped away her tears with his thumb of his other, stroking her face. "I think I understand. You want to go back to him? I thought you said you realized you didn't love him."

"I couldn't go back to him if I wanted. And he means nothing to me, except to keep me from you. I remember the day as if it were yesterday. When I was in that coma or whatever it was after the accident, my whole past assaulted me. I heard your voice, but I was so sad, I just wanted to die. It was then I knew the past did matter, and I couldn't marry the man I love."

"Go on. Why?"

"It was a beautiful summer day just after graduation. A cool front had moved in, and the temperature had dropped to a comfortable degree. A bunch of us decided to have a picnic and spend the day at the lake. Tommy picked me up at about ten o'clock. I had packed a cooler of sandwiches and drinks and felt that maybe this would be a turning point in our relationship. I had decided either we were going to go forward and get engaged, or I was going to break it off and go to college. As I told you, I really didn't know what love was. I don't think any of us did at that time. I thought having someone to do things with and sharing a few intimate moments was love."

"So, you were intimate with him?"

"Intimate? No, not what you're thinking. He knew I was a good girl, so all he did was kiss me and paint a picture of how we would be together forever. He got what he wanted from the other girls he was dating." Ellie reached for a glass of water on her nightstand. "Looking back, I think he was stringing me along. My parents aren't wealthy, but Tommy came from a very poor family. I think he thought if he married me, he would have access to my family's money, and he could manipulate me any way he wanted."

"He's a jerk, Ellie. Even if you don't want me, please, please don't go back to him. He will cause you nothing but heartache, and I've got enough of that for both of us right now."

Ellie looked away and studied the pattern on the coverlet of the bed tracing it with her finger. Her eyes took in every inch of the room. "I'm so sorry. I guess I minimized how all of this would affect me until I had the accident." Her eyes drooped and she had a strange look in her eyes.

"Ellie, I'm dying here. Please just tell me. What happened at the picnic?"

"Okay. So, we had a picnic. I had been lying on a beach towel with sunglasses on, hoping to get a tan. I didn't notice that the boys had brought two coolers full of beer, and they were getting drunk. One of my friends came to me and whispered that the boys were planning to leave us as a prank. She said they were too drunk to drive and asked if I had Tommy's keys. I got up and hugged him and put my hands in his pocket. I grabbed the keys, and he grabbed me." Ellie stopped and seemed to lose her train of thought. Her eyes held a blank look as if she couldn't focus.

"Go on, honey."

"Go where?"

"Did you get the keys from Tommy?"

"Oh, wait. Tommy. He got his keys back and glared at me. That's when he admitted his infidelity. I can still hear his laughter. That's when I told him we were through."

"So, you broke up?"

"Yeah. Everyone had gathered around us. I knew they were going to try to break up our argument. In front of everyone, he grabbed my wrist and twisted until I fell to the ground. Then he screamed to me that no one would ever break up with him. He said this was all my fault, that I'd be sorry and to never forget that. I was in such pain, that I didn't know what happened. He broke my wrist."

"Do you know now what happened after that?"

"I was told he stormed to his car and spun out. One of his friends took me home, and my mother took me to the emergency room. I kept waiting for Tommy to calm down and call me, but the call that came the next morning was not what I expected. It was his dad. He asked if I knew where Tommy was. He never went home that night. Twenty-four hours later, he was declared missing. They found his car three days later in New Orleans by Lake Borgne. He left a note addressed to me. It just said something to the effect of that no one leaves him, and that he was the one leaving me forever. And that I'd have to live with what I'd done trying to break up. I can't remember exactly how he worded it. He also said he had a gypsy fortune teller put a stronger curse on me so I could never marry, or bad things and death would happen to my husband."

"That's horrible. So did they locate him?"

"I'm tired, and my brain is fuzzy. I can't think, and I'm hurting."

"Let me get you a pain pill." Braden went to the bathroom and got the bottle of pain medication. He poured one into Ellie's hand and handed her the glass of water and set the bottle on her nightstand. After a few minutes, he asked, "Can you continue now?"

"With what?"

"With what happened after they found Tommy's car."

"The police talked to all of us. They believe he drowned, either intentionally or accidentally, but that lake area is so deep in areas, they couldn't examine the whole thing. They sent divers down as far as they could go, but nothing turned up. While I wasn't held accountable legally, it still unraveled me emotionally. His family has never heard from him, and his body never washed up. The police think maybe fish ate his remains, or that he was swept out to the Gulf of Mexico. His parents blame me, even though his friends told them Tommy started it."

"What a horrible thing to do."

"They went through the process of having him declared deceased." Ellie closed her eyes.

Braden pressed on, "Do you think he committed suicide?" Ellie didn't respond. Braden gently nudged her arm. "Ellie, I have to know."

"Know what?"

"If Tommy committed suicide."

"I don't know. Part of me thinks he did. Part of me believes he ran into some unscrupulous characters, and they killed him."

"So, you went to college? Do you still keep in touch with his parents?"

"No. They hate me. I couldn't concentrate on school. Instead, I got my real estate license and worked in Jackson. I kept running into his parents, so when my roommate offered me a place to stay here, I moved and stayed with them. They found Tommy's blood in his car and some unknown fingerprints." Ellie's voice broke. "I'm a murderer, Braden. Don't you see, it's the curse of two fortune tellers. That's one of the reasons I can't marry you. I don't want your loving me to cause your death because of the curses."

Braden squeezed her hands. "Ellie, you did not cause any of this. You were trying to get his keys to keep him from driving drunk. You are not a murderer. Even if you had shot him in cold blood, I feel he deserved it, but no matter what you think, nothing will ever affect my love for you. And I don't believe that any of what happened was because of some curses."

"But that's not all."

"What else?"

Ellie seemed to be a little more alert. "When you and my parents went home to get some sleep, the doctor made late rounds. He came in and told me that the internal injuries that had fractured my ribs, had damaged my liver and spleen, and the impact damaged my womb. He told me I may not be able to have children. I am devastated, but for these two reasons, I can't marry you."

"Ellie, I don't care about that. We can always adopt."

"But it wouldn't carry on your bloodline. And I can't do it."

"Will you give me time to process this?"

"I owe you that much. Don't take too long because my heart is breaking, and I need to get this over with as soon as possible. Please don't ask me anything else, and don't tell my parents about the curses."

Braden walked to the back veranda. Sitting on a wicker chair where he and Ellie had shared so many good times, he let his eyes take in the landscape. How could such a peaceful place and the perfect girl for him cloud the atmosphere? Was this place cursed? Were Jim and Grace destined to live a life of despair and never be able to marry? Did Paul Scott somehow put a hex on this place? Braden shook his head. Of course not. Braden realized his thinking was distorted, that's all. Yet, so many things had happened with the hearts they saw and the eerie noises. Braden rose and headed straight to the heart of stones. Sitting on the bench, it was as if he heard Grace speak to him. Her voice was as melodious as a nightingale. A breeze ruffled his hair, and the wind whispered, "Don't give up. Go now. Ellie needs you." Was it her voice, or was he imagining it?

Braden walked into the bedroom. Shock gripped him. The bottle with Ellie's pain pills was knocked over, and the pills were gone. She was slumped to the side of the bed asleep, or was she dead? He rushed to a phone and called the clinic and told them he needed Doctor Purcell to come immediately. "It's a matter of life and death. I think my wife may be dead."

The doctor and a police officer arrived fifteen minutes later. Doctor Purcell took a stethoscope and a blood pressure cuff out of a small black satchel. Ellie did not open her eyes. After a few minutes, he turned to Braden. "Her blood pressure is very low, and her pulse is weak and irregular. Son, we'd better get her to a hospital as soon as we can and pray she makes it. We don't have the facilities here to work on her, and we don't have an ambulance, so you can get her to Vicksburg quicker than waiting for one."

Officer Barton said, "Doctor Purcell, we're on our way! Follow me, Braden."

Doctor Purcell closed his black bag. "Fine. I'll call ahead to the hospital."

Braden picked Ellie up and rushed her to his car. The policeman led the way with his lights flashing, and his siren screaming. Braden gripped the wheel and prayed as hard as he ever had. Ellie's eyes were closed, and she was slumped against the passenger window. This just couldn't be happening. As they entered the hospital's emergency entrance, the policeman waved and sped off. A gurney was waiting for them outside the emergency entrance.

Braden watched as the emergency personnel worked on Ellie. He told them what she had ingested which made their job easier. After what seemed like hours, they admitted Ellie and put her on suicidal watch.

Finding a pay phone, Braden deposited the number of coins, thankful that he had gotten change yesterday at the feed store and dialed Ellie's parents. Cynthia answered. "I don't want to alarm you, and I don't know that you want to upset Preston, but they have just admitted Ellie to the hospital here in Vicksburg. Apparently, she took too many pain pills in a row. I wanted to let you know."

Cynthia gasped and didn't say anything for a long time. Finally, she bombarded him with questions. "Why would she do that? Did you have an argument? Is she critical? Why Vicksburg? Why not here?"

"The policeman led me here. Said it was closer. I don't know if she's critical, but they tell me her vital signs are coming up slowly. And, no, we didn't have an argument. I have no idea why she took all the pills."

"Okay, let me get things together. I don't know if Preston is up to the trip, but if not, I'll be there shortly."

Walking into her room with Preston, Cynthia asked, "Why would she take more medicine than she was supposed to? The more I thought about it, I wonder if she was in pain and trying to get relief, and this overdose was an accident. She should have come back to Jackson to her doctor."

Braden took Cynthia's hand. "Let's walk down the hall and get some coffee. Preston, can we bring you some?"

"No, just water will be fine."

Cynthia didn't want to leave, but she had read Braden's eyes. She followed him out of the door. "There's something you're not telling me."

"Yes. I'm not sure this was an accident. I don't know what came over her. We were fine. She ate lunch that I made and told me we needed to talk. Then she started talking and saying things I couldn't wrap my mind around. In essence, she broke up with me and gave me back her ring." Braden's voice broke.

"What things? Are you telling me she deliberately tried to kill herself?"

Braden nodded. "I don't know, but she took all the pills."

"Why would she break up with you and then take all those pills? Something isn't adding up. Tell me the truth, Braden."

"I'd rather let her tell you. I don't feel it's my place now that she has broken up with me."

Ellie slept the rest of the afternoon. Braden turned to Preston. "Why don't you let me take you to The Sullivan House? I'll cook dinner for all of us. You can stretch out and rest until we hear more news."

Cynthia mouthed, "Thank you."

CHAPTER TWENTY-SIX

When they arrived at The Sullivan House, Doug met them. "I closed up the house. Can I go get something for you to eat?"

"No, Mister Addison is on a strict diet. Thank you so much for seeing about the house." Braden took a package of pork chops from the refrigerator that he had planned for dinner for Ellie. He put them in four individual foil packets with onions, carrots, peas, and a scant number of chopped potatoes on Preston's. Spritzing some olive oil on top, he sealed each packet and put them in the oven. After getting Preston comfortable on the sofa, Braden went into Ellie's room. He searched for a suicide note, but found nothing. Silent sobs shook him as he looked at her bed, still rumpled from moving her. Would this be the last place she would occupy in the house? He needed air. Walking back to the heart of stones and sitting on the bench, he went over everything Ellie had said. None of it made sense, and he certainly did not believe that a psychic medium cursed her. He didn't know how long he had been there, but as he walked back to the house, the smell of dinner jerked him back to reality. He composed himself, woke Preston, and put the contents of a packet on his plate.

"I know Cynthia won't leave Ellie, so I'm going to take dinner to her. Will you be all right here until I get back?"

"Yes, son. I'll be fine. I'd like to be there, too, but I know I would just be a burden since I'm so weak. If you or Cynthia decide to spend the night there, call me, please."

"I will. You would be fine to go, but we don't need you tiring yourself out and maybe ending up in the hospital, too. I can't remember if you've met Doug, our groom, but I'm going to ask him to come stay with you. He's a really nice young man." Braden knew Preston didn't

203

comprehend what had happened with Ellie. He went to the Inn where Doug had pulled out some leftovers.

"Would you mind keeping an eye on Ellie's dad? He has diabetes, but I need to get back to the hospital and relieve Ellie's mom. I also have you a packet of food fixed, so you can put those leftovers back in the refrigerator. I'd like you to eat with Preston." He didn't elaborate on what caused Ellie's hospitalization.

"Sure thing. I can see if he wants to watch TV or play dominoes. My grandmother has diabetes, so I know kind of what to cook for breakfast if I need to stay overnight with him."

"That relieves me a great deal. If he begins to sweat and look confused, there's some orange juice in the refrigerator and a chocolate bar on the counter. See if you can get those down him, and call me if you need me." He gave him the hospital information and Ellie's room number.

Braden sped back to the hospital. Cynthia looked at him in the doorway and pointed to the hall. "She's awake, but she won't say a word to me."

'I'm so sorry. Do they know when she will be released?"

"I'm waiting on the doctor."

An hour after Cynthia finished eating the meal Braden brought her, the doctor entered the room and checked Ellie. He frowned and looked at her chart. He took Ellie's hand. "Ellie, I'm ordering some more tests and blood work. If everything is okay, I'll let you go home tomorrow, but I want to be sure you're okay before I give my final release. If I find you have more issues, we'll deal with that, okay?"

Ellie stared straight ahead. She didn't acknowledge him. He moved out of her eyesight and motioned Cynthia and Braden to the hall. "I don't like her labs. Her platelet count, and her white blood count, along with the pain in her upper left abdomen, her confusion, and lightheadedness are all symptoms that all lead me to believe she may have a ruptured spleen. With her history of a serious car accident, and the resultant injury to the liver, spleen and womb, her suicide attempt may have saved her life."

Braden and Cynthia looked dumbfounded. Cynthia said, "But her accident was two weeks ago. How could her attempt to end her life save it?"

"I understand how this sounds incredulous, but she did not ingest enough medicine to kill her. Had she not been brought in for evaluation, we wouldn't have caught the spleen problem. I believe her fractured ribs perforated the spleen, and I anticipate emergency surgery as soon as I see the updated labs. I didn't want to alarm her, but I'm not sure in her state of mind, she would understand, anyway. I may need you to give consent."

Cynthia looked at him, confusion knitting her brows together. "Then why wasn't this caught when she was in the hospital after the injury?"

"I can't say for sure, but more than likely she didn't move around much when she was in the hospital. At that time, there were no signs of a spleen rupture. But when she started moving around at home or in physical therapy, she may have shifted and caused the ribs to puncture the spleen. It's not uncommon."

Braden put his arm around Cynthia who seemed about to collapse. "Thank you, Doctor. You mentioned her confusion. Could that have caused her suicide attempt?"

"Absolutely. She may have been trying to alleviate the pain by taking more medicine rather than trying to take her life. Or she may have been cognizant of what she wanted to do. At any rate, as I said, she saved her own life. Confusion is one of the symptoms, but I have no doubt after surgery, she will regain her normal functioning."

"Should we try to prepare her for surgery?"

"That would be a good idea."

Cynthia whispered a question, "How serious is the surgery?"

"A ruptured spleen can be life threatening. The surgery, itself, is not any more dangerous than any abdominal surgery. Not doing anything is the serious side of this. Try to relax until I know more. I'll keep you informed."

Walking back into the room, Braden asked, "Do you want me to go get Preston?"

"I'll call him. I think it would be best if he stays at your place. But I'll worry about him all alone, and I know you don't want to leave any more than I do."

"Don't worry about that. Our groom, Doug, is great with people. He is staying with Preston, and I told him to watch him and call if he thinks I need to come home. He knows we may be staying overnight. His grandmother has diabetes, so he knows what to look for and how to cook for him."

Cynthia sighed and exhaled a long breath. "Okay, thank you. That relieves me. Let's tell Ellie, and then I'll go call."

Moving to her bed, Braden stood on one side and Cynthia on the other. Ellie looked pale beneath the white sheets, but she had a peaceful look on her face.

Braden took her hand and rubbed it hard enough that her eyelids fluttered, and Cynthia rubbed her forehead.

"What? Why are you waking me up?"

Cynthia spoke to her, "Braden and I have something to tell you." Cynthia continued rubbing her forehead.

"Darling, they think you have a ruptured spleen, so you are going to surgery. We didn't want you to be surprised." Braden kissed her cheek.

"I'm hungry and thirsty." Ellie's eyes popped wide open. "Surgery?" She threw back the sheet and tried to get up. "Gotta get outta here."

Braden eased her back down. "It's okay, honey. Don't try to get up. We'll be right here."

Cynthia kissed her hand. "Braden's right."

"I want to go home. They are going to kill me."

"And you will go home soon." Braden held onto her arm to restrain her.

Cynthia rang for a nurse to give her something to calm her down.

Within a half hour, the doctor came in. "Ellie, I'm Doctor Miller. I'm going to be doing your surgery, and we are just about ready."

Ellie's eyes were wide with fear. "No." She began to flail her arms and upper body.

The doctor covered her body with his to hold her down. "Ellie, stop moving, please. You are going to hurt yourself worse." Braden helped the doctor hold her down.

Braden began talking to her in a calm voice just as the surgical team walked in. A nurse quietly added a small dose of antianxiety medicine to Ellie's IV. "Ellie, baby, everything's fine. When you wake up, it will all be over." He watched in fear as the surgical team moved Ellie to a gurney and strapped her down. Knowing she was in a panic, he sighed with relief when the medicine took effect and calmed her.

Cynthia and Braden followed the surgical team to the door of the surgical suite, kissed her, and went back to her room. Late afternoon, the doctor walked up to them.

"The surgery went fine, but the spleen was ruptured, her liver and uterus are badly bruised. If all goes well, she should be able to be released in a few days."

Braden shook his hand. "Thank you. What will she need post op?"

"No strenuous exercise or lifting. She should take a shower instead of a bath after her dressings are removed. I'm also going to prescribe an antibiotic as well as some more pain meds. I would rather someone else manage her meds until we are sure her confusion has passed, and that she isn't suicidal any longer. She will sleep for a while now."

Cynthia turned to Braden. "If you don't mind, I think I'll go check on Preston. I'll be back to relieve you."

"Since she will probably sleep for a long time, why don't you just stay and get some rest? You look exhausted."

"Knowing she is out of danger, I may take you up on it."

By late morning the next day, Ellie was awake enough to make eye contact with Braden. He moved to her bedside. "Good morning, sweetheart. How are you feeling?"

"I don't know. I'm in a hospital from the looks of it. What happened?"

"What do you remember? I'll fill in the blanks."

Ellie cleared her throat. Braden gave her a spoonful of ice chips. "I remember someone told me I broke my leg in an accident. And I vaguely remember going home. I don't remember the accident."

"Anything else?"

"Are we alone?"

"Yes. You can tell me everything."

"Just that I had a nightmare and told you all about my past and broke up with you. Tommy was there, and he scared me. He kept telling me not to tell, and he wanted me back. But he looked strange with a splotched tanned skin. I hope I didn't really talk to you."

207

Braden spoke softly. "You did tell me about the ordeal with Tommy and the two other boys. And you broke up with me, but we'll get it all straightened out, and if you are worried about some stupid curses, we'll go to someone to have it reversed. There are plenty of people in New Orleans who would be glad to do that for a fee."

"Could we do that?"

Braden laughed. "Of course, silly girl. You can't get rid of me that easily."

Ellie sighed. "I can't believe I can't remember. It all seems like a dream. Why am I here, and why am I hurting so bad?"

"You've had your spleen removed. Your ribs were puncturing it."

"Oh, when can I go home?"

Just then the doctor walked in. "Hi, Ellie. I heard your question. You may leave the hospital tomorrow if you are doing as well as you are now. I want you to move around some, but don't overdo it."

"I'm sorry, I don't remember you. Did you do my surgery?"

"I did. And I'm glad you don't remember. We like it that way!"

"Thank you." She turned to Braden. "Where is Mom? And Dad?"

"Your mom went to see about your dad. They spent the night at our house."

Ellie squeezed Braden's arm. "When they get here, you need to go get some rest."

When Braden called home, he talked to Cynthia and told her that Ellie was coherent and awake. Cynthia mentioned that they were just getting ready to come to the hospital.

The afternoon was spent filling Ellie in on all the details. Since she didn't remember the accident, they kept details to a minimum and focused instead on the spleen surgery and how she would be able to be back to normal within a few weeks. They told her Andrew Knight came to see her and said that the real estate business had picked up, and he was looking forward to seeing her back at work. The Chamber of Commerce sent a huge bouquet of flowers, and Andrew Knight had a tree planted in the rain forest with her name on it. The engagement and wedding were not mentioned. Everyone felt that would be best handled between the two of them when she got home.

The next afternoon, Braden drove Ellie home and tucked her into bed, gave her the meds she was supposed to take, and started a light supper. Preston went to the parlor to rest, and Cynthia helped Braden in the kitchen. They baked a chicken and served it with mashed cauliflower instead of potatoes, okra, and a salad, to keep the carbs to a minimum for Preston. Braden invited Doug to eat with them, and he gladly accepted. Ellie insisted on going to the table to eat, amid many protests.

"I feel like I've lost out on so many days. I don't want to stay in bed, and the doctor did say I should walk around."

Braden threw up his arms. "That's fine, but I need to help you. You're weaker than you realize, and you're still on crutches."

"Oh, I forgot about that. I was in a wheelchair leaving the hospital, and then you carried me up the steps and put me into bed."

"Yes, and if you insist on getting out of bed, I can carry you to the table."

"No, I want to walk. Will you hand me my crutches?"

Braden helped her stand and walked behind her to the table.

Cynthia smiled. "It's so good to see you up and about."

Preston chimed in, "I agree. I was very worried about you." He turned to Doug. "Young man, you really were helpful to me and kept my blood sugar even."

"Yes, sir. My grandmother is diabetic, so I have a little experience. She lived with us when I was still at home with my parents."

Cynthia nodded. "You prepared a wonderful breakfast with just the things Preston needed. Thank you so much."

"You're welcome."

Preston and Cynthia stayed overnight and then left to go back home. Once they left, Ellie turned to Braden. "You said I told you about my past and why I can't marry you?"

"I think you told me everything. You seemed to blame yourself, even though everyone told you, you weren't responsible. You also told me the doctor said after your accident that you may not be able to have children."

Ellie grew quiet. A lone tear slid down her cheek.

"And I told you then, and I'll tell you now, none of that matters. Now, I think it's time." Braden picked her up and carried her to the parlor. He retrieved her ring from the dish on the mantle and moved in front of her. He bent to one knee and placed Ellie's engagement ring back on her finger. "I'll ask again. Will you marry me? I'll keep asking until you say yes."

"Of course, the answer is yes. I'm relieved that my secret is out. I need to tell my parents, too, I guess. I'm tired of holding on to secrets."

"They already know. You confessed to them a long time ago, but they said you probably didn't remember because you were in shock."

"I'm still worried about the curses. I don't want you hurt or dead."

"I don't believe a word of that malarkey, but if it would make you feel better, I did read some books. I'll go put salt around the house which is supposed to break a curse."

"Yes, please. Put a double amount!"

Braden dutifully went around the house with a box of salt. Just as he finished, he whispered, "Okay, now that will ease her mind, even though I will never believe there were curses, just like I have a hard time believing in ghosts."

Walking back into the house, Braden leaned over and kissed her. "All done!"

"Then I guess it's time to plan a wedding."

CHAPTER TWENTY-SEVEN

Braden had two more weeks before school would start. Ellie had physical therapy three times a week, and he dutifully drove her to Vicksburg for every appointment. After the second week, she was progressing so well, that they gave her specific instructions so that she could do her exercises at home, and would only have to check back in once a month, saving her from having to drive so far each week, and causing Braden not to have to worry about getting a substitute teacher.

Mister Knight had agreed for her to work from home, and he was doing the same. He told her when he checked on the building to lease it again, they had raised the price to almost double. At Ellie's suggestion, they printed a brochure every week with new listings, and Ellie kept in touch with Mister Chandler from Jackson. She did marketing for both offices, and both Andrew Knight and Thomas Chandler combined their offices with Ellie handling the marketing and the commercial accounts. She was able to make more money than she could have working for each of them individually, and both offices prospered exponentially. She and Braden sat down and figured their liabilities and their salaries, and realized that by the first of October, all their bills would be paid along with their indebtedness to Braden's parents, with a sizeable amount left over, once a large commercial commission check came in.

Celebrating tossing the crutches, Ellie made a gourmet meal of roasted pheasant with an herb infused butter glaze, wild rice, baked asparagus, tomato basil soup, and a kale salad. She had draped the dining room table with a vintage linen table cloth that she found in one of the Attic Boxes, as they were now called. With the flatware and the Royal Doulton fine bone china they found earlier, she set a formal table in the English style. Once she had everything ready, she called Braden to the table.

Walking in, Braden looked at the table with the bulbs in the chandelier casting a soft glow to the feast below. He blew out a shallow breath. "I feel like I just stepped back in time, and that I should be dressed in a tux. I can almost feel Miss Daisy standing at the head of the table to serve this gorgeous meal. But this feels like more than just a celebration of being free from the crutches."

Ellie smiled. "I hope it tastes good. Business was slow this morning, so I spent some time going through recipe books. I was thinking we could have a very formal special dinner with guests if they sign up for it. We could charge extra and have our chef serve a gourmet supper such as this. Of course, whatever chef we pick would choose his own menu. I thought we could say something like, "For a special ending to your stay with us, our award-winning chef would be pleased to prepare a gourmet meal that you may share with our owners. It's called Supper with the Sullivans and would feature dishes they may have enjoyed when Oak Hollow was in its heyday. Dress would be optional, but for the full effect, you may select gowns and suits from our wardrobe. Some of the garments were actually worn by the Sullivans and others copied from fashions in that era. Be assured, the clothing is cleaned after each use.""

"That sounds great. You just keep coming up with special attractions. I'll bet some people will be excited to step back into history."

"Yes, that's the idea. We would need to research what a formal dinner would have been in that time. I just came up with this because I figured that they either raised pheasants or had neighbors that did. I'm not sure about the wild rice, but they could have imported it. Or since they were Irish, potatoes might have been served. I am also thinking of hiring a band if our guests would like to attend a ball in our lovely parlor and dining room!"

"I guess we need to start looking for a chef and a band."

"As far as the band, I'm sure I can get some local bands here, or maybe some kids from the high school band class. I'll put some feelers out for a chef. I'm thinking about contacting culinary schools or upscale restaurants to see if they have suggestions. I'll also research how much to pay him or her."

"Our finances, thanks to you, are the best they've ever been. I do keep in touch with my friend, Justin. He might be interested, and he and I once formed a band called The Midnighters."

"Speaking of finances, I really do want a pool and a tennis court."

"I'll look into that since you have your hands full. I think we'll have to wait until spring to start on the outside projects. And I'm just wondering…"

"When the wedding will be?"

"Yes, my darling. Can't we just go get married?"

"No. I still want to have it in the spring. It's too cold now that winter is approaching. I want to concentrate on getting everything finished so we can invite our parents for an official visit. And Nannie said she would like to come, too."

"Okay. I'll try to be patient. I just don't see making a big fuss."

"Braden Cunningham, I'll say it again. I only plan to get married one time, and I am going to have the wedding of my dreams." The look she gave her fiancé silenced him.

Braden ducked his head and grinned. "I think I'll go check on the horses."

Before Braden realized it, autumn had turned to winter. Where had the summer gone? For that matter, where had autumn gone? Two weeks later, Braden came home from school and put his tote bag by the hall table, ready to start his Christmas break. Before he could ask whose car was in the carriageway, an aroma assaulted him, and his stomach began to beg for whatever was cooking. He found Ellie in the kitchen nook with a tall, very distinguished-looking man in a white apron and a hat that billowed out like a hot air balloon ready for takeoff. Ellie jumped up to introduce him.

"Meet our potential new chef. May I present Chef Finn Turner."

Braden rubbed his hands down the side of his trousers before extending his hand. "Pleased to meet you. If you cooked what I'm smelling, I'm very much impressed."

Ellie nodded. "I told him to be prepared to cook and serve a meal. I gave him money, and he had to furnish the ingredients to stay within the budget. He agreed to keep them secret until he started cooking, and he could not ask us for our favorite foods or anything. The only thing he asked me was if we were allergic to anything. I also wanted him to make dinner in this small kitchen to see if he could manage as well as he could in the Big Kitchen."

213

Braden turned to Chef Finn. "Did that make you nervous, sir?"

"Oh, no, sir. I have cooked for some important people and entertained elite crowds in New York City as well as small, intimate dinner parties. I'm confident and comfortable in any kitchen The meal should be ready in fifteen minutes if that is satisfactory?"

Braden grinned. "Fine with me. I'll just freshen up a bit and meet you two in the dining room."

Sitting at the table, Ellie glanced at Braden. She was afraid she had overstepped her bounds by having this man here without consulting Braden. "I'm sorry I didn't warn you he was coming. I had several chefs apply, and I narrowed them down. He is the one that impressed me the most, and he wants to relocate to the south. I hope you're not angry with me."

"Where is he working now? What restaurant?"

"He has been working in New York, but he said it is just too cold there, literally and figuratively, and the competition among chefs is so fierce that he just didn't enjoy it any longer. He gave notice a month ago, so Friday of last week was his last day there. He started driving south as soon as he finished his job."

Braden took Ellie's hand. "I could never be upset with you. If his food is as good as it smells, I think he will have my vote! But how did he get here so fast? Does he have family?"

"I was going to mention to you that he was coming for an interview, but we got busy, and you had all those pre-Christmas parties. It just slipped my mind to tell you. I'm sorry, but to answer your question, I put a few ads in some culinary magazines a week ago. Chef Finn has relatives in Vicksburg and was headed our way to visit them. He stopped for the night halfway here and opened some mail he had picked up in New York. He saw my ad and called me from a hotel on the road to arrange the interview. He arrived yesterday in Vicksburg, spent the night with his relatives, and drove here this morning. His wife and child got a strain of flu that was prevalent in New York and died within days of each other. Another reason he wanted to leave. He is going to have their ashes spread in Vicksburg."

"What impressed you about him?"

214

"He seems genuine. Several who applied seemed too uppity for me. Most of them had demands that I just didn't feel would fit us, not to mention the salary they demanded. I asked him to just prepare an entrée."

Chef Finn appeared holding a tray with two plates. "For your dining pleasure, may I present duck gratin with a cheese souffle and herbed haricot verts. Please enjoy, and when you are finished, it will be my honor to serve a fruit compote to cleanse your palette."

Braden looked at his plate. "He served the duck and the cheese souffle in their own little dishes with the green beans on the side. What was he talking about herbed something?"

Ellie laughed. "The green beans are called haricots verts. This is pretty fancy if you ask me."

"Yes, indeed, but it is also delicious. If he wants the job, he's got it as far as I'm concerned. I was kind of thinking about seeing if Justin would move to Scottsville, but I doubt he would have. He's been looking for a job ever since he just graduated from culinary school."

"Let's keep him in mind. He might want to be a sous chef."

After the fruit compote, they invited Chef Finn to the parlor. An agreement was reached quickly, and he was delighted to move into the Inn that evening. He met Doug, and they seemed to get along fine.

Later sitting by the fire in the parlor, Ellie turned to Braden. "I have also been working on our wedding plans. I'm not really sure I want to wait until spring. How would you feel about a winter wedding?"

"Like Christmas?"

"No, silly, I can't be ready in two weeks. I'm thinking February on Valentine's Day."

Braden grinned. "Hearts. I get it."

"Since we have everything in place, except the swimming pool and tennis courts, I would like to invite our parents before our grand opening January the first. Maybe Christmas here again this year?"

Braden called his parents and sister, and Ellie called her parents. Everyone agreed they wanted to come for Christmas. Even Nannie said she felt like coming.

All the guests arrived early on the morning of Christmas Eve. The weather had turned warmer which made it easier on Nannie's joints. Braden rushed to help her out of the car. Her cheeks were rosy red.

"Are you cold, Nannie?"

"No, I'm just excited to be here. The mansion looks wonderful. I can't wait to see inside."

Braden practically carried her up the steps and situated her in the parlor. Would you like some hot chocolate, Nannie…anyone?"

"That would be lovely. I want to rest a bit and then look at everything. I wish I could make it to the little house by the river, but I don't think my knees would hold up. Where is Ellie?"

"She will be here shortly."

Preston and Mason opted for coffee, and Cynthia, Charity, and Emma chose hot chocolate.

Braden turned to Susan. "Aren't you having anything?"

"Not right now. I need to help Ellie with something."

A few minutes later Chef Finn appeared with a silver tray. Steaming cups of coffee flanked by a sugar bowl and creamer, and hot chocolate that was served with coconut ice cream snowballs on a bed of toasted coconut surrounded by whipped cream warmed everyone.

Braden cleared his throat. "Everyone, please meet and welcome our wonderful chef, Chef Finn Turner."

The chef bowed. "Very pleased to meet all of you."

Nannie looked around, clearly impressed. "I love that you opened up the two rooms. I think if I were younger, I could waltz all around this room!"

Susan excused herself and went upstairs. Ellie had asked Susan to help in showcasing some of the dresses from the Sullivans that she had found in the Attic Box. She chose a rose-colored gown, and Susan put on a festive green one. Susan had asked Braden to put on some Christmas music after the hot chocolate was served, and as it started, everyone let out a gasp as the two young ladies floated down the stairs.

Nannie's eyes teared. "Oh, this takes me back. You look just like pictures I've seen of the Sullivan girls, Grace and Maggie."

Ellie smiled. "We wanted you to have the full effect of our grand opening. Of course, Braden will be in black trousers and a long coat for the actual opening."

Just before lunch, Charity asked Mason to bring in a box from the car. With it sitting in front of her, she opened it. Tissue paper peeked out.

"Braden, I told you I'd tell you about Scottsville when the time was right. I think this is it. So, if I have everyone's attention, I'd like to reveal some of the secrets of this grand old house and the Sullivans who lived here."

Everyone nodded. "Please, Nannie, go on."

CHAPTER TWENTY-EIGHT

Charity took a sip of her hot chocolate, blotted her lips with the linen beverage napkin, and began. "I met the love of my life here. Roman Cunningham was the most handsome man I had ever seen. I would stay here in the summer with my grandparents, and our church invited a youth ministry group from his town near Mobile, Alabama, to hold a three-day revival here. They were staying with some people who agreed to watch over them. Roman was the song leader, and he smiled at me the first night. After the first service, he asked if he could take me to lunch the next day. Missus Porter went with us as a chaperone, and we had a lovely time, but I couldn't tell you one thing we ate. All I saw were Roman's beautiful eyes. We couldn't go out on our own unless the family knew the boy and his family. Not like young folks do these days. For the next two days, I sat on the front row. After the revival, we wrote every week until he moved here, and we got married right here in this very parlor."

Braden's brow knitted together. "So, you knew the Sullivans who lived here?"

"Yes, my grandmother, Hope, and my grandfather, Bruce Walsh, lived here to take care of Abe and Sarah Sullivan when they returned from Ireland." Charity looked hard at Braden to see if he was comprehending her words. My mother, Faith, and my father, Harry Ryan, moved to Vicksburg when I was a baby. We would come back every year for a reunion. We stayed at the little house, as we called it. After we married, Roman and I lived in Alabama."

Mason and Braden exchanged looks as the light dawned with Charity's revelation. Braden spoke. "Do you mean…"

Charity laughed. "Yes, Braden, you are the third generation down from Grace and Jim."

Mason looked dumbfounded. "Why didn't you ever tell me about this?"

Charity had an impish grin on her face. "You never asked. And when I would start to mention something, you said you weren't interested. You thought I made up all those stories, didn't you?"

Mason hung his head and in a low voice, said, "Yes, I did. They sounded like some fairy tale. I wondered more about the Cunningham side of the family."

Ellie excused herself to ask Chef Finn to serve lunch.

"Well, Mason, perhaps that's where you get your carpentry skills, and Braden gets his writing skills."

Braden still looked shocked. "But you don't know if I have writing skills."

"Yes, I do. I have written a book if anyone cares to read it, and when you were just a wee little thing, you'd tell me made-up stories. I knew you have talent. Perhaps you won't wait as long as I did to write."

Ellie sighed. "It's been quite a morning. Lunch is ready."

After Mason said the blessing, Chef Finn served a steaming bowl of French Onion Soup with crusty biscuits followed by roasted chicken, Hasselback potatoes, and a cranberry orange salad. They had asked Doug and Chef Finn to eat with them.

Charity's eyes misted.

"What is it, Nannie?" Braden touched her arm to get her attention.

"It just reminds me of stories my grandmother told me about how Lavitica June and her sister, Bessie would come out and make Christmas dinner for everyone."

Ellie asked, "Did they live in Scottsville?"

"Yes, after the war, they opened a little café. They had a large following of people. Their mama, Miss Daisy, had taught them her famous recipes. They took over here when Miss Daisy was too sick to cook. They were workers and lived here."

Mason asked, "What happened to the rest of them?"

"Let's see if I can remember what I heard all through the years. Oh, yes, Maggie, Grace's younger sister, taught Essie Mae how to design and sew clothes. As soon as she could, she moved to New York and went to work for a large designer shop. Lizzie opened a private school for black students in the little house by the river. Each bedroom was designated a grade. And, of course, Jim and Grace went to Ireland before coming back here with the rest of the family to farm what was left of the land. Jim was a woodworker and made custom furniture for people, so that's passed down to you, Mason, and now Braden. Jim's brother, Willie, helped him farm."

Ellie and Braden exchanged looks. Ellie said, "Who were Bessie, Lizzie, and Willie? We haven't found them in Grace's journals."

"They were workers. That's another story. They were actually Daisy's children that had been sold to a mean man and then to another nice owner before Abe bought them."

Emma looked at Charity. "You look tired. Why don't you go take a nap while we help clean up these dishes?"

Ellie and Braden rushed to help Nannie to her bed. Braden placed a kiss on her hand. "Rest, now, Nannie. Please tell us more when you feel up to it."

"I'm getting out of doing dishes, aren't I? She grinned.

Braden laughed. "Why, yes, you are! But we can always save some for you."

Charity laughed. "I guess I'll pass."

After a nap, Nannie moved into the parlor with the rest of the family. Braden stood up. "Nannie, I have a surprise for you."

"What is it? Don't make me wait too long 'cause I'm not getting any younger sitting here."

"How would you like to see the little house, as you call it? We call it The Inn at Pebble Creek."

"I'd love to see the Inn, but I can't walk that far, I don't think."

"That's the surprise." Braden moved to her, bowed, and offered his hand to her. He and Ellie helped her stand. "Your carriage awaits, m'lady."

Emma had found a carriage reminiscent of the early 1900's in an antique store. They thought it would be nice to have it for buggy rides for the guests. Braden and Doug made a four-handed seat and carried Charity down the steps and helped her into the carriage with Ellie following. Doug drove them to the Inn.

Charity gasped as Doug opened the double doors for them. "Oh, this is beautiful. I love this house. It brings back so many memories. I wish I could go upstairs."

Doug and Braden again made a four-handed seat and carried Charity upstairs. She entered the first bedroom with windows that looked out on the river. "This was my favorite room. My cousin and I had twin beds in here."

"Nannie, we can't see all the rooms because one of them is Chef Finn's room and another one is Doug's."

"But I got to see my favorite!"

Braden looked at Ellie. "This makes me think. I wonder if we should put in elevators?"

"But where? I don't know where we would put one without it taking up valuable space."

Braden's eyes held a faraway look. "We could do an outside glass one that would open to the upstairs on both houses like they've done with some big businesses and hotels."

Ellie sighed. "There goes the swimming pool and tennis court. But would they take away from the historical elements of the houses?"

Charity interrupted. "You could put them on the back of the Big House and the side of the Inn. How much would the elevators cost?"

"I don't know. We'd have to research it." Braden ran his hands through his hair.

Ellie said, "We have enough money for the pool and tennis court, so we could use that if it's enough. And it would increase our guest list for those who couldn't climb stairs."

Charity smoothed her dress. "It would be nice for older guests to have an elevator, especially since most of the bedrooms are upstairs."

Elli brightened. "And if it's glass on the outside, the scenery would be beautiful in the spring and summer...and maybe the fall. Not sure about winter, though."

Back in the Big House, everyone wanted to know more history. Charity situated herself on the sofa in the parlor and held court.

"First, I'll start with Abe and Sarah and then Grace and Jim. I know Grace wrote in journals most of her life. I have some of her later ones, which I'll give to you to complete the little booklet you are doing on the history of the Sullivans, Braden."

"Thank you, Nannie."

"Abe and Sarah had the roughest time just before the Great War Between the States, or the Civil War as it is now called. There was nothing civil about it. It was a blood bath with innocent people mowed down like waist-high weeds. They decided to go back to Ireland before the war broke out, but every time they thought they had a buyer, it fell through.

"They had a young man who came to live with them. He had protected Joseph from getting killed, so they gave him a job. Think his name was Cal. He was a very devout young man and advised them to stay in Scottsville. He had the gifts of discernment and healing and was quite extraordinary. He advised them on numerous occasions, and Abe finally gave him his name and sort of adopted him into the family, so his last name was Sullivan. Anyway, they stayed through the war. This house was used as a command center, rather than a hospital, so that was a blessing. Cal had warned them to build an additional shelter, so that's when they hurried and built the little house where they lived until the war was over. It was kind of strange because Cal just up and left one day with a note of Bible verses in Grace's journal."

Mason noticed Charity getting emotional so he interrupted. "Mother, you seem to be getting tired. I think we should stop for a while and open presents to give your voice a break."

After a light supper of vegetable beef soup, crusty cornbread squares, and a salad, followed by a cherry cobbler with sweetened heavy cream to pour over it, Charity resumed her discourse on the history of Oak Hollow. She pulled a beautiful lavender dress with a lace collar out of the box. There was a note attached, apparently written by Grace. "This is the dress I wore when we announced our engagement. We had a handfasting ceremony with just our parents." Charity laid it on the sofa beside her.

Carefully, she pulled out a sky-blue silk dress. The high-necked bodice was covered with Irish lace that extended to the arms, ending in points over the hands. The skirt of the dress billowed out like a soft cloud. Along the bottom silver embroidered Celtic knots, intertwined with white shamrocks and roses circled the entire hem. Its simplicity was stunning. "This was Grace's wedding gown." She turned back the hem. "Good luck charms were included in most wedding gowns. As you can

223

see, there is a tiny silver horseshoe sewn into the hem for England, an embroidered thistle for Scotland, a shamrock for Ireland, and a daffodil for Wales to honor the entire United Kingdom. Each person who has worn it has their name and date embroidered on the petticoat. It is the same gown her mother, Sarah, wore, and her dau…"

Ellie interrupted. "But I read in her journal that she married in a white dress with a red ribbon sash. Did she have two gowns?"

Charity smiled. "No, she never considered that white dress as a wedding gown. White wedding dresses were considered mourning clothes, and brides who wore white were said to be sad, perhaps for having to marry someone chosen for them. The Scotts didn't dare complain about the white dress, but they were happy for the red sash as that was a happy color for brides. They didn't know, to Grace's way of thinking, it symbolized her blood she shed to rescue the family's failing finances. Blue was thought to represent purity and commitment. This gown has been handed down for generations for any Sullivan girl to wear if she chooses. This gown was what Grace considered her wedding gown when she and Jim married."

The women all rose to feel the beautiful fabric. Emma sighed and addressed Susan. "I doubt you will want to continue the tradition. How I wish you would."

Susan smiled. "We'll see. I need to have a groom first!"

Charity's smile lit up the room. "My mother, Faith, and my grandmother, Hope, also wore this gown just as I did when I married Roman! It's like putting on our history."

Ellie had an idea, but she didn't want to voice it. She would wait until she could get Charity alone. She turned her attention back to Braden's grandmother.

"And," Charity lifted a beautiful white wool cape, "this was her cape." It had a large Celtic cross on the back embroidered in shimmering sky blue with Celtic knots along the hem.

Mason asked, "Mother, what happened to the children? I'm sorry I never got to meet all my cousins."

"I know up to a point, but I've lost contact with a lot of our relatives. Matthew was the artist, as you know. He and Mary had two boys and two girls and moved to Paris where he showed in some prestigious galleries. Maggie and Charles had two girls and one boy. They moved to Jackson, and he built high-end houses. Maggie started a house of fashion there and added a school for designers later. Essie Mae came back and helped her teach. Joe and Becca stayed in Clinton, where he practiced medicine. They had three sons and two daughters."

Braden asked, "But what about Grace?"

"Jim and Grace had two children, a boy named Finn, and my grandmother named Hope. They married in Ireland and had their children there. When Finn was a toddler, and Hope was a baby, they moved back and lived here in the Big House with Abe, Sarah, and my grandparents. Jim and Grace lived here for about two years, I think, until a horrible storm came through. It came out of nowhere so suddenly it caught everyone off guard. Finn was playing outside, and Jim went to find him. He was down by the pecan orchard. Just as he grabbed Finn, a large tree fell and pinned him on top of the young boy. After the storm subsided, Grace found them. Finn was fine, but Jim was knocked out for a while. When they got him to the house, they discovered he had extensive damage. He lost all feeling in his arms and legs and had severe damage to his lungs. He was never the same after that. Grace cared for him for two months night and day, but he couldn't fight any longer, and he passed away. Grace couldn't manage the large house, the farm, and two small children even with my grandfather's help, so she went to live with Maggie and Charles. She said she couldn't bear to be here because she saw Jim every time she turned around. She died at Charles and Maggie's house a month later without ever stepping foot back on Oak Hollow soil until they brought her back to be buried by Jim. Everyone said the day Jim died, Grace did, too, and she passed from a broken heart. Maggie and Charles took Finn and my grandmother in and treated them as their own. Of course, nether Finn or my mother remembered Grace or Jim. My grandparents stayed on here until Abe and Sarah died, and then when they couldn't manage the farm any longer, they moved to Vicksburg to be close to my parents. That's when the mansion was abandoned and went to rack and ruin."

Mason, overcome with emotion cleared his throat. "So, Jim and Grace are buried here?"

"Yes, he told Grace some of the best times he had was singing in the tabernacle. When he knew he was dying, he hardly had enough breath to talk, but he asked Grace to bury him in the tabernacle."

225

Braden asked, "Why didn't they bury them in the circle where they had so many good times?"

"Grace told Maggie that she and Jim wanted to keep the circle as a monument of their love, not a place to mourn."

"Do you think we might find their burial place?" Ellie swiped tears away with her thumbs.

"I'm sure you can. I heard from my cousin a long time ago, that the tabernacle was destroyed by lightning. All you'd have to do is remove all that rotted lumber, and you'd probably find the graves. Each grave had a wooden plaque with a small pink heart made out of the river-washed stones in the middle. Their names were inscribed in the middle of the hearts."

"So, you saw the graves?" Ellie gave Braden a look, and he knew she wanted to find them.

"Yes, Ellie. We used to go back for reunions, as I said, and we'd stay in the Inn and have a memorial the day we left."

Braden rose and stretched. "This is so interesting, Nannie, but you must be very tired."

"I am. But I'm glad you know now why I didn't go into all of this when you were growing up."

"I'm curious, though, how we all ended up in Tuscaloosa."

"Roman and I moved there because he got a job as postmaster. After my grandparents died, my mother and father, Faith and Ryan, moved from Vicksburg to Tuscaloosa to be close to us."

CHAPTER TWENTY-NINE

Ellie stood. "I think we should open our gifts before it gets too late, if that's agreeable to everyone." She knew her father and Braden's grandmother were getting tired.

Chef Finn brought in a tray of his famous hot chocolate and shortbread cookies dusted with red and green sugar.

As was their custom, Braden read the second chapter of Luke while everyone finished their snacks.

Braden and Ellie made short order of distributing the gifts. Everyone had agreed on just small items since they knew Ellie and Braden were saving as much money as they could. Once the gifts were opened, and after laughing and reminiscing, Braden rose and wished everyone a happy Christmas Eve.

Ellie stood by Braden's side and said, "I think it's time to call it a night. When you climb into bed, do not be surprised, but warm metal bed warmers have been placed at the foot of your bed to warm your feet. You can move them to any place in the bed you want to warm. It was a tradition we have chosen to incorporate for our guests. Let us know what you think in the morning!"

Christmas morning found everyone in a jovial mood as they made their way to the dining room. Instead of a tablecloth, Ellie had put placemats for everyone, making sure the Celtic designs around the table were evident. Ellie and Braden had decided to give Chef Finn a break and prepare breakfast in the small kitchen since he was going to have to make a large Christmas dinner in the Big Kitchen. They asked Chef Finn for ideas. They got up at the crack of dawn to start the preparations. They made mini omelets, biscuits and gravy, waffles, grits, bacon, and sausage. They also had a table of sweets including blueberry muffins, apple dumplings, and yogurt with fresh fruit.

Since Doug didn't want to spend time with his family, he and the chef were invited to join them for breakfast and the large dinner.

Sitting at the table, Charity ran her hand over the Celtic designs. "I remember this table."

Emma smiled. "We found it and the little kitchen table in the attic. Ellie and I brought them down and refinished them. Do you know the story behind them?"

"Oh, yes. Abraham had this dining room table designed and presented it to Sarah as her first gift in their new house. The kitchen one with the name Sullivan on it was made from a huge pecan tree that was uprooted during a severe storm that took the life of Abe's parents. He hired a woodworker to design a table from the inner rings of the tree with the edges being cutout pecan leaves. I think it is just as pretty as the dining room table."

Ellie commented, "We love them both, and especially the name Sullivan burned into it."

Mason ran his hands along the Celtic designs as well, his mind working on ideas he had. "Maybe we could make something similar for the Inn, Braden."

Ellie's eyes lit up. "What a great idea. We could burn Cunningham into the edge of the table, and maybe someone a hundred years from now will be as intrigued as we are with the history of what we've done!"

Braden sighed. "Sounds great Ellie, but let's do it later, Dad. We're tired, and we're going to try to open the first of January, so your visit is our first before the grand opening as you requested."

Preston smiled. "It is so nice to hear all the history of this place and for you to include us in your Christmas celebration."

Cynthia nodded her head and turned to Emma. "What a beautiful transformation you and Ellie have created."

"Thank you." Emma's face radiated her pleasure at Cynthia's compliment.

Ellie turned to Chef Finn. "You said your family lived in Mississippi when you were growing up. What town did you say?'

Finn looked a little uncomfortable and cleared his throat. "We lived in Vicksburg, but I have a confession. I searched my ancestry. I was born to Erin and Collin Turner, but I was named after my great grandfather, Finn Sullivan. His father was Jim Sullivan, and his mother was Grace Sullivan. After I came here, I connected the dots and realized that I may be related to your family of Sullivans. Or maybe it was a different family, but it was such a feeling of awe when I came to interview. I haven't asked, but I wonder if I might spread my wife and daughter's ashes down by the river."

Braden, emotion clouding his face, nodded until he found his voice. "Of course, you may. Or, if you prefer, you may bury them on the property."

Charity's hands flew to her face. "I'll bet you are related! This mansion just keeps pulling people back. I wonder if any others will come back. Wouldn't that be grand? Would you and Emma come back, Mason? You own your own business now."

"No, Mom. I don't think so, but I guess I should never say never, huh?"

Braden laughed. "Should we call you Cousin Finn at home and Chef Finn to our guests?"

Finn returned the laughter. "That would suit me. I do feel very much at peace here, and truth be known, I would have accepted any salary you offered because of the feeling I got when I first arrived…like I was home. I do appreciate living in the Inn and the generous salary you are providing."

Charity looked at Ellie. "Have you two set a wedding date?"

Ellie answered, "Yes, we have decided on the fourteenth of February. It will pay tribute to the heart of stones Jim made for Grace, and it's Valentine's Day, a day for lovers. But what we'd like to do after brunch is have a handfasting ceremony to celebrate our engagement."

Charity nodded. "Yes, I love that Irish custom. We must do it."

Braden grinned. "Nannie, since we don't have an officiant, will you do the honors?"

"I'd be delighted."

Charity had asked them to pick three ribbons or cords in colors that mattered to them. They went to Doug because he was always tinkering with something and had learned to braid cords to go on his saddle. He showed them different colors. Ellie chose a sky-blue cord that would remind her of the gown she would wear, Braden chose white to remind him how pure his love for Ellie was, now that white no longer held a negative connotation, and together, they chose purple to remind them of how sacred their vows were.

Ellie and Braden had written simple vows. Standing in front of the parlor fireplace, Ellie embraced her parents and said, "I'm so happy you are here."

Cynthia's voice cracked. "What a blessing."

Emma had carried a camera to the parlor and placed it on her chair.

When they handed Charity the cords, she invited Preston and Cynthia, Emma and Mason, and Susan to drape them over Ellie and Braden's hands. Then she took the cords in one hand, holding on to the other end. She wrapped them in a special way, over and under and made a loose knot. Then she cleared her throat, and Emma took a picture.

"Let me see if I can remember this. I think it goes something like this." She put her hands on top of theirs. "Now that you have joined your hands and made a knot, so that your lives and love are bound one to the other, may this knot always remind you of your commitment and the vows you will make today. May you always renew your love with each day that passes. Remember these hands will love you, these hands will comfort you and wipe away your sadness, these hands will rejoice together in happy times, these hands will give you strength and protection when storms arise, and these hands will tenderly hold your children and each other as you grow old."

Braden looked at Ellie. "I cannot imagine being any happier since you agreed to marry me. I promise to love and cherish you all the days of my life. I promise to try to make each day one of joy, and I will protect you always, with my life if necessary. I will hold you always when times aren't so good, and we'll see them through together. I will be faithful, truthful, and loving, holding nothing back from you. I commit my body, soul, and heart to you forever. These are my vows to you, my betrothed."

Ellie sighed as a tear slipped down her cheek. "I shudder to think I almost lost you, but I am so happy you knew what I really wanted, and that was to be your wife. I promise to be true and faithful, to be with you whatever the future holds, through good times and bad, and I never want to be apart from you. I promise to uphold you in any decision you make and to go where you go. I promise to make our home one of warmth and joy, to be the best wife I can, and to be the best mother if we are blessed with children. I commit my body, soul, and heart to you. These are my vows to you, my betrothed."

Charity ended with a prayer for their happiness, prosperity, and long life.

After the ceremony, Ellie invited Susan to go for a horseback ride. "I'd like to show you the land, the heart of stones, and where we plan to have croquet, the pool, and tennis courts."

"I'm ready." The two girls changed into slacks and sweaters and charged out the door, laughing and giggling. Once they visited with Doug and mounted their horses, Susan took a deep breath. "I want you to know how happy I am that you and Braden are together. He is so into history, and you are a natural decorator, so I think this venture is the best, but…."

"What?"

"It's nothing, really. I just know that Braden gets bored easily, and I just hope he doesn't bail on everything now that the repairs are finished. He always wanted to live in a big city."

Ellie laughed. "I don't think he will. He loves rummaging around in the attic and reading all the papers Abe left behind as well as Grace's journals. Only I fear we have read all of them unless there are some we've missed. And he has been promoted at school to teach English and drama in high school, so he is very excited. And then there's the novel he wants to write, plus the booklet about the Sullivans, not to mention being a host to our guests."

"That's a relief. That should keep him occupied."

They stopped their horses by the woods and tied them to some low hanging branches. "Come, and I'll show you the heart of stones. Braden had it enclosed in acrylic and placed in cement so we can stand on it."

Susan did a quick intake of breath. "It's beautiful, almost like it's alive."

Ellie nodded. "There's one more thing." They were sitting on the wrought iron bench. "I'm wondering if you would be my maid of honor. If you don't want to, I'll understand."

Susan grabbed her in a big hug. "I would love to. I thought you would want your closest friends."

"That's what you're becoming and even more like a sister I never had!"

"I feel that way, too. I guess we'd better get back. I think we are leaving tomorrow, and I need to pack. I've scattered things all over my room."

"There's one last thing. Braden shared that you told him you were thinking of changing careers."

Susan laughed sarcastically and twisted her mouth. "Yes, I haven't said anything to my parents, but being a social worker is a lot of physical and emotional stress."

"I'd love to see what you do sometimes. I understand you place some children in foster homes before they are adopted."

"Yes, and most of the time, it's sad. A few are very cruel, and we try to get the children a new placement, but a lot of them are just perfunctory sitters. It breaks my heart to know I can't always find a good temporary home for them. The thought that all they want is a home to call their own, maybe a toy or two, and someone to hug them."

Tears welled in Ellie's eyes. "I don't think I could do your job. I'd like to visit you and maybe see what a foster home looks like." Ellie didn't mention she wanted to see if she thought adoption would be in their future since she had learned it was unlikely she would be able to conceive.

"I think I could arrange it, but confidentiality is crucial. When would you like to visit and why?"

Ellie had to think fast. "I want to talk to Braden and see if we might qualify as foster parents. I was thinking maybe we could set aside a weekend and invite some foster parents and the children to a free weekend here. I trust you to select the best ones."

"Oh, Ellie, what a generous idea. That would make such an impression on the children. And I can't even begin to tell you how much the adults would relish it. Why don't you come to Birmingham, and I'll arrange for you to see some of the families I deal with? You can come as a potential volunteer and we can decide which families, if any, you would like to invite. That way, I won't be violating any confidentiality."

"How about next weekend? I think Braden is working on a play in his elementary drama class, and he is spending a lot of time with the students. Also, I've never been to Birmingham, and maybe I could get some brochures of businesses there to market for The Sullivan House."

"Good. I'll count on it. Mind you, though, I'm not a cook. I have so enjoyed Chef Finn's meals!"

"Don't worry about that. I know my way around a kitchen, so we won't starve!"

After dinner, Ellie pulled Braden to his bedroom. "I want to run something by you. Susan told me about how sad it is for foster kids. It's a big secret, but she may want to change careers as you know. I want to go with her when she visits her charges, and maybe later, invite a few of the foster parents and the children for a free weekend." Though she couldn't make eye contact, fear covered Ellie's face no matter how hard she tried to conceal it.

"Ellie, I know you. You want to see what children would be like when we decide to adopt. I do like your idea, and I think it's a good thing."

"I just don't know if an adopted child would feel we are the real parents. What if he or she doesn't like us? Should we get a baby or an older child? What if the biological parents want them back?"

Braden embraced her. "Oh, my sweet Ellie. How could any child not long to have you for a mother? And how blessed they would feel. But you have enough on your mind with the wedding, don't you?"

Ellie sighed. "I am fearful that I will fail as a mother."

"You won't, my sweet. Relax. Go next weekend, if that's what you want. I'm busy with school right now. I'll miss you, but I have enough to keep me busy for a few days."

"Okay, I need to go check on a few things. Just don't reveal my real reason, please."

Braden drew her to him and kissed her. "It's our secret."

Ellie went to the kitchen to see if their new maid needed any help cleaning up. They had hired a sous chef to help with the meals, but they had given him and Finn the week off after their guests left. After assuring her everything was fine, she went in search of Charity.

She found her sitting on the sofa with Braden, their heads buried in papers from the Sullivans to get ideas for his novel. He smiled at Ellie. "Nannie is filling in some blanks for me, but I need to go check on Doug and the horses." He reached over and gave her cheek a quick peck. "See you in a little while."

Ellie sat next to Charity. "I have something to ask you, but please be honest with me."

Charity got a faraway look. "You want to wear Grace's real wedding gown?"

"Would you consider that, even though I'm not blood related to the Sullivans?"

"Of course, my dear. Marriage makes you one of us." She paused and had a cute little sparkle in her eye. "But I don't think Braden will want to wear a kilt, even though we do have a tartan, and Jim's is in the box!"

Ellie laughed. "I can pretty much get him to do what I want, but I agree with you! He's not the kilt wearing kind of man! Can we keep it a secret? I want to surprise Braden."

"Of course, and in the bottom of this box are more of Grace's journals. I think I've told you most of what's in there, though. You know I was dubbed the record keeper by the family and the secrets this old house held years ago. I think we all wanted history preserved. And since I like to write, that's what my book is about. And that's why I'm excited that you are resurrecting our history."

"Thank you. I was thinking of having kind of a shadow box and putting Grace's journal in there under glass, but with it opened so they could see her handwriting. I would never reveal a page that held secrets or anything too personal. I would also like to showcase your book!"

Charity got a faraway look in her eyes. "I'm sure it would please Grace for you to be the next one to wear the dress and for Braden to carry on the history. I will leave the box with you, and you can slip the gown and cape out to be cleaned and altered, if necessary, when Braden isn't looking!"

"Thank you so much. I love you. I hope you will be able to come for the wedding."

"I wouldn't miss it."

As soon as everyone left, Ellie went to strip all the beds so the maid could wash them when she came in the next day. She noticed a piece of

paper on top of the dresser in the room
Charity slept in. Picking it up, she saw a note and a check.

The note read. "I want to come more often, and I want an elevator for both houses. Use this money to get them, but if it's not enough, let me know. You had better cash this. Don't make an old woman mad. You know I still have a lot of sass."

Ellie ran to tell Braden.

"That's so like Nannie. I'll call and see how much two would cost and when they can be installed."

CHAPTER THIRTY

On the way home, with Charity asleep in the back seat, Emma turned to Mason and whispered, "So many things have come to light and make sense now. You know we aren't as young as we used to be, and I was thinking maybe we could move a little closer to Scottsville, so your mom could visit as often as she'd like."

"Emma, that would please me since I've found that I have a real connection to the mansion, but I can't leave a business I started, and I have more clients than I thought possible."

"You could sell your business and our house. I just feel your mom needs those memories to come alive when she visits. I think it would give her something to look forward to." Emma thought about her own parents and how much they had sacrificed for her before they were killed in a freak automobile accident the first year after she and Mason married.

"I'll think about it."

"It's the least we can do for her. You know how special she is to me. Like my own mother."

Mason grew quiet. "I know," he whispered.

Mason concentrated on the road, weighed pros and cons of what it would be like to uproot their ties and move away. In order for him to start all over, they'd need to live in Vicksburg or Jackson. Scottsville wasn't large enough to support a construction company. Every time he thought of a reason to honor Emma's wishes, another negative thought would push to the front of his brain. He was tired. He'd think it over at home when he was more rested. He glanced at Emma, her eyes full of hope and love. He made his decision, but he'd go slow and sleep on it to make sure he wasn't making a mistake before he told Emma.

Once they were unpacked and had gotten Charity settled, Mason made an excuse to go to his shop to check on things. He knelt in prayer, "Father, please guide me as to what to do. I feel a sense of duty to my clients, but I want to honor my mother as You said in Your Word, and I want to please my wife as You also said. I'm turning this over to You. In Jesus' name I pray. Amen." He called Preston Addison. "Am I calling at a bad time?"

"No, I work exclusively from home, now, so I can pick and choose how much I work. What's up?"

Mason told him his plans and asked his opinion.

Preston sounded excited. "I think it would be wonderful. The kids…I mean Ellie and Braden could visit both of us if we're in the same city, or we could celebrate together on holidays. I have a few contacts that I could pass on to you that might help you with your business. One is a locally famous builder. Name's Clint Weston. I'm sure he would be delighted with your work. Got a pen? Here's his information."

"Wow. That's more than I expected. I'll phone him, and make an appointment and go for an eye-to-eye meeting. I'm not going to tell Emma until I know if it will work out. Thank you, Preston."

Emma went to Charity's room. "I'd like to know what you really thought about what Ellie and Braden have done with Oak Hollow."

"I was very anxious before we got there. I thought they would have all modern furniture and had turned it into an apartment complex or like a hotel with just rooms for sleeping. When I saw that they had kept most of the furniture that I remember, yet made it more suited to modern living, I fell in love with it. I love that they opened the parlor and dining room, and that they kept the tables. I think they are forward thinking that people would want to have a quiet vacation spot and step back in time."

"Or a wedding."

"Yes. I am looking forward to going to the first wedding there." Charity's eyes sparkled.

"I've mentioned something to Mason, but he seems hesitant to commit to me. This house seems kind of lonely since the kids are gone, and it's almost too much for me to keep up with. I mentioned I wouldn't be opposed to moving closer to Scottsville."

Charity's face lit up. "I'd like that, too. Where were you thinking?"

"Vicksburg or Jackson would be big enough that Mason could start a new company."

"I'm not getting my hopes up, but it would be nice to be able to visit Scottsville more often. Makes me feel a little younger. You know you are such a blessing to me, Emma, and I love you like my own."

"I wanted to tell you my thoughts, but let's keep it to ourselves." Emma suppressed tears.

The next week on Tuesday, Mason came into the kitchen before breakfast. "Emma, I'd like to run something by you. I think there might be some unfinished things at The Sullivan House that I'd like to help Braden with. I may make a hurried trip there and see if I can help him."

"I'll call the sitter for your mom and go with you."

"I'd like that, but I don't think I can take the time to visit. I just need to make sure everything is okay for the opening, and then I'm coming back home. I have a lot of orders to catch up on. I may spend the night, but I'll be home tomorrow." He didn't mention that he was really going to Jackson for an eye-to-eye with Clint Weston and that he had already talked to him on the phone. He also didn't mention that he had put out feelers to sell his business or that he wanted to see if Ellie could find them a home.

"Okay. I know Braden's Christmas break is almost over, and he is due back in school right after the first, so you're probably right that we wouldn't have time to visit."

On the way to Jackson, Mason stopped in Scottsville. When Ellie answered the door, he said, "Hi, Ellie, sorry to drop in unannounced, but I wonder if I might talk to you."

"Of course. Come in." She looked into his eyes, and fear gripped her. Something was wrong. She took a deep breath and prepared herself.

"First is there anything here that needs a final touch before you open?"

"No, just the brochure, the booklet, and a couple of pictures to frame. Why?"

Mason told her about talking to her dad and the information he furnished. "I'm having a meeting with Mister Weston today, but I don't want to say anything to Emma until after I meet with him. I'm wondering

239

if you could keep an eye out for a house that you think might suit our needs."

Ellie exhaled a huge cleansing breath. "That would be wonderful. I do a lot of business in Jackson. What size are you thinking?"

"At least three bedrooms, two baths, and if it had a workshop, that would be a plus. I would also prefer a ranch style. The stairs are getting too much for us. And truth be known, after a hard day in my workshop, it would be nice not to have to climb the stairs."

"Okay, I'll see what I can do. If this all goes through, maybe Emma and I can look at several houses that are available."

"Please, don't say anything to Braden or Emma. Our secret until I see if Clint Weston and I would be a fit. I may come back and spend the night if that's okay?"

"You know you don't need to ask. Mum's the word. Would you like some coffee?"

"No, thank you, honey. If Emma calls, make some excuse for me, okay?"

"I sure will. Be careful, and let me know how it goes." Ellie gave him a quick hug.

Ellie sat in her office checking off things for the wedding. Finn had agreed to make the wedding cake. Ellie knew it would be spectacular because he had worked for two years for a famous baker. Grace's dress and cape had been cleaned, the engagement write up in the Jackson newspaper, invitations sent, and bridesmaid's dresses altered. It was almost scary how everything had come together so easily.

Chef Finn had also run a few ideas by her for the reception. Braden and Ellie had hired a sous chef on a part-time basis since there would be a lot of preparation for the guests as well as the reception when they married. Since Finn would be busy most of every day, she and Braden had encouraged him to move into the bedroom in The Sullivan House that used to be the pantry. They had built a bigger one in the Big Kitchen. The vacant room was large enough for a small sitting room in one corner, and the bath was quite spacious. He readily agreed.

That left the Inn completely vacant because Doug had approached them a month ago and asked if he could buy a bed and turn his break room into a small apartment. Braden and Ellie agreed to enlarge it and make it comfortable for him. They added a small room to house the washer, dryer, and deep freezer so their maid wouldn't have to traipse through Doug's private space.

Braden and Mason installed a couple of cabinets, a sink, a small refrigerator and an apartment-sized stove as well as a window air conditioner. They had hooked up the old cast iron cookstove, so he would have heat in the winter.

Doug wanted to be near the horses, especially one of the prize mares he and Braden had picked up since she was in foal. Braden had thought once a mare bred, they just had to wait. When Doug explained that sometimes a mare giving birth the first time could be problematic, it seemed reasonable for Doug to be close to the horses.

With almost everything in place, Ellie speculated that she could get married today, but she really wanted to do it on Heart Day as she began to think of Valentine's Day. And they needed to get the grand opening over with. She already had four couples who had made reservations, and she had booked the installation of two elevators. They should be in place by the first of February.

Braden walked in from school. He noticed his booklet on the foyer table. A vintage coat rack sat in the corner, probably much like the one the Sullivan's used.

Father Winter seemed determined to persist, but Miss Southern Spring butted heads with her and prevailed with beautiful weather predicted in the seventies, making opening day perfect.

Braden called to Ellie. "Everything looks perfect. Only two more days until we open this beautiful mansion."

"Yes, my darling. We have people coming from Mobile, Baton Rouge, Jackson, and Atlanta. I hope they enjoy the weekend. I need to run something by you, though."

"Okay, what?"

"I've changed the names of the rooms and wanted to see what you think before I gave the final approval for the brochure."

"Okay."

"Upstairs will be rooms named with the names of some of the Sullivans. We could have the rooms named after Grace, Maggie, Matthew, Joseph, and Jim. Then Hope, and Roman. The eighth one, of course, will be ours. Downstairs will be Charity's room and the larger one would be Abe and Sarah's room. Of course, Chef Finn will be in the third one named after his relatives."

"I like it. That gives a more historical element to the place. And Nannie will be beside herself!"

"That's what I thought. So, I'll go ahead and phone the man making the brochures."

"Are Chef Finn and Doug ready for all of this?" A grin spread across Braden's face.

"Doug is a little nervous about people wanting to go horseback riding if they have never been on a horse and whether the horses will be a little skittish around strangers, but he has cleaned up the buggy, and he's hoping they will opt for that. Chef Finn is in his element. I saw him poring over recipes this morning. He loves crowds."

Braden took Ellie's hands. "I have to tell you, sweetheart, I had no idea everything we've done would turn out this well. Our future is in our hands with the good Lord willing."

Ellie smiled. "I do feel blessed, not only that you saw my vision for this lovely home, but that you saw me for who I am and love me anyway!"

"You are easy to love. I just hope I can be the kind of husband you always dreamed of."

Ellie put her hands on each side of Braden's cheeks and pulled him in for a long kiss.

By early afternoon Friday, all of the couples had arrived. Ellie greeted their guests in one of Grace's dresses, and Braden looked quite handsome in black trousers with suspenders and a long coat over a white shirt. The ooh's and aah's as the couple entered put a smile on Ellie's face. After showing them to the rooms they had reserved and giving them time to unwind, Ellie ushered them to the dining room since all four couples had opted for Supper with the Sullivans.

All four ladies chose to dress in one of Grace's dresses, but the men chose simple dress pants and white or pastel shirts. Ellie asked the sous chef to dress in a tux and serve the guests. Menu consisted of creamy pumpkin soup, bacon wrapped quail with Greek lemon potatoes, pimento-wrapped asparagus, and a tangy fruit salad. For dessert, Crème Brulee was offered, torched tableside. Ellie had hired an orchestra to play soft music during dinner and dancing afterward if the guests chose. Ellie wanted an orchestra for their wedding, so this trio would be the entertainment if she liked them. This was to be their debut. As the couples moved into the parlor and began dancing, it was as if Grace and Maggie were having their coming out party with the colorful ballgowns floating around the room.

The next morning during a buffet breakfast, Doug entered and asked if anyone would like to tour the property in a vintage carriage when they finished eating. One couple rose and followed Doug to the stables. The woman grabbed her husband and kissed him.

"This is so exciting. I feel like a new bride going in the buggy to get married."

The man smiled. "Well, if a buggy ride does this to you after almost ten years of marriage, I may have to buy a horse and buggy. I'm glad you're happy, my sweet."

Doug drove them around the perimeter, pointing out the Inn and mentioning that it was for rent for reunions or special occasions. He also suggested that if they wanted to have a picnic, the river bank would be perfect and could be arranged with the chef. Going back toward the stables, he stopped the buggy at the edge of the woods. "There's a special place a little way inside the woods where there is the original heart of stones that you probably read about in the literature. There's a little bench there if you'd like to sit and have some quiet time."

The woman snuggled up to her husband. "I've been thinking, John. Why don't we rent the Inn, invite several friends and celebrate our tenth anniversary in March. Let's go look at the bench and the heart of stones."

"That's a great idea. Or if you get impatient, we could do it on Valentine's Day."

Doug heard the conversation. "Sorry, folks. Valentine's Day is already taken for that weekend."

"Maybe I could pay the couple to have it somewhere else and give us that weekend."

"I don't think any amount of money would persuade them." Doug didn't reveal it was Ellie and Braden's special day.

"Then I guess it will be March. I'd better make reservations while we're here before someone else books it."

Since it was warmer than usual, two of the couples decided to play croquet, one couple chose to walk to the grove and sit on the bench, and the other couple opted for a horse ride with Doug leading the way. It was amazing how the couples bonded over the meals and the shared accommodations. Ellie could hear their conversations in the parlor and was surprised to learn that they all had agreed to come back in the summer. The wives were planning to keep in touch, and the anniversary couple asked them to join them in March. All in all, it was turning out to be a perfect weekend.

Braden motioned to Ellie and pointed her toward the back veranda. "I feel like I can breathe again!"

"Yes, finally! I'm happy that we will show a profit after this first weekend. I thought Finn bought so many groceries, we would be in the poor house, but he is a frugal shopper, and his grocery bill was not as high as I had expected."

"His food is excellent. I hope we can keep him, but I know he could get a better paying job in a big city."

"We talked about that yesterday. He doesn't want to leave. He is totally happy here. There are enough crowds to showcase his cooking, and it's quiet enough to give him some peace. Besides now that we know he is a distant relative, it makes it all the more special."

Ellie sat on the bench in the grove. Braden having the heart of stones encased in clear acrylic plastic and embedded in concrete was a perfect place to stand and recite their vows. She wanted everything to be perfect. The Sullivan Gown, as she now thought of it, was ready, the cake ideas formalized, and the photographer booked. She loved the fact that Braden thought The Sullivan Gown was going to go on a vintage dressmaker's form to adorn a bedroom. He had no idea she was going to wear it. With the winter sun peeping through misty clouds, the birds twilling a soft song, the river gurgling a happy tune, life was wonderful. At last, all was well, and she was thankful that Braden had now accepted her past and had not believed anything the gypsies said. At last, she could put Tommy Butler to rest. He died thinking he could control her by telling her about the fortune tellers. Too bad he would never know she had found out the truth, that they couldn't put a curse on her. Her only concern was whether an adopted child would make Braden happy. From what Susan told her, babies were harder to adopt because everyone wanted one. Ellie vowed to talk to Braden about an older child.

Ellie took off early Tuesday morning to drive to Birmingham to visit Susan.

The next morning, they set out to visit three sets of foster parents. Ellie was introduced as a volunteer.

The first house they visited was wonderful. A mid-fifties woman with her graying hair pulled into a high pony tail opened the door. "Oh, Miss Cunningham, how nice to see you. Come in. Do you have more children for us?"

Susan laughed. "No, Missus Pollock. I'm showing Miss Ellie here some of our clients. She is a volunteer on our team."

"If she's as good as you, we will be delighted. Oh, excuse me. Have a seat. I hear a little one calling." She came back with a baby about a year old. He was clean and healthy looking and laughed at Susan and Ellie. Three other children pushed their way into the living room. They all were happy and crowded around Missus Pollock. "Let me get the children a snack. Would you like to come into the kitchen so we can talk?"

Ellie and Susan followed her. She set out a snack of apple slices and graham crackers with a small glass of milk for each child.

The second house was in a little rundown area. When Missus Fulbright answered the door, her face reflected anger rising up. "Why are you here? You here to spy on me?"

Susan introduced Ellie. "No, Missus Fulbright. I just wanted to introduce Miss Ellie."

"Well, the children are playing."

Ellie heard crying. Susan marched down the hall toward the noise with Ellie following. Four children sat on the floor. They were watching a TV soap opera program, but their faces held blank stares. They were dirty, and one had a runny nose. They looked miserable.

Susan quizzed Missus Fulbright. "Why on earth are you letting the children watch an adult program? Have you taken the child with the runny nose to a doctor?"

"I haven't had time."

Susan looked hard at her. "These children don't look as well cared for as we had hoped. You will be reviewed by another social worker in a week to see if conditions have improved. I urge you to take the sick child to a doctor."

"Oh, go ahead and take my name off the list and find another place for these brats. These kids are a handful to deal with. Get them out of my sight as soon as possible."

Susan made a note.

The third house was in a poorer neighborhood, but the yard was neat, and there was playground equipment visible inside a chain link fence. Missus Morton answered the door. She was a plump woman in a clean white apron, holding a baby in her arms.

"Oh, Miss Cunningham. Please come in. I was just about to serve lunch. Should I wait until after your visit?"

She introduced Ellie. "No, please go ahead. We'll just sit and watch."

Missus Morton served meatloaf, mashed potatoes, green beans, and a slice of buttered bread. A bowl of blueberries and apple slices served as the dessert. As she set the dishes down, she said, "Can you tell Miss Cunningham and Miss Addison what we're having?"

One little boy said, "Chuck wagon meat."

A little girl said, "With a potato pillow for the meat and the green fence posts to keep critters out."

Missus Morton said, "That's right. And what does that teach us?"

Another child raised his hand. "Protein, carburetors and fat, and…uh…oh yeah, vegetables and fruit."

Missus Morton laughed. "Yes, Joey. You almost got it. You can just say carbs. But I'm proud of you." She turned to Ellie. "I'm trying to teach them healthy choices by making it fun. Do you have any questions, Miss Susan?"

Susan spoke, "No, but I'd like to eat at your table!"

Later in the car, Ellie asked, "What will happen with the children in that second house?"

"Those children will be removed as soon as we can find another placement. We have watched her for a while, but foster parents are hard to find. Missus Fulbright is clearly in it for the money. Unfortunately, many fosters are like her. I just showed you the exceptional ones along with one that will lose her privilege."

Ellie felt a tinge of sadness that she couldn't produce a child of her own, but after visiting the foster homes with Susan, the looks of the children were something she would never forget. The younger ones had eyes full of hope, but the older ones in the Fulbright home had a haunted look that revealed scars of more than the beatings or abuse they had suffered. Susan told Ellie many of them had not known cruelty, but the rejection of a forever home was sometimes worse.

"It just breaks my heart, Susan. Please invite the Pollocks and the Mortons to a free weekend the second week in July when it would be warmer so the children could play in the meadow, ride horses, swim, and play croquet. Would that give you time to make arrangements?"

"That would thrill the two couples, and yes, that's enough time."

"I don't know how you do it. I would be crying all the time."

"It's hard. I'm thinking of taking up a new career."

Ellie smiled. "What would you think about helping me at The Sullivan House?"

"I thought you'd never ask. Do you need to run it by Braden?"

"No, we talked about it before I left since you had mentioned you didn't like your job."

"I'll give my notice tomorrow."

When Ellie arrived back home, Braden was putting finishing touches on a light meal.

"You are just in time. Give me a kiss and tell me how it went with Susan."

"It was good, but Braden, my heart goes out to those children, especially the older ones. I hope you are aren't mad at me, but I invited the two nicest couples to a free weekend in July. And Susan will start work in two weeks!"

"I could never be mad at you! Let's make it a weekend the children will never forget."

Ellie smiled. "I love you so much."

"I love you, too, and this is just another example of how wonderful you are to think of these couples and the children."

CHAPTER THIRTY-ONE

Raul Gomez picked up a Jackson newspaper as he had every Sunday for the better part of a year. His eyes burned, and he felt heat rising from the bottom of his feet to his head. He pounded his fists on the ground inside his tent until his hands hurt. Glaring at him on the society page was the engagement announcement of Elizabeth Addison and Braden Cunningham. So, it was a serious relationship. He had scoped out the Addison home almost every night, but there was no sign of Elizabeth.

He smiled. He now knew where Elizabeth was spending her time, and he would switch his surveillance. Making her believe that the gypsies had told her she would bring death or injury to any man she chose had worked well for a long time, especially since two of her former boyfriends had died after she dated them. She was convinced the fortune teller has foretold her future. Sarcastic laughter shook his tent.

He had not counted on her accepting a proposal from this latest one…someone named Braden Cunningham. He took a permanent black marker from his pocket and drew a heart across Ellie's chest in the picture announcing her engagement. He marked an "x" over Braden's picture, but not large enough to obscure his face. This marriage could never happen. She would be Missus Tommy Butler or rather Missus Raul Gomez, or she and Braden would be dead.

When he had spun out in his car that fateful day, he had driven to Lake Borgne in New Orleans, knowing it was deep enough that they couldn't really search properly. He'd waited for the last bus and took it to Brownsville, Texas. It was easy to cross into Matamoros, Mexico in a cab with no trouble. He had intended to lay low for a while, giving Elizabeth time to grieve his death. Trying to relax, he went to bar where a poker game was in full swing. He went over and asked if he could play. A man introduced himself as Pedro Grande and agreed to let Tommy play. They played for several hours. But when Big Pedro started asking

249

questions about why Tommy was in Mexico, what he did for a living, whether he was married, and other personal questions, Tommy became paranoid, wondering if the guy was some kind of bounty hunter. Tommy told him his name was Marco Dunn, and he was taking a break from his job as an engineer in the United States. He and Pedro became friends, and Tommy started gambling weekly. He won a few games off and on, but it seemed the rounds he won all had only meager money. He never put two and two together to realize that Pedro was baiting him, and that's why his jackpots never amounted to much money. Pedro kept calling him son, treating him to expensive restaurants, and buying him new clothes.

Tommy was nervous about a big money game he lost to Pedro. He was running out of money quickly and didn't have enough to pay off his debt. He had to find a job, but as a gringo, his choices would be limited. He went to Pedro to ask him if he knew where he could get a job to pay him for his loss. Pedro said he would forgive him the money he lost if he would come to work for him.

Tommy had no idea what the job would entail. Pedro took him to the back of the bar with two other men and confessed to Tommy that he ran a drug operation. Tommy immediately became frightened because he had heard terrible things about how they operated. But he was already in debt to the drug lord, and he knew his two bodyguards would kill him if he refused the job. There was no recourse but to go to work for him or face execution if he couldn't pay up. And he needed money to get out of Mexico as soon as his debt was paid. He was terrified, and feared for his life, but Pedro was talking, and he needed to pay attention. Big Pedro wanted him to service his customers in Mexico and also the United States since he was a gringo.

Tommy pushed drugs and did what the drug lord demanded for a couple of months, but he was nervous with every deal. He made a great deal of money for Pedro, but he secretly kept some cash back for himself, knowing if he got caught, Big Pedro would kill him.

Tommy was scheduled to go through an initiation on a Saturday to prove his loyalty and to be elevated in the organization. He was to torture and kill a man who broke the drug lord's rule. Tommy knew he was next if they found out he broke the rule and kept some money, so it was time to change his name once again, and flee Mexico. He had watched them murder a man, and he still had nightmares about it. He realized what a dangerous situation he had placed himself in and was scared out of his mind.

Gathering as much courage as he could, Tommy got some rouge and rubbed it all over his face so he would look like he was hot with fever. He went to Big Pedro's house. He knocked, opened the door, and stood a little way back from the doorway. Pedro rose to come to him. Tommy held up his hand to stop him.

"Don't come close to me." Tommy moved back farther and said in a weak voice, "I've been to a curandero. I have a fever and a bad disease. He's going to help me get over it, but I'm contagious, and I don't want you to get this. That's why I'm standing outside."

"You look bad. How long is that going to take? I'll send someone to check on you."

"Don't send anyone. They could get what I have and maybe die. Just have them leave some food outside. I think this should last about a week, but I'll have to throw my clothes away as soon as I get home because the germs on them would keep me from healing. I just hope I have enough money for the medicine and some food. Guess I won't need it if I die, though. If you don't hear from me in a week, check to be sure I'm still alive, please."

Pedro looked him up and down. "A week? What about your runs?"

"I can still do them as soon as I'm healed, but I'm weak and hurting. The curandero told me to go home and stay in bed, not answer the door, drink fluids, and stay away from everyone. I'll let you know when I am able to be near people again." Tommy faked a cough and bent over as if in pain. "I need to go get in bed because I am in pain." Tommy knew Pedro was obsessive about germs, so his story would made perfect sense to the drug lord. He made his face look sad and coughed again. "I'm worried about the job you wanted me to do to prove my loyalty. Can it be put off a few days? I certainly wouldn't mind giving the man my disease, but you would need to be there to observe." Tommy stood up, but winced as if in pain.

Pedro rubbed his chin. "Well, he's not going anywhere, so let's do it when you are cured, so I don't get whatever you've got. What is it?"

Tommy knew a lot of people were coming down with the flu, so he said, "It's some kind of new influenza that is making a lot of people sick. I think some have died."

251

Pedro went to a cabinet and took out a pouch. He scooted it across the floor to the door. "Take this money to pay the curandero for medicine, and there are a few drugs in there for you, too. Buy some new clothes when you get well. Don't come near me until you are healed."

Tommy nodded. "Thank you, Papa Pedro. That's most generous."

Tommy left, went to his room, used black dye to color his hair and the mustache he had grown. He had practiced his Spanish so he knew he had the accent down pat. He packed his clothes, and all his money into a double-lined trash bag, sealed it with strong tape, and tied it around his waist. He knew Pedro had a big poker game going on later that night, so he waited until four o'clock in the morning, and made sure Pedro hadn't posted guards outside his room. He slipped out and walked as fast as he dared to the mouth of the Rio Grande River, about two blocks away.

He slid as gracefully as he could into the cold, black water illuminated by a half-moon, giving him just enough light to get his bearings. Most of the time, the water was no more than knee high, and it would take only a few minutes to reach Boca Chica Beach near Brownsville, Texas. The danger was the uneven bottom and deadly bacteria, but it was a chance he would take. The water got deeper about halfway there, so he had to swim. When he finally emerged on Boca Chica Beach, he bowed down and kissed the sand.

After resting until dawn, he ventured into Brownsville and found a seedy character who did fake IDs and had old cars for sale. Tommy bought the best-looking old car, registered it as Raul Gomez, and started driving to get out of Texas. He didn't want to run into any of his former druggie customers who could report him to Pedro if he didn't have drugs for them. Thankfully, he had more than enough money from Pedro without totally depleting his stash, so he picked up a one-man tent along with a small cooler and a one burner gas camping stove. Arriving in Mississippi, he found a camp site close to the Pearl River near Jackson. Posing as a Mexican with his dyed black hair and liquid tan, he doubted any of his friends would recognize him, but he didn't want to take a chance. Not until the time was right.

Putting all that behind him, Tommy glared at the newspaper once again. "It's time you paid for your mistakes, Miss Elizabeth," he muttered as he folded the engagement announcement and put it in his pocket.

Spying on Elizabeth had been fun. He tried many times to get close enough to her to see if she would recognize him. When she didn't even look his way, Tommy was delighted in a sardonic kind of way. She was not going to marry the school teacher who was living with her. Tommy had told her she could never marry anyone but him.

Granted she thought he was dead, but it would be Cunningham who would die and maybe Elizabeth if she refused to marry him instead of Cunningham.

He was getting good at faking his identity to evade Pedro's goons, but he needed to get his name back to Tommy Butler, so that he could marry Elizabeth. At least, they didn't know his true identity or even his new fake name. Tommy was not going to contact his parents until he could bring Elizabeth to introduce her as his wife or to invite them to her funeral, whichever choice she made. He had to be careful. Confronting Elizabeth and her precious fiancé could get him in trouble with the authorities, and if they checked on his background, they could uncover his drug involvement. He knew the drug lord had men posted all over Texas, and no telling where else, but hopefully not Mississippi.

Tommy did a few odd jobs to add to his money and always asked for payment in cash. He had planned to lay low for a few more months, but now, with the announcement, he had to escalate his plan. He needed to act quickly.

Tommy picked up the phone and called The Sullivan House. Someone named Susan Cunningham answered the phone. Confusion swirled around Tommy's brain. Was she Braden's new wife? Did Elizabeth call off the wedding? He had to find out, but it wouldn't make any difference. He was going to get Elizabeth if she was there. Introducing himself, he cleared his throat and asked in his best Spanish accent for a reservation.

"What day would you like to come, Mister Gomez?"

Tommy didn't want any other guests in the house. "Is pisful there?"

"Oh, yes, sir. There's even a meditation spot outside if you don't mind the cold."

"Tomorrow?"

"Yes, sir. We don't have any people staying this week, so you will be the only one. How many days will you be staying with us?"

"Two, pleez."

"I'm sure you will find it very relaxing here, sir. Will you be making a deposit with a credit card?"

"No, cash."

"Great. We'll see you tomorrow."

Tommy touched up his roots and mustache with black dye and applied more liquid tan. He had secured a revolver from a less than reputable man he met in Brownsville, and he carefully packed it in his bag along with some extra ammunition. He had no intention of staying two days, but there might be a chance that Cunningham was out of town or otherwise unavailable.

The mansion loomed ahead of him, huge and imposing, almost overpowering him as he started down the driveway. Tommy felt it was like a majestic beacon pushing him back. He had surveyed it, always staying back in the trees, but up close, it was like a formidable ghost. "Guess bloodshed won't be welcomed, but I'll try to kill Cunningham outside and not mess up this mansion. After all, this is where Elizabeth and I will live and raise our family," he mumbled. "Be glad I changed my mind to kill your fiancé instead of you, Elizabeth." A smile crossed his face. "Unless you refuse me, and then you're dead, too."

Putting on large sunglasses, a guayabera shirt and a Stetson hat, he entered the mansion, and noticed Elizabeth in some kind of formal that stood out over what must have been twenty petticoats. She moved toward him, extended her hand, and gave him a warm welcome. "Let me show you to your room, sir. We are giving you the best room in the house since you are our only guest. Dinner is at six."

"Gracias, senora." Tommy bowed and kept his voice low, hoping she would not recognize him. He handed Susan cash for two nights.

Elizabeth smiled. Mister Gomez thought she was married, and he was so nice to bow to her. She would be a senora soon. And it was wonderful to have a little extra income from their guest, especially during the week. Usually, their guests only booked for weekends.

Tommy didn't bother to unpack. He wouldn't be here long if he could find Cunningham. His duffel bag was just to make it look like he was staying and to hide his gun. Tommy decided to do a line. He was no hophead and had never done drugs, but he had watched many of Pedro's men do it. Would that give him enough confidence to kill a man? His stomach lurched as he remembered the way the drug lord tortured and killed anyone who got in his way, and he was about to do that to Cunningham, though it would be swift without torture. Sitting for a few minutes, he let the drug take effect and then took a shot of whiskey he had in a flask. A feeling of euphoria slowly crept into his psyche. Securing the revolver in his waistband underneath his guayabera shirt, he decided to walk around to see if he could see Braden. As he neared the stables, he heard male voices. Taking the newspaper announcement from his pocket, he looked hard at Braden's picture. Tiptoeing to the side of the stables, he peeked through a window over the air conditioner. Braden had his back to the door in deep conversation with another man. Although Braden was facing the window, Tommy was sure he didn't notice him. He could shoot him from behind, and Braden or the man he was talking to would never see his face. Perfect.

Braden and Doug had just finished a cup of coffee together. He wanted to see if Doug was still amenable to using his horses to accommodate their guests if The Sullivan House had all the rooms booked. Doug agreed. They stood to shake hands. Braden shook his head. "I almost forgot the real reason I came out here. We have a guest now."

"During the week? That's unusual."

"Yes, but will you saddle a horse? Our guest may want to ride."

"Of course. I hope he has ridden before. I was going to ride around the perimeter to check on everything, so Apollo is already saddled. I saw a strange car in the driveway, so if the guest wants to rid..."

Tommy couldn't wait any longer. This was his chance. He quickly drew his revolver, stole around to the open door of the stables and aimed for Braden's back at heart level. At the last minute, reality took over. Scenes of murdered men in Mexico flooded his brain, and he realized he couldn't kill anyone. He raised the revolver toward the ceiling just as the gun went off.

A slight noise startled Braden, thinking Ellie had come to see what he was doing. As he turned, he saw someone with a revolver aimed at

Doug and him. Instinctively, he shoved Doug to the floor. A shot blasted through the stables and reverberated through the air waves outside.

Tommy had not aimed high enough. He ran to the house. He thought he had hit the ceiling until he saw blood pouring out of Braden. Did he kill him? He saw him fall in a pool of blood over the other man.

He found Elizabeth straightening pictures in the parlor, and as she looked up, he grabbed her. He dragged her down the porch steps to his old car. He had a hard time getting the *Gone-with-the-Wind* dress she was wearing into the passenger seat, and she was screaming. He slapped her. She slumped in the seat.

The gunshot alerted Finn who was preparing lunch for their guest. Before he could react, Doug burst through the door. Adrenalin took over Doug's body. He had to protect Ellie and Susan. Running to the front of the house, he saw Tommy shoving Ellie into his car.

Sprinting toward the back, he yelled, "Braden's been shot! Get him to the doctor NOW! And call the police, Susan. I'm going to follow that man."

Doug raced back to the stables and mounted Apollo. He raced after the man's car. All he could see was dust, but he choked back the fine powder as Apollo galloped faster than he ever had. He seemed to sense trouble. Doug was praying as hard as he could.

"Please, Lord, let me catch them, and please protect Ellie. Give me strength, Lord, please! And please keep Braden alive." Doug suddenly realized that he had no weapon, but maybe he could tackle the man, if he could catch him and get him out of the car. He prayed the police would get there to intercept the man before he and Apollo arrived.

Back in the car, Tommy finally got the car started, jammed his foot on the accelerator, and pushed it to the floor. The car sputtered and paused for a moment before darting forward, kicking up dust, obscuring his vision to see if anyone was following him. He shot to the left onto the road. Elizabeth had grown quiet, but he could see the fear in her eyes, and her hands were shaking as she hugged herself. Her lips moved, but no sound came out of them. She seemed to be praying with her eyes closed. Dropping his accent, he yelled at her. "I told you, you would never marry anyone but me."

Recognition dawned. "Tommy?"

Tommy laughed, evil spewing from his mouth. "Who else? You're never going to marry that guy. I took care of that."

Her mouth felt like cotton, and she could feel her muscles contracting. She willed herself to calm down enough to speak. "What do you mean? And slow down. You're going to get us killed." She needed to buy time.

"I mean, I shot him. He's dead."

Ellie screamed again. Her body shook, her eyes blurred, and confusion swept over her as she went into shock. Punching him in his face and trying to grab the steering wheel, she screeched, "What did you say? Why? How?"

"Shut up!" Tommy backhanded her. Something was wrong with the car. It was sputtering and making coughing sounds. Suddenly it just came to an abrupt halt. How could this be? A cold hard fact dawned on Tommy. He had meant to fill up with fuel, but in his excitement, he forgot. He had run out of gas. Cursing himself, Tommy looked up to see a horse behind him and a police car in front of him. He grabbed his revolver, but Ellie had already shoved the passenger door open. She fell to the ground in a billowing cloud of petticoats.

Doug quickly dismounted and ran, throwing himself over her. Tommy was brandishing his gun in all directions flummoxed in which direction to start shooting.

"Drop the gun, NOW!" The policeman lunged toward Tommy, knocking him down and retrieving the gun, but not before Tommy fired a shot at him. In his agitated state, he missed. They scuffled, but Clyde Barton's police training soon subdued Tommy. He handcuffed him and shoved him into the back of his cruiser. He took his keys and walked over to see about Ellie.

CHAPTER THIRTY-TWO

Doug raised himself off of Ellie, but sat with his arms wrapped around her. She was crying hysterically, and her face was reddened on both sides where Tommy had hit her twice. Her whole body was trembling.

"He...he...killed Braden." She started wailing.

Doug soothed her enough for her to gain her composure. He recognized the officer.

"Ellie, you have to calm down so we can help the police. We don't know for sure if Braden is dead." Doug knew with the amount of blood he saw, there was a possibility Braden had succumbed. At least Ellie would have Susan, Finn, and himself to help her.

Ellie composed herself enough to talk to Officer Barton.

"I know this is hard, ma'am, but I need to ask a few questions. Do you know this man?"

"Yes, sir. This is a man I dated in high school. Everyone thought he was dead. He is apparently using a different name, but his real name is Thomas Butler. He may have other aliases for all I know. I didn't recognize him with dark hair and a Mexican accent."

Doug stepped up. "You remember Elizabeth Addison, Clyde." Together, they situated Ellie sideways in Tommy's front seat. The car door was still open.

The officer addressed Ellie. "Yes, I know you from the Chamber meetings. I just didn't expect to see you in a...a...formal dress."

Ellie brushed her hair from her face, but didn't comment.

Clyde asked her, "Do you know his next of kin, and how we can locate them?"

Before Ellie could speak, her car shot passed them. Braden was slumped over the dash holding a towel to his neck. Finn was speeding away from them.

259

Doug interrupted Clyde. "Ellie, Finn just passed us. Braden was sitting up, so he's alive as of right now."

Again, Clyde gently pressed Ellie. "Do you know his next of kin?"

Ellie had her head in her hands. She was in shock, but managed to say, "Yes, but he said he killed my fiancé, and I need go to him, please!" Her hands were shaking, and tears mixed with the dust made streaks down her cheeks. Doug wasn't sure she comprehended the fact that Braden was alive. He handed her a bandana he had in the back pocket of his jeans. "It's not a fancy handkerchief, but it's clean." Ellie wiped her face.

Clyde Barton asked Doug who had been shot.

Doug looked at the policeman. "His name is Braden Cunningham. He and Miss Ellie own The Sullivan House and he's a teacher at the elementary school. I asked their chef, Finn Turner, to get him to the clinic. I believe he was alive when I left to follow this Butler guy."

Ellie screamed, "Please take me to Braden."

"Okay, Miss Ellie. I hate to do this to you, but it's the quickest way to get you to your fiancé. Will you be all right to ride in the front of my cruiser; otherwise, I guess Doug can put you on his horse and ride to the clinic." Eyeing her petticoats and with the cloud of white net, he doubted she would be able to even get on the horse. He waited.

"Ye…ye…yes, sir. I'm fine. I just need to get to Braden."

Just as she settled in the front seat, Tommy yelled through the bars separating him from the front of the cruiser. "You'll never marry him, Elizabeth! Never! Do you hear me? I'll kill both of us, but you will never marry anyone else but me, or we'll die together!"

Clyde raised his voice, "That's enough, Butler. You've got enough trouble without threatening murder. At this rate, you won't see the light of day for a long time." He read him his Miranda Rights.

Doug mounted Apollo and sped to the clinic, praying for Braden the entire way.

Ellie was shaking, but managed to compose herself long enough to get out of the car and into the clinic with Clyde's help. He spoke in a whisper to the receptionist and took Ellie's arm. She turned to see Finn sitting in the waiting room. She rushed to him.

"Is he…."

"He's alive. He was bleeding heavily, but I got him here in record time. Doc is with him, now. Sorry I took your car, but it was the closest one."

Clyde urged her forward. He led her to a white, sterile room where Braden lay still and pale on a gurney with a large bandage on his neck. Ellie rushed to him and looked up at the doctor.

Doc Williams smiled. "He's lost a lot of blood, but he's a healthy young man. The bullet barely missed his carotid artery, so he will recover. I just finished stitching him up. He's a little groggy from the medicine I gave him."

Ellie let out a big sigh and looked toward the ceiling. "Thank you, Father God, for saving him." She put her hand over Braden's exposed hand. She gave it a light squeeze. Then she turned to the doctor. "Thank you, too. You saved the most important man in my life."

Braden's eyes fluttered open. "Ellie?" Then he drifted back to sleep.

Clyde addressed the doctor. "Are you thinking of transporting him to a hospital?"

'No, he won't need any surgery that I can see. The bullet made a clean exit, but he's a mighty lucky man. The Man upstairs must have had him in His hands. I'll keep him here until he wakes up, and then he can go home."

"Let me know if you need anything. Right now, I've got a man to book." He turned to Ellie. "Do you need me to take you home?"

"No, sir. Our chef has my car, but I'm not going until Braden can leave."

Clyde moved to the waiting room and saw Doug. "Someone needs to notify Mister Cunningham's next of kin."

Doug walked Clyde out to the cruiser. "I'm sure Susan, Braden's sister, has called their parents, but if not, I will."

"Thank you. It would be better coming from family than me. When Miss Ellie's up to it, I need to get a statement and as much information as she can give me about this man."

"Sure thing. I'm just glad there were no other guests at The Sullivan House."

"The Lord works in mysterious ways." Clyde tipped his cap and left.

261

Two hours later, Braden woke up. The last thing he remembered was hearing a gun going off and seeing a man in the doorway of the stables. He must have been shot, but he hadn't felt pain. He looked around and realized he was in the clinic. He saw Ellie sitting next to him. Suddenly his neck hurt. He raised his hand and felt the bandage.

"What happened? Is Doug okay?"

Ellie explained a shortened version of the events. "But now that you're awake, I think Doc will release you, so I can take you home."

"Okay."

Finn and Doug got Braden into the front seat of Ellie's car. She sat in the back. Surprisingly, most of the blood stains were on Braden's clothes and the dash.

Braden looked at the dash and commented, "Glad you didn't take my T-bird. Guess I have to clean up Ellie's car."

Finn smiled. "Yes, boss, I made it a point not to take your precious car." He glanced at Braden. "Actually, Ellie's car was the closest."

Braden was weak, but he managed to walk up the stairs onto the porch and into the house. Ellie and Finn got him into the elevator and upstairs to his bed.

As Ellie straightened a blanket over Braden, she said, "I hope we don't ever see that man again, but I'm glad we have the elevator."

Finn said, "We won't see him again. The policeman told me he would make sure."

"I wonder why he waited until now to surface?" Braden's face registered concern.

Ellie sighed. "I don't know. He had a wild look about him and wasn't really coherent when I was riding in the cruiser. He was talking nonstop as if he'd had too much coffee to drink or something. I'll need to give a statement as soon as I'm sure you are okay."

Braden laughed. "I'll bet you made a pretty picture in that big dress."

"I guess I did. Thankfully, it isn't ripped or anything, but I did get a few stares from people in the waiting room. I can have it cleaned, but I want to put on my regular clothes now." Ellie went to her room and took off the dress and petticoats. She freshened up, put on her own clothes and went to find Doug.

He met her as he was coming in from putting Apollo in the Stables. "Well, we've had quite a day, haven't we?"

"Yes. I'm just wondering if you know why he shot Braden or if he said anything?"

"I have no idea. I had just saddled Apollo to check out the perimeter, and all of a sudden, Braden knocked me down and fell on top of me. I heard the gunshot and saw the man running toward the house. When I realized Braden was shot, I got from under him, ran, yelled to Susan to call the police and told Finn to get Braden to the doctor. We're lucky Tommy turned left toward town and not right. He would have been headed toward Jackson. And it was just by the grace of God that his car stopped."

"Why did it?"

"Apparently, he ran out of gas! Didn't think his plan through, apparently."

"Yes, the Lord answers prayers. I was praying as hard as I could for Braden and myself. Has anyone contacted Emma and Mason?"

"Yes, Susan took care of it. They're on their way."

"Thank you. I guess I'll go to the police station now. I want to get this over with."

"Not by yourself. Either Finn or I will take you."

"Okay, I'll go tell Braden. I'll go with you. Finn needs to cook something for Braden."

Fifteen minutes later, Ellie and Doug left for the station.

Entering the station, the receptionist paged Clyde. He rounded the corner before Ellie and Doug had time to sit down.

"Thank you for coming. Raul Gomez or Tommy Butler or Marco Dunn, or whatever other alias he's using, is wanted for dealing drugs and attempted murder...twice. Once when he shot Braden Cunningham and then firing at me when I arrested him. He also threatened you, Miss Ellie, in my presence. Right now, jail is the safest place for him. Mexico wants him extradited, but since he dealt some drugs in the United States a few times, I don't think they have a leg to stand on. Believe me, Tommy Butler does not want to be in jail in Mexico. And certainly not at the cruel hands of the Mexico mafia."

"May I see him?"

"Yes, but I want someone with you. Doug?"

"Yes, sir."

Ellie stood back from the bars. "I have one question for you, Tommy. Why did you wait until now to come out of hiding?"

Tommy looked up from the cot where he was sitting with his head in his hands, his elbows on his thighs, staring straight ahead. The look in his eyes had turned from anger to terror. He rose and went to the bars. He seemed to have calmed down somewhat, but he grabbed the bars to steady himself.

"Ellie, all I've thought about is you. I guess I thought if I couldn't have you, no one could. I'm sorry I killed your fiancé. At the last minute, I realized what I was about to do, and I raised my revolver, but I guess it went off before I raised it up high enough. I've seen that man with you, but I didn't think you were serious until I saw your announcement. I'm sorry for a lot of things. I've watched you for months, and I never saw you and Cunningham acting romantic. I've spied on you many times. I thought I had plenty of time to make enough money so you would see that you needed to be with me. When I found out you bought that big mansion and a guy was living with you, I just went crazy."

"Are your parents on their way here to see you?"

"I don't know. I didn't give the policeman their names."

"I think it's only fair they know. Would you like for me to call them?"

"Why are you being so nice? I just killed your fiancé."

"How did you know I was engaged?"

"I saw it in the Jackson newspaper. That's when my anger took over, and all I could think about was that he was not going to have you."

"I'll call them when I get back home. I know they will be as shocked as I was. I can't believe you fooled me."

"I only said two words to you in my Spanish accent."

Ellie thought back. That was true. He had called her senora.

Tommy reached out his hand to her. "Will you come back again? I'm scared."

Ellie ignored his hand. "You should be. But you'll get a fair trial."

"Not that. I got mixed up with a drug lord in Mexico. He is a vicious person. I know how they torture and kill people, so I figure I'm next, especially if they extradite me."

"I don't think that will happen. But I need to go now and give a statement. And by the way, my fiancé is alive."

"Well, that lets me off of a murder charge." He didn't apologize for shooting Braden.

Ellie walked into the lobby and told the receptionist she was ready to give a statement.

CHAPTER THIRTY-THREE

Ellie pulled Grace's journals out of the box Charity had left behind. She was sitting next to Braden's bed. "I thought I'd read more of Grace's journals. I think your grandmother told us most of it, but I enjoy seeing Grace's handwriting. Makes me feel closer to her."

"Yes, I enjoy reading and hearing about her life."

The doorbell rang. Chef Finn came up the stairs. "Ellie, there's a Mister and Missus Butler to see you. They're in the parlor. Shall I send them away?"

"No, I'll see them." She bent and gave Braden a kiss. "You stay put."

Entering the parlor, she saw the reddened eyes of Missus Butler, and Mister Butler looked as if he'd seen a ghost. Ellie crossed the room and extended her hand.

"What brings you here? I thought you'd be at the jail with Tommy."

Mister Butler spoke, "We've just come from there, but both Ruby and I feel we owe you an apology. We blamed you for our son's death, and we were wrong. Will you please forgive us?"

"I think it was a shock to everyone when they found his car by the lake. I have lived with the guilt, thinking I drove him to take his life, but I'm glad he's alive. I am sure you saw it in the paper that I am engaged to a wonderful man who is upstairs at this moment recovering from the bullet that Tommy put in him. And yes, I forgive you. That's what Jesus would do, and I think He is the one who saved us."

"Yes, we heard about Braden Cunningham, and please let him know how sorry we are, and we wish him a quick recovery. We are going back home tonight to get the best lawyer we can for Tommy. He doesn't seem like the same boy we knew."

"He's been through a lot. I think he needs more than a lawyer. Prayers for him would help, too, along with a therapist."

"Yes, we are also going to see if we can get a therapist if the jail will let us."

Ruby rose with her husband behind her. She extended her arms, and Ellie gave her a hug. "Thank you for seeing us and for calling us. Please know our door is always open to you and Braden when you are in Jackson. Maybe we'll come for a weekend and rent a room from you."

Ellie smiled. She didn't want them anywhere near her, but she would not turn down paying guests. "Anytime."

Braden insisted on getting up. With help, he made it downstairs to the breakfast nook. Finn served a large steak, baked potato, and salad. "They say beef will build up blood. I hope this is satisfactory for a meal."

Braden grinned. "Oh, I think I might have to have several of these because I'm sure my blood needs a lot of building up!"

Finn laughed. "You're back to yourself!"

"Maybe you could fix me a steak sandwich to take to school tomorrow for lunch. I don't want to miss any more work because I want to take a week off when we get married."

Ellie pulled Braden to the parlor. "I've read more in Grace's journal and know more about Bessie, Lizzie, and Willie."

Braden's smile lit up his face. "Nannie said they were Daisy's children, and that was another story."

"They were Daisy's children, but she had been told they died by the mean man who raped her over and over. They were eventually purchased by a guy by the name of Noble that bought Walnut Hill."

"Confirms what Hiram told us. Did Daisy ever meet them?"

"Oh yes. Abe Sullivan bought them from Mister Noble so he could keep all of Daisy's children together. They, along with Jim, Lavitica June, and Essie Mae were all products of Daisy's rape, so Jim and his siblings were all mulatto."

"So, Daisy's husband, Jeremiah was not the father of any of them?"

"No. But he never found out, at least not that I have found in the journals. I'm wondering if maybe being beaten may have rendered him

268

impotent. I did find out the Sullivans and their workers went through the Civil War, and the Sullivans did finally make it back to Ireland."

"Start reading that part."

"Okay, here goes. Jim and I finally arrived in Cork. I don't think I have ever seen my mother so happy. She came alive once we got rested. She and Papa spent the entire day going from one relative to another. The house that Charles built is perfect. Matthew and Joseph are going to take Mary and Becca to see relatives tomorrow, and Jim and I will go with Mama the day after that. I am nervous, but I hope they will accept Jim. It's nice for the entire family to be together in one house."

Braden nodded. "I can almost see the whole family there. Sorry to interrupt. Carry on."

Ellie cleared her throat and started reading the next page. "Jim and I met the relatives. No one said a word about Jim being a mulatto. Funny thing is, Papa was asked if he was Castilian because of his light coloring! The men have all met and decided that the best thing to do would be for Jim to help Charles with a construction business. Many houses and buildings were damaged or deserted during the rains that turned all the fields to mush. Joseph is going to set up a small clinic, and Matthew is busy deciding how to arrange a gallery in a building that was empty. I can't wait to get married, but we have to go through some paperwork first."

Braden remarked, "That is so interesting. Looking at some of the pictures that Nannie had of Grace and Jim, he did have very fine features. I guess he got that from the man who raped his mama."

"I guess. I know you're tired, and so am I. I think we should turn in. I wish I could move my bed back into your room."

"I do, too, but it won't be long until we can sleep in one bed. I'm counting the days."

"Everything is ready except you need to be measured for your tux and have your guys do the same."

"Maybe if I'm up to it, we'll go next weekend. I forgot to tell you in all the turmoil that I had a phone call from Justin. He's had a hard time in Dallas finding a job, even as a sous chef. He's coming for a visit, and I have asked him to be my best man. Since you said Finn's sous chef quit, maybe we could offer the job to Justin. I've also asked Doug and Finn to stand up with me. You said keep it small."

"I like that. As far as Justin is concerned, I think it would depend on Finn and whether they could work together. We will definitely need someone if we stay full. I've asked Susan to be my maid of honor and two of my friends to be bridesmaids. Do you know a little girl at school who would like to be a flower girl and a boy for ring bearer?"

"I'll look into it. I have a couple of kids in mind."

"Their parents would, of course, be part of the wedding party with free rooms."

"I'm sure that will seal the deal. People have been asking me about our house." Braden threw back his head and laughed.

Ellie's brow accordioned into a frown. "I had a call from our attorney. Tommy's trial has been set for April first. Couldn't be a more fitting date!"

"That will be well after the wedding, so that's good. April Fool's Day. Bet his lawyers didn't think about that."

Susan made her way to the stables after work. She knocked on the apartment door and shifted from one foot to the next until Doug opened the door. "Susan, I wasn't expecting you. Is something wrong in the house?"

"No, I just thought I'd see if you think it's too late to take a ride?"

"Come in and have a cup of coffee. You know it's a little late in the day to ride."

Susan moved to a chair opposite Doug. She couldn't help but notice in his t-shirt, his muscles stood out, accentuating his broad shoulders and very handsome face. She loved the way a lock of his hair always fell just above his eye. And his blue eyes were like a sapphire pool she could dive into. He was speaking.

"You said the other day you would like to know more about the care of horses. I could give you some quick facts if you'd like." He sat a cup of coffee in front of her. "I'll need to saddle a horse if you want an evening ride at dusk, but I wouldn't suggest that."

Susan tried hard to keep the blush she felt creeping up. "I'd like to learn. Maybe we could go for a ride in the morning." She put her hands around the mug of coffee to hide them from shaking. She didn't really want to ride. She wanted to spend time with Doug. "And I've been

270

meaning to ask you, why do you want me to research leather stores in the library?"

"I'll let you in on a secret. I would like to learn to make saddles and also boots."

"I won't tell, but why keep it a secret? I'm sure Braden wouldn't mind. It sounds really exciting. Maybe I could watch you work."

Susan's thoughts traveled back in time. It seemed that Doug was in the house a lot. He was either getting items to stock his refrigerator with snacks and beverages, or some days he just pulled up a chair when Susan wasn't busy at her desk, and they'd talk. She had felt herself being attracted to him, but dismissed it, thinking he probably had a girlfriend. Things had been so busy, she really hadn't counted their visits, and she knew Ellie hadn't, either since she had mentioned she thought he was checking on supplies for the horses or turning in receipts, or had some other reason to be in the house talking to Susan.

Doug broke the silence. "Maybe you could help me understand the books I've ordered." He paused and rose to pace the room. After a few minutes, he returned to his chair. "Susan, I may be out of line, but I've never heard you mention a boyfriend."

Susan knew he didn't need her to help him, but maybe it was a cover for something else. She quickly answered, "No, there's no one."

"Then, would you like to go to a movie in town Saturday evening? If you're not comfortable, just tell me."

Susan's heart leapfrogged into her throat. Finding her voice, she said, "I would love that. I've been wanting to see the movie that's showing."

"Good, let's have an early dinner before the movie."

"Sounds wonderful. I'll let you get back to whatever you were doing." Susan floated to the house, giggling like a school girl with her first crush.

Saturday dawned bright and warmer than usual. Susan was in a dither trying to decide what to wear. Ellie saw her pulling one dress after another from her closet and putting them on her bed.

"So, you and Doug are going to dinner and a movie?" Ellie's eyes were twinkling.

"Yes, but just as friends. Don't read anything into it."

271

Braden leaned against the doorframe. "I just came from the stables. Doug seems as nervous as a dog treeing a squirrel." Braden had a mischievous smile on his lips. "Going to a movie, huh? Is there something I should know, little sis?"

Susan blushed. "No! It's just a night out...with a friend."

Braden locked eyes with her. "Ellie and I have watched you two for a while, and you have just confirmed our suspicions. We think there's more to it than just a casual friendship."

"Stop, Braden. I have to decide what to wear. Now leave me alone, please."

"Knowing how long you take in the bathroom, you'd better start getting ready now."

"That was in high school. I'm faster now."

Ellie and Braden moved out of the room and into the breakfast nook. Ellie opened the refrigerator and took out a pitcher of tea. She put ice in two glasses and poured the tea. Setting them on the table, she looked at Braden, and they burst out laughing. "Do you think they will really fall for each other?"

Braden wiped his eyes. "I think they already have, but they don't know it, yet."

"I guess they'll find out soon enough." Ellie laughed out loud.

Doug went to the house to see if Susan was ready. She was sitting in the parlor in a pale-yellow dress with a white cardigan. Doug's breath caught in his throat. She looked like sunshine and radiated happiness that warmed his whole body. "Shall we go?" He helped her with her coat.

At dinner, Doug was surprised to find that he and Susan chose the same entree from the menu. "Guess like minds, huh?"

Susan smiled. "The more we talk, the more I think we have in common."

"I've noticed that, too."

After the movie, riding home, Susan turned in her seat to face Doug. "I really had a nice time tonight. You're very easy to talk to. Thank you for inviting me."

So many things Doug wanted to say tore at his brain, but he knew he should take things slow. "You're good company, Susan. I've wanted us to do this for a long time, but I thought you had someone in your life."

"I thought the same about you!"

Doug walked her to the door, gave her a long hug and brushed her cheek with his lips. "See you tomorrow."

Every Thursday, Susan and Doug would spend time together, either going to dinner or to a movie. They both discovered they liked bowling, and Doug would drive to either Jackson or Vicksburg to a bowling alley a couple of times a month. They couldn't date on the weekend because that's when most of the guests arrived so they had to get creative through the week.

CHAPTER THIRTY-FOUR

The rest of winter backed out as spring heralded her majesty with beautiful flowers, greened pastures, sot breezes, and gently swaying branches where leaves were beginning to erupt. February scored unusually warm weather, and Valentine's Day dawned exceptionally pleasant.

After a fitful night's sleep, Ellie moved to a window opposite her bed and brushed her hair out of her eyes. Murmuring she said, "I thought I'd be nervous today, but I think I'm more excited." She threw on a robe and stood on the first step of the stairs to see if she heard voices. Susan came up the stairs.

"I was just coming to see if you are awake. Finn has a lovely breakfast waiting on you."

"I don't want to see Braden."

"You won't. He slept at the Inn. Doug and Justin stayed with him. Both of our families are in the dining room. Do you want to eat with them or in your room?"

"Is Nannie here?"

"Yes, as spry as can be!"

"I'll throw on something and eat with them. The wedding isn't until five, so I have plenty of time for you to do my makeup and hair. So, Justin is here?"

Susan smiled. "Yes, he got here last night. He seems really nice, and I'm glad he's here with Braden. Doug said Braden is as nervous as a horse in an earthquake!"

"I wonder if he's eaten?"

"No, but Finn said he was going to take Doug and Braden a tray."

"What about Justin?"

"He's helping Finn. I heard them laughing, so I assume they are getting along fine."

As Ellie walked into the dining room, both families clapped, the men rose, and smiles lit every face.

Cynthia jumped up and hugged her daughter. "Happy wedding day, sweetheart. You are getting a wonderful man to be your husband."

Ellie beamed. "I feel like God orchestrated this whole thing. The house, Braden coming to town, my guilt over Tommy, and now knowing he can't hurt anyone any longer. It's not just coincidence, as far as I'm concerned."

Mason stood. "You're right. Emma and I have wondered for years if Braden would find someone and if we would accept his choice. He didn't have a lot of girlfriends in high school, as you know." Mason cleared his throat as an ebbtide rose from his stomach and almost drowned his voice. "But, Ellie, you are perfect for him, and I pray he will be perfect for you. We couldn't be happier. Welcome to the Cunningham family!"

Ellie smiled. "Thank you. I don't think Braden or I would have thought this possible when we first met, but we've both changed and relaxed."

Emma said, "And let love blossom just as this mansion has come to life, vibrant with your love."

Finn and Justin walked in and served breakfast. Ellie locked eyes with Justin.

"Thank you for coming. I know having you stand up with Braden will make this wedding extra special."

"Thank you. It's nice to meet you. I love this place. And the kitchen is superb. It's wonderful to work with Chef Finn."

Finn was smiling. "Good to have you. We work well together."

All the guests assembled in the parlor just before five o'clock. Every third person was handed an old-fashioned lantern with a candle inside. They would make a processional down to the orchard, all except Nannie and Preston.

Upstairs, Susan did Ellie's hair and makeup, and Ellie's friends took care of the dress. Katherine slipped The Sullivan Gown over Ellie's head. Lori put Ellie's shoes on and secured her blue and white garter. The girls helped each other to get into Grace and Maggie's pastel gowns.

Shivers ran up and down Ellie's spine as she imagined herself wearing the same gown that had been worn by so many Sullivan women.

It seemed to glow. Susan held the white floor-length cape and draped it around Ellie's shoulders.

Ellie wanted Finn to make a three-tiered wedding cake with blue flowers draped down the sides, and a little bride and groom she found on top. As a final preparation, she had hired a three-piece orchestra, who would set up just outside the circle and then move inside for the reception.

After the guests had left, Ellie and her attendants descended the stairs. When Charity saw Ellie, her hand flew to her mouth. Tears glistened in her eyes. "You are beautiful. This brings back so many memories of my own wedding and so much hope for the future, my dear."

Preston wiped his eyes. "I don't think I have ever seen you so radiant. I may not be able to give you away."

"Thank you, Nannie. Thank you, Daddy. Now let's go get married."

Doug had the buggy ready to drive Nannie and the attendants to the wedding site before returning for Preston and Ellie. As soon as they were seated in the buggy, Ellie heard the strains of "Canon in D Major" by Pachelbel.

As the processional neared the orchard, Ellie saw people walking with the lanterns and taking their seats after hanging the lanterns on special hooked poles. An arched white trellis intertwined with greenery and baby's breath marked the entrance to the bridal path. Pots of white roses and blue hydrangeas flanked each side of the path leading to a small gazebo that would house the wedding party. Ellie carried one of Grace's journals with a single white rose on top, tied with a blue ribbon.

As Ellie walked through the trellis on Preston's arm, loud gasps emitted from the audience. Braden's eyes took in the beauty of his bride, and tears threatened. He swallowed hard, forcing them back down. It was as if time stood still, and Grace Sullivan was walking down the aisle. He couldn't believe Ellie was wearing the gown that had been passed down for so many generations. So, she had kept this a secret from him, but he smiled, knowing he had a surprise for her, too.

The ceremony was short and personal. Braden and Ellie had decided to recite the vows they repeated at their handfasting. As soon as the minister pronounced them husband and wife, he ended the ceremony. The weather was turning a little nippy.

Following the wedding, Nannie and Preston rode back in the carriage, and Justin and Finn rushed toward the Big Kitchen. The orchestra led the recessional playing "Beethoven's 9th Symphony" as Ellie and Braden walked behind them. As they neared the house, the orchestra slipped into the house ahead of the wedding party.

No one saw the lone figure hidden behind a large oak tree. Tommy Butler wiped a tear from his eye and made his way back to the road. "It should have been me, but I've messed up my life. At least she's happy," he said to the trees as he walked back to his father's car.

Since his dad had gotten him out on bail, Tommy had determined to change his life. He had been going to church, had been baptized, and was attending a Bible study every week. There was no sense in trying to find a job until after the verdict of his trial.

As Braden and Ellie reached the top step, Ellie could barely wait to see what Finn and Justin would serve. She had made some suggestions, but left the final menu up to Finn. She was anxious to see if Finn had made her cake the way she wanted it.

Braden bent and gave Ellie a quick kiss at the entrance to the house. Everyone clapped and cheered. Before he opened the door, he raised his hand.

"I've been told there is one more detail before my bride enters, so please excuse me for a few minutes." Strains of music filtered from the house onto sound waves gently wrapping around each guest in the happy atmosphere.

Ellie frowned. What could have happened? Did Finn not finish the cake? Were the extra chairs not set up? It had been so perfect so far. What was wrong?

Within a few minutes, Braden opened the door. Ellie and everyone else broke into laughter. He stood, decked out in the Sullivan kilt! He offered his arm, and Ellie not trying to suppress her giggles, moved inside with everyone following. They moved to the parlor where an area had been reserved for dancing. Ellie could see through to the dining room where a magnificent three-tiered cake stood in the middle of a beautiful buffet. She squinted her eyes. Instead of the bride and groom she had purchased for the top, there was a bride dressed in a replica of Grace's gown and a groom in a Sullivan kilt! She turned to Braden.

"When did you have the topper made?"

He smiled. "I didn't. Nannie did that."

"And you're in a kilt!"

"Jim's to be exact! I wanted to surprise you! But I wouldn't have done this for anyone else!"

"Well, you certainly did surprise me."

Ellie glanced at Charity who had a mischievous grin. "Told you I can keep secrets!"

Finn and Justin had outdone themselves and served a delicious meal. Tables had been set up in the parlor as well as the dining room. Since the only guests had been family and a few close friends, there was room for everyone. Finn had hired waiters who wore tuxedos and white gloves for the occasion. The orchestra situated in the study continued playing softly as the guests took their seats.

The first course consisted of onion soup or a clear broth cabbage soup. The salad course featured either apple fennel slaw or a caprese salad. The main course provided a choice of roasted duck confit croquettes or prime rib roast with horseradish aioli, twice whipped mashed potatoes, herbed Yorkshire pudding, lemony asparagus, and spinach gratin. Yeast rolls and Irish butter completed the entrée. Iced tea and Champagne accompanied the meal, the flutes ready for a toast.

When everyone was seated, Mason and Preston rose. Preston recited an Irish blessing.

"May love and laughter light your days and warm your hearth and home. May God and faithful friends be yours wherever you may roam. May peace and plenty bless your world with joy that long endures."

Mason held his flute high that had been filled with Champagne. "To Ellie and Braden for a long and happy life together. God bless you. Cheers."

Everyone clinked their flutes and yelled, "Cheers."

Dessert was the wedding cake with each layer a different flavor, consisting of chocolate, coconut, and vanilla. Guests clapped as Braden and Ellie cut a piece and fed each other.

Following the large meal, tables were removed from the parlor, and chairs were situated along the walls. Guests were invited to dance or just listen to the orchestra playing. Ellie and Braden moved to the center of the room for their first dance. They had practiced the Viennese waltz for

279

days. Strains of "The Blue Danube Waltz" drifted from the study as they began their dance. Halfway in, the newlyweds stopped. Braden bowed, and Ellie curtsied. Ellie went to sit beside Preston and her mother.

Braden went to Charity, bowed and escorted her to waltz around the parlor one time. Her eyes sparkled the whole time, and the smile was something no one would forget.

"This is what I've been living for! To see you happy and married to a wonderful girl."

"You'll always be my best girl, Nannie! Are you sure you're up to dancing?"

"Glad it's a slow waltz. I made a vow to dance at your wedding a long time ago, and nothing would stop me. I'm doing it! My swimming has helped my legs."

"Looks like Susan and Doug may be the next couple to marry."

Charity giggled. "Hope I'll be able to attend that wedding, too."

Braden led Charity back to her seat, then moved to his mother. He bowed and escorted her to the dance floor, and Ellie and Preston waltzed about halfway around the dance floor.

Braden and Ellie then danced to "The Twelfth of Never," their song.

Braden held his bride as they danced. "I can't imagine a more beautiful wedding. I see now why all the details. I love you so much."

"And I love you!"

The orchestra played a few more songs, and most of the younger guests danced while the older ones just listened to memories the music brought back.

As the clock wound down to ten o'clock, Braden raised his hand.

"It's been the best night ever for us. So, as a surprise, we'd like to ask you to join with us singing one last song. Justin had slipped behind Braden and all at once, they broke out their guitars. Suddenly they belted out, "Goodnight Irene" except they substituted Ellie for Irene in the lyrics. The crowd sang along with them, laughing and singing. It was a happy ending to a wonderful celebration.

Laughter and music filled the air as everyone got ready to leave or go to their rooms.

Braden and Ellie changed clothes. Braden was more than happy to get out of his kilt, and Ellie wanted to change as well. They decided to spend their first night in Vicksburg in a quaint little hotel next to their favorite restaurant.

Braden picked up Ellie and carried her across the threshold. "I know this isn't our home, but when we go back to the Big House, I'll carry you over the threshold there, too! I want to make sure that will insure good luck for our life together."

"Braden, I didn't realize that I could ever be this happy. And now I am one of the Sullivans the same as you."

"You looked beautiful in Grace's gown. What a surprise that was for me. I thought I was the only one with a surprise!"

Ellie laughed. "Yes, Nannie gave her blessing for me to wear it, and she is going to have our names and date put on the petticoat. And obviously she kept your secret, too!"

"It didn't take much to convince her I wanted to wear the kilt. I wish you could have seen her face when I mentioned it."

"I think being so much a part of our wedding was a special honor to her and those who came before us."

The next morning, Braden and Ellie got up early and drove back to The Sullivan House to say goodbye to those who stayed overnight. After a hearty breakfast, everyone made their way to their cars, and one by one, they followed each other down the drive.

"Looks like a caravan!" Braden remarked as he and Ellie waved from the porch.

Justin joined them. "Are you sure I'm not overstaying my welcome?"

Braden looked at Ellie. They burst out laughing. Ellie finally found her voice. "I guess if you'd like to stay around a while, we might find an opening for you as a sous chef."

"Really?"

Braden clapped him on the shoulder. "Yes, Ellie and I talked to Finn, and he would be delighted. We'll discuss salary later if you're interested."

"I'd been thinking I jumped into the wrong profession when I couldn't find a job in Dallas except for fast food joints, and somehow gourmet food doesn't fare well in those."

Braden laughed. "When I got here, I thought I had made the wrong career choice, too, but there's something endearing about a small town."

"I never thought either one of us would want a town like this, but it's growing on me. Dallas is big and noisy!"

Justin looked at Ellie. "I really enjoyed meeting Lori. She and I hit it off right away. Is she from here?"

"No, she's from Jackson, which isn't that far from here. She's a friend from high school days. Want me to put in a good word for you?"

"Sure, but don't make a big production out of it. I don't want her to think I'm too eager!"

Braden laughed. "Of course, you know we may have to fill in for the orchestra if they aren't available."

The phone ringing summoned Ellie back inside.

CHAPTER THIRTY-FIVE

She almost dropped the phone when she heard the voice on the other end. "Tommy, why are you calling? You are still in jail, aren't you?"

"No, my dad got me out on bail a long time ago. Listen, please, and don't hang up."

"You'd better make it quick."

"Okay." He told her about his conversion and how his life had changed. "I know my trial is coming up in April, and I am resigned to spend the rest of my life in prison. But to save my soul, I asked God to forgive me. I'd like to ask your forgiveness, too."

"Tommy, I've known you a long time. Your personality changed that day at the lake, and again when you came here to shoot Braden. But if you are truly sorry, then as the Bible says, I forgive you. Just don't ask me to do it seventy times seven as Jesus said."

"I won't. Thank you. Look, I know you and Braden are going to testify against me, and I don't blame you. I deserve it. May I speak to Braden? I need to ask his forgiveness as well."

Ellie squinted her eyes shut. Had Tommy really repented? Taking a deep breath, she said, "Let me ask him."

Going to the front veranda, she told Braden about how Tommy had supposedly changed. "He wants to talk to you."

"I guess I could see what he says." He took the phone from Ellie, but held it between them.

"Braden, I would like to ask your forgiveness. I have given my life to Christ now, and I am planning to pursue a divinity degree while in prison. I know I can't atone for what I did, but maybe if I can reach out to other prisoners with the truth of God's Word, then my mistakes can be turned to something good."

Braden inhaled a deep breath. What should he say? Was Tommy serious? Should he forgive him? He thought of Nannie and his upbringing in the church. "If you really mean it, then I forgive you. Just do not hurt my wife, or there will be consequences."

"Thank you. I sincerely hope you and Elizabeth will be happy. I won't bother you again, and please know I am not trying to persuade you to change your testimony at my trial. Thank you, Braden. Now my soul can rest." The line went dead.

Ellie moved into Braden's arms. "That was weird. I heard most of what he said, but I wonder if he's serious?"

"Maybe you should call his parents."

"I won't have to. They have booked a stay next weekend."

"Are you okay with that?"

"They have asked for forgiveness, also, and I agreed. We can use the money, and I can be nice for a weekend! They were very sweet to me until Tommy went missing."

Braden pulled Ellie close to his chest. "I don't know about you, but I'm glad we have the wedding behind us."

"Yes, it was everything I imagined, and more."

"I wish you hadn't booked the Butlers for next weekend. I thought maybe we could get away somewhere for a few days and then later have a real honeymoon."

Ellie said, "Susan and Doug can watch the house for a few days during the week, and maybe Finn could take a few days off. He really worked hard on this wedding. It would give Justin a crash course in being chef for a week! I think we could slip away for a day or two."

"That's a great idea! I hope Susan and Doug don't get married before we have a honeymoon. But thinking about it, spring is almost here. As Tennyson said, "In the spring a young man's fancy lightly turns to thoughts of love.""

Ellie smiled. "Perfect. Susan and Doug did look pretty cozy on the dance floor. Where shall we go?"

"You name it."

"I'm tired, and I know you are, so why not just go back to Vicksburg? There are some things we could do, and I love that restaurant."

"That suits me. I'll call and make reservations."

After a three-day hiatus, resting and eating to their heart's content, Mister and Missus Braden Cunningham returned home. Walking into the house, Ellie found Susan.

"Did we have more reservations call in? And did Doug have any trouble with the horses?"

Susan blushed. "Yes, three more couples. One couple wants to come on Wednesday and leave Friday."

"That's odd. I take it from the expression on your face, you and Doug had a good time?"

Susan extended her left hand. A beautiful oval diamond sparkled from her ring finger. "Yes, we did."

Braden overheard the conversation. "Did you say someone booked in the middle of the week?"

"Yes, they said they work weekends."

Ellie looked at Braden and blew out a breath. "A lot happened when we were gone! Susan is engaged!"

"How do you know that?"

"Because she has a diamond ring on her finger! Men!" She pulled Susan to the kitchen for a cup of coffee. "Tell me everything."

"Doug planned a picnic. He found a grassy spot and had put a quilt down with a basket of food and a pitcher of lemonade. I had no idea he had done that. He asked me to go horseback riding and led me to a place down by the river. When I saw what he had set up, I was hoping it was something special. We dismounted, and before I could sit down, he dropped to one knee and asked me to marry him."

"That is so romantic. Have you set a date?"

"No, he wants to save up more money."

"Are you planning to leave us?"

"No, Doug was going to ask if you would mind if we live in the Inn? You can still rent it out for reunions, and we could stay in his apartment if people rent the Inn. He wants to run it by Braden, so don't say anything."

"I think that would be perfect. Finn has moved back into the house, so you and Doug would be the only ones living there, and if we have reunions, you could oversee the guests to make sure they are comfortable."

The days flew by until Saturday morning. Joe and Ruby Butler arrived, and much to Ellie's relief, they didn't speak of Tommy. They took a buggy ride, and mostly rested, either in their room or on the veranda. They did go to the Circle of the Heart, as it was now known.

Sunday afternoon, after church, Ellie approached them on the back veranda. She looked at Ruby. "I've noticed you haven't mentioned Tommy."

"We didn't want to cause you any discomfort, dear. We just wanted to come and rest and get away from everything for a little while. It's only a couple of weeks until the trial. Joe and I also went to the Circle and renewed our vows. It is a hard time for us, and we know sometimes this kind of news can push married people apart. We need to stand strong for our son."

Ellie wiped tears from her face. "I'm happy you did that. It's a place of spiritual peace for us. There is also a large bolder by the river. It is called The Blessing Stone, and we sometimes go there to pray."

Joe took his wife's hand. "We've been working with Tommy's attorney. After we saw this place when we came to visit, I thought it would be a quiet place to bring Ruby before all the chaos of the trial starts…that is, if you would have us."

Ruby smiled. "And of course, we've always loved you. I'm afraid we didn't show it when Tommy went missing. We had thought you would be our daughter-in-law."

Ellie's frown knitted her brows together. "You do know, they expect Braden and me to testify?"

Joe's expression changed. Sadness covered his face. "Yes, we know that. We want you to feel free to tell the truth, and we will deal with the verdict, whatever it may be. We are not here to try to coerce you to change your testimony or even to talk about Tommy."

Braden and Ellie talked about Tommy after the Butlers left. They had taken the horses out for a ride and stopped by the river. Braden turned his head and looked deep into Ellie's eyes, trying to read her thoughts.

They dismounted and walked their horses along the bank of the river, each wrapped up in their own thoughts. Braden broke the silence.

"Have you thought about what you will say at the trial?"

"Yes, I've been wondering what you are going to say before I tell you what I think because you are the victim."

Braden took a deep breath and exhaled. "I know Tommy wanted to kill me at first, and he very well could have, but raising his gun at the last minute saved my life. Based on what we saw in his room, he was on drugs and alcohol. I'm no worse for wear, and if he has sobered up and wants to be a minister, I can't see relegating him to prison."

"You're the one he shot, but for me, I feel he has learned his lesson. Ruby said he wants to start a prison ministry whether he is an inmate or not. Just like he said. And he did tell me at the last minute, he knew he couldn't go through with killing you. He tried to move the gun up."

Braden stopped by a large bolder. "Let's pray here at The Blessing Stone as Grace called it."

"I told the Butlers about it."

Holding hands, they knelt at the stone and both prayed for wisdom to do the right thing. Once they prayed, Braden said, "I just feel like the Lord wants me to ask for leniency for Tommy."

Tears moistened Ellie's eyes. "That's very generous of you, Braden, and one of the reasons I love you so much. You are able to love your enemy. I have the same feeling as you do."

Braden pulled Ellie to her feet, and they headed back with the horses. "I'll call our attorney tomorrow and tell him what we have decided. He can take it from there."

Over breakfast the next day, Braden poured a second cup of coffee for both of them. "I don't know if you heard the phone, but that was Kenneth Tyler. He thinks we've gone soft in the head, but he said he would abide by our choice and call Tommy's attorney."

"I guess I was outside. We don't have long to wait. I know the Butlers are as nervous as a fly in a spider's web." Ellie gathered their dishes and put them in the sink as Finn and Justin were finishing their breakfast.

"I could have gathered the dishes, Ellie." Justin rose to take the last few dishes from her.

Ellie grinned. "Well, next time. I didn't think it was a sous chef's job or the chef's place, either."

Justin grinned. "I love my job, and I love large gatherings."

"Finn stoked his chin. That makes two of us."

"We are booked solid through the summer, so you two will have a lot of fun!"

Back at the table, Ellie stirred her lukewarm coffee and quizzed Braden. "Has Doug talked to you about their wedding plans?"

"I meant to say something to you. I told him he and Susan could live in the Inn for as long as they want to. He told me he has bid on a couple of more horses for us. If he gets them, we may have some foals before long."

Ellie laughed. "So, we'll have a side business breeding horses?" Her eyes sparkled.

"I hope you will agree to sell them!"

The morning of the last day of March dawned bright and sunny. Braden had taken a couple of days off and busied himself with their luggage. Ellie finished dressing and headed to give Susan last minute instructions.

"So, you're staying with Mom and Dad while the trial is going on?"

"That's the plan. I am not looking forward to this at all."

"Is it a jury trial?"

"I don't know. We haven't heard." She gave Susan a quick hug.

"The trial should have been here, shouldn't it? This is where he shot Braden." Susan looked confused.

"They asked for a change of venue in case they did decide on a jury because they have a better pool in Jackson."

"Keep us posted if you need us."

As Ellie and Braden entered the courtroom, Ellie noticed Tommy sitting quietly, staring straight ahead. Braden took his seat beside their attorney. She was relieved it wasn't a jury trial, so maybe it wouldn't take so much time. She took a seat on the front row behind Braden.

When the court was called to order, both attorneys asked to approach the bench. Kenneth Tyler told the judge that Braden had decided not to pursue the lawsuit. The judge looked at Tyler and asked, "Was your client coerced in any way to come to this conclusion? This is a serious crime if Mr. Butler is found guilty. He's been charged with attempted murder of Mister Cunningham and Officer Barton, and one count of threatening Missus Cunningham."

"Yes, your honor, my client is well aware of the gravity of this lawsuit. I tried to talk him out of it, but he insists."

"That leaves Missus Cunningham and Officer Barton. I need to know their decisions before we proceed."

Kenneth Tyler spoke. "They are both in the courtroom, Your Honor. Shall we ask them to testify?"

"I'll see all litigants in my chambers." He rose and motioned for Braden, Tommy, Ellie, and Officer Barton to follow.

They sat in maroon leather chairs arranged in a semi-circle around a large oak desk as the judge took his place behind his desk. A court reporter swore them in. The judge questioned Braden and asked why he did not want to pursue the case.

"You honor, I believe Tommy Butler was on drugs when he shot me. He has since become a Christian and has asked my wife and me to forgive him. We feel he deserves a second chance to turn his life around because he told my wife, Elizabeth Addison Cunningham that he changed his mind at the last minute, and the gun went off before he raised it enough not to hurt me."

The judge turned to Ellie and Clyde Barton. "And I'll hear what you two have to say. Officer Barton?"

"Your Honor, Thomas Butler was in an agitated state and almost incoherent when I arrested him. He fired his revolver at me and threatened Missus Cunningham on the way to the jail, but he had settled down by the time we got there. After he was put into a cell, we observed him closely because he seemed very depressed, and I was afraid he would hang himself, so he was put under suicide prevention observation. He tested positive for drugs and alcohol. As soon as he got settled, he asked me for a Bible. At first, I thought it was a ploy to look good in court, but I found him sobbing and praying. I am happy to drop the charges on my behalf."

The judge turned to Ellie. "And what do you have to say?"

Ellie cleared her throat. "Your Honor, I've known Thomas Butler for a very long time. When I first knew him, he was nice and sweet to me, but then he turned arrogant and self-centered. After his arrest, he has changed and become more focused on other people. I believe if given the chance, he could have a more positive influence on others rather than sitting in a jail cell. I would be willing to give him that chance."

The judge looked hard at each of the four plaintiffs. "Were any of you coerced into dropping this case?"

One by one, under oath, they all replied they had not.

The judge shook his head and turned to Tommy. "You are one fortunate man, Mister Butler. Not many people would be as generous."

"Yes, your honor. I am aware of that. I didn't know Mister Cunningham wasn't going to go forward with the case until a few days ago, and I had no idea that Officer Barton and Elizabeth Cunningham felt the same. I believe the Lord has answered my prayers, and I am very grateful to all of them as well as this court."

"Mister Butler, you will have to pay court costs, and serve an extended parole period. You will also have to spend a few weeks in prison because it is the law, but I can dismiss that with the time you spent in jail. You will also have to pay for Mister Cunningham's medical bills."

Braden spoke up. "Your honor, I would like for the case to be dismissed with prejudice."

Ellie and Clyde nodded their heads.

"Very well. Against my better judgment and with that said, I will dismiss the case with prejudice." He shook his head again and pounded his desk with his gavel. "Case dismissed."

As they prepared to leave, Tommy walked over to Braden, Clyde, and Ellie and shook hands with each of them. "I've never known anyone to be so generous. Thank you doesn't seem adequate, but I am eternally grateful."

Braden smiled. "Good luck, Tommy. I do hope you have turned your life around."

Office Barton locked eyes with Tommy. "Don't give me a reason to rescind my decision."

Ellie's face held memories of the past. "Don't prove us wrong, either. Go forward to a new life, but don't forget your past."

Tommy raised his right hand. "By the grace of our loving Father, you all have been His answer to my prayers. I shall never forget your kindness."

By the time Ellie and Braden drove home, it seemed as if the air was a little clearer and the sun a little brighter. Ellie reached over and put her hand on Braden's arm. "We did the right thing, didn't we?"

Braden smiled. "Yes, sweetheart, we did."

CHAPTER THIRTY-SIX

Two weeks later, Braden went to the post office before going home after school. There was an envelope addressed to him. He opened it, and a check fell out. It was from the County Clerk noting payment by Thomas Butler for the medical bills Braden had submitted. There was also a thank you note to both Ellie and him.

Ellie looked at the note. "Nice of him to send a thank you."

"Yes, I wonder if he really is going to pursue a divinity degree?"

"I talked to Ruby Butler the other day. She said Tommy was going to college full time, and that he would have his degree in another year. In the meantime, he has apparently started a small church in their basement. She said the music gets kind of loud with a band playing, but they aren't complaining."

"That's good. Anything else?"

"Yes, she said he's met a girl from one of his classes, and they have started seeing each other."

"I didn't know girls got a divinity degree."

"Ruby said she wants to be a missionary."

"Sounds like you had quite a conversation."

"We did. I harbor no ill will toward any of them. I believe Tommy learned his lesson when he thought he had killed you. I'm sorry I didn't tell you. I got busy, and it slipped my mind."

"I wonder if he is serious about the girl?"

"According to Ruby they are engaged."

"Well, that's sudden. You haven't talked to Tommy?"

"No."

Braden looked over the calendar. "Looks like we're booked all summer except for one weekend. I'm glad we took a few days to go to

Vicksburg when we did. Let's take a that week off and have a real honeymoon. I owe you that."

Ellie was trying hard not to laugh, but she couldn't keep her lips in a straight line.

Braden looked at her. "What? You're grinning like a monkey with a peanut."

Ellie burst out laughing. "Well, that weekend is taken."

"What? It's not marked in the reservation book."

"You need to go be fitted for a tux the first of June to attend a wedding right here."

"Tux?" Suddenly, it dawned. "Susan and Doug?"

"Yes, my darling. They want us to stand up with them. Doug was going to ask you, but I couldn't keep the secret. The wedding is the seventh of June."

"Couldn't happen to a nicer couple."

"That's not all."

"What else? I must have missed a lot of news."

We had a wedding invitation also from Tommy and his fiancée, Denise. I don't know that we want to go, but I thought it was nice to invite us."

"Yes, it is. I guess they are both in school. "When is that wedding?"

"June the second in Jackson." Ellie looked at Braden to see his reaction.

"It's up to you whether we go." Braden sighed.

"I'd like to meet Denise and lend our support to Tommy. From what Ruby said, I believe Tommy is now on the right path."

"I've started on my novel, but so many things keep happening that I want to put in it, it's going to be nine hundred pages!"

Ellie laughed. "Are you going to tell the story of Oak Hollow and then our life here?"

"I thought I would just fictionalize everything, but there are so many true things. Maybe I'll make it nonfiction."

"I can't wait to read it."

"Hopefully, Grace's journals, my book, and your journaling will be time for this grand old mansion to live in infamy."

Ellie laughed. "Yes, President Franklin Roosevelt, may you be correct."

Braden returned the laughter. "That was a brilliant speech but a sad time."

The summer was speeding by as if it were on roller skates. With two weddings and all the rooms booked, Ellie and Braden hardly had time to say hello to one another. Finn and Justin seemed to be glued to the kitchen, but from the happy sounds of music and laughter drifting from the Big Kitchen to the main house, happiness and peace had finally overtaken the negativity of the past few months.

Doug and Susan's wedding was small with only their families and Braden's mom, dad, and grandmother there. They married in the gazebo just like Ellie and Braden, and much to the family's delight, Susan wore The Sullivan Gown and cape. Doug refused the kilt and wore a suit and cowboy boots. Finn and Justin prepared a great sit-down dinner, and everyone commented on how delicious the food tasted. All Doug wanted was a steak and baked potato, but Susan said she would like something a little fancier, so Finn and Justin were charged with making both of them happy.

In the end, they served a sit-down meal. First course was shrimp cocktails for an appetizer. A sweet potato and carrot soup with crusty bread sticks followed. The entrées were a grilled T-bone steak to honor Doug's wishes and a parmesan crusted Cornish game hen for Susan. Both were accompanied by a baked potato with toppings of butter, pepper jack cheese, sour cream, and fresh spring onion ends placed under the broiler until the cheese melted. A fresh corn salad followed as the next course. Dessert was a triple layer chocolate mocha cake with a rich cream cheese frosting.

For their honeymoon, they went to Gulf Port beach for five days. Doug had rented a house right on the beach. It had a hot tub and a swimming pool with a beautiful view of the gulf. Every morning, Doug got up, brewed coffee, and served Susan in bed. They usually had a quick breakfast and then lounged on the beach or tried their hand at surfing.

Sitting on the beach after getting bounced off their surf boards, Susan played with the sand. Doug turned to face her.

"Having fun?"

"Oh, yes. The water is beautiful, but it doesn't taste so great when it splashes into my mouth! Guess this is when I need to keep my mouth shut!"

"Those waves have a mind of their own. I got plenty of salt water, too. Getting up the nose is not the best way to clean out the sinuses!"

Susan's demeanor changed, and she stopped digging in the sand. "Doug, I know you have gone to a lot of expense and trouble to fulfill my dream of a beach honeymoon, and I am loving it. Treating me like a queen is something I could get used to pretty quickly, but I have another request."

"What might that be? Have I overlooked something you said you wanted to do?"

"No, darling. I said I just wanted to sit on the beach and soak up the sun, but that's selfish on my part, so I was wondering if we could start home a day early and stop by a small little shop."

"You want to go shopping?"

"No, I've arranged a meeting for you."

"Meeting? I don't understand."

"The man owns a shop and makes saddles, boots and belts. He has agreed to meet with you and answer questions you might have."

"Really?" Doug's eyes lit up almost as bright as when he said his vows to Susan. "You are too good to me."

"I see your million-dollar smile when saddles are mentioned. As I told you, you could have a side business and sell your saddles."

Walking into the small shop on their way home, the scent of leather permeated the room, and Doug stood for a moment taking it all in. Saddles and tack stood proudly on display, and Doug was almost mesmerized. From the back of the shop, an older man shuffled forward, a smile covering his wrinkled face.

"Welcome. You must be Doug Mabry. I'm known as Duke Taylor." He extended his hand to both Doug and Susan.

Doug regained his composure. "I am really happy to meet you. Are you sure you don't mind a novice like me asking you some questions?"

The old man laughed. "Son, individual saddle makers are a dying bunch, and it is my pleasure to see a young man like you interested in the art. It *is* an art, you know."

"Yes, sir. I know."

The old man turned to smiled. "My wife is up to the house yonder making some lunch, and she said for your missus to come up there and sit a spell with her while we talk business…that is, if you want to." He looked toward Susan.

Susan smiled. "I'd like that very much." The old man pointed her to the back door.

Knocking on the screen door of the rambling farm house, Susan immediately recognized the smell of baked apples.

"Come right on in, young lady. I just took a cobbler out of the oven. Name's Lucille."

"Susan." She extended her hand.

"Oh, land sakes, none of that formal stuff. Get over here and give me a hug."

"Mister Taylor said I might come visit with you while my husband asks your husband a million questions."

"Well, I can tell you, Duke will be in hog heaven. He'll probably enjoy their visit more than your mister."

"Is there anything I can help you with? Mister Taylor said you were cooking lunch."

"Oh, no, dearie, I've already got all the vegetables cooked. Just waitin' on the roast. Do you like to quilt? I'm just starting a new one."

Susan explained how they lived in an antebellum home, and that they found some quilts in the attic that must have been made in the 1800's.

"Oh, goodness, I'd sure like to see them. I have some my grandmother made a long time ago. They're priceless. You take good care of them."

"Yes, ma'am. I don't know the first thing about how to make them."

Lucille took Susan's arm and led her into the living room. A large frame hung from the ceiling with a quilt in the middle.

"This here's the quilt me and my ladies are makin' for the old folks' home. Come see." She lowered the quilt frame.

Susan looked at the stitches and was surprised that someone could make such tiny stitches. Before she could say anything, Lucille pulled her to a large sewing box full of scraps. "See these squares? They look like trash, but when they're sewed together, they make a quilt. This is the next

297

one our group will quilt." She produced a picture of the pattern from a quilting magazine.

Susan looked at some of the scraps that were sewn together. "These look so pretty. They don't look like scraps at all. They look like a fabric picture."

"Quiltin's an art, you see? To make something pretty out of something that looks like it should go in the trash."

"I think I might like to try my hand at this."

"Either find you a quilting bee, that's what we call it, or get you a good book with some patterns."

"I could do this while Doug is making saddles. He's not much on being idle, so after work, I could sit and make a quilt. Thank you for showing me. Maybe I can persuade my sister-in-law to do this, too."

"Maybe I'll get you hooked, and you'll come back, and sit with us someday."

"I just might take you up on it."

On the way home, Doug was excited and talked so fast, Susan had to ask him to slow down. "I take it you got a lot of information?"

"I did, but the neat thing is, he said if I needed to get some forms, he would help me and that I could come anytime I had a day off, and he'd work with me. He's going to tell me the best places to get leather, too."

"That's great."

"But I'm talking your head off. Did you and Lucille get along? You were talking at lunch about something I didn't quite understand."

"It was a quilting bee."

"Is that a special kind of bee? Do they make honey?"

"No, it's a bunch of women getting together who like to quilt. I am really intrigued about learning."

Doug smiled at her and reached over and put his hand on hers. "So, we are both going to learn something new in our spare time."

"Yeah, like we have a lot of that!"

"Weekdays aren't too busy, so maybe we can squeeze some time in."

Ellie and Braden postponed their honeymoon until the last week of August since they needed to help with all the guests, and other obligations kept cropping up.

They went to Tommy's wedding. Denise was a petite little thing, about the same size as Ellie, and they hit it off right away. They were going to honeymoon in The Philippines where they were both going to be missionaries. At the wedding, Tommy joked and addressed the small gathering. "Don't throw rice. We may have to take it with us because I know Filipinos eat lots of it!"

Tommy thanked Braden and Ellie again. "I'm going to be gone a long time, but I can finish my degree in a home study. If you feel like keeping us posted on any news from here, we would appreciate it."

Denise came up and put her arm around Tommy. "Thank you so much for coming. Tommy has shared his story with me, and I am very grateful that you two have been so kind. And please keep in touch…unless that's too awkward for you."

Ellie smiled. "Of course, we'll let you know any news we hear. It's nice to know you are both happy."

Later driving home, Braden looked at Ellie. "Maybe if Tommy had come to his senses a lot sooner, you might have stayed with him. He's really nice, now."

"I'm glad he's changed, but I don't think I was ever really in love with him. When I found out he had cheated on me so many times, I knew I didn't want him as a husband. I don't think he loved me, either. I was just another notch on his belt, and he wanted to control me and thought he would have access to my parents' money. But if you had told me he would become a minister, I would have told you that wouldn't happen until glaciers floated in the Mississippi. And I don't think he would have changed without the trauma he's been through."

"He said they are leaving as soon as the summer session of college is over, so I guess sometime in August."

"I wanted to run something by you. Now that we have some money, what would you think about air conditioning the Big Kitchen? That window unit blows on the food and it's hard to keep hot dishes warm."

"Great idea! I know both Finn and Justin will appreciate it. By the way, do you think Finn misses not having someone special in his life?"

Ellie sighed. "I don't know. I've thought about it a lot. At least there are a lot of pretty girls at church. Maybe one of them will catch his eye. But I don't think he is through grieving."

299

"One caught Justin's eye at our wedding. He and Lori Franklin are dating."

"So, he said. And Lori mentioned it to me the other day."

Things finally settled down by September. Though they had missed going on a honeymoon, they both agreed they were happier staying at home. Braden was delighted to be teaching in high school, and they had two new foals born. Doug came into the house often to spend time with Susan.

Ellie watched them and knew they were as happy as she and Braden were.

One morning over breakfast, Ellie was looking over the ledger when hunger pains prompted her to the kitchen and a bowl of oatmeal. Suddenly, she felt very hot, and the oatmeal tasted terrible. She rushed from the room and threw up. After rinsing her mouth, she went back to the kitchen. Finn had left breakfast up to Justin, and he was very concerned that the oatmeal had given her food poisoning. He tasted it, and it tasted fine.

"I'm so sorry, Ellie. I didn't do anything different than what we usually do."

"Don't worry about it, Justin. I think it's really stress with all the guests we've had. I've barely been able to keep up with the bills and reservations, and without Susan's help, I don't know what we'd do."

Finn came in and pulled up a chair. "May I have a word with you?"

CHAPTER THIRTY-SEVEN

"Yes, of course. What's on your mind?" Fear gripped Ellie, afraid Finn was going to turn in his resignation. Still feeling a bit queasy, she focused on his eyes.

"I'm wondering if I could have a weekend off to go see my relatives in Vicksburg."

"No, you most certainly cannot. You are due a paid vacation, and you have earned two weeks, so if you want to take them one at a time, that's fine. If you want to stay two weeks, you can!"

Finn finally relaxed. "Thank you so much. I hate leaving all of this to Justin with no help. He may be overwhelmed with so many mouths to feed."

"We don't have a lot of bookings until the end of the month, and I need to brush up on my skills. Susan and I can be Justin's sous chefs!" Justin rolled his eyes.

The next morning, Susan came in for breakfast, and she and Ellie started talking. Suddenly, both of them felt nauseous. Susan excused herself and went to the bathroom.

"Are you okay?" Ellie decided that it must be the brand of oatmeal that they were eating because she felt the same way she did the day before. She turned to Susan. "I'm going to ask Justin what brand of oatmeal he is serving. It's making both of us sick."

Susan grinned. "I'm not sick, Ellie."

"You're not? You threw up."

"I'm pregnant."

Ellie had a smile as big as Texas. "That's wonderful. I'm going shopping right away. Just wish we knew what you're having."

Susan said, "Doug and I both wanted children right away, so this is a blessing."

"Maybe I'm having sympathy pains with you. You know Braden and I are going to be parents, too."

"Are you pregnant?"

"No, you know that's not a possibility. We are picking up a precious little girl who is available for adoption. She's six years old. Both of her parents were killed in an accident when she was only three months old. Of course, it will take several months to finalize the papers. The good news is we have already been approved, but it will depend on whether we are all comfortable with each other."

"Wonderful. What's her name?"

"Annabelle Rose. We are going to pick her up Friday. I just hope she won't be intimidated with us, and I hope they've told her she is being adopted. I've picked out some clothes for her, but I want to take her shopping."

"I noticed you have been going into town a lot, but most of the time, I'm off before you come home, so I never asked you about it. I guess you were buying girly things!"

"Yes, come into her room, and I'll show you. I want to get your opinion."

They moved to the room next to their bedroom. Ellie opened the closet. Susan gasped at the beautiful things Ellie had picked out.

"Everything is perfect. I think she will love them."

Just then the phone rang, and Susan went to answer it. It was for a reservation.

Ellie poured a cup of hot tea and when it had steeped, she took it to the bench in the grove. Sitting where Grace and Jim fell in love always gave her a peaceful feeling, and she let her thoughts ramble. She and Braden had met Annabelle three times when they went to Jackson. She was a beautiful child with bright blue eyes and skin as soft as a newborn baby. She had long blonde hair that cascaded in ringlets almost down to her waist. She was shy and didn't interact with them on the first visit, but when she found out, she was going to be living with them as potential parents until she could be adopted legally, she opened up a little more on the second visit.

Apparently, according to the social worker, she had been living with her maternal grandmother, who was suffering from cancer and didn't feel she could keep her any longer. The grandmother had been in and out of the hospital, and the side effects of chemo were brutal. She could barely maintain herself, so Annabelle was put into f care. The family who fostered her were not the nurturing kind, and Annabelle had withdrawn into a shell. Her paternal grandmother had died before Annabelle was born, so she had no other surviving relatives.

The second time Ellie and Braden went to see her, her eyes looked less sad, and she actually smiled. She answered questions, but they could tell it was hard for her. The third time, when they told her they would be back in a week to get her, she looked relieved but somewhat apprehensive.

On Friday, Braden got a substitute teacher, and he and Ellie went to pick up Annabelle. Ellie had laid dresses and a couple of pair of jeans on Annabelle's bed. She would buy shoes and other essentials when Annabelle could pick out what she liked. Ellie had put an extra patchwork quilt on Annabelle's bed and couldn't wait for her new daughter to decide out how she wanted to decorate her room.

Driving toward Jackson, Ellie was as nervous as a cat caught in a thunderstorm. Braden wasn't much better. He pulled the car over just before they entered the city. Ellie's eyes reflected her confusion. "Is something wrong with the car?"

"No. We're both nervous wrecks. I can only imagine how Annabelle feels. I thought we'd take a few minutes to pray and ask God's guidance as we bring our beautiful child home."

Tears formed in Ellie's eyes. "You are so thoughtful, Braden, and such a strong Christian." She bowed her head and listened to her husband say the most heartfelt prayer she had ever heard. Once he finished, Ellie calmed down.

They arrived at the foster parent's house and met the social worker. Annabelle was ready with her backpack and a small suitcase. After a few introductory sentences, Ellie stooped down to Annabelle's level and asked, "Are you ready to go see your new room in your new home?"

Annabelle nodded and twisted her fingers together, but didn't meet Ellie's eyes.

On the way back to Scottsville, Ellie sat in the back seat with Annabelle. She rambled about the mansion, and told her about buying her some new clothes. She mentioned Finn and Justin and also Susan and Doug. When she told her about the young foals and the horses, Annabelle's eyes lit up.

"I think you will like the horses and their babies called foals. You can help Uncle Doug feed them if you'd like."

Annabelle said in a low voice, "I'd like that. I've never seen a horse in real life."

"Well, they are very sweet horses, and Uncle Doug will teach you to ride if you decide you want to learn."

Annabelle smiled.

Arriving home, met them as they came into the house. She looked at Annabelle. "Hello. I'm Susan. I'm your new aunt. I'm so glad you're home. You are going to love it here."

Annabelle smiled and ducked her head.

Braden followed behind with her small suitcase.

Unpacking, Ellie was shocked that the child had very few clothes, and what she did have were faded and out of style. Some had been patched, but they were not pretty. The grandmother had done the best she could, but Ellie had found out from the social worker that Annabelle got teased at school. No wonder from the looks of her clothes.

Ellie opened the closet and showed what she had bought to Annabelle. Her eyes took in all the clothes as if she were counting them. She turned a questioning look to Ellie.

"Yes, sweetheart, these are yours, and when you feel like it, we'll go shopping, and you can pick out some more. Would you like that?"

Annabelle ran her hands over the sashes of the dresses, caressing them as if they were fine silk.

"Come now. I want you to meet Uncle Finn, Uncle Justin, and Uncle Doug. They are your new uncles."

In the kitchen, Finn had made homemade ice cream, and when he heard them outside the Big Kitchen, he scooped out a double portion into a bowl and had it waiting.

"I'm so glad to meet you, Miss Annabelle. I made some fresh strawberry ice cream for you."

Annabelle sat down at the table as Finn put it in front of her.

"Thank you," she whispered before lifting a spoonful to her mouth. "Do you like strawberries?"

"Yes, sir."

Ellie sat beside her. "Finish your ice cream, and we'll go see Uncle Doug and the horses.

Entering the stables, Annabelle went up to the horses, but gripped Ellie's hand so hard, she thought this tiny girl would break all her bones. "Don't be scared, honey. They are very sweet." She patted one of the horses on his shoulder. He bent his head, and Ellie helped Annabelle rub his face. After ten minutes, she nuzzled her face to Apollo's. Doug and Ellie exchanged glances.

"Apollo loves to give rides. Would you like to go riding?"

Fear took residence in Annabelle's tiny face as she backed away. Doug saw it right away. "How about this? I'll get in the saddle, and your new mama can hand you up to me, and we'll ride for a little while. I'll hold you tight so you won't fall."

"Yes, sir, please."

They started off at a slow pace. Doug felt her relax and lean into the saddle as if she'd been riding all her life. "You're a natural horsewoman, Miss Annabelle. I think Apollo has just adopted you just like Miss Ellie and Mister Braden have adopted you!"

"Faster, please?"

"Okay, here we go." Doug spurred Apollo into a canter.

Annabelle loved the feel of the breeze blowing her golden curls away from her face, and the rhythm of the horse's gait soothed her as nothing had for a long time. She wondered if the Cunninghams were really going to adopt her. She missed her grandmother, but the last few months, she had been shuffled from one place to another when Granny had to go to the hospital. She didn't know how to pray, but she had heard that Jesus loves children, and she hoped He would find it in His heart to let her stay here forever.

After a few days, Ellie and Braden sat with Annabelle in the breakfast nook. She had opened up a little, but they wanted to make her feel more at home.

Ellie took Annabelle's hands. "Sweetheart, you are what we have been dreaming of for such a long time. When I pictured the child Jesus would give us, I wanted a little girl with blonde hair and beautiful blue eyes, like mine. He answered our prayers when you became available for adoption, but I never dreamed you would be so beautiful. You are exactly what I asked for in my prayers. I love you so much."

Braden wiped his eyes. "I didn't know you would be so perfect, either. God has answered our prayers. You two girls are the most important things in my life. We had agreed to let you stay home for a while to get used to us and your new surroundings, but it is time now for you to go to school. I teach in the building next to where you will be, so you can always come and get me if anyone is ugly to you, or if you get scared. I'll tell your teacher to let you come to me."

Annabelle's cast her eyes downward, and she scrunched her eyes to keep from crying.

Ellie thought she knew how she felt. "Honey, we know you had a wonderful mother and father, even though you don't remember them. Your grandmother gave us all the pictures she had of them and told us a little about them when we visited her before we picked you up from the foster home. It is okay if you'd like to keep some pictures of them in your room, but we need to decide what you will call us. Can you think about it?"

Annabelle raised her head and looked at Ellie and then at Braden. In a tentative voice she said, "Mama and Daddy?"

"That would be wonderful. Okay, that's settled. Since today is Saturday, if you want to, you can go to the stables and ride Apollo if Uncle Doug isn't busy."

Annabelle whispered, "I don't like school. Do I have to go?"

Ellie smiled. "Yes. I think you will like it here. You will have new clothes and meet new friends. If someone is ugly to you, like Daddy told you, just go tell him."

"Really?"

Braden spoke up. "Yes, really. No one is going to bully my beautiful daughter."

Annabelle seemed relieved. "May I go now and see the horses?" She hugged both Ellie and Braden, which surprised all three of them.

306

Sunday evening, Ellie and Annabelle picked out a beautiful pink t-shirt with a horse on the front and a pretty pink tiered skirt and laid them on Annabelle's dresser. She had pink socks and white tennis shoes, so she could just slip her clothes on the next morning for her first day of her new school.

Braden woke her gently the next morning, and together, they went into the breakfast nook for warm pancakes with syrup and whipped cream on top. Riding to school, Braden asked, "Are you nervous to be going to a new school?"

"A little. I've been to lots of schools when Granny was in the hospital."

"You'll do fine. You look very beautiful, and I hope you have a wonderful day. He led her to her room and introduced her to her new teacher, Missus Adams.

After school, Braden went to her room to walk her out. "How was your first day?"

Annabelle's eyes were sparkling. "I love it. The kids were so nice. I met a new friend named Karen who helped me learn how to play jacks at recess. And Polly pushed me in the swing and showed me how to go high. Missus Adams is very pretty and sweet. She told me I was a good student."

Braden grinned. That was the most Annabelle had talked since she came to live with them. When they got home, Justin had made her a snack of cheese and crackers with a glass of milk. As soon as she finished, she changed into her old jeans and went to find Doug. She started asking some questions, and as she became less intimidated, she asked, "When may I ride Apollo by myself?"

"I'll talk to your daddy and see what he thinks, but for now we'll ride together."

After they rode for a half hour, Annabelle went inside to talk to Ellie, and Doug went to find Braden. He was down by the orchard looking at some rotting lumber that used to be some structure. "Hey there, got a minute?"

"Sure, what's up? Is it Annabelle? Is she driving you crazy?"

"Just the opposite. Braden, she's a natural. I have never seen a child take to a horse like she has to Apollo, and he is the same way. I'm telling you I think he smiles every time he sees her. She wants to ride by herself, but I wanted to get your permission before I agreed."

"Are you comfortable with her riding alone?" Braden's face reflected his alarm.

"I'd want to saddle up and ride alongside of her for a while, but I think she and Apollo would both think I'm crazy." Doug chuckled.

"She's so little, she can't reach the stirrups, so how would she be able to ride?"

"I can adjust the stirrups if you agree."

"Let me talk to Ellie." Braden wiped his hands on his jeans as he started for the house to clean up.

That night at dinner, Braden broached the subject with Ellie. "Annabelle wants to ride by herself, and Doug thinks she ready for a trial run. What do you think?"

Ellie's face turned pale as if all the blood had drained from it. "Oh, my goodness, Annabelle, you are so little."

"But Uncle Doug would be beside me. Please?"

It was the first thing Annabelle had ever asked. Ellie shook her head dispelling the fear that had terrified her. "Braden, what do you think?"

"I guess if Doug rides beside her, and she only walks or maybe trots, we might try it."

He turned to Annabelle. "You know you could get hurt very badly if you fall off or if you try to go too fast at first. Will you promise your mama and me you will do exactly as Uncle Doug tells you?"

"Yes sir. I promise."

Ellie looked at Doug. "You feel sure about this?"

"I do. She's a natural. I want you to come out and watch us the first time."

"Can we go now, please?" Annabelle put her napkin on the table.

Ellie smiled. "No, sweetheart, it's bath time, and time for our bedtime story before you go to sleep, but I'll tell you what. When you get home from school tomorrow, we'll try it if Daddy agrees. I want to go watch, though, so I can see for myself."

After her bath, Ellie and Braden went in to read her a story. Almost all her books were about horses. "Are you tired of the same stories over and over again? Maybe you can get some books from Daddy's library."

Ellie was pulling up the cover over Annabelle's lap as she sat in bed. She looked a little restless.

Braden patted the cover over her legs. "Are you too excited to go to sleep?"

"A little. I wanted to ask if you would take a picture of me and Apollo and also one of our whole family. I'm happy I have you for parents. You're the best in the whole wide world. I want to put the pictures Granny gave you up somewhere and put pictures of us in my room. I don't remember my other mama and daddy."

Ellie couldn't speak. Braden coughed to clear the boulder that rose from his chest to his throat. "That can be arranged as soon as you want, sweetheart."

CHAPTER THIRTY-EIGHT

The next afternoon, Ellie sat in a lawn chair near the stables and watched Doug on one side, Braden on the other, with Annabelle in the middle. They came around to where Ellie could see them. What a sight they were. On Doug's command, Annabelle loosened the reins and clicked her tongue for Apollo to start walking. Ellie watched them go around in a large circle and back to where she was. Annabelle bent over Apollo's neck and then looked at Braden. "Can we go a little faster, Daddy?"

"It's May I, and you need to ask Uncle Doug."

Doug nodded. "Just a canter, Annabelle. No faster, okay?"

"Yes, sir." She took off ahead of them, but slowed to let them catch up. She was bent over, talking to Apollo and laughing.

After their ride, Doug went into the Big House and sat down with Braden and Ellie while Annabelle took a bath. "I've really observed her when she rides Apollo. She instinctively knows how to sit a horse, and though her little legs aren't quite long enough, she uses them well to direct Apollo. I've talked to some horse friends of mine, and there is an excellent dressage teacher in Vicksburg. I know that's a long way to take her for lessons, but it might be a good idea to see what they offer and see what they think about her skill. Of course, Annabelle may not want to take those kinds of classes. There's also barrel racing, but I think that's too dangerous at her age."

"Oh, my goodness. I want to do what is best for her, but that seems a long way to go for lessons." Ellie had her hands on the side of her face as if shielding it from words she didn't want to hear.

"I just wanted to run it by you. I haven't said anything to Annabelle."

In Annabelle's bedroom, Ellie was pulling up Annabelle's covers, and Braden was trying to find a book they could read that they hadn't read a thousand times. He'd memorized most of them as had Annabelle.

"I don't want a story time tonight. I want to talk."

"Okay, sweetheart, what is it?"

"You know what the kids at school are calling me?"

Dread spread through Ellie's body. She steeled herself. "What?"

"Rosie. They said that's what I am…sweet and pretty like a rose, so they changed it to Rosie. Isn't that cool?"

"Very cool." Braden was smiling. In only two weeks, Annabelle had made monumental changes. She was coming out of her shell and seemed open and trusting."

"You know what else?"

Braden smiled. "No, what else?"

"I'm a hippophile!"

Ellie looked puzzled. Does that mean you like hippos as well as horses?"

Annabelle laughed. "No, it means lover of horses. Did you know when Uncle Doug lets Apollo out to eat grass in the field, he stops and follows me wherever I go? Sometimes we just go to the river. I sit on that big rock, and he stands there like he's protecting me. I think I can read his thoughts, and he can read mine. I love him so much."

Ellie bent and adjusted the covers. "I think that's wonderful, sweetheart. But you know we don't like you going to the river until you learn to swim. Now let's say your prayers and go to sleep. Tomorrow's Friday, so you can stay up a little later. But you know you're not to get too close to the river, right?"

"Yes ma'am. I love you, Mama. I love you, Daddy."

They both gave her a kiss and a snuggle hug, as she called it.

Later in their room, Braden sensed something was wrong. Ellie had not been herself lately. She seemed tired and appeared to be forcing all her energy into taking care of Rosie as she now wanted to be called.

Rosie had said since this was a new life, she wanted to use her new name, and Rosie Cunningham sounded better and shorter than Annabelle Cunningham.

Braden reached over and pulled Ellie to him as he straightened the covers over their laps. "I sense something's wrong, honey. Are you okay? Is Anna...Rosie becoming too much for you?"

"Oh, no. I love her, and she is no trouble at all." She burst into tears.

"Tell me, sweetheart."

"I am afraid I have cancer."

"Cancer? Where did that come from?"

"I'm tired all the time, I have been having some abdominal pains, I'm losing weight, but I have no appetite, and I'm nauseated a lot of the time. I read in a magazine those were the symptoms of cancer. I don't want to leave you and Annabelle, I mean Rosie."

"We are going to the doctor tomorrow. I'm taking the day off from school. I'll get Doug to pick up Annabelle."

Braden called the next morning and told the receptionist it was urgent that his wife have an appointment. We think it may be something serious."

He hung up the phone and turned to Ellie. "We have an appointment at noon. The doctor is going to take his lunch break to see you."

"I don't want him to miss lunch."

"I don't want you worried or me, either."

Once they entered the doctor's office, Ellie told Braden she wanted to go in alone because she didn't want both of them to be shocked at the same time.

"No, I insist on going in with you." Just then the nurse called her. Braden rose.

The nurse said, "She's going to the lab, sir."

"Oh, I see."

Inside the lab, Ellie told the nurse, "I'd like to see the doctor alone. My husband doesn't take bad news very well when it concerns me."

Braden was getting nervous. Ellie had been gone thirty minutes. He didn't know much about labs, but he didn't think that was the amount of time it took, but maybe it was a special cancer test. He paced until he heard a door click. Ellie was grinning from ear to ear and holding a piece of paper.

"So, I take it, you don't have cancer?"

"No, but we need to stop by the pharmacy so I can get some vitamins."

"And that will cure you?"

"No, darling, not for about seven more months." She began laughing.

"Seven months?"

"Being pregnant isn't an illness, Braden."

"I know." Suddenly his face went pale, his hands trembled. "Oh, are you saying…"

"Yes!"

"Didn't you have an idea?"

"Well, I've missed monthlies before, so I didn't think a thing about it, especially since I was told I couldn't get pregnant."

"We don't want Annabelle to think this baby will cause us to want her any less."

"I've thought about that. I'll talk to her." Ellie started laughing again.

"I'm glad you are so happy, and I am really relieved. I prayed the whole time you were in there."

Ellie paused for a moment. "I was just thinking. Susan is due about the same time I am."

"I guess you two can compare notes as you go along. How are we going to tell Annabelle?"

Ellie rubbed her temple. "I'll think of something. Maybe we should investigate those horse lessons for her. That would mean so much to her."

"We can ask Doug and maybe take her tomorrow if they're open on Saturday."

When Rosie came home from school, she hugged Ellie and Braden and ran to her room to change. Braden stopped her.

"Rosie, we need to talk, okay?"

Immediately her little eyes clouded. "Am I in trouble? What did I do?" Tears welled in her eyes.

"Oh, no, sweetheart. I think you are going to like this talk." Braden pulled her onto his lap. "You see, Uncle Doug and I have been watching you with Apollo. We don't know what to think about it, but you and that horse have something special."

"Yes, we do, Daddy. Please don't take him away…or me, either."

Ellie couldn't stand it. "Listen carefully to Daddy, sweetheart. This is a good thing."

Rosie took a deep breath. "Okay." She swiped her eyes with the back of her hands.

Braden continued, "As I was saying, you are a natural with Apollo. We think maybe you might like to take dressage lessons. Dressage means…"

"I know what that is, Daddy. I've been reading books about horses from your school library, and Uncle Finn and Uncle Justin have helped me with some of the words. I know all about eventing and show jumping and dressage. Uncle Doug has explained a lot to me."

"Well, okay, then. There is a teacher in Vicksburg. She may want to use her own horse to train you, and then maybe you can train Apollo."

Suddenly Braden couldn't breathe. He was smothered in a six-year-old's hugs and kisses.

"Yes, yes. Wait until I tell Uncle Doug."

"So, we have an appointment tomorrow afternoon to visit Miss Lillie to see what we need to do."

"Oh, by the way, Mama. I'm not Rosie any more. I'm Annabelle again."

"Okay, why is that?"

"When Uncle Doug was explaining about dressage to me, I got to thinking that if you let me take lessons, when I'm a famous equestrienne, that's what they call girl equestrians, the man who announces me would need to refer to me as Annabelle, not Rosie because that would be confusing since it's not really my name."

Ellie smiled. "Okay, Annabelle it is, then. You have been reading a lot of big words lately."

"Yes, because I'm almost seven, you know."

Meeting with Miss Lillie Strickland Saturday afternoon was more than Ellie and Braden could hope for. She related to Annabelle in a way that built up their daughter's confidence. She put her in a dressage saddle that was for children her age and watched as Annabelle settled into the seat. Even though she had never been on that horse, she leaned over the neck, patted it and started whispering to the horse. Lillie walked her around the arena and observed her from every angle. When they came back, Annabelle slipped from the horse, patted him on the neck and gave him a treat Miss Lillie had given her. The horse, Snowflake, nuzzled her, and Annabelle laughed.

Lillie turned to Braden and Ellie. "She's a natural. I have never had a pupil, young or old react to a horse as quickly as she does, and Snowflake is usually more reserved around children. I'd like to put her on another horse, Duster, who isn't as kid friendly. I'll be right beside her, but I want to see how she and Duster react. The same thing happened. Annabelle rode like a champion, and Duster put his face close to hers for his treat.

"She will do well in my class. She's already surpassed most children her age. I know it is a long way to come, but I think she would do well with my advanced classes on Saturday morning. I'll try her, and if it's too much too soon, we'll move down to a class for her age group."

"Should we bring the horse she usually rides?"

"No, I would rather train her on one of mine until she has more experience. Then as she progresses, we'll talk about bringing your horse, but be aware, it takes years to train a horse and rider to trust each other and perform well."

Arrangements were made, and one little girl was the happiest she had ever been, except when she was adopted. When they left to go home, she looked up at both parents and said, "I'm so glad Jesus heard me. I have the best parents in the world." She hopped into the back seat before she saw tears rise in Ellie and Braden's eyes.

Ellie turned in her seat far enough to see Annabelle's face. "You know, Annabelle, Jesus is a pretty good guy. Growing up, all I wanted was two babies to call my own. Now Jesus has given you to us, and we love you so much, but sometimes if you are an only child, it can get a little boring. So, Jesus must have known we need another child to keep you company."

"You're going to adopt another child?"

"No, sweetheart, I'm going to have a baby."

"Oh." A tiny frown knitted her brows together."

"You'll have a playmate as the baby gets a little bigger, but you will always be number one in our eyes because you are the first child we have."

"I don't know much about babies."

"We'll learn together. That's why we wanted a six-year-old because I don't know much about babies, either."

"I'll read about it. Uncle Finn can help me with the big words, and I'll tell you all about it."

"That would be wonderful." Ellie glanced at Braden. He was having a hard time not to burst out laughing."

"I hope it's a boy."

"You do?" Ellie looked surprised. "I would think you would want a sister."

"Not unless she minds me. Karen has a little sister, and she says she is always getting into her stuff without her permission."

"Well, if we have a girl, we'll make sure she minds you, okay?"

"Okay. But I still want a brother."

After tucking Annabelle in, Ellie and Braden went to the breakfast nook, and Braden made a fresh pot of coffee. "You can have coffee, can't you?"

"Yes, just no alcohol."

"That's easy. You don't drink."

"I think I did a good job of explaining to Annabelle."

"It was perfect. We haven't had a lot of time to talk lately, but I wanted to tell you, I saw some pink stones when I was moving the wood where Nannie told me she thought the tabernacle was, but I can't be sure I found anything. Wouldn't it be wonderful if that is where Grace and Jim are buried?"

"After church tomorrow, can we go look?" Ellie's eyes sparkled like diamonds as the sun lit up the kitchen.

"That's what I was going to suggest."

"I'm going to take a soft paint brush and try to brush the stones so I don't disrupt them."

"Just like an archeologist."

"If we find them, maybe we could make a little curb around them and put a small fountain or bird bath and flowers there."

"That sounds perfect. And if Nannie wants any of our family moved here, we could make it a family plot."

Ellie sighed. "I'm glad it's where there's a view of the river. Moving the family here would be a wonderful memorial to happier times at Oak Hollow."

"Yes, according to Nannie, after Grace died, she was buried here, but Abe and Sarah are buried beside Maggie and Charles on their property. We could locate their grandchildren and see about bringing the whole family here."

"That sounds wonderful."

CHAPTER THIRTY-NINE

Sitting on the back veranda, Ellie asked, "Is there anything we can do to help your parents and Nannie get settled after their move?"

"No, finding them the house and my help with the big furniture is all we needed to do. Antique furniture is heavy, and I was about to hire someone to help us."

"I was worried about both of you."

'As you know, Mom had to remodel it, even though it was perfect, but she's known for knocking out walls and rearranging the whole inside! That's why it took so long, but they're happy and all settled now."

"Good thing your dad knows so much about construction, or it would have cost a fortune. I couldn't help but laugh when your dad and Nannie thought it was perfect, and your mom was going around marking walls She knocked all the walls clear down to the studs! She was in her element."

"She had plenty of money to do it since you sold their home for so much more than they thought it was worth, and giving them a couple of months to vacate their old home was perfect. I'm glad we can visit them more often. Nannie is happier than I've seen her in a long time. She was right there watching us move stuff out of the old house and into the new one, giving instructions for where to place things in her room. What I do feel bad about, though, is that we never had a real honeymoon."

"What we had was perfect! And I'm thrilled that your mom is going to be working with a realtor to do interior decorating."

"Yes, she is taking classes to get a certificate."

Working side by side to uncover the grave sites while Annabelle played in the orchard, Ellie realized how happy their lives had turned out. She watched Braden stack the rotten wood into a pile in the open meadow and start a fire. He had already removed most of the lumber, and Ellie was on her hands and knees removing small twigs and larger rocks. Annabelle was fascinated with the fire, but Ellie had warned her not to

319

get too close. How fortunate that she was a child who never broke rules. Recalling how Grace had been so proper most of her life, Annabelle was her little Grace. Ellie saw a small rectangular piece of wood. Bending closely, she could barely make out the name. It was Jim's grave!

"Braden, come quickly." Ellie was yelling. "I found it, I found it."

"Really?" He rushed over and bent to see what Ellie was talking about. "I do believe you have found Jim's, now let's find Grace's."

By dinner time, Ellie and Braden had uncovered both graves, but the wooden plaques were almost rotted, so they planned to have flat cement plaques with the stones they uncovered in the center and their names and dates engraved on silver metal plates in the center of the hearts. They would have to replace some of the stones, just like they did with the heart of stones in the circle, but it would be a permanent monument.

Getting up and brushing off her jeans, she followed Braden to the stables to get Annabelle who had tired of playing in the orchard and had taken a long ride on Apollo. Doug had been correct. Annabelle had some kind of rapport with every horse she encountered. She looked up as Annabelle came running to her and threw her arms around Ellie's waist.

"Mama, Miss Lillie says I need a helmet. Can we please go get me one?"

Ellie put her arms around her daughter and swung her in a circle. "Yes, my darling. I don't think Scottsville has a store with helmets, but we can go early Saturday and get one in Vicksburg. I thought we might get you some riding attire also."

Annabelle clapped her hands and jumped up and down. "I'm going to be the best dressage rider in the whole wide world."

Braden laughed and picked up his daughter and swung her up to straddle his neck. She put her hands over his eyes.

"Hey, you. I can't see."

Annabelle laughed and moved her hands to his forehead.

Ellie loved fall when the trees would turn, but a harsh winter was forecast, so the leaves might not get a chance to show off their gorgeous colors. Thoughts bombarded her, thinking of what the workers and even the Sullivans went through with no electricity, proper heat, or bathrooms. Having to get up every winter morning and get the fireplaces going was not something she could imagine doing, much less going to an outhouse. And what slaves on other plantations had to endure tore at her heart.

Shaking her head, she concentrated on the small little bundle of joy growing inside her. A smile curved her lips.

Saturday morning dawned cold and damp, and Ellie shivered as she grabbed her robe to go to the breakfast nook. She knew she was the last one up, and sure enough, Braden and Annabelle were sitting at the table. Susan had just come in and was shedding her coat, ready to go to work.

She turned. "Good morning, everyone, I could use a cup of that coffee I smell!"

Ellie poured two cups and set one in front of Susan. "How are you feeling?"

"Feeling great. I have a new hobby, and I was going to talk to you about it when you have time."

"You've got my curiosity up. How about when we get back from Annabelle's dressage lesson?"

Braden rose to refill his cup. "I want to know what's going on with Doug. He seems preoccupied with something, and every time we have a slack week, y'all are off to somewhere, but he won't tell me where you're going. He just has that silly lopsided grin."

Susan laughed. "It's a good thing you haven't been to the apartment in the stables lately, or you'd know."

"Well, what is it?"

The door flew open, and Doug stomped his feet on the porch before entering.

Susan raised her voice. "Shut that door. It's cold out there."

"Yes, ma'am."

"You're just in time. Braden has been questioning me, and I had to cover for you."

Doug laughed. "Okay, we might as well confess. On the way back from the beach, we stopped in a little town and met a couple named Lucille and Duke Taylor. He's a saddle maker, and he's helping me learn the trade."

Susan turned to Ellie. "And Lucille is teaching me to quilt. That's what I was going to talk to you about when you got back."

Braden filled a cup for Doug. "I'd like to see what you're working on."

"Come on. I'll show you if you have time."

321

"I've got a few minutes before we have to leave for school."

They walked to the apartment in the stables, and Doug opened the door. It looked as if a saddle shop had taken over. The smell of leather punctuated the room, a smell Braden loved.

"I didn't want to say anything in front of Annabelle, but I'm working on a special dressage saddle for her. I've kind of measured her from the way she sits in the saddle on Apollo, and Duke is helping me. Should be ready in time for her birthday. The other forms are saddles that I'm going to cover in leather."

"Annabelle will be thrilled, but you've only got a little over a month to finish it. Ellie said she wants to invite her whole class. I guess we'll have a lot of kids wanting horse rides."

"I could lead them around in a circle, so they'd be safe and yet experience the thrill of a horse ride."

"That's a great idea. I'll run it by the girls."

"Not a word until it's finished."

Braden ran his hand over the strange looking saddle and noticed Doug had burned Annabelle's name on one side of the saddle. "Mum's the word. Now that I know what you're up to, I'm most relieved and surprised at the same time. I kind of thought you two were planning to move."

"You couldn't make us!"

After Annabelle's lesson, Ellie went into the house, and Braden and Annabelle went to the stables. Susan brought out a basket with some of the scraps sewn together. Ellie picked up a long length of pieces. "This is amazing. I'd like to help you."

"I'd like that. If we get good enough, Lucille said we can sell them for a lot of money."

"We may just want to keep them."

"Don't tell Annabelle, but I want to make one for her. I'm looking for fabric with horses on it. We can do it together."

"I'll look in Vicksburg while Annabelle and Braden are at her lesson next week. That would be a nice birthday present if we can get it finished in time."

"We've got a month. I'll bet we can do it. How are her lessons going?"

"She has a competition in two weeks, so we're going to look for her attire. She's excited. Lillie says she has jumped ahead of all her other advanced students. She didn't say, but I think Annabelle is her favorite!"

"Isn't she too young for competition?"

Ellie laughed. "Technically, yes, and since children under twelve can't compete in real competition, Miss Lillie has set up a similar competition for her students."

"I'm going to tell you a secret." She looked around to be sure Annabelle wasn't in earshot. They could hear her in her room singing. "Doug is making her a saddle. That's what he's been doing."

Ellie's hands flew to her mouth. "I'm so glad you aren't leaving us."

"Never. We've got two babies coming. We need to help each other!"

"Yes, will you help me with her birthday party?"

"Of course!"

The next week, Ellie found the perfect fabrics for their quilt for Annabelle, and she and Susan worked each night after Annabelle was in bed in order to get it finished before her birthday.

Braden and Annabelle both missed school on Friday so that Annabelle could practice all day on Apollo. Even though the horse had not been trained as a dressage horse, Annabelle had taught him some of the things she learned at Miss Lillie's. Annabelle was able to get him to follow her commands. How she wished she could ride Apollo in the competition, but she knew if she had any chance at a win, she would have to ride Snowflake. She loved Snowflake, but not as much as she loved Apollo.

Two weeks later, Saturday dawned cold but as bright as Annabelle's spirits. She could not wait to put on her new riding attire with her beautiful black helmet. Mommy and Daddy had bought her a new saddle blanket to go on Snowflake. It had her name on it.

As they entered the holding area, Miss Lillie walked up to them. She bent down and addressed Annabelle. "I see you've brought a good luck blanket for Snowflake. I want to caution you. Do not think about winning. Think about how much you and Snowflake like performing. The rest will take care of itself. Okay?"

"Okay, Miss Lillie, but I am excited."

"I know, but don't let it interfere with what you and Snowflake know how to do. And remember, you are still young. Most riders do not place their first time out, especially almost seven-year-olds, so if you don't place, don't be disappointed. And remember your salutes. Before and after."

Lillie turned to Ellie and Braden. "I've set up this competition as close to an authentic one as I could, and I have hired professional judges to be here. It's my best way of assessing how well I'm doing as a teacher and how well my students are doing."

Annabelle kissed her family before they went to the viewing area.

A frown marred Braden's handsome face, and Ellie needed to know what he was thinking. "Are you worried?"

"Not about Annabelle not doing well. Just that if she doesn't place, I hope she won't be disappointed. If she is, I hope that new Irish Sport horse I bought will ease her disappointment."

Ellie sighed, "And if he doesn't excite her, we've spent a lot of money for nothing."

Doug helped Susan to a seat in the bleachers and asked, "When will he be delivered?"

"Next week. I said we could go get him, but James Ford said he would be happy to bring him. I hope we get more bookings to pay for the him."

Susan overheard their conversation. "I looked at the books yesterday. We do have three weekend bookings this month, and surprisingly, we have all of October weekends filled. We have a few scattered bookings for weekdays, too, so I think you will be fine."

Ellie shifted in her seat to get more comfortable. "I know you and I aren't showing, Susan, but I think I'm having more flutters of pain than you are."

"I'm making up for it with the morning sickness, or should I say all day sickness! Maybe we can make a couple of quilts to sell. Doug has already sold a saddle that he's finished, so things are looking up."

Everyone grew quiet as the first rider entered the arena. He did well, but it was not a winning performance. Annabelle was seventh in line. The horses ahead of her had points taken off. None of them seemed to be in great form, and most of the young riders appeared stiff.

Ellie looked at Braden. "Maybe the riders are just nervous, even though this isn't real competition."

"Maybe, or maybe we are just used to our Little Miss Perfection!"

Annabelle entered, and when her name was announced, Ellie thought her heart would burst. Her tiny daughter looked so regal sitting tall and straight astride Snowflake. Ellie watched her bend down, pat Snowflake's neck and say something to him. Then it was time. Annabelle sat relaxed and confident as she saluted the head judge and started her test.

Doug remarked, "She is doing well. Snowflake doesn't seem as antsy as the horses before him. They're not perfect, but I think she will get a high mark."

Braden said, "I hope so. She's a trooper, though, so I'm hoping she does well with the other tests."

The day warmed to a brisk sixty degrees by the time the competition was over. Annabelle placed eighth overall. She was thrilled.

"Uncle Doug, did you see us do the right turn? That's what Snowflake always has trouble with."

"I sure did. She did well."

"Daddy, did you watch when we did the loop?"

"Yes, honey, we all watched. You and Snowflake outrode a lot of the other horses."

"I know. I whispered to her before we started not to get nervous, and I told her just to have fun, and that I love her."

Ellie smiled. "Good girl."

"Miss Lillie is so proud of me. I wish I had placed at least third, but eighth is really good for my first time."

Ellie hugged her. "Yes, that is excellent, and I'm glad you know that."

"I've got to go now and brush Snowflake to get him ready to go back to his stall. We're going to have to get my riding habit cleaned! It was dusty out there."

Ellie laughed. "It does look a little bit worse for wear."

As they walked to the car, Annabelle said, "I had to really brush Snowflake because that dust blew up so fast, and I didn't want the bridle to hurt him with the dust on his skin."

Braden took her helmet and opened the door for her.

On the way home, Ellie reached for Braden's right arm and touched it gently to get his attention. "Have you and Doug made an area for the children to ride for the birthday party?"

"It's almost finished."

The next Saturday afternoon after Annabelle's dressage lesson, fifteen children accompanied by their parents converged on The Sullivan House for Annabelle's seventh birthday party. Several parents asked for a tour of the property. Ellie announced that she would give a short tour while the children went to the circle to either ride Apollo or watch. Presents were stacked in the parlor where a table had been set up with a beautiful cake frosted brown around the sides to represent dirt. Green icing on the top represented grass, and a little white picket fence encircled the perimeter. Ellie had found a ceramic horse resembling Apollo to go on the top, and it appeared to be grazing on the "grass" icing. Ellie jumped up and down when she saw it. The inside had one chocolate layer and one vanilla. Chef Finn with his big white hat served hot dogs or hamburgers with chips. Punch and iced tea were the drink options. Most adults chose tea while most of the children chose the punch. After playing a few games indoors, the children went outside to the special area set up for a slow horse ride. Most men followed them, but the women wanted a tour.

After the horse rides, the children watched Annabelle open her presents and then feasted on cake and ice cream. Annabelle especially liked the quilt Ellie and Susan made for her. She thanked each guest for their presents and two and a half hours later, the house was quiet again.

CHAPTER FORTY

Sunday morning Doug walked into the kitchen. "Annabelle, I have something I want to show you."

"But Uncle Justin is making me a waffle."

Justin smiled. "It can wait. I'll keep it warm."

The whole family made a beeline for the stables. Doug opened the door and right in front of them, sat Annabelle's saddle on a wooden form, gleaming from the overhead light.

Annabelle looked and ran to it, speechless. She bent and smelled the leather and ran her hand over her name. Finally, she recovered enough to exclaim, "Uncle Doug, did you make this? Did you put my name on it?"

"Sure did. You like it? Happy Birthday a day late! I figured you had enough excitement yesterday, so I wanted to wait until today to show you."

"I love it. Can we take it with us next Saturday for my class?"

Braden spoke up. "You need to ride Apollo with it for a couple of days to be sure it fits you. But we can take it with us to show Miss Lillie. While Doug gets it ready, you need to finish your breakfast so we won't be late for Sunday School."

"It will fit. I want to sit on it."

Braden lifted her up and put her on the saddle which was resting on a wooden form. "Just for a few minutes."

"It's perfect. I love how it feels. Can I skip Sunday School and try it out? Please?"

"Okay, just this once. Eat your breakfast, and then you may ride for a while."

Sitting in the breakfast nook, Ellie had Grace's journals spread out on the table. "I read more in Grace's journals."

"Did you discover more than what Nannie told us?"

"Yes. She talks a lot about the Civil War. Big plantations were hurting financially, slaves were running like crazy to get to the North, and the war was escalating."

"I can't imagine how scary that could be. I know if slave hunters found them, they enforced horrific punishment."

"Grace said she never understood why they punished them and then expected them to work extra long hours. Abe was very concerned and came up with a plan. He and Sarah had come across from Ireland with Albert and Eileen Winthrop and visited them as often as they could. Albert, who ran goods up and down the Mississippi River in his boat told Abe he could carry slaves to freedom with the idea if he was stopped, he could say they were sold, and he was delivering them. Of course, the women worried that Abe and Albert would be caught, but they did get some slaves to Illinois, which was a free state. Of course, everyone was nervous and worried."

"If they had been caught, Abe and Albert would have been in big trouble, and Jim might have been killed." Braden shook his head to clear out the visions of the horrors of some of the lives of the slaves and the nonstop evils of a war that tore the country apart for a long time.

"What a history this mansion has, Braden. So many joys and also sadness."

"It does, and I'm taking notes for my book. I have a lot already, but I also want to redo the little booklet I made earlier. We seem to be finding out more news every time we pick up Grace's journals."

"As the war intensified, Grace described the plight of most of the women left behind when the men went to war. There were a few brave souls who followed their husbands to do laundry and help with the meals, but most stayed home with their children."

"I wonder if they were able to maintain the plantations?"

"I'll read this passage to you." Ellie refreshed their coffee and started reading. "Cal was right. The war has come. I'm very worried. There aren't enough slaves to help the women who are left. Mama, Maggie, and I take baskets of food every week to a drop off point in town. Most women know how to can and store vegetables from their gardens, but with young children, they don't have a lot of time, and they have no help. We are fortunate that Papa and Matthew can't go to war. Papa doesn't want the plantation left to Matthew to run with his weak legs. I'm scared for Joseph and Charles. They both enlisted soon after the war came here."

Braden rubbed his temples. "I wonder if they perished?"

"Let me read more." She scanned a few pages. "Here it says that both Joseph and Charles were wounded, but they survived."

"That's a relief. "

"I'll tell you more if I find something interesting."

"I'll go see what Doug is up to. Susan is in Annabelle's room listening to a vivid description of the contest, even though Susan was there."

"She loves an audience."

"I'm going to see if Doug has heard anything about the horse."

"Do you know his name?"

"I think James Ford said his name is Brave Eagle. He's going to bring him Friday. That will give Annabelle time to get used to him over the weekend. There's kind of a sad story about the reason he's selling the horse."

Ellie's hand flew to her mouth. "Surely someone didn't get hurt?"

"No, James spent a fortune on training and going all over the country for his daughter to perform dressage, show jumping, and also eventing, so the horse is well trained. When his daughter turned sixteen, she sashayed into their living room, and announced that now that she could drive, she didn't want to participate any longer in equestrian activities." Braden smiled. "But her loss is Annabelle's gain."

"I hope if this horse is a good fit, that the girl doesn't want him back."

"She won't. She persuaded her dad to open a horse training business. They teach riding lessons as well as all the rest of the equestrian skills. His daughter helps on weekends, and when she graduates from college, she plans to come back and help full time so that eventually she can take over the business."

"Then it all ended up well. I guess if Miss Lillie ever quits, we have another option."

Annabelle dashed into the kitchen. "Aunt Susan said she would like to go riding with me. She was going to ask you."

"Since there aren't many guests, I think that would be okay." Ellie motioned to Annabelle to come sit for a minute. "I know you are anxious to see Apollo, so promise you won't run off and leave Aunt Susan in the lurch! Remember, she has a little one in her tummy."

"Yes, ma'am."

The week seemed to dive head long into Friday. Ellie remembered that James Ford was delivering Brave Eagle. "I hope he comes before school is out, so Annabelle will be surprised when she comes home from school."

"I asked him to, and it shouldn't be a problem since he lives just outside of Jackson."

Annabelle walked slowly into the kitchen rubbing her eyes. Her hair looked like a family of rats had taken residence.

"Morning," she mumbled as she plopped down in her chair.

Finn put a bowl of grits along with bacon and a fried egg on a plate."

Ellie's eyes locked on Annabelle's face. "I hope you have a wonderful day at school today. You know it won't be long until Christmas break."

Annabelle perked up. "Then I get to ride Apollo as often as I want."

Ellie cautioned, "As long as it's not too cold."

When Annabelle and Braden walked in from school, Ellie, Susan, and Doug were in the kitchen having a cup of coffee. Braden stood behind Annabelle and eye quizzed Doug.

Doug grinned and pushed his cup back a little, nodding to let Braden know the horse had arrived.

Annabelle started to sit down. "Uncle Justin, do you have a snack for me?"

"Oh, my. Let me see what I can do. You may have to wait a few minutes." He nodded to Braden also.

Braden took Annabelle's hand. "Let's go check on the horses while Uncle Justin gets your snack ready."

Annabelle looked a little disappointed, but she rose to follow her father. Of course, Susan, Ellie, Justin, and Finn followed also.

Doug turned to Annabelle and said, "Let's go look at that stall down at the end."

Annabelle noticed it wasn't empty. She raced to it. There stood a beautiful Irish Sport horse, his jet-black coat shining from the light beaming down from the bright rays of sun dancing on his back. He stood straight and tall, almost like a regal statue. Annabelle looked at the horse, then at everyone around her. The puzzled look on her face caused an eruption of laughter.

"What's so funny? Did you buy another horse, Uncle Doug?"

Braden stepped up. "No, sweetheart. Your mama and I bought this horse. He's your new dressage horse. Isn't he beautiful?"

"For real? I was going to ask if I could use Apollo."

"Honey, Brave Eagle has already been trained and is the breed of horse a lot of dressage equestriennes are riding. Brave Eagle was trained by a professional for a young girl, but she got tired of competing as she got older."

"So, you bought him? Why can't I use Apollo?"

Braden sensed a reluctance on Annabelle's taking up with the horse. "Apollo can certainly be trained, and he knows a lot of the movements, but it will take years to get him ready for everything he would be asked to do. Apollo could be your pleasure horse. Brave Eagle has also been trained for eventing as well as dressage."

Just then, Brave Eagle whinnied and lowered his head. Annabelle moved closer to him. "I think he's scared since he's in a new place." She started talking to him in a soft voice and pressed her face to his. "You're okay. You are a brave horse, just like your name. You and I are going to become best friends, and I'll bet you and Apollo and the other horses will accept you into their family."

Doug interjected. "You know Eagle in Native American language means courage, wisdom, and strength."

Annabelle smiled as the horse nudged her shoulder. "See that's why you are so perfect for dressage. I can't wait to ride you."

Doug said, "She's done it again. She just has a way with horses. He's calmed down, and I swear, he's smiling. If we ever decided to raise thoroughbreds, she'd be an awesome asset."

Braden held up his hands. "Whoa, we've got our hands full. We certainly don't have time or money to train a racehorse."

Doug laughed. "Just a thought. It might be fun to go to the Kentucky Derby!"

Susan shook her head. "Annabelle, how on earth do you do that?"

Annabelle smiled as she rubbed Brave Eagle's cheek. "I just try to be calm and whisper that I love them. I think they can sense it."

Ellie said, "It's time for dinner."

"But, Mama, can't I ride Eagle for a little while?"

"Honey, tomorrow's Saturday, and you have a lesson. So, are we shortening his name to Eagle?"

"Yes. Except in competition. Then we will use his full name. I like it a lot. It reminds me of a warrior."

The bigger Susan and Ellie got, the longer winter seemed to hang on. Ellie's feet had begun to swell, and the doctor told her to prop them up.

Ellie shuffled into the office. "Susan, you are so lucky. Your feet aren't swelling like mine."

Susan sighed. "I'll trade with you. I can't eat breakfast any longer because I still have morning sickness every single day and sometimes at night."

"I guess babies have a mind of their own. Since Braden hired the new maid, and with you in charge of the office, I have very little to do."

"Yes, Dotty is a lifesaver. Thank you for letting her clean the Inn as well."

"I can't believe we have had so many guests this winter. So many have come from the frozen north, but our weather hasn't been the best to lure them."

"I know. I'm surprised, too. We do have a gentleman coming this afternoon."

Ellie had a stricken look on her face. "By himself? I hope it's not someone like Tommy."

"I don't think so. I wonder if he is a long lost relative."

"Why would you say that?"

"His last name is Sullivan."

"Wouldn't that be a coincidence? Another one of our relatives coming home like Nannie said." Ellie visibly relaxed.

"It's a fairly common name. I doubt he's related, though. I just wish I knew our babies' gender. I could go ahead and shop for clothes. Doug, of course, wants a boy, but I really don't care."

"Braden wants a boy, too, but he is so enamored with Annabelle, he says another girl would be fine. I would kind of like to have a boy to carry on the name." Ellie adjusted her maternity skirt. "Spring can't come soon enough. I hope March goes out like a lamb, and the weather warms up before we have these babies. Do you have time to go sit in the parlor and work on some pieces for a quilt?"

Susan sighed. "You read my mind. I thought we might make one for each of the babies."

"But what color?" Ellie was rolling colors around in her head.

"I think just neutrals. That way, it would suit either a boy or a girl."

Braden had started calling their daughter Belle, and they had formed a bond just as strong as she had with Ellie.

"You could never tell that Belle, as we now call her, is not your natural daughter. You look like the pictures of her biological mother, and she looks like you!"

"That makes me happy. Her grandmother is very ill, and Braden and I don't know if we should take her for a visit, or if it would upset her. The grandmother is on very strong pain medicine, and sleeps most of the time, so I don't know if she even feels up to a visit. The social worker who called me said the hospital believes she will pass within the next two weeks."

"Talk to Belle and see what she says. She told me when she first came and started talking to us that her grandmother didn't want her to talk because it tired her. Belle said she was glad she could be with people who weren't sick."

Ellie nodded. "I think I will talk to her and see what she wants to do. I'll also talk to the social worker and get her advice."

When Belle came in from a long day of riding, she was exuberant. "Eagle is the best! I love him almost as much as I love Apollo. I rode both of them today. I'm worried about Apollo. He doesn't seem like he feels good, or he's jealous. After I tacked him down and brushed him, he laid down in his stall. Uncle Doug is looking at him."

"Dinner is almost ready, so maybe he will tell us what he thinks while we eat. In the meantime, I need to talk to you about your grandmother."

"Which one? I have three of them. Grandmother Ophelia, Grandmother Cynthia, and Grandmother Emma, plus Nannie."

"Grandmother Ophelia. You know she's sick."

"Yes, that's why she was kind of mean to me, but I do love her."

"She didn't intend to be mean to you, honey. She was just in pain. She's really sick this time, and she may not get over this sickness."

"You mean she'll die?"

"I'm afraid so. Would you like to go visit her one last time?"

Belle thought for a few minutes. "I don't want to go. I would rather remember her like she was before she got sick. Dying scares me. But I don't want her to think I don't love her."

"Grandmother Ophelia told the social worker almost exactly what you said. She wants you to remember the good times you had. I just wanted to ask. Will you go tell Uncle Doug dinner is ready?"

CHAPTER FORTY-ONE

Braden had spent a good portion of the day with Hiram to decide what to plant and which fields to use. Braden weary-footed it into the kitchen and addressed Ellie. "The old man was worried that cotton harvesting would upset the guests, but I told him to go ahead."

"I wanted to talk to you. Belle doesn't want to go to see her grandmother, and I think she is old enough to make that decision. What do you think?"

"I agree. It seems as if we hardly have time to talk any more. We need to make more time for us."

"True, but too much going on. We had a note from Tommy today. He and Denise can't go to The Philippines. It would violate his parole, so instead, they are going to move the small church he has started to a vacant building in Jackson."

"I didn't think about the parole."

Belle bounded into the parlor. Her eyes were shining, and she could barely contain her excitement.

Braden smiled. "You look excited. How was it riding Eagle today?"

"Oh, Daddy, he is wonderful. I took turns riding Apollo and then Eagle. Horses know how you feel, and I don't want Apollo to feel left out. But then Apollo acted tired."

"That's good that you are thinking about Apollo's feelings."

Susan pulled herself up to go ask Finn about dinner. Suddenly she looked panic stricken and sat back down. Ellie ran to her. "Are you all right?"

"Just a sharp pain, and I feel lightheaded."

Ellie helped her to the bed in one of the downstairs bedrooms and asked Braden to go get Doug.

The doorbell chimed. Braden was torn. He needed to answer the door, and he needed to tell Doug about Susan.

Braden called Finn in and hurriedly asked him to get Doug.

Doug was in with Apollo when Finn found him. "I was checking on Apollo. He seems restless. Is dinner ready?"

"Not quite, I think Susan needs you. She had a little pain, and Ellie has put her in bed."

"Is it labor?" Angst swept over Doug, and he broke out in a sweat.

"I don't know. My wife had a Caesarean Section, so I don't know about labor."

Doug broke into a run and barged into the bedroom. "Are you in labor?"

"I don't know. I'm scared." Her face twisted into a grimace.

Doug stuck his head out of the door. "Ellie, call Doctor Purcell."

"I have already called him. He should be here shortly. Is she still in pain?"

"Yes. I hope you told the doctor to hurry."

Justin had come in with all the commotion. "Can I help with something?"

Braden said, "I don't know. Right now, I need to get the door. You might sit with Annabelle. Ellie is in with Doug and Susan."

Braden moved quickly to the door, thinking it was the doctor. Instead, their guest, Mister Sullivan stood there. He was an elderly man with white hair and the most translucent gray eyes Braden had ever seen. He was smiling, and kindness radiated from him.

"Welcome." Braden picked up the man's small suitcase and showed him to his room. "We're having a bit of a problem with my sister, and our doctor is on his way, so dinner may be late."

"I'm in no hurry. I'll just freshen up. Thank you for bringing up my suitcase."

"You are welcome to wait for dinner in the parlor, or if you would rather avoid all the chaos, our chef could let you know when dinner is ready, and we could serve you in your room if you'd like."

"Thank you. I hope your sister is not seriously ill."

"She's pregnant and having some pains. The doctor should be here shortly."

"Let me know if I can be of help." Mister Sullivan smiled.

336

"Thank you." Braden backed out of the room and closed the door. "What an odd thing to say," he muttered. "I guess if he is a doctor, he would have said so."

Justin and Finn were putting the finishing touches on dinner.

No one saw Mister Sullivan come downstairs, He sat in one of the corner chairs in the parlor. Belle sat in the chair across from him.

The old man turned to her. "You're a very pretty young lady."

"I'm an equestrienne. Do you know what that means?"

"I believe I do. Do you do dressage or eventing?"

Belle told him about Brave Eagle. "He's wonderful, and my daddy was so nice to buy him for me, but I really love Apollo more. He's my pleasure horse."

"And he's a good horse."

"I'm hungry. I wonder when Uncle Finn will call us to eat?"

"It will be a little while. I think your daddy is talking to him now."

Doug was trying to hide his fear, so he bent and kissed Susan on her forehead, hoping she couldn't see his worry."

"I don't know if these pains are labor or something else. It's too early to deliver." Susan winced as another pain hit her.

Ellie brushed Susan's hair behind her ear. "The doctor should be here soon."

Doug attempted to calm Susan, but he knew she could read him like a book.

"You're scared too, aren't you?" Tears and fear marked Susan's face.

"A little. Not knowing if this is normal makes me worried."

Doctor Purcell arrived, and Ellie showed him to the bedroom. The doctor asked Doug and Ellie to leave while he examined Susan. "I'll be out in a few minutes, and we can talk."

Doug went to the parlor to wait. He paced in front of the fireplace.

It didn't take long before Doctor Purcell emerged. "The pain is not what I'm worried about. What concerns me is I believe she could be going into early labor. The good news is they are not coming at regular intervals. Watch her, and if she starts having contractions on a regular

337

basis, or if the pain intensifies, then take her to the ER, and I'll attend to her there. Let's hope it's false labor. I gave her a mild sedative."

"But it's too early. What did you say? What is false labor?"

"It is when a woman has what feels like labor, but it isn't. Medical term for it is Braxton Hicks. I don't think anything is imminent. Just watch her through the night, and let me know of any changes. This could possibly be labor, but I doubt it." He shook Doug's hand and made his exit.

As he walked to his car, Doctor Purcell uttered a prayer. "Father in Heaven, please watch over Susan. It's too early for the baby to arrive. Please send your healing to her and protect her and the baby. In Jesus' name I pray. Amen."

Ellie covered Susan with an afghan and went to the parlor to let Doug and Susan have some alone time.

In all the commotion, Braden had forgotten their guest and moved toward him. Ellie walked up to Braden and put her arm around his waist. He turned to Mister Sullivan. "I'm so sorry I haven't introduced you. Mister Sullivan, may I present my wife, Elizabeth Cunningham, known lovingly around here as Ellie. Ellie, this is our guest, Mister Sullivan."

They shook hands. Ellie said, "Pleased to meet you. It's nice to have someone with the same name as our home."

"The pleasure is mine. We don't need to stand on formality. Just call me Cal."

The name. Cal. Sullivan. Grace's journal. Braden's veins turned to ice, and goosebumps caused the hair to stand up on his arms. He glanced at Ellie and saw the same reaction. It could not be the same Cal that Grace wrote about and said her father felt like he was his son. That was too long ago. But it gave him a weird feeling.

Doug came out of the bedroom to see if Finn could prepare something for Susan to eat. The parlor had taken on an eerily quiet atmosphere, and Doug felt as if he had been trapped in some sort of strange time warp. Braden and Ellie stood rigid, and a blank look occupied both of their faces. They looked like statues that time had frozen in place. He approached them. "Is everything all right? You and Ellie look like you've seen a ghost."

338

Braden's eyes were glazed, and Ellie stood staring transfixed. Neither spoke.

Doug introduced himself to Cal. "What's going on? These two look terrified." Immediately his thoughts went to Tommy, and he wondered if this man had threatened Braden or Ellie.

"I'm afraid my name has shocked them. It's nice to meet you."

"I get it. The name Sullivan, and this is The Sullivan House." Doug touched Braden's arm. "Are you okay? I was going to see when Finn will be serving dinner. I think maybe Susan needs to eat something."

Braden shook his head to come back to reality. "Tell him we are ready when he is."

Over dinner, Ellie explained that a family named Sullivan had lived in their house for many years, and they had a young man who came to live with them named Cal. "I'm sure we upset you with our behavior. I would like to apologize."

"No need, Miss Ellie. I'm sure the Sullivans passed many years ago."

"Yes."

Belle looked at Braden. "Daddy, Mister Cal knows all about dressage. We had a nice talk."

"Well, thank you for entertaining our guest." He turned to Cal. "I hope she didn't bore you."

"Not at all. She is a very special child."

Doug strode in from the Susan's bedside after delivering her meal, a wild look in his eyes. "I'm scared. Ellie, can you come? Her pains are getting closer together."

"Of course, but I don't know what I can do."

Cal spoke up. "Not to interrupt you, but how close are they? I have some medical knowledge."

"Twelve minutes right on the nose." Doug's hands were shaking.

Cal said, "Would you like for me to take a look at her?"

"Sure, if you can help. I'm thinking I should take her to the ER."

Cal rose as if in a trance and seemed to float to the bedroom. The rest of the family stood around watching him. He folded his hands in a prayer position, mumbled something incomprehensible, and gently placed one hand on Susan's bulging tummy and one hand on her head.

Suddenly Susan's eyes radiated a glowing light, and a peaceful countenance replaced her worried look.

Cal turned to Doug. "She will be fine. There is nothing to worry about. It is not time for the baby to come. Her pains are little pockets of gas that are rumbling around in her abdomen. She will be fine once she eats."

Susan's eyes grew wide. "I don't know what you did, Mister Sullivan, but I felt warmth and have no pain now."

Shock reverberated through her Ellie's spine. This couldn't be, could it? Surely this was not the same Cal that had lived with the Sullivans. He would be dead by now, unless….

She didn't want to think about it.

Doug reacted to the scene. "Thank you so much. I don't know what you did, but Susan looks so much better."

"It was a small thing. I was able to relax her. She should eat a light supper and drink plenty of water. I'll wait in the parlor unless there is something else I can do."

Doug said, "I'm sorry that this may have ruined your stay with us. I've never seen so much trouble going on in one night."

"Do not worry about me. I needed a few days to rest, and I will certainly be able to do that once I retire to my room. I am eager to walk around surrounded by the beautiful trees in the orchard. I believe there is a special place I was told about. A circle, I believe?"

Ellie spoke, "Yes, we call it The Circle of the Heart. There is a story about it in our brochure. And there is a bench there you can sit on. How long are you staying, sir?"

"I've booked the room for a week. So, I'll be leaving next Wednesday."

Everyone moved out of the bedroom except Doug.

Susan took Doug's hand. "Help me up. I'm hungry."

"Do you think that's wise?"

"I feel fine."

Susan resumed her regular duties on Thursday morning. Ellie came in to look at the reservation book. "How are you feeling?"

"Fine. I don't know why I'm not worried about having this baby early, but Mister Cal said I won't have the baby until it's time. How does he know?"

"I don't know. All I can think of is that somehow, he must have some medical training. He couldn't be the same Cal that lived for a while with Abe and Sarah. He performed healings and seemed to know when some events were going to happen. He just disappeared without saying a word. I wonder if he is related to that Cal. I remember Nannie saying something about all the relatives are returning. Finn, then Dad and Mom Cunningham, and Nannie. Maybe he is a long-lost cousin of the Sullivan's Cal."

"Maybe, but it is strange that I instantly felt better. I saw him take his coffee cup and move toward the orchard. Maybe he will find the heart of stones."

"Or maybe he knows exactly where it is." Ellie felt a shiver go up her spine.

On Saturday, Belle invited Mister Cal to go with them to watch her practice. In the car, her excitement lightened the mood after Susan's scare.

"Mister Cal, do think Apollo is as pretty as Eagle?"

"I think they are both pretty and very nice horses. Has Apollo calmed down? Your uncle told me he was restless."

"I think he's restless because he is going to miss Brave Eagle. We're taking him to board at Miss Lillie's so he and I can train together."

"You will do well. I'm sure you will place at the next competition."

When they got back from Belle's practice, Belle ran to the stables to see Apollo. Before anyone had time to sit down, Belle ran back into the house. "Daddy, Apollo is laying down and won't get up. He looks sick."

Ellie gently corrected her daughter. "He's lying down, not laying down. Braden, go see what you think."

Belle's eyes filled with tears. "Where is Uncle Doug?"

"It's Saturday. He's not working today since Mister Cal didn't want to go horseback riding, so he's probably with Aunt Susan at the Inn."

Braden hugged Belle. "We'll get Uncle Doug to look at him. I'm going to the stables."

341

"I'm going, too, Daddy. Mommy, call Uncle Doug on the phone, please."

Braden followed Belle to the stables, but he couldn't rouse Apollo, either. Going back outside, he saw Doug rushing toward him. Doug went into Apollo's stall and examined the horse.

Braden and Belle stayed outside the stall waiting for Doug to finish looking at Apollo. Braden asked, "What's wrong with Apollo?"

"Can we talk?"

"Sure."

"Outside. Belle, will you go ask Uncle Finn to put on some coffee?"

"Yes, sir. But then I'm coming back."

Braden saw the stern look on Doug's face. "What is it?"

"We need to call the vet. I can't be sure, but Apollo may have colic."

"Is that serious?"

"Can be."

Braden went into the house to use the telephone. Belle ran to him. "Is Apollo okay?"

Braden held his hand over the receiver. "I think he's okay, but we want to be sure, so I'm calling Doctor Blackwell."

CHAPTER FORTY-TWO

Belle paced from one end of the parlor to the other. Finally, Doctor Blackwell rang the doorbell. He entered and went straight to the stables with Doug and Braden following. Ellie held Belle back.

"I want to go." Belle's face pleaded with Ellie. Tears streamed down her face.

"We don't want too many people with Apollo so the vet has plenty of room to see about him. As soon as we know what is wrong, we'll tell you, and then you can go see Apollo."

Belle sighed a big breath. "Okay." She wiped her eyes.

In the stables, Braden asked, "What's your diagnosis, Doc?"

"I need to know if the horse has passed manure today?"

"Doug, do you know?"

"No, but he hasn't eaten much in the last few days. That's why I thought it was colic."

"I'm afraid you are correct. It's not the worst I've seen, but he's in a lot of pain."

Braden stuck his hands into his front pockets, a nervous habit he had. "What can you do?"

"At this stage, there's not much to do. If he gets any worse, surgery is an option, but the prognosis isn't good for survival even with surgery. I've given him a large dose of Mineral Oil and a mild tranquillizer to ease the pain."

"We can't lose him. Belle would be devastated."

"I hope his symptoms will abate so he won't require further treatment, but it can be serious. You need to watch him through the night and call me if he gets worse or starts thrashing around. He needs to be walked." They shook hands. "Thank you, Doc."

"Glad to come. I'll just leave from here."

343

Cal had come downstairs to find a book in the fully stocked bookcase in the study. He saw Doctor Blackwell leaving.

"Was that a doctor?"

Belle burst into sobs. "It was the vet. Apollo is sick. You made Aunt Susan better. Can you help Apollo?"

Cal looked at Braden.

"Doctor Blackwell feels the horse has colic."

"I used to care for horses, so if you would like for me to look at him, I would be happy to give you a second opinion. Maybe that would ease Annabelle's worries. I don't know that I can help, but I'll try."

"Yes, please." Braden led the way to Apollo's stall.

Belle grabbed Cal's arm, pulling him forward. "Please, please hurry."

"Okay, sweetheart. I'm going as fast as I can. Remember I'm very old."

Belle led Cal to Apollo's stall. He was on his side, thrashing around, and looking at his flank, but he kind of perked up when Belle went in and spoke to him in a low, soothing voice. Cal went in and knelt in front of the horse. He put one hand on the horse's belly and his other hand on Apollo's head. Again, he closed his eyes and mumbled something. It took a few minutes for Apollo to react.

Gradually. Apollo settled down. Belle stayed by him until Cal opened his eyes and spoke. "Can you ask your uncle Doug where to get some fresh warm water for Apollo?"

Belle watched him. "Is he going to get cured? What's taking so long?"

Cal rubbed Apollo's muzzle, but spoke to Belle. "Sometimes for healing to work, you must pray in Jesus' name because the Bible says if you ask for anything in Jesus' name, it will be given to you. Do you understand?"

"You mean I can just tell Jesus I want to win the dressage competition, and I will?"

"No, dear, it means that whatever we ask for should glorify God. And you know God has a plan for each of us. Sometimes when our prayers aren't answered, God doesn't feel like what we ask for is in our best interests, and sometimes He has a different plan for us. So, instead of asking to win the competition, that might not be God's plan for you. We can pray for Apollo, and that's what I do when I make people feel better, but the Lord is the great physician."

"So, is it wrong to pray for Apollo?"

"No, because God knows that you have a tender heart, and you're not asking for something selfishly, but praying for Apollo to get well because you love him. And God knows how badly you want Apollo to get well."

"But you healed Aunt Susan. Can't you heal Apollo?"

"I don't heal anyone, sweetheart. I pray when I lay hands on people who don't feel well. But it's up to God if it fits His plan. Never be upset with God if your prayers aren't answered the way you want, okay? And you wouldn't want Apollo to be in pain if he can't get better, so if God feels it's best for Apollo to go to horse's heaven, then I don't want you to be upset."

"Okay. I think I understand."

"Now go with Uncle Doug and get some fresh water for Apollo, okay? And then he needs to be walked and not fed until he passes some manure."

"Yes, sir."

As soon as Cal went back to the house, Apollo struggled, and managed to stand. Doug took Belle's hand and together they prayed for Apollo and then got some fresh water for him. He appeared pain free and started drinking large amounts of water.

"Belle, sweetheart, I'll walk Apollo, but it's about time for dinner, so you go on in."

"If he gets worse, will you come tell us?"

"Of course."

That evening after dinner, Ellie found Cal in the parlor reading a book. "I don't want to interrupt you, but may I ask you a question?"

Cal placed the book in his lap. "Of course."

"Are you related to the Cal that lived with the Sullivans in this house all those years ago?"

"That was a long time ago. I grew up with a minister and his wife in a small home in Louisiana. I was left on their doorstep. I haven't done any kind of genealogy study."

"But how do you have the same name?"

345

"When I came to them many years ago, their name was Sullivan. They had done some searching for relatives. They found out about the Sullivans here and a young man named Cal who had gifts of healing and prophecy. They could not find where they were related, but as I grew, they discovered I had the same gifts as that Cal had. They had always called me Boy because they said when I was old enough, I could choose my name. Together, we chose Cal Sullivan."

"Didn't they adopt you?"

"No, in those days, you could just take someone in without adopting, so they just never got around to the adopting process."

"Did you ever find your birth mother or father?"

"There was no need. I was content."

"But you are so much like what I read about in Grace's journal. Could you be…."

Cal smiled. "That's a very nice compliment. Shall we leave it at that?"

The next morning, Susan and Ellie were sewing quilt pieces together. Ellie relayed her conversation with Susan. "You know, he never answered me directly, but I wonder if he could be the same Cal."

"You think he may be an angel?"

"Angels don't die. I don't know, but he acts the same way Grace described their Cal."

"Finn is about to serve breakfast. Let's ask Cal when he comes down what our babies will be. I've had no more pain or morning sickness."

"This is his last day, so hopefully, he will be down in a few minutes. I think that's a good idea because then we can start shopping for gender-specific baby clothes."

Finn went to Cal's room to announce breakfast, knocked on the door, and waited. Minutes passed. Finn knocked again and called his name. "Maybe he's out talking to Doug," he mumbled. He went to the stables. Doug hadn't seen him.

Doug read Finn's face and saw concern. "Maybe we should go check his room to see if he's okay."

Together they went to the room and knocked. No answer. Trying the door, they were surprised it wasn't locked. Doug pushed the door open a few inches and called. No answer. They tiptoed in quietly in case Cal was sleeping. The bed was turned down, the towels were folded on the counter in the bathroom, ready to be washed, but no Cal.

There was an envelope on the pillow. Doug picked it up, and he and Finn went to find the family.

They found Susan and Ellie with Braden in the parlor. Doug asked, "Has Cal paid his bill?"

"Yes, he paid up front. Why?"

"He is nowhere to be found."

Cal was gone just like a whisper uttered on a silent night. Vanished.

Ellie shared a look with her husband. "He's disappeared, just like that Cal did many years ago. Maybe we can track down his address from his credit card."

Susan sighed. "He paid cash."

"What about a phone number? He had to call to make reservations."

"It was from a hotel in New Orleans."

Ellie's hands flew to her mouth. "New Orleans is where Joseph Sullivan met him when that Cal saved his life. Joseph sent him to Oak Hollow. Grace said that's when they named him Cal."

Braden rose and helped Belle with her coat. "I thought it strange he had no car. He said he got here in a taxi. I guess we'll never know. I was up early. He didn't use the phone this morning, and I didn't hear or see a taxi come for him. Maybe he walked to the end of the carriageway to get in the taxi. He probably made arrangements ahead of time, but Belle and I need to leave for school."

After they left, Ellie remembered the envelope. She carefully opened it and pulled out the note. She turned to Susan. "This note says, 'Thank you for your hospitality. Always ask in prayer any question you have. God will hear you. He says in His Word in Psalm 91:11: For He shall give His angels charge over thee, to keep thee in all thy ways. Things will be fine if you put your trust in the Lord. Love, Cal.'"

Susan's eyes reflected her shock. "Ellie, I believe he is an angel."

Ellie smiled. "I believe that, too. Angels don't age as far as I know, so he could have been with the Sullivans."

Winter finally gave up its hold on spring. Flowers bloomed profusely, trees dressed themselves in various shades of green and some sported flowers, temperatures warmed up, and gentle breezes ushered in the perfect backdrop for two special babies to make their appearance. Luke Cunningham made his grand appearance on the eighth day of April, much to the delight of his sister, Annabelle.

"I told you I wanted a brother. He's going to be so much fun. I hope he grows up fast so we can play together. And he won't be getting into my stuff! I can teach him to ride."

"It won't be too long, but you will have to be patient. And you know, your aunt Susan is going to have a baby in May, so you'll have two babies to play with."

Luke was the best baby. Having no experience, Ellie had called her mother or Emma every day asking questions to be sure she was taking care of Luke correctly. Both mothers assured her she was handling the new baby and Annabelle perfectly.

Susan waddled into the laundry room the first day of May where Ellie was folding diapers. "You are such a good mother. I'm so glad you had Luke before me, so you can help me. I feel like a cow."

"That's how I felt right before Luke was born. I've had a lot of help, as you know. I'll be glad to share whatever I've found out. Both my mother and Mama Emma have told me Luke is an exceptional baby. I'm glad he isn't fussy, and that we have moved to the Inn with you and Doug to maintain a peaceful, quiet atmosphere for our guests." Ellie placed the folded diapers into a basket.

"Yes, that will make it easier on both of us. And I'm sure no guest wants to hear baby cries while they are here!" Susan rubbed her expanded stomach.

"Belle is thrilled to be near Doug and learn from him. She told me the other day, she wants Doug to show her how to make saddles. She is definitely our little horse lady."

"He's doing very well with his side business. He's sold three already." Suddenly shock registered on Susan's face. She whispered, "I'm so sorry. I'm embarrassed. I think I just wet my pants."

Ellie observed the small puddle on the floor. "My dear, your water just broke. I'll go tell Doug. You are about to have a baby."

"Do you think I'll be able to make it to the hospital? I don't have any pain right now."

"You'll be fine. Doctor Purcell at the clinic is excellent at delivering babies!"

Early morning, May the second, Mark Mabry was born, crying loud enough for the whole hospital to hear according to Doug. He turned out to have colic, and every adult in the Inn took turns walking him. By the time Susan was ready to pull her hair out, he settled down.

Sitting with Susan on the veranda on a bright summer day, Ellie shifted Luke to her shoulder to burp him. "I'm sitting here thinking. I believe we have restored Oak Hollow, now The Sullivan House, to her former glory. Braden's book is finished, he's able to be home full time, we have two precious children, and wonderful friends. What could be better?"

"I feel the same. I know you have recorded all the things that you and Braden have done to the house. It's almost like Grace's journal has turned into your journal. I hope you keep it up and leave it for those that come after us. Doug's business is flourishing, he's teaching pyrography to some 4-H boys, as well as Belle, before teaching them saddle making, and he is thrilled with being a father. Life is good."

"Pyrography is the technique he uses to burn designs into his saddles?"

"Yeah. You and I have been blessed abundantly."

Ellie smiled. "I pray this mansion will, indeed, create more memories after we're gone. I will keep up the journal. I think Grace would want that. Too bad we don't have the ability to see into the future."

Susan nodded. "I wish Cal was still here. I have never forgotten what he did for me."

Ellie had a faraway look in her eyes. "For all of us. Kind of like he knew when he was needed."

Braden and Doug walked up. Braden bent and kissed Ellie on the forehead. Taking Luke in his arms, he said, "We've had some ups and downs, but this journey, bringing Oak Hollow to life. and preserving the Sullivan legacy will stand as a legend for many generations to come, and to think this is part of my heritage. We are blessed beyond measure, and I believe we have found favor with the Lord."

ACKNOWLEDGEMENTS

I would like to thank my faithful readers for waiting patiently for me to finish this novel. You make my day each time you ask when it would be ready.

Thank you for the members of my Sunday School class, the Naomi Class, and for those wonderful women who tell me how much they enjoy clean, Christian writing.

Thank you to Rosie Humphrey, Real Estate Guru and Interior Decorator Extraordinaire for letting me "borrow" you to create Emma. My love always to you.

I am so blessed to have a top-notch proofreader. Thank you from the bottom of my heart to Linda Barrett. You make me look good!

My writing would not be nearly as good without my mentor and muse, James Olson, a multi-talented, award-winning author. Thank you a million times over. You will never know how much I treasure your friendship.

And to my biggest fan, my sister, Patricia and her husband, John Nelson. Your support and love mean more than I can say. I love you both.

Where would I be without my wonderful daughter, Jennifer Bullard, who encourages me, helps me, inspires me, loves me, and plots new adventures with me. Your editing, proofreading, formatting, cover art, and suggestions made this book shine. You're my best love!

And what a blessing and encouragement my beloved grandchildren are. Morgan, Trevor, and Hannah, you are my special loves. You have given birth to Annabelle Rose who believed with all her heart, she could anything with grit and determination.

Though he will never know, a very special Texas thoroughbred, Wild on Ice inspired me to include Apollo, Snowflake, and Brave Eagle, even though they were not racehorses. My heart goes out to the owners, trainers, and jockey when Wild on Ice sustained a fatal injury. It made

351

me sad when he didn't get to run in the Kentucky Derby. RIP beautiful athlete.

Most of all, I thank my Lord and Savior for loving me, saving me, and letting me live another day. My prayer is that everyone will know the joy of salvation that only Jesus can grant.

ABOUT THE AUTHOR

Lanna Richards lives in Texas and took up writing many years ago, writing her first three-act play when she was nine. She is an award-winning poet, but turned to novels to while away her retirement years. Her hobbies include sewing, reading, cooking, decorating, and getting into little adventures along the way. Living with her daughter, son-in-law, and her special granddaughter, Hannah, has provided her countless hours of pleasure, and they keep her in line!

Adding two sweet fur babies to the mix makes for extra fun, snuggles, and some exercise letting them in and out to explore the world many times a day!

Look for the first two novels in this series on Amazon. (*Heart of Stones* and *An Uncertain Horizon*).

www.ingramcontent.com/pod-product-compliance
Lightning Source LLC
Chambersburg PA
CBHW021526250626
47154CB00006BA/1988